Richard Laymon wrote over thirty [...]
May 2001 *The Travelling Vampire Sh[...]*
Best Horror Novel, a prize for which Laymon [...]
shortlisted with *Flesh, Funland, A Good, Secret Place* (Best Anthology)
and *A Writer's Tale* (Best Non-fiction). Laymon's works include the
books of the Beast House Chronicles: *The Cellar, The Beast House* and
*The Midnight Tour*. Some of his recent novels have been *Night in the
Lonesome October, No Sanctuary* and *Amara*.

A native of Chicago, Laymon attended Willamette University in
Salem, Oregon, and took an MA in English Literature from Loyola
University, Los Angeles. In 2000, he was elected President of the Horror
Writers Association. He died in February 2001.

Laymon's fiction is published in the United Kingdom by Headline,
and in the United States by Leisure Books and Cemetery Dance
Publications. To learn more, visit the Laymon website at: http://
rlk.cjb.net

'A gut-crunching writer' *Time Out*

'Incapable of writing a disappointing book' *New York Review of Science
Fiction*

'No one writes like Laymon and you're going to have a good time with
anything he writes' Dean Koontz

'One of the best, and most underrated, writers working in the genre
today' *Cemetery Dance*

'This author knows how to sock it to the reader' *The Times*

'This is an author that does not pull his punches . . . A gripping, and at
times genuinely shocking, read' *SFX Magazine*

# The Woods are Dark

and

# Out are the Lights

THE WOODS ARE DARK first published in Great Britain in 1983
by New English Library

First printed in this edition in 1991 by HEADLINE BOOK PUBLISHING

OUT ARE THE LIGHTS first published in Great Britain in 1982
by New English Library

'Bad News' first published in Great Britain in 1991 in BEST NEW HORROW,
ed Jones and Campbell, Robinson Publishing

This edition of OUT ARE THE LIGHTS AND OTHER TALES
published in 1993 by HEADLINE BOOK PUBLISHING

First published in this omnibus edition in 2006
by HEADLINE BOOK PUBLISHING

A HEADLINE paperback

1

ISBN 0 7553 3169 9

Typeset in Janson by Avon DataSet Ltd, Bidford on Avon, Warwickshire

Printed and bound in Great Britain by
Mackays of Chatham plc, Chatham, Kent

Headline's policy is to use papers that are natural, renewable and recyclable
products and made from wood grown in sustainable forests. The logging and
manufacturing processes are expected to conform to the environmental
regulations of the country of origin.

HEADLINE BOOK PUBLISHING
A division of Hodder Headline
338 Euston Road
London NW1 3BH

www.headline.co.uk
www.hodderheadline.com

# The Woods are Dark

# Chapter One

Neala O'Hare slowed her MG as the narrow road curved. The evening sun was no longer behind her. Shadows of the high trees threw their dark capes across the road, hiding it. She pulled off her sunglasses.

'Here, would you stow these in the glove compartment?'

Sherri, in the passenger seat, took the glasses. She opened the glove compartment. 'Christ, I'm starving. You don't suppose we'll run into a McDonalds?'

'I've got some gorp in my pack.'

'Gorp? Thanks anyway. I'd rather . . .' She suddenly gasped.

Neala saw it, too. She hit the brakes.

Her friend thrust a hand against the windshield as the car jerked to a stop.

In front of them, the legless thing dragged itself over the road with powerful, hairy arms.

'What the fuck *is* it?' Sherri muttered.

Neala shook her head.

Then it faced them.

Neala's hands clenched the steering wheel. Stunned, she tried to figure out what she was seeing. It hardly looked like the face of a man.

The thing turned. It started to drag itself toward the car.

'Get out of here!' Sherri cried. 'Quick! Back up!'

'What *is* it?' Neala asked.

'Let's *go!*'

Neala backed up, but slowly, just enough to keep away from the approaching creature. She couldn't take her eyes off its bloated face.

'Run it over!' Sherri snapped.

She shook her head. 'I can't. It's a man. I think it's a man.'

'Who cares? For Godsake, run it over and let's get the fuck out of here!'

It sat up, balancing on its torso, freeing its arms. It leered at Neala.

'Oh God,' Sherri muttered.

It fumbled at an opening in its furry vest. A pocket? It pulled out a severed human hand, kissed its palm, and tossed it. The hand flipped toward Neala. She ducked her head, felt it in her hair, and knocked it aside. It fell into the gap between the bucket seats.

The legless thing scuttled off the road and disappeared into the forest.

Neala looked down at the hand, at its crooked fingers, its coral painted nails, the white band of skin where a wedding ring used to be. Lunging sideways, she threw herself over her door and vomited onto the pavement. When she was done, she turned to her friend.

'We've gotta get rid of it,' Sherri said.

'I . . .'

Snarling as if enraged, Sherri clutched the hand by its fingers and flung it from the car. 'God!' She rubbed her hand furiously on her shorts.

Neala sped away.

As she drove, her mind repeated the incident again and again. She needed to make sense of it, but no matter how she concentrated, it wouldn't fall into a pattern she could accept. The scene belonged in a nightmare, not on a peaceful road on the way to Yosemite.

She was glad to see a town ahead – not much of a town, to be sure. Up in these areas, though, they rarely were.

'Maybe they've got a police department,' she said.

'You're not planning to stop!'

'We ought to tell somebody.'

'Tell Father Higgins, for Godsake. Save it for confession. Jesus, let's get the hell out of here.'

'We can't just forget about it.'

'Forget about it? Every time I shut my eyes, I'm going to be looking into that repulsive, gloating . . .' Sherri jerked her head sharply as if to shake the picture apart. 'God, I'm *never* gonna forget about it. But we don't have to go around making a big deal of it, okay? Let's just keep it to ourselves. It's water over the dam, you know?'

They had already left half the town behind. Ahead of them, Neala saw a bait shop, Terk's Diner, and the Sunshine Motor Inn.

'Why don't we stop at the diner?' Neala suggested.

'Let's not.'

'Come on. It's late. You just said you're starving.'

'I lost my appetite.'

'Please. I'd sure like to get out of the car and relax, at least. Try to think it out. Talk it over. Besides, there's no telling when we'll hit another restaurant.'

'You call this a restaurant?'

'Hey, this is your kind of joint. Probably filthy with greasy spoons and "characters."'

Sherri managed a smile. 'Okay. But let's keep the freak to ourselves.'

Neala turned onto the gravel parking area, and shut down the engine. 'Let's batten down the hatches,' Neala said. 'It'll be dark when we get out.' They latched the roof into place, rolled

3

up the windows, and locked the doors. Before starting across the gravel, Neala stretched.

She was stiff from the long day in the car. Standing on tiptoes, shoulders straining back, she felt the luxury of her tensing muscles. The movement pulled her shirt taut across her chest. She liked its feel against her nipples, and thought how long it had been since she'd felt the eager touch of a man's fingers or tongue on her breasts.

Maybe, up in Yosemite; she'd get lucky.

Meet a rugged Mountain Man.

One for Sherri, too. I'm not selfish.

'I feel almost human again,' she said, meeting Sherri behind the car.

They crossed the gravel lot to the entrance of the diner. Sherri pulled open the screen door, and they walked in.

Neala liked the warmth. The familiar aromas made her long for a cheeseburger and French fries. 'Counter?' she asked, seeing a pair of empty stools at the end. The other half a dozen were occupied.

'Let's take a table,' Sherri said, surprising her. Sherri usually preferred the counter, where she struck up conversations with nearby strangers.

Not tonight, apparently.

They slid into booths at a side table, facing each other. Sherri's eyes briefly met Neala's, then lowered.

'Buck up, pardner,' Neala said.

'Sure thing.'

'Don't be this way. Please.'

'Oh, how should I be?'

'Be the gutsy champ we all know and admire.'

That didn't even get a smile from Sherri.

Neala needed that smile. She'd never felt so stunned, so

alone. This was a hell of a time for Sherri to go silent and glum.

'Would it help if I apologize?' Neala asked.

'It's not your fault.'

'It was my idea to go backpacking.'

'The freak wasn't your idea.'

'That's for. damn sure. But if we'd stayed home . . .'

'It's all right. Forget it.'

The waitress came. 'Sorry to keep you folks waiting,' she said. She set water glasses on the table, and handed out menus.

When she left, they studied the menus. Usually, they would talk over the offerings, maybe decide to split an order of fries or onion rings, discuss whether to 'blow it' and have milk shakes. Tonight, they kept silence.

Neala picked at a speck of yellow food on the menu, then wished she hadn't touched it.

The waitress returned. 'Ready to order?'

Neala nodded. 'I'll have one of your Terkburger Specials and iced tea.' She watched the gaunt, unsmiling woman write it down.

Can't anyone smile tonight? she wondered.

This gal ought to be happy as a lark, with a ring like that on her pinky.

'A patty melt,' Sherri said. 'Fries, and a Pepsi.'

The woman nodded. She took the menus, and walked away.

Sherri watched her, frowning.

'Did you get a load of her ring?' Neala asked, hoping to break the somber mood.

'How could I miss it? The thing nearly blinded me.'

'Do you suppose it was glass?'

'Looked real enough to me. I'm no expert, though. Besides, I left my jeweler's loop at home.'

5

Neala laughed, and saw the hint of a smile on Sherri's face. 'It looked like a wedding ring,' she said.

'Wrong finger. Wrong hand, too. She probably outgrew it.'

'Her? She was nothing but bones.'

'Maybe it's a friendship ring,' Sherri suggested. 'I could use a friend like that. Money coming out his wazoo. If I were that gal, I'd blow this burg in about two seconds. Grab hold of the guy, and light out for the big city.'

When the waitress brought their supper, they both watched her hand.

'What do you think?' Neala asked when she was gone.

'I think it's real.'

Neala bit into her Terkburger: a thick patty on a sesame seed bun. Juice spilled down her chin. She back-handed it off, and reached for a napkin. 'Delicious,' she said.

'Same here,' said Sherri. Strings of limp onion dangled from the sides of her sandwich.

'Onion breath.'

'You planning to kiss me?' Sherri asked.

'Not tonight.'

'Gee whiz, and I had my heart set on it.'

'You're sure going to stink up the tent. Maybe we'd better sleep under the stars.'

'What if it rains?' Sherri asked through a mouthful that muffled her words.

'Then we get wet.'

'I wouldn't like that.'

'Better than onion gas in the tent.'

'Yeah?' Sherri pulled off the top slab of rye bread, pinched a matted glob of onions, and dropped it onto Neala's plate. 'You have some, too. Insurance.'

6

Laughing, Neala piled the onions onto her Terkburger and ate.

Soon, their plates were empty. Neala thought about returning to the car. She didn't want to.

'How about dessert?' Sherri asked, as if she were in no hurry to leave, either.

'Good idea.'

This was no time to worry about calories. Neala never worried much about them, regardless; she had no trouble keeping her trim figure. Still, gloppy desserts made her guilty. Tonight, it would be worth the guilt to postpone returning to the car.

They both ordered hot fudge sundaes. They ate slowly, picking at the mounds of ice cream, the thick warm syrup, the whipped cream sprinkled with chopped nuts.

'This'll add an inch to my hips,' Sherri said. She was several inches taller than Neala, with broad shoulders, prominent breasts, and big hips. She wasn't fat, but an additional inch on her hips wouldn't be that noticeable. Neala decided to keep the observation to herself.

'We'll work it all off, this week,' she said.

'A great way to spend a vacation, working our asses off.'

'You'll love it.'

'Sure I will. I'll love it plenty if Robert Redford wanders over to our campfire and I bowl him over with my wit and charm, and he drags me off with him. My luck, though, he'd fall for you.'

'I'd share.'

'Promise?'

When the sundaes were gone, they ordered coffee.

After this, Neala thought, we'll have to go. Back to the car. Back to the narrow, dark road and the woods.

7

We can't stay here all night.

She watched the waitress shut the main, wooden door. Through the window, she saw that dusk had fallen. The gravel of the parking lot was a gray blur. Across the road, the sign of the Sunshine Motor Inn blinked gloomy blue. It showed a vacancy.

Her eyes met Sherri's.

'No way,' Sherri said.

'I know. I don't want to stay, either. I don't want to go and I don't want to stay.'

'We'll feel a lot better when we've put some miles behind us.'

Neala nodded agreement.

'But before we do another thing, the kid here's gonna hit the John.'

While she was gone, Neala had another cup of coffee.

She came back, and Neala went. The toilet, at the rear of the diner, was clean and pleasant. Ought to be, Neala thought; the place is run by a bunch of tycoons.

She returned to the table. Sherri had already put down the tip. They took the bill to the cash register. This meal was Neala's turn.

She bought two foil-wrapped mints for the road.

The waitress poured change into her hand. 'Don't be strangers,' she said.

Sherri reached for the knob, and tried to turn it. The knob didn't move. She tried again. 'Hey, Miss?' she called to the waitress.

The heads of everyone at the counter turned toward them.

'Hey Miss, the door's stuck.'

The customers stared. A couple of the younger ones smiled, but most looked grim.

'Ain't stuck, honey. It's locked.'

Neala felt a tight pull of fear in her bowels.

'How about *un*locking it?' Sherri asked.

'Afraid I can't do that.'

'Yeah? Why the fuck not?'

' 'Cause you're here to stay, you two.'

With a big grin, the waitress turned to the other customers – the same customers, Neala suddenly realized, who'd been at the counter when they entered, so long ago.

Silently, four of the men climbed off their stools.

# Chapter Two

Lander Dills cut his high beams as a car appeared around a bend. When it was gone, he pressed them on again, doubling the brightness of the road and forest ahead.

'This is the forest primeval,' he announced. 'The murmuring pines and the hemlocks.'

'That's Dad doing his *Evangeline* routine,' said Cordelia in the back seat, explaining him to Ben. 'He gets poetically inspired at frequent intervals.'

'Fine with me,' Ben said.

Good fellow, Ben. Didn't know an iamb from a dactyl, and couldn't care less, but at least he seemed reasonably intelligent and polite. Lander, a high school teacher, had seen enough of the other kind to last him a dozen lifetimes.

His daughter had good taste in boyfriends, thank the gods.

9

'Longfellow knew his stuff,' Lander said. 'The forest primeval. You can feel it in your bones – the silence, the isolation. Out there, nothing has changed for a thousand years. "Down by the dank tarn of Auber, in the ghoul-haunted woodland of Weir."'

'The Poe routine,' Cordelia said.

'I wouldn't mind his motel routine, about now,' said Ruth.

'Mom's horny, too.'

'That's not what I meant, Cordie, and you know it!'

Cordelia and Ben were laughing. The motel routine. With a pang, Lander pictured his daughter under Ben, naked and moaning. From the way the two acted, he was certain they had gone the whole route. It made him feel sick, as if he'd lost something precious. She was eighteen, though. Old enough to know what she was doing, to make her own choices. He couldn't stop her. He wouldn't try. But it hurt him.

'We should be coming into a Barlow pretty soon,' Ruth said, shining her flashlight at a roadmap on her lap. 'How about stopping there?'

'Don't you want to try for Mule Ear Lake?' Lander asked.

'We're *hours* away, honey. It'll be midnight, at least, and we told Mr Elsworth we'd be there by nine. He'll probably be asleep. Besides, we've been on the road all day.'

'If we *had* been on the road all day, we'd be there by now.'

'Here we go,' Cordelia said. 'The general. His idea of a vacation is hitting the road before sun-up.'

'Well, I'd be happy to stay in Barlow, myself,' he said, 'I'm just looking out for you people.' He grinned through the darkness at Ruth. 'You do realize, I hope, there won't be a Hyatt.'

'As long as we have clean sheets . . .'

'Would you kids rather stop, or go on through to the cabin?'

'Let's stop,' Cordelia said. 'It'll be fun.'

'Either way's fine with me, Mr Dills.'

'Well, we'll see,' he said.

He wouldn't argue the point. Not worth the trouble. He was pleased enough to assume the role of leader, but only so long as nobody tampered with his decisions. His decision, from the start, had been to drive on through. Now, he'd been over-ruled.

With some satisfaction, and telling nobody, he switched his role from leader to chauffeur.

If they want to run the show, let them. He would sit back, relieved of responsibility, and watch. More than likely, they would botch it.

Soon, he came to the town of Barlow. He drove past a closed gas station, a general store, Phillips' Hardware. Just ahead, on the right, was Terk's Diner. Across the road was the Sunshine Motor Inn. Its flashing blue sign read, 'Vacancy.'

'Is this where you want to stop?' he asked, slowing down. It wasn't a regular motel, at all, but a cluster of cottages behind a shabby office. A motor court.

'I don't know,' Ruth said. She sounded dubious.

Lander grinned.

'What do you think?' she asked him.

'It's up to you. Should we give it a try?'

'What do you think, kids?' Ruth asked.

'I don't know,' said Cordelia. 'It looks kind of creepy, to me.'

Lander stopped the car in the middle of the road. He waited, watching his rear-view mirror in case a car should come along.

'Shall we?' Ruth asked him.

'If you want to.'

'You're a lot of help,' she complained.

'Give the word, and we'll stay here.'

'Okay,' Ruth said. 'Let's give it a try.'

11

Flipping on his turn signal, Lander drove across the road and stopped beside the lighted office. 'You might as well wait in here.'

'Hold it,' Ruth said. 'What are you going to do?'

'Register.'

'You know what I mean.'

'I don't think we can all fit in one of these hovels, do you?'

She shook her head.

'So I'll get two. Boys in one, girls in the other.'

'Oh *Dad*!'

'No,' he said. 'I'm perfectly willing to spend the night here, if that's what everyone wants, but I won't sponsor your sexual escapades.'

'Lander!'

'God, Dad!'

'That was uncalled for,' Ruth said.

He'd expected a showdown over the sleeping arrangements for the trip. He should have handled it beforehand, but he'd hoped to avoid it, somehow. 'I'm sorry,' he said, 'but that's how I feel. As long as we're all together, they won't be sharing a bedroom. Not here, and not at the cabin.'

'That's great,' Cordelia muttered. 'Just great.'

'It's either that, or I turn this buggy around and we call the whole thing off.'

'That's fine with me,' Cordelia said.

'It's not fine with me,' said Ruth. 'We came up here for a good time, and that's what were going to have. I happen to agree with your father. We never allowed Ben to spend the night with you at home, and I don't see any reason to start now, simply because we're on vacation. If you were married, it would be a different kettle of fish, but . . .'

'Marriage. A license to screw.'

'If you think that,' Lander said, 'you've got a lot more growing up to do.'

'I agree with your parents,' Ben said.

'Thanks a bunch.'

'Not about growing up. I mean, you know.'

Cordelia sighed. 'What's this, gang up on Cordie night?'

'I'll get the rooms,' Lander said. He was glad to leave the car, and the argument.

Bells jingled as he entered the office. He waited several moments at the deserted counter. Then a door opened, off to the side. A man came out of the dimly lighted room beyond. The door started to swing shut, but stopped, leaving a three-inch gap. Half a face appeared behind the gap, looking out at Lander with a single eye.

'Room?' asked the man. He seemed pleasant enough. Chubby and bald, with a cherubic smile, he looked like he should be doing skits on a television comedy show.

'Uh, yes,' Lander said. 'Two rooms.'

The eye behind the door watched him, only a slit of it showing through the fleshy lid.

'There are four of us. Do you have connecting rooms?'

'Nothing like that, sorry. We can put you all up in one room, though, if you want. We've got one, sleeps three. We can wheel in an extra bed.'

'No, that's all right. Do you have two rooms available?'

'Sure do.' He smiled. 'Want to fill out a guest registration card?'

As Lander filled in the requested information, his hand shook slightly. That person in the doorway . . .

Twice, he looked up. The face was still pressed to the crack. It was an ancient face. He couldn't tell whether it belonged to a

13

man or woman. The eye blinked, dripping fluid from its corners.

He finished the card, and handed it back along with his MasterCard.

The man ran it through the machine. 'That'll be $42.50 for the rooms. One night. Check out time is noon. Want to sign here?'

Lander signed the bill.

He looked up at the door. It was shut.

'All set, Mr Dills.' The man bent down and came up with two keys. 'That's bungalows three and twelve.'

'Are they close together?'

'Well, one's just behind the office here. The other's back a ways.'

'Do you have any that aren't so far apart?'

'It's the best I can do for you, Mr Dills. We've got a pretty good crowd, tonight.'

'Okay. That'll be fine. Thanks.'

'Enjoy your stay with us.'

Lander nodded. He pulled open the door and stepped outside, relieved to get away from the office.

He climbed into the car.

'Well?' Ruth asked.

'Got 'em. Three and twelve.' His hand hesitated on the ignition key.

What's wrong?'

'Nothing, I guess. Probably the guy's mother.'

'What?'

'Some old buzzard kept watching me while I was in there. It spooked me a bit. She – he – whatever, kept staring at me through a crack in the door.'

'Dad!' Cordelia sounded frightened.

'I'm sure she's perfectly harmless,' Ruth said.

'Yeah,' said Lander. He started the car, and drove slowly into the dark courtyard, taking some comfort from the presence of the other cars parked nearby, glad his family wasn't alone at this God-awful motel.

# Chapter Three

As two men held Neala from behind, the waitress took her purse and tossed it onto the counter. A teenaged girl grabbed it, and started looking through its contents.

'She's got cool shoes,' said a freckled boy beside the girl. 'Let's see 'em.'

'They won't fit you,' the girl said.

'Might. 'Sides, she don't need 'em.'

The waitress knelt, and pulled off one of Neala's running shoes. Neala didn't try to stop the woman. The last time she'd protested, one of the men had bent her arm backwards. Sherri, who'd given them a rough time at first, got punched in the stomach for her trouble. Neala figured she would let them have whatever they wanted, and hope for the best.

The waitress tossed the shoes to the boy. He caught them, and climbed onto the counter to try them on.

Neala's wristwatch went next. Then her school ring from Loyola-Marymount. The waitress dropped them into her apron pocket, where they clinked in the loose change from her tips. Her rough hands tugged the neck of Neala's old workshirt. The top button popped off and skittered across the floor. Normally, she wore a gold chain necklace. She was glad she'd left it home for the backpacking trip.

The woman flicked the hair away from Neala's ears, mumbled about finding no earrings, and slapped her.

Then she sidestepped and repeated the process with Sherri, taking her purse, her sandals, her two rings. Sherri had no watch, but her crucifix hung by a gold chain at her throat. The waitress carefully opened the clasp, then dropped the chain into her apron pocket. Sherri cried out, squirming in the arms of the two big men as the waitress ripped the gold loop earrings from her pierced lobes.

'That it?' asked one of the men holding Sherri.

'Guess so,' the waitress said.

Neala heard a metallic rattle. Her left arm was jerked down. A handcuff hit her wrist. It latched shut with a quick ratchet sound. The second cuff locked around Sherri's wrist.

'Okay ladies, let's go.'

Someone pushed Sherri. She stumbled forward, snapping the chain taut, tugging Neala's cuff. The sharp edges bit into Neala's wrist. She lurched forward, trying to stay close to Sherri so it wouldn't happen again.

'I'm going along,' the freckled boy said.

'Pervert,' said the girl.

He jumped down from the counter, wearing Neala's shoes, and raced to the rear door of the diner. He held it open while the men guided Sherri through, then Neala.

'Where are you taking us?' Sherri asked. She sounded, to Neala, remarkably calm.

The men didn't answer. From the start, they'd said very little. All four stayed quiet and solemn, as if carrying out an unpleasant necessity.

The boy ran ahead of them. At the rear of an old pickup truck, he tried to open the tailgate. He was still working on it, without success, when one of the men arrived and gave him a hand. Together, they dropped the gate. It fell with a clamor that resounded in the night's stillness.

The boy scampered onto the truck bed. The man walked to the cab. As he climbed in, the others pushed Neala and Sherri toward the pickup's rear gate.

'This is kidnapping, you know,' Sherri told them.

'That's the least of your troubles, sister.'

They were tugged and lifted onto the metal floor of the truck bed. A man on the ground swung up the gate. It crashed into place. He latched it, climbed aboard, and sat down at Neala's feet.

The truck started to move, lurching over the rutted lot. Neala's head banged the floor. She lifted it.

'Stay down,' said the man beside her.

After a turn and a final sharp bounce, the truck steadied out.

We're on the highway, Neala realized. Heading west. Back the way we came.

'Where are you taking us?' Sherri asked.

'Not far,' said the man beside her.

'You're going to kill us, aren't you?'

The question made Neala's stomach hurt. Why couldn't Sherri keep her mouth shut!

'Not us,' the man said.

'I want to check them out,' said the boy.

'Help yourself.'

'For Christsake, Shaw,' said the man beside Neala.

'Ah, let the kid,' argued the one at her feet. 'No harm done.'

'It isn't right.'

'So what the hell *is* right?'

17

'He's pushing twelve,' said Shaw – the boy's father? 'He needs the education.'

'Every time we get a good young one, Timmy's at her. It's disgusting.'

'Going queer, Robbins?'

'I just don't think it's right. Do you? We don't have to turn into a bunch of savages, for Christsake. Next thing you know, we'll be the ones raping and . . .'

'That ain't allowed, and you know it,' Shaw said.

'It's the next step, damn it! We let Timmy do whatever he wants, next thing you know he'll be screwing 'em.'

'No I won't,' Timmy pouted.

'He knows better than that.'

'You ever tell him what they did to Weiss?'

Silence.

'I don't want to scare you, kid, but we used to have a guy named Weiss on these runs.'

'Shut up, Robbins.'

'Weiss knew better, too. He knew the rules.'

'Robbins!'

'Let him tell,' said the man at Neala's feet. 'The kid better know, for his own good.'

'We had this really beautiful gal, about six years back. Weiss couldn't stand it. We should've stopped him. I don't know why we didn't, but I guess we were tempted, ourselves, and figured we wouldn't mind watching him. Safe enough, just watching. Anyway, he had her right here in the truck.'

'He *screwed* her?' Timmy asked. Neala heard eagerness in the boy's voice.

'A few days later, he vanished. Weiss and his whole family: his wife and three kids. They vanished in the middle of the night, right out of their home.'

'Maybe they ran away,' Timmy suggested.

'No. The Krulls got 'em.'

'How do you know?'

'We found evidence,' Shaw explained.

'So just remember Weiss, when you get an urge to start exploring our ladies here.'

'It's okay, long as I don't screw 'em.'

'Christ, kid, where are your brains?'

'Knock that off,' Shaw snapped.

'Dad can I?'

'Let him,' said the man at Neala's feet.

'Just a little?' Timmy asked.

'You want to end up like Weiss?' Robbins asked.

'Long as I don't screw 'em . . .'

'Shit,' Robbins muttered.

'We're almost there,' Shaw said. 'Go ahead, but don't dawdle.'

Timmy crawled to Sherri's head. Kneeling, he leaned over her.

'Don't touch me, kid,' she snarled. 'I'll kill you, I swear it.'

Timmy looked at his father.

'Just shut up, sister.'

'Yeah!' Timmy said. 'You're just a big ox anyway. Who'd *want* to feel you up?'

He suddenly lunged onto Neala, his belly pressing her face, his hands pulling her shirt from her waist. She felt his hands rubbing her belly, pushing under the waist of her corduroys, one reaching inside her panties and moving in deep, fingers pressing and entering her.

With her free right hand, she hammered the center of Timmy's back. He jerked with the impact. Then a spasm of coughing shook his body. His hand went away. So did the pressure of his belly on Neala's face.

'Damn it, Robbins!' Shaw shouted. 'You shouldn't have let her do that!'

'She caught me off guard.'

Timmy knelt above her, shaking as he coughed.

'Goddamn bastard,' Shaw muttered.

The boy was crying, now. He suddenly gasped, 'You!' and punched Neala's face with a small, hard fist. She flung up her arm to stop the next blow, but Robbins had already shoved Timmy. The boy tumbled backwards.

'That's enough,' Robbins said.

'Dad!'

'Nobody touches my boy pal!'

'Yeah? I do. The kid's out of hand. He's starting to act like a shit, and I'm not going to let it go on. Not while I'm on this run.'

The man at Neala's feet said, 'What's got into you, Robbins? All the kid wanted was to cop a little feel. How come you're so touchy, all of a sudden? Last week, you were helping him. You stepped on that gal's hand, remember?'

'I don't feel so great about that, either.'

'What the fuck, did you get religion or something?'

'Something.'

The pickup lurched as it turned onto a dirt road. Overhead, the woods closed in, shutting out the moonlight.

# Chapter Four

'Who's for a nightcap?' Lander asked, once they'd carried the suitcases into cottage twelve.

'You mean a Pepsi?' Cordelia asked.

'Whatever you like. Pepsi, 7-Up, hard stuff. We'll hoist a couple to fortify Ben and me for the long trek back to three.'

'Dad's trying to mollify us,' she told Ben.

Lander opened his Travel Bar. 'Vodka for me,' he said, smiling at his daughter's remark. After all, she was right. She may be a smart-aleck and over-sexed, but she wasn't stupid. 'A Manhattan?' he asked Ruth.

'That'll hit the spot.'

'What's your pleasure, Ben?'

Cordelia smirked at the boy. 'Don't get your hopes up,' she said. 'You won't be getting that, tonight.'

Lander was pleased to see Ben blush.

'Just a Pepsi, I guess.'

'We don't have any ice,' Ruth told them.

Cordelia smiled. 'I saw a machine by the office.'

'I'll go get some,' Ben volunteered.

'Good man.'

'I'll go with you,' Cordelia said. At the door, she turned to Lander. 'Don't worry, Dad, we won't indulge in sexual escapades.'

They left.

Lander poured rye into one of the glasses from his case. He opened the small Vermouth bottle.

'You sure opened a can of worms,' Ruth said.

'It's Vermouth.'

She ignored his attempt at humor.

'The *can*,' Lander explained, 'was open already. I only tried to put a lid on it. Not even that, really. If they want to have at it, let them do it on the sly. It's more fun that way, anyhow. "Stolen sweets are best."'

'I don't know,' Ruth said. 'Maybe we should let them share a room. They are eighteen, you know. In a couple of months, they'll both be going off to Santa Barbara, and we won't have any say in what they do.'

'All the more reason to have our say now.'


'Over here,' Cordie whispered. She pulled Ben toward a dark path between two of the cottages.

'We'd better get the ice.'

'What's the hurry?'

'They'll be waiting.'

'Let 'em wait. Come on. This'll be our only chance to be alone, tonight.'

'Just for a minute,' Ben said. 'We don't want to get your dad angry.'

'Speak for yourself.'

'Did you really think he'd let us sleep together?'

'God no. Dad? It was worth a try, though.' She led Ben into the shadows. Wrapping her arms around him, she lightly touched her lips to his mouth. He seemed hesitant, at first – preoccupied. She kissed him more deeply, opening her mouth, sucking his tongue into her.

Ben pulled her tightly against him, and she felt his erection against her belly. If only she were wearing a skirt instead of these tight jeans! Moaning with frustration, she rubbed against him. His leg bent. She rode his upthrust thigh, grinding herself against it, slipping a hand down the front of his pants. One of his hands went inside her blouse. It squeezed her breast through the thin sheath of her bra.

Abruptly, his whole body shook. He bit her tongue. His hand clenched, shooting pain through her breast. He pumped warm fluid into her hand, and dropped to his knees.

Behind him, hammer poised for another blow, stood a grinning, toothless old woman.

'It's sure taking them a long time,' Lander complained. He swirled his warm vodka, and sipped it.

'They haven't been alone all day.'

'You'd think they could exercise a little restraint.'

'They're in love, honey.'

'I know, I know.'

Ruth sat down on the bed beside him. 'You're not exactly the world champ at exercising restraint, yourself. Remember the night on the porch glider?'

He laughed softly. 'I thought sure your dad would catch us.'

'And how you brought a can of oil the next night?'

'I wonder if they ever noticed the squeak was gone.'

'I sure did.'

'I oiled you both that night.'

'Geez, Lander!' She gave him a playful shove.

'I noticed you stopped squeaking, too.'

'You're awful!'

They kissed. Her lips were pliant and warm and familiar. He felt the gentle pressure of her hand on his leg. 'Hey,' he said, 'we'd better not get started.'

'Better not,' she echoed. 'Guess we'll have to exercise restraint.'

'That's not what I'd like to exercise,' he said.

23

She pushed him, laughing. 'How about *you* getting the ice? It'll keep you out of mischief.'

'Yeah, and maybe I'll run into the love-birds.' He picked up the room key and went out the door. Outside, he tried the knob to be sure it was locked. He climbed down the wooden stairs and scanned the three small duplexes across the driveway. No sign of Cordelia or Ben. He glanced into the car. Not there.

From the middle of the dirt driveway, he had a good view of all six cottages, the office and the main road. Turning, he looked behind him. The drive ended, and the forest began.

The forest primeval. The murmuring pines and the hemlocks . . .

Maybe they went in there for a tumble in the hemlocks. Joking about it didn't help.

It's no joke, your own daughter having a tumble.

*Roll me over in the clover . . .*

He pictured Cordelia on her back, Ben pumping. It made his stomach hurt.

*Roll me over lay me down and do it again.*

I'm obsessed, he thought.

Jealous?

Crap.

Where *are* they?

Could they get into one of the cottages? He studied each, turning as he walked, sometimes walking backwards. Six duplexes. Twelve rooms in all. Lights on in the windows of about half. Cars were parked in front of several others. Real clunkers. One, he noticed – an ancient, battered Buick Special – even had a flat tire. One of its windows was down.

He shook his head. No. They wouldn't dare make out in a stranger's car.

Stopping, he eyed each car with new suspicion. Four, not

counting his own. The kids could be in any of them, rutting on the back seat.

*Rutting?*

Shame burned Lander's face as he changed direction and walked across the dirt to the Buick. He moved close enough to see that the back seat was empty, then veered away and approached the next car.

A Maverick. Its right rear corner was badly bashed as if a metal-eating monster had taken a bite from it. Stepping closer, he glanced into the back seat. A dark shape jumped, and sprang through the far window. A cat. Lander laughed softly at his own fright. He patted his chest, where his heart pounded frantically, and looked again into the car. Baby shoes hung from the rear-view mirror. His eyes lowered to the steering column. Something weird there. With a quick glance around to be sure he wasn't being watched, he opened the passenger door and leaned across the seat.

On the steering column where the ignition should be, he saw only a round hole.

Strange, all right.

He climbed out, silently shut the door, and stepped to the front. His fingers searched beneath the lip of the hood. He found the latch and released it. He raised the hood, hinges squawking.

No battery.

No radiator, no fan belt, no carburetor, no air cleaner. The engine had been cannibalized.

'Jesus,' he muttered, and lowered the hood.

He ran across the driveway to a dilapidated Grand Prix. Raised its hood. Gazed into the darkness where the engine should have been, and found no engine at all. The car was an empty shell.

What kind of a motel was this, leaving useless cars in front of its room like – decoys?

With a sudden chill of dread, Lander wondered if the entire place was deserted: lights left on in rooms, hulks of cars rolled into place like props in a play . . .

*The play is the tragedy Man* – good old Poe, popping up when you need him least – *it's hero, the Conqueror Worm:*

A play. Its stage constructed by the smiling man in the office – by the strange, ancient person lurking behind his door.

'Cordelia!' Lander shouted. 'Cordelia! Ben!' He waited, listening for a reply. He heard wind in the trees, crickets and distant frogs, the sounds of birds singing in the night as if nothing were wrong, the laughter of a television audience.

At the end of the courtyard, a door swung open. Ruth stepped out. 'Lander! What's wrong?'

He ran to her.

'For heaven's . . .'

He pushed her inside and shut the door.

'What is it, what's wrong?' Her frightened eyes begged him for a quick answer. 'The kids?'

'I didn't see them. I don't know where they are, but something's wrong here. All those cars, they're fakes.'

'I don't . . .' She shook her head.

'I don't know what's going on, but . . . Remember Norman Bates?'

'Who?'

'Anthony Perkins. *Psycho*? The hotel . . .'

'Lander, stop it!'

'I don't think this is a real motel, at all. I think it's some kind of a trap.'

'No!'

Lander leaned against the door and rubbed his face. Always a

26

pacifist, he'd detested firearms. Now he wished to God he had one.

'What'll we do?' Ruth asked.

'I don't know.'

'Cordelia's out there!'

'Look, maybe I'm wrong. Maybe it's all . . . innocent, and the kids are out in the woods, or something, having the time of their lives. I don't know.'

In a quiet voice tight with control, Ruth said, 'We'd damn well better find out.'

'How?'

'We'll march ourselves right over to the office . . .'

'Oh, that's a great idea.'

'What do you suggest?'

He looked at the telephone, and immediately gave up the idea. No way to call out for help, not without going through the motel switchboard, 'We could go for help,' he muttered. 'There must be police, a sheriff . . .'

Ruth reached for the doorknob.

He grabbed her wrist.

'I'm going out there and find my daughter,' she said. 'Now let go of me.'

'Wait! We've got to think.'

'My ass! While you're thinking, God-knows-what could be happening to Cordie.' She jerked her hand free and gripped the knob. She tugged the door open.

Lander dropped backwards, slamming it shut. 'Damn it Ruth!'

'Let me out!'

The telephone rang, its harsh clamor sending a shock of alarm through Lander. Ruth's head snapped sideways. They both stood motionless, staring at the black instrument as it blared again.

27

Lander suddenly rushed to it. As it rang a third time, he picked it up. 'Hello?'

'Mr Dills, this is Roy in the office.'

'Yes?'

'Your daughter's here with me. She would like a word with you.'

Lander waited his eyes on Ruth.

'What is it?' she mouthed, the words barely coming out.

Lander shrugged.

'Daddy?' His daughter's voice was shrill with panic.

'Honey, what's wrong?'

'Oh Dad! They . . . Ben! I think he's dead!'

'Where are you?'

'No. Don't come. They'll kill you.'

'Are you in the office?'

'Don't let them get you!'

He motioned to Ruth. 'Here, your mother wants to talk to you.'

She hurried across the room. He handed her the phone. 'Hello, Cordie?'

'Keep her talking,' Lander whispered.

Ruth nodded.

He ran to the door, jerked it open, and rushed out. Something – a wire? – snagged his foot. As he pitched headlong, he glimpsed a grinning old woman sitting crosslegged on the hood of his car, cradling a hammer. He slammed into the dirt by the wheel.

With a squeal of delight, the woman pounced.

# Chapter Five

The pickup truck lurched over a rough, dirt road. After the flare-up about Timmy, the men had kept a cold silence.

Neala wished they would talk, even fight. Their quarrel over the horny creep of a kid had pulled her mind away from thoughts of her own situation. Now, the distraction was gone. Her fear returned, black and paralyzing with images of rape and slaughter.

She began to cry. She didn't want to, didn't want the men to see her weakness, didn't want Sherri to draw more fear from her own desolation. She couldn't help it, though. She felt alone and helpless. Like the time she was lost in the woods.

She'd been only six, then, but she still remembered how it felt. Her family had been camping near Spider Lake in Wisconsin, Dad told scary stories by the campfire while they all drank hot chocolate. The hot chocolate did it: she woke in the middle of the night with a horrible strain on her bladder. She shook Betty awake, but her older sister refused to budge from the sleeping bag.

Neala had to go so badly she didn't bother to dress. Wearing only her underpants, she crept out of the pup-tent. The chilly breeze made her shake. She crossed the campsite barefoot, the ground moist and cold under her feet.

Her dad had dug a hole, off behind the camp. A 'latrine,' he called it. Neala had been there several times, but not at night.

She wandered far into the dark woods, searching for the latrine. She couldn't find it. Finally, she gave up and squatted beside a birch tree. Relieved, she headed back for camp. She thought she knew just where it was. But she walked and walked.

When she came to a strange, moonlit pasture, she knew she was lost. She called for Mom and Dad. She called for Betty. Nobody came.

That's when it hit her: the awful fear of being alone and helpless in the night. She wandered the pasture, blind with tears, wailing her anguish, hoping they would hear and come for her.

But what if someone else heard, and not her parents? One of those boogy-men Dad talked about at the campfire? Or the awful Wendigo? Or a witch like the one that tried to eat Hansel and Gretel?

Covering her mouth to stop the squalling, she ran from the pasture. In the woods, she ran as fast as she could, not daring to look back because something horrible might be chasing her. Roots tripped her. Webs stuck to her bare skin. Switches whipped her. But she kept running until she broke into another clearing and saw the moonlit car.

*Their* car.

They'd left it behind, and hiked a long way before making camp. She wasn't sure which way.

The doors were locked, so she crawled underneath the car. The grass beneath it was dry. She lay there, and shivered through the night, waiting.

Waiting for the boogy-man to reach under and drag her out. Waiting for the Hairy Hand to grab her, for the Wendigo to fling the car aside and sink its talons into her bare back and carry her away into the stratosphere, her feet burning to ashes with the speed of its flight.

In the morning, when Dad found her, he cried. They both cried, because everything had turned out all right, after all.

And they lived happily ever after, Neala thought, until four men and a boy put the girl into a pickup truck and drove her to a secret place in the woods, and . . .

The truck stopped.

Robbins and Shaw climbed out. 'You wait here,' Shaw told his son.

The man at Neala's feet jumped over the tailgate, and unlatched it. The gate swung down with a groan and clank. He grabbed Neala's ankles and pulled. She slid along the metal floor.

Timmy, crawling at her head, reached down suddenly and tore open her shirt. She tried to knock him away with her one free hand, but he was too quick. He squeezed her breasts as if he wanted to rip them off. Neala cried out. Her fist caught him in the face so hard it hurt her knuckles, and he fell backwards, crying.

Then she was on her feet behind the truck, Sherri at her side.

'Are you all right?' Sherri asked.

'Shut up,' Shaw said.

'Let's go,' said Robbins. His grip on Neala's arm was firm, but not painful like that of the other man.

They walked to the front of the truck. The driver had left the headlights on. The beams lit a path through a clearing, a clearing not too different from the one where Neala had wandered, lost, as a child – though that was two thousand miles away, and twenty years ago.

After a distance, the downward slanting headbeams seemed to bury themselves. The field ahead lay in darkness.

'Why the hell didn't you park closer?' Shaw whispered to the driver.

'Shut up.'

'Man, they're probably all around us.'

'They don't attack delivery parties,' said the man on Neala's right.

31

'Always a first time, Phillips.'

'I wouldn't sweat it.'

'I still don't see why he had to park so goddamn far away.'

'I felt like it,' the driver said. 'How about shutting your face?'

Ahead, a line of six trees stood in the clearing. Neala stared at them. They were tall and thin-trunked. Their high branches, reaching into the moonlight, were bare of leaves.

They shouldn't be bare, not in summer. They should be full, their leaves fluttering in the breeze.

The trees are dead, Neala realized.

Six dead trees all in a row.

'No,' she said.

'It's all right,' Robbins whispered.

'No, don't take us there. Please.' She tried to hold back, but the men thrust her forward.

'Just take it easy,' Robbins said.

'Please! They're dead! I don't want to go there. Please!'

Plain stunned her right leg as Phillips shot a knee into it. 'Now hold it down, hon,' he said.

'You okay?' Robbins asked.

'No!'

'Christ, Phillips.'

'You've really got it bad pal. You better watch yourself.'

'Everybody shut up,' the driver snapped.

Under one of the trees they stopped.

'Lean back,' Robbins said.

'I don't . . .'

Phillips shoved Neala. Her back and head hit the trunk. Phillips held her while Shaw and the driver pushed Sherri against the same tree. She heard a rattle of handcuffs. Then the driver grabbed her right arm, pulled it backwards, and snapped the bracelet into place. Craning her neck, she saw that it was now cuffed to Sherri.

They stood back to back, hands joined, the trunk of the tree between them.

'That does it,' said the driver. He reached to his throat where something hung on a chain. He raised it to his mouth. A whistle. He blew a long, shrill note that pierced the night like the cry of a terrible bird. Then the whistle dropped from his lips. 'Let's haul ass,' he said.

Three of the men ran. The one called Robbins backed away, shaking his head. 'Sorry,' he muttered. Turning, he followed the others in their race to the pickup truck. Their sprinting forms flicked through the headlights. Then they disappeared behind the brightness. Neala heard doors bump shut, heard the tailgate bang into place. The engine rumbled to life. The headbeams swung sideways and away. For a while, the red tail lights jiggled. Then they vanished.

'Hope the fuckers rot in hell,' Sherri said.

# Chapter Six

The pickup stopped in front of Robbins' house, and he jumped to the pavement.

'Have yourself a good one,' Shaw said, apparently trying to make up for his earlier behavior.

'You too,' Robbins said.

Timmy sat quietly beside his father.

'Say goodnight to Mr Robbins,' Shaw told him.

'Night,' Timmy muttered.

'Yeah.'

The truck pulled away. Robbins unlatched his front gate. He crossed the lawn toward his dark house, and sat on the porch stairs. Folding his arms over his knees, he stared at the ground.

Damn it, there was just something about that one woman – the smaller one. He'd been making delivery runs for years, ever since he turned eighteen, but he'd never felt like this before.

He'd never felt this way about any woman. Sure, there were a few he liked well enough, and some who claimed to love him. He could take his pick, whenever he got an urge to hit the sheets. But none like this.

This woman was different. Just to sit close to her, to hold her hand, to talk with her quietly through the night . . .

By morning, she would probably be dead.

He could feel the loss, already, like a hallow in his chest.

Never to see her again.

If it were just himself, he'd go back there, maybe. He could get away, all right. They'd come for Peggy and Jenny, though.

Everybody'd have to leave. The whole family.

So why not? If they could get past the boundary, they'd be all right. He could take the woman to Los Angeles, maybe . . .

*You're dreaming her life away!*

Leaping to his feet, he rushed across the porch and threw open the front door. His hand hit the switch. Blinking in the sudden brightness, he crossed the room to his gun case. He took down his 30-30 Winchester, picked up a box of cartridges, and ran outside.

His old Pontiac was parked on the street. He sped two blocks to his sister's house, and ran to the screen door. He knocked hard, then entered.

'Peggy!'

She came out of the kitchen, worry on her thin face.

'For Petesakes, John . . .'

'I need to talk to you. Outside.'

Hank appeared in the kitchen doorway. He eyed Robbins with suspicion. 'What's up?' he asked.

'Nothing. Just want a word with Peg.'

Hank's eyes narrowed. 'Big secret, huh?'

'She'll tell you all about it.' Robbins grabbed his sister's arm and pulled her out the door. He hurried across the lawn, dragging her along.

'We're getting out of here tonight,' he said.

'What?'

'Tonight's run. There was a girl. I'm going back for her.'

'Johnny, no!'

'I have to.'

'Dear God!' Oh dear God!'

'Listen, we're getting out of here. All of us.'

'No!'

'I'll get back here as soon as I can. Have Hank and Jenny ready to go.'

'Hank won't leave. You know that. He wouldn't leave here for the world.'

'That's his worry, then.'

'John, you can't do this to us!'

'Do you want to spend the rest of your life here? Do you, Peg? Do you want Jenny to grow up the way we did? Do you want her turned into a murderer like the rest of us?'

She was crying, the tears glistening in her eyes and streaming down her cheeks. 'We can't leave!'

'You *will*!'

'But Hank!'

'If he won't come along, the hell with him. You'd be better off without him anyway.'

'I suppose, but . . .'

'He can't stop you.' Johnny hugged his sister tightly. 'Don't worry, okay? We'll make it.'

She shook her head. 'Don't do this to us. Oh please, Johnny, don't!'

'Half an hour,' he said, and climbed into his car.

# Chapter Seven

'We've got to get out of here,' Neala said.

'Just how do you plan to arrange it?'

'I don't *know*.' Neala's voice cracked into a sob. She turned her hands, rattling the cuffs that held her prisoner against the tree.

'We'd better think of something quick,' Sherri said. 'That whistle was some kind of a signal.'

'Maybe we can pull free.'

'Let's give it a try.'

They worked their wrists against the barkless tree behind them.

'Mine are both awfully tight,' Sherri said.

'My left seems just a bit . . .'

'Oh Jesus!' Sherri gasped, her voice dropping to a whisper.

'What's wrong?'

'Someone's in the tree.'

Neala looked to her right, tipping back her head.

'No, the other way. Beside us.'

She turned to the left. She raised her eyes up the weathered trunk to the high branches. At first, she saw only jagged limbs, pale in the moonlight like bones stripped of their flesh. Then one of them moved, and she realized it was a leg. A second leg dangled beside it. She followed them upward to a bare hip and torso, a head with shaggy hair. If there were breasts, she couldn't see them. 'Is he alive?' Neala whispered.

'I can't tell. Looks dead to me.'

Neala continued to squint upward. The figure seemed to be straddling a branch, arms at his sides. His head was tilted downward, as if he were watching her. 'I think one of the legs moved,' she said. 'Could've been the wind, I guess.'

'I hope so.'

'You hope he's dead?' Neala asked.

'Hell yes. How would you like him to come down for us?'

'God, don't say that.'

'He's probably one of *them*, whatever the fuck they are. I mean, why else would he be out here?'

Neala didn't answer. She stared at the high, motionless figure until the sound of a car engine drew her eyes away. Across the clearing, headlights appeared.

'They're coming back!'

As the headlights approached, Neala saw that they were higher than those of the pickup. 'It's someone else,' she said. 'In a van, I think.'

'Just as well,' Sherri said.

It came through the darkness, not stopping where the pickup

had stopped. Its beams skittered over the ground as if seeking out Neala. They lit her and stayed, dimming just slightly when the engine shut off.

'What's going on?' Sherri asked.

'I can't see,' Neala whispered, squinting past the headlights. 'Someone just got out. He went to the back, I think.'

'End of the line,' said a man's cheerful voice. 'All out that's getting out.'

A woman cackled.

'I think we'd better do as they say.' A man's voice. Frightened.

'Daddy!'

'Here hold onto Ben's wrist.'

'What do you want with us?' a woman demanded.

More raspy chuckles.

'I know what Rose Petal wants,' said the cheerful man. 'She wants to pound your brains out with her hammer. I'll let her, too, if you don't make it snappy.'

'Bastard.' From the girl. Then she cried out with pain.

'Damn it, leave her alone!'

'We haven't got all night.'

Several figures appeared in the darkness beyond the head-lights. As they came forward, Neala saw four in a line, all cuffed together. A woman was at one side, then a man. The person at his other side was down. He and a girl each held a hand of the fallen one, dragging the limp body between them.

'Look,' said the woman.

'Hi,' Neala said.

'Step to the right,' said the cheerful man. Neala could see him, now, behind the others. He was chubby, and carried a pistol. An old, hunched woman scuttled along at his side, swinging a hammer overhead.

'Hello, young lady,' said the man with the gun. Walking

around the group, he stepped up to Neala. He looked at her, grinning. With the barrel of his pistol, he pushed one side of Neala's blouse out of the way. She felt the cool muzzle stroke her nipple. 'You're a nice one. Very nice. Little Timmy got at you, I'll wager.'

'Leave me alone,' she said.

'Ah, little Timmy. Tiny Tim. He "knows where it's at," so to speak.' The man laughed, and used his hand on her other breast, cupping it, squeezing as if to test its firmness, flicking the nipple. 'Mmmm. Sometimes, I do envy those Krulls. Yes I do. Give me a little taste.' Crouching, he licked her nipple. Neala kicked. He grunted at the impact and danced away, clutching his thigh. 'Oh ho! Lucky for you, lucky for you!' He whirled toward the four chained onlookers. 'Almost got me in the 'nads!'

Neala cried out, 'No!' as he spun around, raised his pistol, and aimed toward her face. He fired. The slug smacked into the tree above her head. He lowered his aim, and fired again. The bullet ripped through the crotch of her corduroys, just missing Neala.

'Ha ha! Owed you one.' He turned away. 'Okay folks show's over. Make a circle around that tree.'

As they followed instructions, the old woman started hobbling toward Neala.

'Get away!' Neala shrieked.

Rose Petal swung the hammer as if to show off her form. Tilting her head sideways, she laughed. She limped around to the back of the tree.

'You touch me,' Sherri snapped, 'and I'll kill you.' More laughter from the old woman.

'Get away! Damn you! I'll kill you, you . . . OW! Goddamn you!'

The cuffs cut into Neala's wrist as Sherri twisted and kicked.

39

The old woman squealed with delight, and Neala saw her skipping sideways out of Sherri's range. Neala kicked and missed. Prancing forward, Rose Petal swung the hammer. It pounded Neala's shoulder.

A high-pitched whistle made the hag turn away.

'Let's be off, sweets,' said the chubby man.

Side by side, they hurried to the van. The doors shut. The engine turned over and the van backed up. It didn't turn around; it rolled backward across the clearing and disappeared into the woods.

'Now what?' asked the girl beneath the other tree. All four were in a circle around it, hands joined as if playing 'Ring Around the Rosie.'

'Young ladies,' the man called. 'Do you know what's going on?'

Neala shook her head.

'They just – kidnapped us!' he said. 'Right out of the motel.'

'We were at the coffee shop,' Sherri told him.

'Do you know why they brought us here?' asked the woman.

'For the Krulls,' Sherri said.

'The what?'

'Krulls. I don't know. Krulls? We're sacrifices or something.'

'That's crazy,' the man said.

'Don't I know it,' Sherri muttered.

'It's crazy,' the man repeated.

'You're damn right,' Sherri said. 'Look, we've gotta get out of here. These things are gonna come for us. One's already here.' She pointed at the tree high above the four strangers.

Neala looked, along with the others, and saw the pale figure suddenly swing downward, dropping from branch to branch.

'Oh my God!'

Screams and shouts of panic erupted from those beneath the

tree as it scurried down the trunk. They threw themselves outward, trying to get away, and yelled in pain as the cuffs tore into their wrists. The unconscious one, arms jerked by those at his sides, raised his head. The others didn't seem to notice. They leaped and squirmed as the naked man dropped into their circle.

He pounced on the woman's back, his weight knocking her forward until the ring of arms stopped her. She recoiled backward. The whole circle fell.

The strange, bony man was pinned beneath her. Neala saw his legs wrap the woman's hips. His hands appeared beneath her outstretched arms and wildly tore her blouse as she thrashed above him. He jerked the blouse off her shoulders. His mouth clamped down on her left shoulder, and she screamed.

Then he was writhing out from under her. He crawled to her kicking feet. Kneeling over her, he grabbed one.

'Hey!'

He raised his head, mouth gaping, and looked toward the woods behind him.

Neala looked, too.

A man was running toward them.

The naked man stood. His shaggy head jerked from side to side, as if he hoped to find help. Then, with a bellow that made Neala's skin shrivel, he raced toward the intruder.

The other man stopped. He raised a rifle. Its detonation slammed through the night and the naked man pitched forward.

# Chapter Eight

Robbins sprinted past the body. Ignoring the shouts from the group of four, he headed toward the tree with the two women. He slung the rifle over his shoulder and dug a hand into his pocket. He pulled out a key.

'We're getting out of here.'

The woman he wanted stared at him, looking confused.

He stepped to her right side, and unlocked the cuff.

'You're one of the men from the truck,' she said.

'That's right. I'm taking you out of here. I've got a car off in the trees.' He stepped past her, and started unlocking the cuff on her other wrist. 'Are you a good runner?' he asked.

She shrugged.

'What's your name?'

'Neala.'

I'm Johnny Robbins.'

'I'm Sherri,' said the bigger woman, appearing from behind the tree. She held out her hands, empty bracelets dangling from the wrists. 'Do me a favor, huh?'

Quickly, he removed the cuffs. Unslinging his rifle, he scanned the perimeters of the clearing. Over the shouts of the other captives, he could hear the howling of distant Krulls. No sign of them, though.

'Okay,' he said. 'This way.'

'Wait,' Neala said. 'We can't leave *them*.' She nodded toward the others.

'The hell we can't. Let's go.' He grabbed Neala's arm, but she jerked free.

'I'm not going without them.'

'Shit,' her friend said.

Neala whirled on her. 'What's the matter with you? How can you even *think* of leaving these people?'

'To save my sweet ass, for Godsake.'

'We can't!'

Robbins groaned. It was stupid to waste time freeing the others. The delay could be fatal. But if he didn't give it a shot, he wouldn't stand much of a chance with Neala. 'All right,' he said. 'Stick close.'

They followed him to the other tree.

'Everybody shut up!' he snapped at the four.

They went silent. He stepped in front of the older male.

'You'll have to take care of the others,' he said, unlocking the right wrist. 'I'll leave you the key. We're going on ahead. If I can, I'll hold the car for you.' The other cuff fell loose. He slapped the key into the man's palm. 'Good luck.' He turned to Neala. 'Okay?'

'Okay.'

'Let's haul it.'

They started to run. Robbins took the lead, holding back to stay with the women. They were much slower than he'd hoped. Damn it, he should have parked the car closer. He'd left it much too far away, wanting to come in silently on foot. Sneak in, sneak out. With luck, he might have taken Neala out quickly, without a sound, and been on the road before anyone knew. If he hadn't shot that one bastard . . .

They were almost to the edge of the clearing when Neala grabbed his arm. 'Wait,' she gasped. 'We've got to wait.'

'What?'

She pointed to the group that was still at the distant row of

43

trees, the man busy unlocking cuffs. 'Forget 'em,' Robbins snapped.

'How'll they find the car?'

'Doesn't matter. Come on.'

'Christ, Neala!' Sherri snarled.

'Look!' Robbins pointed at a far-off figure loping across the field toward the group. 'There's another. Another.' Scanning the clearing, he could make out half a dozen dark shapes: some running, others limping, another scurrying across the ground like a crab.

'Oh my God!' Neala gasped.

'In a few more minutes, there'll be dozens. They'll get us, too, if we stick around much longer.' He pulled Neala into the woods. She tried to struggle free, at first. Then she was running close behind him. He dashed between the dark posts of tree trunks, kicked his way through waist-high bushes, dodged thickets too dense to penetrate, leapt onto the back of a fallen tree and jumped down to its other side.

Pausing while the women caught up, he listened.

The howling had stopped, but he heard Krulls nearby: feet crushing foliage, wheezing breath, the gibber of their strange language.

'Almost there,' he whispered.

'They're everywhere,' Sherri muttered. 'We'll never make it.'

'We'll make it.'

They kept running. Finally, they reached the roadhead where Robbins had left his car. He scanned the area. 'We're all right,' he said. 'Come on.'

Crouching low, he ran to the car. The women stayed close behind him. He grabbed the nearest handle. He was about to tug the door open, but a movement caught his eye. He looked up.

The face in the car window twisted, showing teeth.

Neala yelped with fright.

Robbins stared at the face. It was badly scarred.

The nose was a ragged flap, as if it had been chewed off in a fight.

There were five other faces inside the car, all turned his way.

Something clutched his foot. He lurched backwards, knocking into the girls, kicking the hand that had him by the ankle. Three Krulls started squirming out from under the car.

The doors opened.

Robbins rammed his rifle to his shoulder, took quick aim at the noseless face, and fired. The top of the head flew off.

'Let's go!' he yelled.

'Where?'

He fired again; this time taking out the eye of one by the rear door.

'Run! For Christsake, run!'

Free of the cuffs, they ran. Lander led the way, taking them across the clearing toward the place where the other three had vanished into the timber.

He took them that way in spite of the gunshots, in spite of the woman moving toward them from that direction. She was alone, a stooped old crone with white hair and pendulous breasts flapping down to her waist. She was armed with a machete, but her crippled back prevented her from moving fast. Lander simply planned to run around her.

'Dad!'

With a quick glance around, he saw a man on the heels of Cordelia. Two more were close behind. Ben dropped back and threw a shoulder block into the nearest one. They both tumbled sideways.

Looking ahead, Lander saw the old woman hobbling toward him. He lunged sideways as the machete slashed. He heard it cut through the air, saw it flash past his cheek, felt the breath of its close passage. He tripped and fell. The crone came after him, swinging. She stood over him. Raised the machete.

Whimpering, Lander shut his eyes tightly.

The blade didn't fall.

'Lander!' He looked. Ruth was behind the old woman, clutching the upraised arm, dragging her backwards.

He clambered to his feet. He drove a knee into the sagging belly. Foul breath blew into his face. Reaching up with both hands, he twisted the machete loose.

He hacked sideways, careful to miss Ruth's arm across the hag's throat. The blade slashed into one of the hanging breasts. Horrified, he watched the pale sack of flesh fall away.

Ruth let go as the woman dropped to her knees, screaming. Lander swung the machete straight down. It missed the center of the head, glanced off, took away half the scalp, and chopped into the shoulder. He tried again, this time splitting the head.

With a quick jerk, he pulled the blade free. He ran to where Ben and Cordelia were struggling with three men. One had Cordelia around the waist, trying to lift her. She kicked backward and squirmed. Lander circled, but the man turned, too, keeping Cordelia in the way. Finally, Lander threw himself against his daughter. The man stumbled and fell. As he hit the ground, Cordelia twisted free and Lander swung. The blade bit into an upthrust arm. The man bellowed with pain. He rolled out of the way, and Lander's next blow missed. Then he was on his feet and running.

Lander turned to Ben. The boy sat astraddle one, punching down at the face. A second man was behind Ben, about to bash him with a club. Lander's machete caught the standing one in the spine. With a cry, the man jerked stiff and dropped his club. A white club. A bone with a ball-joint at one end.

'Dad!' Cordelia called.

He tried to pull the machete free. It was stuck in the man's back.

'Dad, My God!'

Ruth was already far away, forty or fifty yards away, almost to the edge of the forest – slung over the shoulder of a tall, pale figure.

Lander whirled around. 'Ben, get off!'

Ben rolled away. The half-conscious man raised his head. Lander kicked it hard, and the man went limp.

He turned in time to see Ruth disappear into the woods.

'Stay close to me!' he yelled, and began the chase.

Just to the right, three people ran out from among the trees.

'Over there!' Lander called to them. 'Over there! He's got my wife!' The two groups met, and entered the timber.

# Chapter Nine

Peg quietly pushed open the door, half expecting to find Jenny asleep. Instead, the girl was propped up with pillows, reading a mystery. Her bare feet were crossed at the ankles. Peg realized, vaguely, that her daughter had nearly outgrown the pink pajamas, that Christmas would be too long to wait . . .

'What's up?' Jenny asked.

Peg shut the door. 'I want you to get dressed.'

'Now?'

'Right now.'

The girl wrinkled her nose. 'I don't get it.'

'We're going on a trip.'

'We *are*?' Her delight only lasted an instant. Then she frowned. 'Where are we going?'

'Away with Uncle John. Now hurry up and get dressed. Jeans and a blouse are fine.'

Jenny's eyes widened. She pressed the open book to her belly, and leaned forward. In a voice hushed and eager with conspiracy she said, 'It's Hank. We're running away from Hank!'

'We're not running away. We're just going on a vacation.'

'Don't worry, I won't tell.' Jenny swung herself off the bed. 'Where're we going? How about Los Angeles?' She flung her pajama shirt aside as she headed for the closet. 'Wouldn't you just love to go to Disneyland? We can go there, can't we?'

'Sure,' Peg said.

'Which bluse should I wear?'

'The plaid's fine.'

Jenny pulled the plaid blouse off its hanger. She slid her arms inside as she hurried toward the dresser. The sight of her small, pointed breasts reminded Peg that they'd planned to go shopping, this week, for a bra. Jenny's first. Now, that would have to wait.

Like everything else.

With John's visit, their normal world had come to an unexpected, abrupt halt. Nothing would ever be the same.

It hadn't been such a great life, up to now. She'd often dreamed of changing it, of leaving Hank, of taking Jenny far away. Now, she only wished that it could go on in the same old way.

It couldn't. John had dropped the bomb.

Trembling, she sat on the corner of Jenny's bed.

'Are you sick or something?' Jenny asked.

'I'm okay.'

'You look like you're gonna die.'

A chill crawled up Peg's back. 'Don't say that.'

'We've got to make sure and go to the Haunted House.'

'Huh?'

'And Space Mountain.' She kicked off her pajama bottoms, and stepped into her cotton underpants. 'Uncle John'll take me, if you don't want to. I'll be the only one in class who's been on Space Mountain. Harriet Hayer went to Disneyland, but her dad wouldn't let her. He's a creep, even if he is the mayor.'

Jenny fastened her jeans, and sat on the bed to pull on her socks. Peg put an arm around her.

'What happens if Hank catches us?'

'He won't.'

'Where is he?'

'Watching TV'

'Want me to climb out the window? We can both climb out. Is Uncle John coming in his car?'

'Yes.'

'When?'

'Any minute.'

'We ought to fix Hank's car. I could give it a flat tire. You want me to? Then he can't chase us.'

'No, you don't have to.'

'It'd be easy.'

'It's all right.'

Jenny finished tying her sneakers, and turned to Peg. 'We're never going to come back ever, are we?'

Peg shook her head.

'I didn't think so.' She shrugged her small shoulders. 'Oh well.'

'What?'

'Nothing. It's just that . . . well, Robbie Taylor, he was going to take me bowling tomorrow. I guess I won't ever see him again, huh?'

Peg brushed her fingers through Jenny's soft, brown hair.

'Or Marilou, either.' Her lips began to tremble, and tears filled her eyes. She looked at Peg, blinking, as if waiting for an answer that would make everything all right again.

Peg had no answer for her. 'Come on,' she said, and led the girl to the window. Silently, she slid the window up. The screen remained, its frame hooked into place at the bottom. She flicked open the hooks, and pushed. The snug frame didn't budge.

'You have to whack it,' Jenny told her.

'If we make any noise . . .'

'I'll do it.' Jenny wiped the tears off her face. Then she went to her bed for the book. Holding its upper edge against the frame, she struck the bottom sharply with her palm. The screen popped outward. 'Now it just slides out,' she said.

'Can you do it?'

'Sure.'

Peg held her by the hips while Jenny gripped the sides of the screen, and pulled.

'It's stuck.'

'For Godsake, don't drop it!'

'I . . .'

It suddenly fell free. Jenny gasped. The screen crashed into the bushes below the window and banged into the wall. 'Oh no,' she muttered. She turned to Peg, shaking her head. 'I'm sorry, Mom. I didn't mean to, honest. It just slipped.'

'It's all right, honey.'

'Maybe he didn't hear it.'

'Maybe not.'

Jenny leaned out the window.

'Bitch!'

Hank, just outside, grabbed the front of her blouse and jerked her through the window. Peg reached for the girl's feet. Too late. Hank flung her to the ground.

'You bastard!' Peg cried.

Hank grinned up at her. Then he turned away. Crouching over Jenny, he grabbed her by the collar and belt.

'Leave her alone!'

'Try and stop me.'

He raised the struggling girl waist-high, and dropped her.

'No!' Peg shrieked. She threw a leg over the window sill and started to climb out. Hank clutched her arm. He tugged. He wrenched the arm as if trying to drive her head into the ground, but her shoulder hit first. He shoved her onto her back, and sat on her. Pinning her hands to the ground, he bounced on her belly.

'Okay,' he said. He was breathless above her, and sweating. 'Okay, what's going on. Huh? What're you trying to pull?'

'Nothing.'

'Nothing? You and the kid were running off!'

'No.'

'You want me to hurt the kid?'

'Hank, for Godsake!'

'Set her hair on fire?'

'You bastard!'

'Where were you going? To Phillips?'

'No.'

'That shithead has always been after your ass.'

'It wasn't him!'

51

'Then who?'

'Nobody.'

'Okay, the kid gets it.'

As he scurried off Peg, she grabbed his foot. He kicked free and rushed to Jenny. The girl was still face down. He grabbed a handful of hair and lifted it from her back. His other hand snatched a butane lighter from his shirt pocket.

'No!' Peg yelled. 'I'll tell, I'll tell!'

She crawled toward him.

Hank thumbed the lighter. A flame spurted high.

'It was John! He's coming for us! He went out to the Killing Trees for a woman, and he's going to take us away!'

Hank grinned. 'Oh yeah? Not anymore, he's not.'

# Chapter Ten

Neala's feet throbbed with pain. Dozens of times, she cursed that little prick, Timmy, for taking her shoes. The pain and anger helped her hold onto reality as she followed the man named Robbins to his car, found it full of Krulls like a strange family about to embark on a vacation, watched him shoot two of them dead, and ran for her life away from the car.

Finding the other group again had been a relief, at first. Strength in numbers. But the man, Lander, didn't care about staying quiet or hiding. He wanted only to find his wife, even if it got the rest of them killed.

'We'll never find her,' Robbins said after ten minutes of wandering through the dense trees. 'We'd better give it up and try to make our way to the mam road.'

'Go ahead,' Lander snapped. 'Who needs you?'

'You'll get your kids killed.'

'I've got to find my wife.'

'She's probably dead already.'

'No.'

'How can we possibly find her?' asked the girl. She sounded desperate, on the edge of tears.

'We can't if we don't try,' Lander said. 'We can't if we do nothing but cower in the bushes like whipped curs.'

'It's our only chance,' Robbins said.

' "A coward dies many times. A brave man never tastes of death but once." '

'I'm with Mr Dills,' said the boy. 'We've got to save her, even if it means taking some extra chances.'

'Fuck it,' Sherri said. 'I'm not gonna risk my ass . . .'

Lander yelped as a pale figure dropped out of a tree. The knees rammed his shoulders, driving him down. Neala saw a knife in the upraised hand. Robbins fired. A hole appeared between the small breasts. The girl tumbled forward and hit the ground face first.

'Holy fucking shit!' Sherri gasped.

Neala stared down at the body. The girl was naked. Blood gushed from the ragged hole in her back.

'Let's go,' Robbins snapped. 'The shot'll bring 'em running.'

He pulled Neala by the hand.

They ran. They ran for a long distance. Neala's feet throbbed with pain as she kept pace with Robbins, but she didn't complain or slow down. For the first time since her capture at the diner, she felt hopeful. She was no longer anyone's prisoner, Robbins seemed determined to save her, and the Krulls had dropped out of sight. Maybe she would survive the night, after all.

Finally, when she thought she could run no farther, Robbins stopped.

'We'll just . . . catch our breath,' he gasped.

Neala nodded.

Sherri, who'd been running a short distance behind her, caught up. She sagged against a tree trunk.

'Where're the others?' Robbins asked.

'Coming.' Sherri flopped an arm sideways. 'Back there someplace. Christ on a crutch, I can hardly move.'

Neala heard the crunch of rushing feet. Off to the left. She raised her voice to call out. 'Ov . . .' Robbins clapped a hand across her mouth.

'Shhhh.'

His hand had a pungent odor like gunsmoke.

'Might not be them,' he whispered.

'Hey!' called a voice. The boy's voice. 'Where'd you all go?'

Robbins nodded and dropped his hand.

'Over here,' Neala called.

A few moments later, the boy and girl joined them.

'Sorry,' gasped the boy. 'Got a little lost.'

'Dad?' The girl staggered as if lost in a dark room. 'Dad? Where are you?' She looked at Robbins. 'Where's my dad?'

'I haven't seen him.'

She turned to the boy. 'Oh God, Ben, what'll we do?'

'He'll show up. We'll just wait.'

'Five minutes,' Robbins said. 'Who's got a watch?'

The girl raised her hand, and Neala saw a band on her wrist. For a moment, she was puzzled that the watch hadn't been stolen, back in town. Then she thought about Rose Petal. No surprise, really, that the old bag didn't care about such loot. Too

54

far gone for that. Her big thrill was bouncing her hammer off skulls. And that guy, the sadistic . . .

'What's the time?' Robbins asked.

The girl pressed a button. Red numbers glowed at her wrist. 'Ten thirty-two.'

'We'll give him till ten forty'

'Then what?' the girl asked.

'Then we move fast.'

'Maybe *you* do.'

'We're giving him eight minutes.' Robbins' voice was a quiet, calm whisper. 'If he hasn't shown up by then, he probably won't show at all. He either got lost, or the Krulls nailed him. Either way, we could stick around here till we've got Krulls crawling up our . . . till they get us, and it won't do your father any good.'

'Well, I'm not leaving.'

'That's up to you.'

'Maybe he'll get here in time,' the boy said.

The talking stopped. They waited.

Neala looked into the trees. Except for a few shreds of moonlight, the woods were as dark as a shut closet. The father was out there, someplace. But she didn't expect him to show up. If anyone came out of there, it wouldn't be him.

She rubbed her arms. She turned, staring into the darkness. If anyone came out . . .

She stepped close to a tree, and leaned back against it. The bark felt rough through her shirt. It felt good.

At least they can't come up behind me, she thought.

Robbins asked the time.

'Ten thirty-five,' whispered the girl.

Only *three* minutes had passed.

Neala moaned. She crossed her arms. Her nipples were erect and aching, as if she had a chill. She covered them with her hands, and the comforting warm pressure eased the tightness.

Off to the right, a twig popped.

Neala looked in that direction. She saw only trees and bushes and darkness. Nothing moved. No more sounds came.

But she kept her eyes on that patch of darkness. She barely breathed.

Because someone was out there watching.

She could feel him. She could almost see him, but not quite. Someone.

Someone not the girl's father.

# Chapter Eleven

'Just sit there,' Hank ordered.

Peg lowered herself again to the sofa, where Hank had shoved her after dragging her inside the house.

He stood across the room, holding Jenny by the hair. Jenny, on her knees, kept sobbing. 'Don't move an inch,' he warned her. Then he let go of her hair, and dialed the phone. When he finished dialing, he gripped it again.

'Yes. This is Hank Stover. I've got a situation here. Is Chief Murdoch around? . . . No? Well, send out one of the boys, would you? . . . No, nothing like that. I've got matters well in hand.' He grinned at his joke, and wrenched Jenny's hair. 'That's 833 Nussbaum Road . . . Right. I appreciate it.'

He hung up, and pulled Jenny to her feet. 'Okay, go sit with your mother.'

She sat beside Peg and leaned against her, crying softly. Peg put her arm around the girl.

'You did it this time,' Hank said. 'You and your damn brother. You're gonna get us *all* killed, you know that?' Shaking his head, he leanded back against the wall and folded his arms. 'That guy's really done it. Christ, you don't monkey with the Krulls. They're gonna come for us, you know that, don't you?'

'That's why we have to leave.'

'Yeah. Leave, my ass. What we'll do, we'll grab your hotshot brother when he shows up. That's what we'll do. We'll take him to the Trees. Maybe that'll be enough. Some brother you got. Flushes us all down the shitter for a piece of tail.'

'Don't you *want* to get out of here?'

'I like it here fine, thanks. I've got a good business . . .'

'Sure. Selling dead people's cars.'

He jabbed a finger at her. 'Not in front of the kid, damn it!'

'You think she doesn't know? She knows. Tell him,' Peg said to the girl.

Jenny shook her head.

'Tell him!' she snapped.

'I know!' Jenny blurted.

'Know what?' Hank asked.

'You get the cars . . . from the people we give to the Krulls.'

'Who told you that?'

'Everyone knows.'

He lunged toward her and raised a fist. Jenny covered her face. 'Lois Murdoch!' she yelled.

'Charlie's kid?'

'Yes. She said you get to keep part of the money, and her dad gets part, and part goes to the town.'

'It's no big secret,' Peg added.

'Hey, that's perfectly all right by me. They all get their share. It's not like I'm the only one taking advantage of the situation.'

'You more than most.'

'Yeah? Well I didn't see you complaining when you got the dishwasher. Or the TV for the bedroom. Or the . . .'

'You could've got a clean job.'

'Sure. Like your sainted brother, the grease monkey?'

'He's a fine mechanic. His money hasn't got blood on it.'

'Ah. He's pure as the falling snow. Except he's been a Delivery Man since he was eighteen.' Hank smirked. 'He's a *real* sweet guy.'

'He didn't have a choice.'

'Sure. They held a gun to his head. Don't give me that. Know why he's a Delivery Man? 'Cause he likes it. He gets off on the power.'

'You don't know what you're talking about.'

'Don't I? There's nothing he likes better than getting his paws on those . . .'

The doorbell rang.

'Don't move,' he warned. He went to the door and opened it. 'Come on in.'

Looking over her shoulder, Peg saw Dave Fielding enter. At twenty-three, he was the youngest man in the Barlow Police Department. He fidgeted, and smiled uneasily at Peg and Jenny.

'What seems to be the trouble, Mr Stover?'

'John Robbins.'

'I see.' He had trouble unbuttoning his shirt pocket. He pulled out a note pad, and a Bic pen. He wrote on the pad as Hank continued.

'Robbins is my wife's brother. What happened, I caught her trying to sneak out tonight with her daughter.'

'*Her* daughter?'

'By a previous marriage.'

'Her father,' Peg said, 'is . . . he disappeared.'

'I see.' Fielding glanced at Hank. 'So you're the girl's step-father.'

'Right. Now I caught the two of them trying to sneak out. It seems that Robbins went back to the Trees, Tonight . . .'

'He's a Delivery Man, isn't he?'

'Right. He apparently got the hots for a gal, tonight, and went back to the trees to rescue her.'

'*Jesus*,' Fielding muttered. He glanced at Peg, and blushed.

'After he gets the gal, he's planning to come back for Peg and the kid, and they're all gonna make a break for it.'

'Wow.'

'What I think we should do is grab him when he shows up . . .'

'And take him out to the Trees,' Fielding finished.

'Right.'

'When do you expect him?'

'Any time, now. It's been about an hour.'

'You realize, he probably won't show up.'

'Knowing Robbins, he might pull it off.'

Fielding shook his head and slipped the pad into his uniform pocket. 'If he does come, we'll need some back-up.'

'You'd better get your car out of sight, too.'

'That goes without saying. Now, may I use your phone?'

'Right over there.'

Fielding stepped over to the telephone, and dialed.

Jenny leaned close to Peg's ear. 'I've got to *go*,' she whispered.

'Can't you hold it?'

'No.'

'Hank, Jenny has to use the bathroom.'

'Wait'll the cop's done.'

'Fielding,' he said into the phone. I need a back-up team over at the Stover place.' He checked his note pad '833 Nussbaum . . . Marks and Haycraft are fine. Tell 'em to hurry.' He hung up.

'Now can I go?' Jenny asked.

'You want to watch my wife?' Hank asked Fielding. 'I'll take the kid to the John.'

'I don't want *you* to come!'

'Tough tittie. I'm not gonna have you sneaking out.'

'No! You'll watch!'

She turned to Fielding. 'He's a pervert! He's always spying on me.'

Hank's face turned purple. 'You lying little bitch, what're you trying to pull?'

'It's just 'cause it's the truth!'

Hank's fists clenched, but he stayed back. He looked at Fielding. 'You know why she's doing this? She wants you to take her to the john. I don't know what she's got up her sleeve, but she's a clever kid. She's always reading books, you know? Mysteries and stuff. Thinks she's Nancy Drew.'

'You want me to take her?' Fielding asked. His face was red.

'Help yourself. But watch out.'

Fielding gestured to the girl. 'Come on, then.'

She gave Hank a smug glance, and hurried to Fielding's side.

'There's a window,' Hank warned. 'Don't let her shut the door.'

Jenny took hold of Fielding's hand, and led him away. Hank shook his head. He turned to Peg. 'She's gonna pull something, just wait and see.'

Fielding entered the bathroom and went to the window on its far wall. It was plenty big enough for the girl to climb out, but the screen was firmly in place. He shut the window and latched it.

'All right,' he said.

'Can I shut the door?' she asked.

'Okay. But I'll only give you half a minute. Then I'm coming in, whether you're ready or not.'

'What if I lock the door?' She grinned up at him.

'I'd have to break it down.'

'That'd be neat.'

'I'd rather not have to.'

'Okay.' She shut the door.

Fielding listened for the click of the lock, but it didn't come. He raised his left arm. The second- hand of his wristwatch moved slowly past the numbers. After thirty seconds, he knocked lightly. 'Time's up.'

'I'm almost done.'

'Hurry it up.'

The toilet flushed. He heard water run for a moment. Then the door opened. She smiled up at him.

'Hank really would've watched, you know. He's sick in the head.'

'Come on, let's get going.'

'Can I tell you a secret?' She wiggled a finger, and glanced nervously down the hallway. 'I've gotta whisper.'

Fielding shrugged, and crouched down. Her lips tickled his ear. 'You know what Hank does to me?' she whispered. 'Late at night, he comes sneaking into my bedroom, sometimes, and he . . .'

The girl's hand moved swiftly. Fielding felt a strange, hot line across his throat. For an instant, he thought she'd scratched him with a fingernail. Then blood sprayed her face. His blood. He shoved her away. He tried to stand. Dizzy, he lurched toward the wall. The spray of blood moved as he did, and painted the wall.

He staggered back. He reached for his revolver, but his hand seemed too clumsy to unsnap the leather guard. Then he was staring at the ceiling. Blood showered down, filling his eyes, and he didn't have the strength to wipe it away.

Jenny slipped the injector blade into the pocket of her blouse and dropped to her knees beside the policeman. She popped open a snap that held his revolver inside its holster. She pulled the revolver out.

Standing, she looked down at the man. Blood still ran from his slit throat, but it no longer gushed.

She felt sick.

He'd seemed like a nice man.

But he would have helped kill Uncle John. He had to be stopped. It was the right thing to do. The right thing.

She suddenly doubled over and vomited. The spasms tore at her insides. Her eyes filled with tears.

*I've got to stop!*

*I've got to . . .*

Another contraction hit, sending a gush through her mouth and nostrils. A motion down the hallway caught her eyes. Blinking tears away, she looked up.

Hank ran toward her.

With both hands, she raised the revolver.

'No!' He stopped. 'Don't shoot! You did right! Now we can make our getaway.'

The first bullet knocked a leg out from under him. Jenny watched him flop. He lay on his belly, raising himself with his arms.

'Jenny, please!'

She took careful aim at his face, and pulled the trigger five times very quickly, staring through the white smoke as pieces of his head exploded away and hit the walls.

# Chapter Twelve

The roar of gunshots pounded through Peg's head. She raised her face off the carpet and looked toward the hallway.

*Jenny!*

*Jenny's down there!*

She pushed herself to her hands and knees. Grabbing the edge of the coffee table, she struggled to her feet. She straightened up. She wobbled a bit, still dizzy from the blow to her temple. Hank, hearing the commotion in the hall, had slammed her with a beer bottle to keep her from running. She stepped over the still unbroken bottle, and staggered toward the hallway.

A tattered layer of smoke hung over the bodies, swirling in the air currents as Jenny rushed from Hank's body to Fielding's. Peg glanced down at the body of her husband. His head . . . she quickly looked away, and saw the tiny, bright blade in his outstretched hand.

'Come here,' Jenny said. 'But don't step in the blood.'

'Jenny?'

'We've gotta get out of here,' the girl said. She wrapped Fielding's fingers around the revolver grips.

Peg watched, stunned and confused. Jenny was sheathed with

blood, her hair matted with it, her shirt splattered. 'Are . . . are you hurt?'

The girl smirked. 'They didn't touch me. I blew it, though. Boy, did I blow it. If I'd kept out of the blood, we could've stuck around and played innocent.'

'What are . . .?'

'We've got to split. Come on. The back door.'

Peg followed her daughter into the kitchen. The girl hurried to the sink, turned on the water, and rinsed her hands.

'Shouldn't we hurry?' Peg asked.

'I figure they won't get here in under five minutes, so we've got a couple left.' She dried her hands on a paper towel and stuffed the wadded towel into her pocket.

Amazed, Peg watched Jenny step over to the silverware drawer and pull it open as casually as if she were preparing to set the dinner table. Her hand came out with four steak knives.

'What are those for?'

'In case . . .'

The doorbell rang, knotting Peg's stomach with fear. Jenny rushed to the kitchen door, opened it silently, and pointed out.

They raced through the yard to the tool shed in the rear, and ran behind it. Jenny stopped. She leaned back against the wall.

'Where'll we go?' Peg asked. For a moment, she thought how strange it was to be relying on her twelve-year-old daughter. But the girl seemed to know what she was doing. She'd always had a lot of common sense and nerve – too much nerve, Peg often thought.

'To Phillips?' Jenny asked.

Peg stared at her. 'What do you mean?'

'Hank said . . .'

'I know what he said, and it's not true.'

64

'Come *on*, Mom. I'm not a baby. I know you've been going with someone.'

'That's enough!'

'If it's not Phillips, who is it?'

'None of your business young lady.'

'Look, we need help. We can't just wander around the streets, for gosh sakes. We need a hideout or a car, one or the other. Do you know how to hot-wire a car?'

'Of course not.'

'Me neither. They do it in books all the time, but I can't. I tried on Hank's car a couple times, but – I don't know – there's more to it than meets the eye. I think we'd better try Phillips.'

'What about John? He'll come by, and . . .'

'And see the cop cars, and keep going. Here, take these.' Jenny gave her two of the steak knives. 'Hide them.' She watched Jenny lift a cuff of her jeans and slip a knife into her sock. The other went into her hip pocket, handle first.

Peg was wearing a sleeveless, belted dress. Her feet were bare in her sandals. She shook her head. 'Where?'

'Have you got panties on?'

'Of course.'

Jenny patted her hips. 'Put them at the sides.'

Peg lifted her dress and slipped a knife under each side of her panties. The blades were cool on her skin. She adjusted the knives until she could no longer feel their sharp, serrated edges. 'Okay,' she said.

'Now let's go to Phillips.'

'Jenny!'

'Mom, they'll take us to the Killing Trees.'

'But . . .

'Do you want the Krulls to get us? My gosh, you *know* what they'll do!'

'Just rumors,' she mumbled.

'Well, I believe them, don't you? If Phillips loves you, he'll help us. Now come on!'

Jenny pushed away from the wall and hurried to the gate. She unlatched it and opened it an inch. She peered through the gap, opened the gate wider, and stuck her head out. After looking both ways, she glanced back at Peg. 'The alley's clear,' she whispered.

Peg followed her through the gate. They rushed across the dark alley and ducked beside a telephone pole. 'Where's his house?' Jenny asked.

'Third and Division.'

'Geez, that's the other side of town.'

'I know that.'

'We can't make it that far, not even cutting through yards. They'd be sure to . . . I've *got* it!'

'What?'

'Tucker Grady. He's on vacation. I saw him drive off in his jeep yesterday. He's a bachelor. His house'll be deserted.'

'So?'

'It's deserted. We can use it.'

'You mean, break in?'

'Sure. Why not?'

'It's against the . . .' The look on Jenny's face stopped her. Against the law. A hell of a thing to worry about at a time like this. 'Do you think we can get in?' she asked.

'No sweat. Come on.'

They made their way cautiously down the alley, staying close to the left side. They were nearly to the end of the block when a car turned in. Jenny pulled Peg down. They ducked behind a pair of garbage cans. The car moved slowly toward them.

'Bet it's a cop car,' Jenny whispered.

'Do you think they saw us?'

'It would've sped up.'

Peg hunched lower as the car approached. She heard its radio crackle and sputter, heard the loud, staccato voice of the dispatcher blasting unintelligible phrases. The wheels crunched over the crumbling macadam less then a yard away. She caught a whiff of cigar smoke. The car kept moving. The sweet cigar odor faded along with the sounds of the radio.

'Don't move till they're out of the alley,' Jenny warned. 'The rear-view mirror.'

When the sounds of the car were gone, Jenny stood. She leaned over the top of her trash can and peered down the alley. 'It's okay,' she whispered.

They ran the rest of the way. Tucker Grady's house was second from the last. The yard wasn't fenced. A thick hedge of bushes shielded it from *the alley*. Near Grady's trash cans, Jenny found a space through the bushes.

They entered the back yard. The rear windows of the small, single-story house were dark.

'Are you sure it's empty?' Peg asked.

'It better be.'

Staying low, they rushed through the yard. Jenny crept up the steps to the screened-in porch. She took the knife from her back pocket, slit the screen, and reached in to unlock the door. They entered the porch.

Peg stood just inside the screen door, holding it open, ready to dash out if the door of the house should suddenly burst open. She held her breath as Jenny tried the knob.

'Locked.'

The girl stepped back, and looked along the wall of the house. 'Ah-ha,' she said. She climbed onto an old couch against the wall, stood on its back, and tried to force open a small, high window. It didn't budge. Jumping to the floor, she glanced around. She stepped over to a bumper pool table in the corner. Two cue sticks lay across its top. She picked up one, and returned to the couch. Standing on its cushion, she thumped the cue's heavy end against the glass as if taking aim, then drew back and shot it forward, smashing a hole through the window.

Peg cringed at the sudden noise. Her eyes darted to the door.

Jenny, standing on the couch, also watched the door. She held the cue stick overhead like a club, ready to bash anyone who might come out.

The door stayed shut.

Jenny set the cue aside. Climbing onto the back of the couch, she reached through the broken window and unlocked it. She slid the window up.

'I'll go through,' she whispered, 'and open the door for you.'

'Don't cut yourself, honey. Do you want a boost?'

'Nah,' Jenny said, and climbed head first through the window. In moments, she was gone.

Peg waited in the dark porch. She looked at the open window and wished she had gone into the house instead of Jenny. She should have been the one. It wasn't right, letting Jenny take such risks. If harm came to her . . .

What was taking her so long?

Peg stepped toward the window. It looked high and small. Jenny had climbed through it easily, but it wouldn't be so simple for Peg.

She decided to give her daughter another minute. Slowly, she began counting to sixty.

One, two three, four . . . She heard footsteps inside. Five, six . . . The lock clacked and the door swung open. Jenny smiled out at her.

'What took you so long?' Peg whispered.

'I hurried as fast as I could.'

'It's okay. I was just worried.' She entered the kitchen, and shut the door.

'There's only one thing,' Jenny said.

'What?'

'Someone's in the bedroom.'

'Oh God!'

'It's just some old lady. Besides, she's asleep.'

'Let's get out of here!'

'No, it's all right.'

'What if she wakes up?'

'There's two of us, and only one of her. Besides she's ancient. And . . .' Jenny opened a lower button of her blouse and reached inside. 'I got these. They were next to her bed.'

Peg stared through the darkness. 'Glasses?'

'Yeah. And a hearing aid. Without these, she's useless.' Jenny set them on the kitchen table beside a ring of keys. She nodded toward the wall. 'There's the phone. Why don't you call Phillips and have him pick us up?'

Peg reached down to the table. The keys jangled as she picked them up. She clutched them tightly to stop the noise. Then she opened her hand, and carefully studied them.

'What're you doing?' Jenny asked.

'There are keys here for two cars.'

'Hey! I'll bet the other's around here someplace!'

'Let's check the garage,' Peg said. 'We'll drive right out of Barlow, and keep on going.'

'Disneyland, here we come!'

# Chapter Thirteen

Cordie glanced at the red numbers on her wristwatch. 'Okay, it's ten thirty. You guys are gonna leave now, right?'

'There's no point waiting any longer,' Robbins said.

'You're right.' Cordie took a deep, trembling breath. 'What're you gonna do, try and get to a road?'

'Eventually. We'll keep heading east and try to get out of Krull territory.'

'Yeah, well, good luck. You too, Ben.'

'Cordie?'

She wiped her sweaty hands on her jeans, and looked away. Ben took a step toward her. 'No. Don't, Ben. You go with the others.' She turned and ran. She heard quick footsteps, and knew that Ben was following. She ran harder. Damn it, he wasn't supposed to come. 'Go with *them*!' she called over her shoulder.

Reaching out, Ben grabbed her shoulder. He dragged her to a stop.

The others were out of sight.

'What do you want to do?' Ben asked, 'get yourself killed?'

'I can't leave. Mom and Dad are out here. I've got to find them.'

'I'll go with you, then.'

'No, don't.'

'I haven't got a choice, have I?'

'Go with the others. They're headed out. They've got a gun.'

'I can't.'

'Ben please.'

'I can't leave you. The same reason you can't leave your parents. I love you, I guess.'

70

'Oh Ben.' She pulled him tightly against herself. She kissed his mouth. Twisting a handful of his hair, she pulled back his head. 'I hope you don't regret it,' she muttered.

'I won't.'

'Let's find my folks and get our tails out of here.'

'This way,' Robbins said.

'Shouldn't we go after them?' Neala asked.

'They made their choice.'

'We're better off without them,' Sherri said.

'Come on.'

Neala, still with her back to the tree, squinted at the place in the darkness that had kept her filled with dread. She didn't move.

'Neala?'

'No, there's . . . Over there. Someone's hiding.'

'I'll check.'

'No!'

'Don't worry.' He walked toward the place unslinging his rifle and holding it ready.

'No! Don't, Johnny! Let's just go.'

He looked back at her. She thought she saw a smile on his face.

'Let's just go,' she said more softly.

'All right.' He turned away from the place Neala feared, and walked toward her.

She watched behind him. Her heart lurched as she glimpsed a quick movement. Something pale. A face? Whatever she'd seen, it vanished in an instant.

Johnny, seeing her alarm, looked back.

'It's nothing,' Neala said.

'You sure?'

Sherri stepped up beside Johnny, blocking Neala's view. 'What're we standing around for?'

71

Neala shook her head.

'I'll take up the rear,' Johnny said. 'We'll head east.' He pointed in the direction they'd been heading before they stopped. 'That way. Not much civilization out there, but we'll be okay once we get clear of Krull territory.'

'How far's that?' Sherri asked.

'About twenty miles.'

'Oh shit.'

'Let's get started.'

'Neala pushed herself away from the tree. She glanced behind Johnny and Sherri, but saw nothing in the darkness.

She led the way. Sherri followed, staying close, and Johnny kept behind Sherri. At first, she ran too fast for the terrain. She tripped, and Sherri stumbled over her, stepping on her leg.

'You all right?' Sherri asked, gently helping her up.

'I'll live.'

'Don't count on it.'

'Thanks a heap.'

Sherri patted her rump 'Think nothing of it.'

With Sherri in the lead, this time, they started running again. Neala ran more slowly than before. She tried to watch where her feet were landing, but the darkness hid all but glimpses of the ground.

The second time she tripped, she saw what did it.

A hand.

She yelped as she dived forward. The ground slammed her breathless. Rough hands turned her over, and a bony, white-skinned creature scurried up her body.

A man. A hairless man with the hollow face of a death's-head. He bit her mouth, and wetness dripped from his eyes.

Neala heard an awful thud. The head jerked away from her. The man flopped off, onto his back. She gazed at his erection, a loathsome thing like a rigid, pale snake. Then Johnny blocked her view. The rifle butt smashed into the horrible face, breaking through it.

'It's all right,' Johnny whispered. He helped her up.

Neala shook her head. She wiped tears from her eyes. Her shirt hung open, leaving her right breast uncovered. She closed the shirt. Not before noticing the fingernail scratches. They felt like burns on her skin.

'Did he hurt you?' Johnny asked.

'A little. I think I'm okay.'

'The filthy pig,' Sherri muttered. She stepped close to the body. 'Christ, look at him.'

Neala didn't.

'A fucking albino.'

Neala tried to fasten her shirt. The buttons were gone, so she overlapped the front and tucked it in.

'Shit,' Sherri said, still inspecting the body.

'We'd better get moving,' Johnny said.

# Chapter Fourteen

In Tucker Grady's garage, they found a Dodge Dart. They went to its rear, and Jenny reached for the handle of the garage door.

'That won't work,' Peg told the girl. 'It's on remote control.'

'Oh no.'

'What's wrong with that?'

'It'll make enough racket to wake the dead – *and* the old woman.'

'Well?' Peg asked.

'We won't get any headstart if she starts screaming her head off or calls the cops or something. We'd better go in and tie her up.'

'My Lord, Jenny.'

'Come on, she's older than God. She can't hurt us.'

'Hadn't we better just get going?'

Jenny frowned at her. 'Do you want to blow everything?'

'I . . .'

'Let's take care of the old bat. Nothing to it.'

They left the garage, and re-entered the house through its back door. Jenny led the way through the kitchen and up a hallway so dark that Peg couldn't see her at all. Reaching out, she touched her daughter's back. She found Jenny's shoulder, and hung on.

'Right here,' Jenny whispered.

Peg heard a door moan open. Jenny moved sideways. Peg followed, her arm brushing the doorframe.

The room filled with light. Squinting against the sudden brightness, she saw Jenny's hand on the wall switch.

On the bed, an old woman was sitting upright, her eyes wide open, her bony arms held out. 'Took yer merry time,' she said in a high, brittle voice.

Jenny glanced around at Peg, confusion on her face.

'I knew you'd get to Heggie, one fine night. Felt it in my bones, I did. Don't know what kept you.'

Jenny walked toward the closet.

'Nobody there, young fella. I'm all alone. Been all alone since fifty-two when you took away my darling Brian.'

'What about Tucker?' Jenny asked.

'Took who? My Brian, my only Brian. You took him to yer trees. Oh Lord, you took him. You took him to yer trees.'

Jenny stepped into the closet and came out with a quilted robe.

'Took him for the dirty Krulls.'

She slipped a cloth belt off the robe, and walked toward the bed.

'I knew you'd come for me,' Heggie said, bobbing her head as Jenny tied her hands. 'I been waiting. I been figuring. I'll be a merry treat for the heathens.' She giggled. 'Trick or treat, trick or treat. Want to know my secret? Promise to keep mum?' She winked a pale eye at Jenny.

'Cross my heart,' the girl said loudly, and knotted the belt.

'Snake poison.' She giggled again. '*Rattlesnake* poison. Venom. Get it? I'm *full* of it. Full of it. Been dosing myself since fifty-two. Yessir. Full of it.' She hissed like a snake. 'Poison meat.'

Jenny glanced at Peg, fear in her eyes. Then she turned back to the old woman. 'We'll be right back.'

'Taking me to yer trees. Yessir. A merry treat for the dirty Krulls.'

Jenny hurried out of the bedroom. With a shaky hand, she brushed hair away from her forehead. Peg put a hand on her shoulder.

'She's nuts huh?'

'I guess so,' Peg said.

'Gosh.'

The garage door rumbled up, and Peg backed the Dodge down the driveway. She noticed Jenny looking toward the house. She looked, too. In one of the windows, a light was on. It must be the bedroom, she thought.

Jenny wrinkled her nose.

'What's wrong?'

'Crazy people. They make me nervous I guess.'

With a nod, Peg pulled onto the street. 'Better strap yourself in.'

'Do you really think she did it? Gave herself snake venom?'

Peg shrugged.

'I mean, that's weird. It's scary.' She snapped her seatbelt into place. 'Not a bad idea, though. Wonder where she keeps the snakes. I didn't see any around the house.' She opened the glove compartment. 'None in there.' She put one of her knives – the one she'd taken from her rear pocket before sitting in the car – into the glove compartment.

'Here, do something with these.'

Peg fumbled blindly on her lap, and picked up her two knives.

'Better keep one on you,' Jenny said.

'We won't need them now.'

'You never can tell.'

She handed one of the knives to Jenny, and left the other on her lap.

'Do you need the headlights?' Jenny asked.

Peg killed them. The pavement ahead went dark, but the street lamps gave enough light to steer by. She drove slowly, staying on Grove because it ran parallel to the highway. At the end of town, it stopped. She turned left, and stopped at the highway. Terk's Diner, on the corner, was closed for the night. Across the highway, the blue neon VACANCY sign of the Sunshine Motor Inn went dark, and blinked on again.

Far down the highway, headlights appeared. Peg's stomach knotted. She shifted to reverse and sped backwards, swinging the rear of the car toward the curb. She hit the brake pedal. The car jerked to a stop, and she turned off the engine.

'Get down!'

They both ducked low in their seats.

From the roar of the engine, she doubted that the approaching vehicle was a passenger car. It sounded more like a truck. She raised her head enough to peek out. A trailer truck plowed by.

Quickly, she started the engine and pulled onto the highway behind it.

'Los Angeles is *that* way,' Jenny protested.

'We'll worry about that later,' Peg said. 'Let's stay with the truck.'

She floored the gas pedal, trying to catch up, but the truck was too fast. It kept pulling away. She followed it around a curve, leaving Barlow behind. Without street lamps, she could barely see the road. She stayed in the middle of the highway. Soon, she found herself gaining on the truck. If she got close enough, she could simply follow in its wake, letting its taillights show her the way.

Its brake lights flashed on.

It slowed quickly. Peg moved up close behind it.

'It's gonna stop!' Jenny warned.

'My God, what . . .?'

Steering across the center line, she saw lights ahead of the truck. Headlights. Parked cars. She swung behind the truck.

'A roadblock,' she muttered.

Jenny moaned.

Peg stepped on the brake. As the car jerked to a stop, she watched the truck pull slowly away.

'What'll we do?' Jenny asked.

She shook her head.

'They'll have it blocked the other way, too.'

'I know, I know.'

'Let's go back to Grady's.'

She wondered if she dare try Phillips. He might help. Or he might not. He claimed to love her, but . . .

'Oh geez, they've seen us!'

Stunned, Peg saw a car speed past the truck. Its headlights on high-beam, were blinding.

'Oh God!'

'Turn around!'

'It'll hit us!' she shrieked but her foot stomped the gas pedal and she jerked the steering wheel, swinging broadside to the onrushing car. She gritted her teeth, waiting for the impact as the force of the U-turn shoved her sideways. She straightened the wheel. Headlights burst in her rearview mirror. She mashed the accelerator. The car shook and bucked. She saw that her right tires were off the pavement. She eased left, bringing them onto the road.

'He's still gaining!' Jenny yelled. She was twisted around, looking out the rear window. 'He's right on our tail!'

She sped through the center of town, all its shops closed and dark, its only traffic signal blinking yellow. She shot beneath the light. Just ahead, a startled cat leaped and sprinted to safety.

'Stop!' Jenny said. 'Stop the car!'

'What?'

'We'll hit the other roadblock.'

'But . . .'

'Just stop.'

She took her foot off the gas. Slowly the car lost speed. The trailing car stayed close behind.

'We'll make *them* get out,' Jenny said. 'Whatever you do, don't get out. Do just what I say. There's only two of them, I think.'

As the car stopped, Jenny reached into the glove compartment. She took out the two knives, and gave one to Peg. The other, she slipped inside her blouse.

'Stick it in your armpit,' she said. 'Clamp your arm down.'

'I . . .'

The car pulled alongside. She recognized the boy in the passenger seat. Timmy Shaw. He met her eyes, then looked past her at Jenny and smiled. A vicious, mocking smile.

'Hi-ya Jenny,' he called.

As the car slid by, Peg opened a button and reached inside her dress top. She tucked the knife handle into her right armpit, and lowered her arm to hold the knife in place. Then she reached forward awkwardly to turn off the engine.

'Leave it going,' Jenny whispered.

The car stopped in front of them, and backed up until it bumped. Both doors opened. Jack Shaw climbed out the driver's side, and Timmy came out the other.

'Okay,' Jenny said. 'Back up, real quick, then run over the old guy.'

Peg turned to her daughter, shocked. 'I can't do that.'

'Geez Mom!'

'I just . . .!'

'They'll take us to the Trees!'

'But I . . .'

Shaw pulled open her door. 'Step on out, Mrs Stover.'

'You too,' the boy told Jenny.

Keeping her arm tight against her side, Peg climbed from the car. As she stood, she felt movement on her lap. The second knife! It hit the pavement with a clatter.

Shaw gazed at the knife. Then he smirked at Peg, shaking his head. 'Dumb,' he said, and smashed a fist into her belly.

She doubled. The road slammed her knees and she sprawled forward, sucking for air that wouldn't come.

Jenny, still sitting in the car, watched her mom go down.

'Come on,' Timmy muttered, grabbing the shoulder of her blouse.

'Leave go!'

He jerked her sideways. As she fell, she grabbed the door handle. The knife dropped from under her arm, slid down the in side of her blouse, and fell to the gravel. She let go of the door. She dropped to the ground, planning to reach for the knife.

Before she could move, the boy gripped her arms. He dragged her clear, gravel scraping her back. Then she felt the soft wetness of grass. She squirmed, trying to pull free. Timmy dropped onto her outstretched arms. His knees pounded like spikes into her arms, nailing them to the ground. After the first blast of pain faded, she felt his hands on her breasts.

'Timmy, what're you doing back there?'

The hands continued to rub and squeeze.

'Bring her over here.'

'In a minute,' Timmy called.

'Right now.'

He leaned farther forward, his hands sliding down her chest and belly. They tugged at her belt.

'Timmy!'

The boy unbuttoned her jeans. He slid the zipper down. Then he was lifted away and shoved aside. 'Damn it, you little twerp! We've got a job to do!'

'I only wanted a little feel,' he pouted.

Jenny rolled onto her side and drew her knees up.

'Just a feel, that's all.'

'Let's get her into the car,' the man said, sounding disgusted.

'Why don't we keep 'em, Dad?'

'You know better than that.'

'We could take 'em someplace and screw 'em.'

'And get the Krulls on us? Where's your brain, boy? Never mind, I *know* damn well – it's swinging between your legs.'

'Nobody'd have to know, Dad. We can kill 'em when we're done, and hide their bodies. I'd sure like to screw Jenny, Dad. Please?'

'Forget it. Now give me a hand.'

Kneeling, Timmy's father rolled Jenny onto her back. She opened her eyes. The broad, grim face was just above her. With a growl, she rammed the knife at his eye. It hit low, ripping open his face from cheekbone to chin.

He wailed. He grabbed his cheek and lurched backward but Jenny caught his arm. She hung on and blindly stabbed overhead, the knife jolting as it hit bone. She struck again. This time, the blade went into softnes. The man shrieked and fell.

Letting go, Jenny rolled off him. She glimpsed his gouting face and neck, then looked up at the boy.

Timmy's stunned eyes met hers. Then he spun around and ran. At the rear of the car, he tripped and fell sprawling.

Jenny saw her mother lying on the road, an arm outstretched.

'No!' Peg cried.

Jenny rushed past, ignoring her, and leaped onto Timmy.

The knife plunged. The boy squealed.

'No! That's enough! Don't *kill* him!'

The knife went down again.

Peg squirmed forward, dragging her useless legs, the cuffs on her ankle scraping along the pavement.

The boy stopped screaming.

Jenny raced by, knelt over Jack Shaw's body, and searched his pockets. Moments later, she was kneeling at Peg's feet.

'You . . . you didn't have to . . . slaughter them.'

'Didn't I?' Jenny asked, and unlocked the cuffs.

# Chapter Fifteen

Cordie climbed onto the trunk of a fallen tree. She held a dead limb to steady herself, and gazed ahead. Nothing was visible in the darkness except more trees.

Ben climbed up beside her. 'Which way?' he asked.

'I guess it doesn't matter. I mean, they might be anywhere.' Cordie couldn't keep the despair out of her voice.

'Do you want to go back?'

'Go back where?'

'Try to find the others again.'

'Oh, you know right where they are?'

'Not exactly, but . . .'

'How the hell are we supposed to find them, then? Just turn around and start walking? That'll do a lot of good.' She sat on the trunk and scooted forward, her legs stretching toward the unseen ground. She pushed off. Not hard enough. A rough jutting stub of branch jabbed and scraped her back as she dropped. 'Damn!' She stumbled forward, grabbing at her back.

'You hurt?'

'Yes, Shit shit shit!'

Ben leaped down.

'God *damn*!'

'Let me see,' he said.

She turned away and lifted the back of her blouse.

'Its just a scratch.'

'Kiss it and make it well. But *gently*.' She felt the soft touch of his lips on her back.

'Better?'

'Yeah. Thanks.'

He stood beside her, and she took hold of his hand.

She studied the dark wilderness. 'I don't know, Ben. They might be anywhere.'

'We'll just keep going.' He shrugged. 'Not much else we can do.'

'If we could just find that clearing . . . I thought it was this way, but . . .' She shook her head. 'None of this looks familiar.'

'I don't think we've gone far enough, yet.'

'Maybe not.'

'It's a big clearing. We'll probably run into it.'

'I sup . . .'

She staggered back as a naked boy leaped from behind a tree. He planted himself in their way, crouching slightly, one hand forward. The hand held a knife. Cordie and Ben backed away, but the boy stepped forward, staying close to them.

'Run?' Ben whispered.

'Let's get his knife. He's just a kid.' Cordie lowered her eyes, hoping to spot something she could use as a weapon. The ground was too dark. But her heel knocked into a hard object. She stooped and felt for it. Her fingertips found a moist surface of bark. She grabbed, clutched a thick branch, and lifted. It started to pull free from the ground, but one end stayed down.

The damn thing was a dozen feet long!

As she let it go, the boy lunged. His knife flicked at her face. She threw out an arm to block it. The blade sliced into her forearm. Then Ben was on the boy, pulling him back, reaching for the knife hand. He couldn't get a grip on it, but Cordie grabbed the wrist with both hands. She twisted sharply. The arm made a sound like crackling gristle. The boy cried out. The knife fell.

Cordie dropped to her hands and knees while Ben struggled

to hold the writhing boy. She raked the moist ground cover. Found the knife. Got to her feet. Braced herself. 'Okay, hold him.'

She pressed the point against the boy's belly. He stopped moving.

'Where do you live?' Cordie asked.

The boy growled. His upper lip curled, baring his teeth.

'I don't think he understands,'

Ben said. 'Yeah. Maybe not.' She leaned close to the boy. 'Do you speak English?'

Again, the boy growled. 'The kid's an animal,' Ben muttered.

'Kid. I'm looking for my parents, my mom and dad. Do you know where they are? Where do you take the people you catch? Do you have a camp or something?'

'He can't talk.'

'What'll we do with him?' Cordie asked.

Ben shrugged. 'I don't know if we ought to let him go. No telling what he might do.'

'Well, I don't think I'm up to butchering him. Are you?'

'Ben sighed. 'I guess not.'

'Hey, let's have your belt. We can loop it around his neck, maybe use it like a leash, see where he takes us.'

'We can give it a try.'

Keeping one arm clamped around the boy's neck, Ben unfastened his belt and yanked it free. As he held it out to Cordie, she passed the knife to him.

She slipped the broad, leather tip through the buckle, and dropped the loop over the boy's head. Ben forced the belt down the thin neck. Cordie jerked it taut.

'Okay,' she said. 'Let him go and we'll see.'

Ben let go.

The boy leaped at Cordie. She sidestepped, tugging the belt, and swung him off his feet. He sprawled, choking. He clawed at his throat, but Cordie stepped on his back and kept the belt tight. He rolled. Cordie's foot skidded off. Balance lost, she fell. The belt flew from her hands.

She saw Ben kick. His shoe slammed into the boy's face, and the boy went down.

'He's out,' Ben said after nudging the body.

'Dead?'

'Just unconscious, I think.'

They took the time to bandage Cordie's cut arm.

Ben used the tail of his shirt, slicing it off with the boy's knife and tying it around Cordie's wound.

Then Cordie knelt beside the boy. She loosened the belt. Touching his neck, she found his pulsebeat. 'Let's just leave him while he's still conked out,' she said.

'Fine with me.'

Leaving the boy, they ran through the trees. They had gone no more than fifty yard when a voice cried out the single word, 'Krull!'

Not the voice of the boy.

It came from behind. Cordie stopped, and turned.

'What was that?' she whispered.

'I don't . . .'

The shriek of the boy ripped into her ears.

Ben grabbed her arm. 'Come on.'

They ran a few steps. Then Cordie pulled free. 'Wait.' She crouched behind a tree and pulled Ben down beside her. 'What'd that sound like?' she whispered.

'Like a maniac.'

'I mean, didn't it sound like somebody yelled, "Krull," and then maybe killed the kid?'

'Sure did.'

'Maybe he'll help us.'

'You're nuts.'

'No really. I mean, *we're* not Krulls. Maybe he's trying to get away from here too, just like us.'

'Not just like us. You heard him, for Christsake. He hardly sounded human.'

'It'd be . . .' Her voice froze in her throat as she heard the quiet crushingof underbrush.

Ben's hand tightened in hers.

A tall, broad shape strode between the tress. In one hand, it held a machete. From the other swung the head of the boy.

A strangled whimper escaped from Cordie.

Ben lunged away, pulling her hand. She jerked it free. Ben glanced back.

The awful voice roared, '*Krull*!'

Ben ran.

Cordie staying down saw dark shape after him.

Then there was only forest. She heard the crashing footfalls.

Ben yelled, 'No! Please!'

She covered her ears.

Ben's final cry was cut short.

She curled at the base of the trunk, and hugged her knees, and listened to the woods.

# Chapter Sixteen

'Holy shit, a cabin!'

Robbins caught up to Neala. They stopped beside Sherri, and looked through the trees.

Near the end of a long,moon-washed clearing stood a cabin of logs.

'Not bad,' Robins said. 'Let's have a look.'

He went first, steping into the open and pausing to scan the area. The clearing was larger than a football field. Watching the edges of the forest, he saw no movement. The cabin looked dark and deserted. 'Stay close,' he said.

Neala stepped to his right side, Sherri to his left. He started forward, rifle ready. The ground felt springy under his boots. A cool breeze stirred across his bare arms.

He looked at Neala. She was limping. Her mouth was pressed shut as if she were biting into the pain. She looked very brave and very vulnerable. He wanted to hold her.

She saw him looking, and made a smile.

'How're the feet?' he asked.

'They've seen better nights.'

He turned to Sherri. 'Gonna make it?'

'First chance I get,' she said, and laughed sourly.

As they moved closer to the cabin, Robbins saw that it stood in a field of pickets. Each of the tall poles had a crossbar like the armbones of a scarecrow. Each was topped with a dark ball.

Sherri grabbed his arm and pulled him to a halt. 'Oh shit,' she gasped. 'Oh fucking shit!'

'They're *heads*,' Neala whispered.

Robbins squinted at the top of the nearest pole. The sphere on top was a head, all right, its dark hair drifting in the breeze. He looked from one pole to another. A head was impaled on each. 'Good God,' he said. He took a step forward.

Sherri tugged his arm. 'We're not going in there!'

He turned to Neala.

She shook her head, her face twisted with disgust.

'The cabin,' he said.

'I don't want to,' Neala told him in a voice like a terrified child.

Turning around, he saw movement in the woods. A face appeared beside an aspen. He raised his rifle and took aim, but the face slipped sideways. It vanished behind the trunk.

To the left, a pale body darted between trees.

Sherri groaned loudly.

'Let's go for the cabin,' Robbins said.

Neala squeezed his arm.

A knife arched through the night, flipping end over end, its blade flashing moonlight. Robbins shoved Neala. She stumbled sideways as the knife whipped by. Robbins rushed to her.

'Let's go,' he said, pulling her up.

'God, it would've . . .'

'It didn't.'

They raced toward the cabin. Sherri caught up. A dozen feet before the first stake, Robbins dropped Neala's arm and snatched the knife from the ground. 'Take this,' he said. He looked back.

He saw no one.

Then he led the way among the poles, ducking beneath the cross-bars. The pikes were close together. He moved carefully, afraid of bumping them, but his rifle butt knocked into one. The staff wobbled. Something dropped from above and Neala, behind him, gasped with horror. He wanted to look around, but the staffs enclosed him like a cage. He couldn't turn without tipping others.

'You all right?' he called back.

No answer.

'Neala?'

'I'm okay,' she whispered.

'Sherri?'

'*Get us out of here!*'

'How's the rear?' The words were out before he realized his mistake. 'Forget . . .'

'*Yaaaaah*'

He raised himself. His shoulder hit a cross-bar. The staff wobbled in the loose earth. He clutched it to stop it from falling. Then he pivoted and looked back. Neala was still crouched low. Sherri, a distance behind her, was standing upright, back toward him, shoulders level with the cross-bars, head just below the other heads. Robbins watched her, and knew she wasn't checking the rear for Krulls. She was gazing at the impaled heads. Dozens of them. Surrounding her. Pressing close like a hideous mob.

'Sherri!' he shouted.

She whirled around. Knocked into a pole. It fell against another, and that one tipped, and suddenly a dozen staffs were swaying and falling, their grisly ornaments jerking toward each other as if to share a secret, others thudding together, some falling and rolling.

Sherri looked at it all, then at Robbins. Her eyes and mouth were dark holes in her moonlit face.

Neala started to rise. Robbins pushed her head down. 'Don't look,' he said.

'Sherri, just come on forward.'

She didn't move.

'Sherri!'

'I can't.'

'Stay right here,' he said to Neala.

Crouching below the cross-bars, he made his way through the forest of pikes. When he got close to Sherri, he found the crosses standing at crazy angles. He tried to lift one out of the way. A weathered head, little more than a skull with patches of hair trailing in the breeze, wobbled in front of his face. Sickened, he dropped the pike.

He stood facing Sherri. She was several feet away.

A tangle of sticks and heads separated them. Keeping his eyes on her, he began moving forward, stepping high, his boots smashing the frail crosses to the ground. Twice, he stepped on heads. One crushed. The other tipped like a rock and nearly sent him sprawling. He caught his balance, choked with horror at the thought of falling into such things.

Then he had Sherri by the arm.

He looked beyond her. Nobody was in pursuit.

'You all right?'

She answered with a whimper.

Holding her arm, he pulled her through the trampled mesh.

'Shut your eyes,' he said. He looked back to make sure they were shut. Then he pulled her forward again. He told her to hold onto his belt. When he reached the first upright cross, he kicked it aside. The head flew off, but he didn't watch. Another cross stood in his way. Cursing, he used his rifle butt to knock it aside. He moved fast, smashing the barriers down.

'Neala, keep your eyes shut. We're coming up behind you.'

He Slammed the sticks out of his way. They crashed into others, heads flying.

When he was close to Neala, he uprooted three of the crosses and flung them to the sides. He stepped past her. 'Grab onto Sherri. Keep your eyes shut and hang on.'

'Johnny, what . . .?'

'I'm getting us to that cabin.'

He shot his foot forward, kicking down a frail stick. It took down the one in front of it, and that one tore down another. As they fell, he plowed ahead and knocked down more. He swung his rifle. The butt smashed through one cross after another. He swung high and it clubbed a head. He swept low. The pikes scattered. Then there were no more in front of him. The cabin door was yards away.

Robbins turned, and saw the path he'd battered through the barrier. The passage was bordered by half-fallen crosses that teetered at strange angles.

'It's all right,' he said.

The women stood and looked back. Sherri covered her mouth. Neala quickly turned away.

Robbins walked to the cabin door. It had no knob. A leather thong hung out. He pulled it, and heard a squeak of wood inside as the latch lifted. He pushed the door. It swung open.

'Hello?' he called into the darkness.

No answer came.

He stepped through the doorway. The air smelled gamey. It felt warm and damp. He peered through the darkness. He could see nothing.

Reaching into his pants pocket, he found his book of matches. He flipped open the cover, tore a match loose, and struck it. The head flared. He squinted against the sudden brightness, and turned in a full circle. Satisfied no one was lurking in the small room, he shook out the match and returned to the door.

'It's okay. Come on in.'

Neala and Sherri entered. Robbins pulled the door shut, cutting off the moonlight. The wooden latch dropped into place. He struck another match. In its fluttering light, he quickly searched for a lamp. He found a candle holder protruding from a wall, and lit it. Each wall had a candle. He lit them all. Their tips fluttered, filling the room with shadows.

'Must be a bed,' Sherri muttered, looking down at a nest of fur pelts. She sat on it, rubbed her hands cautiously over the top, then lay back and sighed.

Neala stood in the center of the room. She turned slowly. Her eyes moved up to Robbins' face.

'I think we should get out of here,' she said.

'We need the rest,' Robbins said. 'This place'll be easy to defend.'

Sherri raised her head. 'I'm not going out there again.'

'But . . .' Neala nervously rubbed her mouth.

'Whoever lives here, he must be the one who put up the heads.'

'I don't want to hear this,' Sherri said.

'What if he comes back?'

# Chapter Seventeen

Art Phillips came to the door in his boxer shorts. 'Peg?' he asked.

She stepped into the dark foyer, Jenny close behind. Art shut the door. He turned on a bright overhead light, and gaped at them. '*Jesus* what happened?'

'We're in trouble,' Peg said.

'I can see that.' He shook his head, frowning, and rubbed one eye. His hair was mussed from sleep. 'What kind of trouble? Come on in here, let's sit down. *Jesus!*'

They followed him into the living room. Peg stared at his pale, freckled back. His shorts hung low, showing the cleavage of his rump. Only two days ago, she'd hooked a finger into that groove, and tugged his shorts down. He'd fallen onto his bed, the shorts around his knees, and rolled onto his back, and she'd taken him into her mouth . . . Only two days ago. And yet, she was afraid now to ask him for help.

He turned to Jenny. 'Is that blood?'

Jenny nodded.

'Are you hurt?'

She smiled strangely. 'It's not my blood.'

'Whose?'

'Ask Mom.'

'Do you want to go wash up?' he asked her. 'Take a shower, why don't you?'

'Okay. Thanks.'

He pointed the way to the bathroom, and rubbed the back of his head as he watched her leave.

'Now what happened, Peg?'

'I left Hank.'

'What do you mean? Here, sit down.' He dropped onto the couch, and patted the cushion beside him. Peg sat down. He rubbed the back of her neck.

'I decided to run away from Hank, tonight. But he caught me and Jenny sneaking out. He . . . He was hurting Jenny. I had to stop him. He kept beating on her . . . I think I killed him.'

*'You killed Hank?'*

'I stabbed him,' she said. She found it easy to lie. Art

continued to stroke her neck. He said nothing. Peg could hear the distant spray of the shower.

'Where were you planning to go?' he finally asked.

'Just away. Los Angeles, maybe.'

'Are you nuts? You can't leave Barlow.'

'I *killed* him, Art.'

'There're other ways. Plead self-defense or something. You can't leave Barlow. That's suicide.'

'Not if you help us.'

He quickly took his hand off her neck. 'No way.'

'With your security pass . . .'

'That won't do you any good. Not if they're looking for you. They'll have roadblocks at each end of town . . .'

'They already do. Jenny had an idea, though. We could hide in the trunk of your car. They wouldn't look in the trunk, would they?'

'They might.' He leaned back, folding his hands behind his head, and stared at the ceiling. 'You've really done it to me.'

'I know. I'm sorry.'

'If I don't turn you in, and anyone finds out you were here . . .'

'Nobody has to know.'

'They'll know, all right. And then they'll come after me.'

'That's the whole thing, Art. Leave with us, and never come back. They can't hurt you, then. You haven't got any family. You'll be free and safe, and you'll never have to worry about the Krulls again. Wouldn't you like that? Aren't you tired of living in fear?'

'Don't give me that "living in fear" shit. Don't you watch the news? That world out there is full of maniacs. Jesus, they kill you for no reason. Nobody's safe out there. It ain't like that in Barlow. You can walk around the block, here, without getting snatched or raped or your brains blown out. You don't have to lock your doors at night to keep all the freaks out. So don't tell me about living in fear. You got nothing to worry about, here in Barlow, as long as you play by the rules.'

'But if you break the rules . . .'

'Then you're up shit creek.'

She stared down at her folded hands. They felt cold and heavy on her lap. 'Is it true, what they say about the Krulls?'

'Depends what you heard.'

'Oh God, Art!' Her hands blurred as tears filled her eyes and she began to cry, hunching over and sobbing loudly.

Art stroked her back. 'Take it easy,' he said. 'Hey, come on take it easy. Nothing to cry about.'

'I'm . . . Oh God, I'm so frightened!'

'Hey, don't cry.'

'If you won't help . . . Jenny's so . . . she's just a child. How can you . . . how can you do that to her?'

'Do what?'

'Give her to the Krulls.'

'Look, turn yourself in. Plead self-defense. Everyone knows what a bastard Hank was. You'll get acquitted, and that'll be that. You don't have to worry about the Krulls, at all. They haven't got a thing to do with it, if you just forget this dumb idea of running away.'

'You don't understand,' she sobbed.

'Look, give John a call. He'll tell you.'

'I can't. He's . . . He went to the Trees, tonight.'

'I know. I was with him.'

'No, I mean later. He went back.'

'What?' Art asked, his voice suddenly low and hard.

'He went back to free some girl.'

'You're kidding.'

'That's why . . . why we have to leave.'

'That idiot!' he snapped. 'That damned idiot! I *knew* he wasn't right, tonight. The way he kept sticking up for that gal. I knew something was off. What on earth could . . . how could he *do* a thing like that? Put you on the line like that? And Jenny? My God didn't he know he was cutting your throats?'

'He planned to come for us.'

'But he didn't.'

'Peg shrugged. 'He might've. He had to go before . . .'

'No. No way. The Krulls got him, sure as hell. And now they'll want you and Jenny. The immediate family.'

'Are we "immediate family"?'

'You're all John's got. They have to set an example, and you're it.'

'It isn't fair.'

'So what is? I'm sorry, Peg. I'm really sorry.'

He got up from the couch. Peg lifted her head. She wiped the tears from her eyes. 'You won't help us?'

'I wish I could, hon.'

'I thought you . . . cared for me.'

'I do. I like you a lot, you know that. But you can't expect me to throw my life away, can you?'

'If you drive us out and don't come back . . .'

'No way.' He stepped across the room to the telephone.

Peg's shaking hands fumbled with the buttons of her dress.

'None of that, now.'

She stood and walked slowly toward him, working on the buttons.

'Come on, don't make a fool of yourself.' He picked up the phone and looked down to dial.

Peg reached inside her dress. The knife lay loose at her side, held up by her tight belt. She gripped its handle.

Art began to dial.

She pulled out the knife. 'Stop,' she said.

Art saw the knife. He smirked, and kept on dialing. 'Put that down,' he said, 'before I take it away and make you eat it.'

'Put down the phone,' said another voice.

He looked past Peg.

She turned her head, and saw Jenny in the hallway. The girl's face and clothes were still dark with dried blood. In her hand was a big, bedroom pillow.

In the background, the shower continued to run with a sound like leaves in a strong wind.

'I took a look around,' Jenny said. She grinned with one side of her face. 'Guess what I found.'

'Hey now,' Art muttered. He put down the telephone.

'You were going to turn us in, you creep.'

'No, I . . .'

A muffled shot stopped his words. The pillow jerked. A hole blossomed in its white case, spouting feathers.

With a yell, Art grabbed his left forearm.

'No!' Peg cried. She rushed toward him.

'Mom, get away!'

'No! I won't let you kill him, I won't let you! No!'

'For gosh sakes, Mom.'

Art fell to his knees, whimpering.

Peg, standing in front of him, stared at her daughter. Jenny dropped the pillow. In her hand was a small, nickle-plated automatic.

'All right,' Jenny said. 'I'll keep him covered, and you tie him up. Gag him, too.'

# Chapter Eighteen

Neala sat under a candle, her back against a wall, and watched Johnny search the cabin.

He checked the walls first. They were hung with deer skins, probably to keep the winds out. He lifted each pelt, and looked beneath it.

When he finished the walls, he stepped to the fireplace. A black pot hung over the dead coals. He swung it out, took off the lid, and sniffed. Gagging, he jammed the lid into place.

Sherri, asleep on her pile of furs, groaned and rolled onto her side.

'What is it?' Neala whispered to Johnny.

'Spoiled.'

He returned the pot to its hook. He pushed his hand into the ashes beneath it. 'Cold,' he said. Brushing off his hand, he stood. He hefted a metal fireplace poker. It looked solid and heavy to Neala. He swung it a few times as if testing its weight, then put it back. For a few moments, he inspected the sooty billows, a broom, a stool with a wicker seat. Then he turned away.

He wandered the cabin floor, his feet silent on the thick layers of fur that covered it.

'What're you looking for?' Neala asked.

'Anything we can use.' He shook his head. 'The place is bare. Except for that.' He nodded toward the covered pot.

'What do we need?'

'Food and water. A couple of guns would be nice.'

From the corner came Sherri's voice. 'While you're dreaming, how about a chopper to haul us the fuck outa here?'

'Maybe there's another room,' Neala suggested.

'I already checked. No other doors.'

'Another shack? Out back, maybe?'

'I'll take a look.' He went to the door, picked up his rifle, and raised the latch. He pulled the door open.

His body was a black, strong shape against the pale darkness outside. He seemed alert and dangerous, peering into the night. Then he glanced back. 'See you later,' he said, and Neala heard in his voice the bravery of a frightened boy.

He reached in to pull the door shut.

'Just a second,' Neala said.

He waited while she got to her feet and joined him outside.

Her eyes wandered over the dozens of frail crosses and heads. She saw the path Johnny had battered through them.

'Let's go around back,' Johnny said.

They walked close to the cabin. At its corner, Neala saw more crosses, more heads. At the rear, still more. But no other buildings. The small, square cabin stood alone.

They completed the circle, and stopped by the door.

'I'll stay out for a while,' Johnny said. 'You go on in and get some sleep.'

Neala hesitated. Maybe the man wanted time by himself. More likely, though, he was just trying to be nice, offering to stand guard while she slept.

'I want to stay with you,' she said.

'Well . . .'

'If you want to be alone . . '

'No, it's all right.' He grinned. 'You think I want to be alone with all this?' He eyed the field of heads. 'What if they start talking to me?'

'Do you think they might?'

'Not if we keep the conversation up.'

'Can we sit down?'

They sat on the ground. Neala crossed her ankles, and leaned back against the logs of the cabin. They felt scratchy through her shirt. She kept her eyes down as she talked. 'I want to thank you,' she said. 'I don't know what's going on, or why you did it, but you saved our lives.'

'Well . . .'

She waited for him to continue, but he said nothing more. 'Why *did* you come back for us?'

'Who knows?'

'You must.'

'Yeah. I guess I do.'

'Tell me.'

'I guess I didn't want to see you die.'

She eased sideways until she felt him against her shoulder. She was strongly attracted to this man; it confused her. He was part of the scheme that brought her into this nightmare. Perhaps she ought to loathe him for that. She couldn't. He was powerful and deadly, but vulnerable in a way that made her want to hold him close.

'Why me?' she asked.

'I don't know. There's something . . . I knew what they'd do to you. The thought of you being hurt . . '

'What about Sherri? Suppose I hadn't been along. Would you have left her to be killed?'

'Yes.'

'Why?'

'It's the way things are done in Barlow. It's the way we've always done things from the start.'

'How did it start?' She looked at him. He met her eyes, then turned away to scan the area.

'I'm not sure anyone knows,' he said. 'Apparently, the Krulls were here first. Nobody seems to know where they came from. Plenty of theories, though. Some say they're the Devil's children, some say a stone-age tribe of some kind.'

'If they're stone-age, where'd they get the steel weapons?'

'From us. We give them what they want. Except guns.'

Neala shook her head.

'Anyway. My high school history teacher had a theory that the Krulls are descendents of a band of Vikings that came up the Pacific coast and worked their way up the delta.'

'What do you think?'

'I think they might've descended from some crazy old mountain man – a demented Daniel Boone.' She saw a wry grin as he shrugged. 'What the hell, nobody knows. I've got a neighbor, Joanne Early, who thinks they're Martians. Whatever they are, they're in control. They used to raid town about once a month, but then our forefathers got smart and started delivering strangers to them. That worked out nicely, because the townspeople robbed the folks before taking them out.'

'They're still at it,' Neala said, looking down at one of her bare, bloody feet.

'Both sides get something out of it. And as long as the Krulls get eight or ten victims a month, they leave us alone.'

'Hasn't anyone ever tried to stop them?'

'There've been a few attempts. Not many, though. A fellow named MacQuiddy went in, once, with a bunch of men from town. They called themselves the Glorious Fourteen. That was back in the thirties. For a time, back then, word was out that Barlow was a good place to avoid. Travelers stopped coming through, and our people stopped taking victims out to the forest. So the Krulls came into town, one night. They snatched a dozen of our women and children. The Glorious Fourteen went in to rescue them, and never came out.'

Neala watched his eyes roam over the field of heads. 'Nobody ever comes out,' he said.

'Will we?'

'We'll sure give it a try.' Johnny put an arm across her shoulders, and she leaned her head against him.

She felt good, being with Johnny.

Better than she'd felt with any man since Derek. That was nearly two years ago. The break-up had left her stunned. She spent six months living like a hermit: hating Derek, hating all men, yet dwelling on the times they'd had together and dreaming of his return as if she enjoyed the twist of pain that such thoughts brought to her.

When the loneliness finally drove her from the house, she met only desperate men. They wanted her body close to them in the night, because they had the loneliness, too. Many tried to be cool: they talked big, and drove Porsches, and pretended. Others displayed their sensitivity like a raw wound, whiners pleading for attention. Few and far between were the normal guys, the confident ones she might want to know better.

She suspected most were already married – busy raising children and dogs.

And now, here was Johnny Robbins. You couldn't say he was normal, not after growing up in a town like Barlow and doing the terrible things he'd done. But he was strong and confident. He could be gentle. And he spoke straight.

He was so different from those other men – so solid, someone to rely on.

Someone she might love.

Her eyes filled with tears. She sniffed, and Johnny looked at her.

'I'm sorry,' she said.

'Don't be sorry.'

'It's just all so horrible.'

'I know.' His hand stroked her hair, the side of her wet face.

'We'll never get a chance to know each other, Johnny. I mean, to spend time and do things.'

'We'll get the chance,' he said.

She shook her head. A sob wracked her body.

'We will. You can count on it.'

His face moved close to hers. He looked into her eyes, and smiled gently, and pressed his mouth to hers.

# Chapter Nineteen

Cordie lay on the ground, curled up and shivering at the foot of the tree, afraid to move. She stayed that way for a long time.

Hours must have passed since she'd seen the dark shape stride through the trees. Hours since she'd heard Ben's pleading, terrified voice. God, he must've died an awful death.

The thing had come her way, and passed her by.

But it might be lurking near.

She couldn't stay on the ground much longer. She had to urinate badly, and she didn't want to wet herself.

Finally, she rolled onto her belly. She raised her head. Her eyes searched the forest. The air had a blue-gray cast, and she could see a long distance into the surrounding timber.

With sudden dread, she realized that the night's protective darkness was gone.

She got to her knees. Her right arm, numb from being crushed by her body for so long, hung useless at her side. Slowly, feeling returned to the arm. It tingled and burned. She shook it. She flexed her fingers. When the arm felt usable again, she stood up.

She turned slowly, studying the woods. She seemed to be alone.

Quickly, she lowered her pants and squatted. Her stream sounded terribly loud hitting the leafy ground. Eyes on the woods, she wished the noise would end. But she wasn't willing to stop the flow; getting rid of the aching tightness felt so good. Finally, she finished. She stood and pulled up her pants.

For a few moments, she stared in the direction that Ben had run. She didn't want to see his body. She couldn't just leave, though. Not without knowing, for sure, that he was dead. To know with absolute certainty, she had to see him.

She walked slowly, trying to move with total silence. In spite of her care, each footstep caused a quiet crush of the forest debris. Not much of a sound. But enough for others to hear. Too much. She took longer strides. Though her footsteps were louder, that way, she wouldn't need as many to reach her goal.

A goal she didn't want to reach. She wanted only to hide.

But she *had* to find out.

She kept moving. She knew just where to look. All night, in her mind, she had seen Ben dart into the trees, heard him running, heard his voice. He hadn't gone far. No farther than the distance, back home, between the front door and the kitchen.

When she saw his legs, she stopped. He was on his back, one leg straight out, the other bent sideways at the knee in a position that looked painful. The rest of Ben was hidden behind a tree.

His pants were all covered with blood.

'Ben?' she asked. The word came out as quiet as a breath.

But much too loud.

She took a step, and saw more: the lap of his pants, the bloody stomach of his shirt. She inched closer. The tree uncovered more: his chest, his outflung right arm. With another step, she would see if . . .

No!

She took a step backward until the tree concealed all but his legs. She stared at them. They were blurred by her sudden tears.

Those shoes.

She'd flung one out the car window at a drive-in movie, last week.

'Oh Ben,' she moaned.

Then she ran. She knew she was making too much noise, but she didn't care.

Let them get me. *Let* them!

She ran hard. Away from Ben. Running blindly, tears in her eyes, head thrown back. Better to look at the sky, the blue morning sky, than whatever might be coming to kill her.

She crashed into a thicket. Its limbs gripped her legs, but she churned through, kicking and grunting. It couldn't hold her back. As she broke free, though, it caught her trailing foot. It tripped her. She plunged forward, shrieked, and twisted wildly to keep from falling onto a naked boy.

The boy who'd attacked her last night.

The one slaughtered only minutes before Ben.

She hit the ground. Got to her hands and knees. Glanced at the body. Saw blood and ants, and the pulpy stump of neck where his head should have been.

Scrambling to her feet, she ran. She knew she was making too much noise.

Now, she cared.

As soon as she was well away from the body, she stopped. She looked around.

There!

A dense thicket, off to the right.

She rushed to the high cluster of bushes. She circled it, trying to see inside. The closely packed, leafy branches blocked her view.

Perfect!

Dropping onto her belly, she squirmed forward. She pushed her way through leaves and springy, low-hanging tendrils. Deeper and deeper into the thicket.

Finally, she stopped. She looked to each side, and saw no hint of the outside world. She rolled. Directly above, she could see a few tiny patches of sky.

Something tickled her arm.

She looked.

An ant.

Her fingertip got it. The ant left a tiny smear on her skin.

'Not yet,' she muttered.

# Chapter Twenty

Neala woke up. Her head was on Johnny's lap. They were still outside, Johnny sitting with his back to the cabin wall.

He smiled down at Neala. His eyes were bloodshot. His face, dark with a day's growth of whiskers, was torn by scratches and streaked with the brown stains of dry blood.

Reaching up, she touched his rough cheek.

'Guess I could use a shave,' he said.

'And sleep. Did you get any sleep at all?'

'What's sleep?'

His hand caressed Neala's forehead. It felt big and warm and comforting. She drew it down to her mouth, and kissed it. Then she slipped it inside her shirt. She closed her eyes as the hand moved lightly over her breasts. It stroked the skin of her belly. She felt his hardness push against the back of her head. The hand returned to her breasts, less gentle now, squeezing and plying her rigid nipples.

She moved his hand away, and stood. Her stiff muscles ached and burned as she stretched. She smiled down at Johnny. He watched as if he knew what would happen next.

She opened her shirt, and slipped it off.

'Are you sure?' Johnny asked. 'Here?'

She kept her eyes on Johnny. If she turned to the field of impaled heads, she knew she could not go through with it. 'Here's the only place we have,' she said.

'Inside.'

'Sherri.' She tugged at her belt and opened it. 'Here's fine. In the sunlight.' She unfastened her corduroys, and slid them down her legs. Stepping out of them, she stood before Johnny, clad only in her brief panties. She slipped them off. The morning breeze licked her skin. The sun was warm.

Neala opened her eyes when the cabin door squeaked open. Sherri stepped out.

'You done?' Sherri asked, her voice sarcastic.

'For Godsake!'

'Oh, don't pay any attention to me.'

'Get out of here! What's the *matter* with you!'

Shaking her head, Sherri gazed into the distance. 'Nothing's the matter with *me*. I just wonder about you two.'

'If you'll go inside for a minute,' Johnny said, 'we'll finish up and get dressed.' His voice was calm.

'Don't you like an audience?'

'Damn it, Sherri!'

'Well, you've got one. Just thought I'd let you know.' She pointed.

Neala turned her head. 'Oh God,' she moaned. She gripped Johnny's sides.

'They've been out there since you started,' Sherri said. 'Just a couple, at first. Must be fifteen or twenty now. I guess they liked the show.'

Johnny raised himself. He was still inside her, still erect. With a look of tenderness and regret, he slowly slid out. Moving on his knees, he grabbed his rifle. He stood, shouldered it, and aimed toward the scattered group beyond the barrier of heads.

Neala began to gather the cast-off clothes. She glanced up. Sherri was staring at her. 'Give me a hand, damn it!'

Nodding, Sherri crouched and picked up Johnny's boots, his socks, his pants. That took care of it. Neala rushed ahead of her into the cabin.

Sherri stopped in the doorway, and looked out. She stayed in the doorway as Johnny moved toward it.

Dropping her bundle of clothes, Neala grabbed Sherri's arm and tugged her inside.

Sherri swung around. 'Leave me alone!'

'Sherri, for Godsake, you're acting . . .'

Sherri clutched Neala's hair and jerked her head back. 'Shut up,' she hissed. 'Just shut your fucking mouth!'

# Chapter Twenty-one

'I'll take the gag off,' Peg said. 'But you have to promise not to yell.'

Art nodded.

Peg set down the .22 automatic, and got up from the kitchen table. She stepped behind Art. Crouching, she checked the ropes binding his hands and feet to the metal chair. They were secure.

She picked a corner of the wide tape loose from the side of his face, got a firm grip, and tugged. The tape peeled off. Opening his mouth, Art worked the handkerchief forward. Peg pinched the wet ball of cloth and removed it.

'Thanks,' he gasped. 'Can I have a drink?'

'I suppose.'

'Coffee.'

She stepped over to the cupboard and reached up for a coffee mug.

'I'm sure sorry about last night,' he said.

'I'll bet you are.' She poured coffee into the mug, and added a tablespoon of sugar. At the refrigerator, she put in a splash of cream.

'I am sorry,' he said. 'I was just so shocked, you know? I wasn't thinking.'

Peg lifted the mug to his mouth. He sipped from it. She tilted it higher. Coffee spilled from its corners and streamed down his chin.

'Sorry,' she mumbled.

Flustered, she put down the mug. She grabbed a napkin and wiped the trails of wetness from his chin, his neck, his chest.

Spots had even dribbled onto his lap. His penis showed through the slit of his boxer shorts. Quickly, Peg stepped away.

'Jenny would've killed me,' he said.

'I know.'

'You saved my life.'

'I'm not sure why.'

'I owe you, Peg.'

'What's that supposed to mean?'

'It means I'll do what you asked. I'll drive you and Jenny out of here.'

'I don't know.'

'Well *Jesus*, isn't that what you want?'

'I'll have to ask Jenny.'

'*Ask* her?'

'She's better at these things than me.'

'She's a kid. What does she know?'

'She seems to know a lot about surviving.'

'Okay. So ask her.'

'She's sleeping.'

'Wake her up. You want to get out of here don't you?'

'I think I'll just let her sleep. She'll wake up in due time.'

'Let me have some more coffee then, okay?'

Peg stepped again to the table, and lifted the mug. 'We'll take it slow and easy this time,' she said.

This time, not a drop spilled.

'Thanks, hon,' Art said. 'You know, if you really wanted to help me, you'd let me out of this chair.'

'Oh sure.'

'It's been hours. My arm's just killing me.'

'Your arm's hardly scratched.'

'That's easy for you to say, you're not the one who's shot.'

'I bandaged it, Art. I saw it. It's nothing. A scratch.'

'It hurts like hell.'

'Well, you'll just have to live with it.'

'You're gonna have to untie me, anyway.'

'Oh why's that?'

'How else am I gonna drive you and Jenny out of here?'

# Chapter Twenty-two

Waking up, Cordie stared through the tangled roof of bushes. She listened, afraid to move.

She heard running. She heard the jabber of voices. She heard harsh laughter. From the sounds, she guessed that half a dozen teenaged kids were nearby.

The thicket no longer felt like a refuge. Now it was a trap.

She wanted to get out, to run . . .

They might hear her, though. They might hear her crawling over the matted leaves and twigs, and get to her before she was free. Trapped in the mesh of bushes, she would be helpless. A game for the kids.

Play with her.

Taunt her, cut her, set her on fire.

She listened to their vicious laughter, their squeals.

All around the thicket.

As if they knew she was there.

She wanted to curl up on her side and hug her knees to her breasts. She didn't dare. Instead, she pressed her legs tightly together. She pressed her arms to her sides. She stared at the morning sky through a cross-work of limbs.

And waited.

The kids argued in sharp, high voices. Someone chuckled. Bushes rustled.

Cordie's rigid body trembled. Her neck ached with stiffening muscles.

*They know I'm here!*

How *could* they?

She heard the sounds of someone crawling inside the thicket. Coming for her.

She sucked in her breath and held it, trying not to scream.

All other sounds stopped.

They're listening, she thought. They're all out there listening, waiting.

Cordie raised her head. She looked down her body, past her shoes, and saw a face appear. The face of a girl. A blonde girl with twigs in her wild hair. A girl with blood smeared on her lips, her cheeks, her chin.

She was young. Fourteen or fifteen. Her tanned shoulders were bare.

As the girl crawled closer, Cordie heard herself gulping quick short breaths. Swallowing, she choked and gasped for air.

The girl moved alongside Cordie. The skin of her back was cross-hatched with scratches and smudges of dirt. Her buttocks were bleeding from scratches like the rake-marks of fingernails.

She sat up and crossed her legs. 'I'm Lily,' she said. 'What's your name?'

Cordie mumbled her name.

'What?'

'Cordelia.'

'That's a weirdo name.' She wrinkled her nose. 'What kind of weirdo name is that?'

'Who *are* you?'

'Lily.'

'You're one of *them*?'

'Sure.' Lily scratched one of her breasts. 'I've been with 'em a couple of years. It's fun.'

'Fun?'

'Shit yes!' She giggled. 'No school, nobody telling you what to do, fucking all the time. It's great. You'll like it.'

Cordie shook her head.

'You'll love it, really.'

'You're murderers.'

'Sure. It's a gas. Anyway, you're suppose to come out.'

'What for?'

The girl smiled and shrugged. 'You don't want to stay in here.' Leaning forward, she propped her elbows on her knees. She whispered, 'If you don't come out, the boys, they'll have to come *in*. They won't like that. They'd have to crawl. So you'd better just come out with me.'

Cordie shook her head.

'They'll get real mad. It'll spoil your chance.'

'Chance of what?'

'Joining up. They just won't let you, if they're pissed.'

'What happens if I join up?'

'Then we don't kill you.'

'But what *happens*?'

'Well, after the boys look you over, you've gotta get initiated. Then you're one of us, and you can live in the woods like we do.'

Cordie rested her head on the ground. She stared through the lacework of branches at pale and cloudless bits of sky. 'If I join up, they won't kill me?'

'Not if they like you.'

'I have to . . . make them like me?'

'Righto.'

'And then they won't kill me?'

'You'll be one of us. That's how I joined up. That's how a lot of us did.'

'All I have to do is go out there, and . . . What do they want to do, screw me?'

'Sure.'

'So they screw me, and that's it? They won't kill me or anything?'

'Yeah. That's about all. Then we'll take you to the village, see. You'll have to go through some shit there, but it's nothing. Old Grar has to give you the okay, stuff like that. Nothing to worry about. Come on.'

Cordie lay still, afraid to move.

The village, she thought. They'll take me to the village. Maybe that's where Mom and Dad . . .

'Move it!'

God she didn't want to go out there!

'The guys are gonna get tired of waiting.'

'Okay,' she said.

'You first.'

She forced herself to move. She turned around and began to squirm forward on her belly, head down.

What if Lily was lying?

What if they planned to kill her?

But she had no choice.

She kept inching forward.

Then she saw them. Three of them. Teenaged boys. Squatting naked in the sunlight just outside the bushes, staring in at her.

She stopped, cramped with fear, and looked back at Lily.

'Keep going.'

She shook her head.

'Go on.'

'No!'

'At the sound of crushing foliage she snapped her head forward. Two of the boys were scurrying toward her, smashing aside the bushes in their way.

'No!' she shrieked.

She kept shrieking as they grabbed her arms and dragged her from the thicket.

# Chapter Twenty-three

'Why don't they come?' Neala asked, whispering so she wouldn't wake Johnny.

'You sound like you want 'em to,' Sherri said.

'Hardly.' She was dressed and standing in the doorway, watching the distant Krulls. Several times, she had tried to count them. They kept moving, though – some vanishing into the timber, others appearing. She counted twenty, twenty-four, nineteen, twenty-six. They seemed to be doing nothing special. Just milling about. She couldn't see them well because of the crosses and heads.

'It's like they're waiting for something,' Neala said.

'Yeah. For us. Why don't we shut the door?'

'We've got to keep watch.'

'We can,' Sherri said. She closed and latched the door. 'Over here.' She stepped sideways through the darkness, and lifted one of the deer skins draping the front wall. Sunlight spilled through gaps between the logs.

So this is how Sherri spied on us, Neala thought. Anger and humiliation began to burn in her. How much had Sherri watched? The whole thing? Had it turned her on?

God, how could she sink that low!

Reaching up, Sherri yanked the deer skin loose. She flung it aside. 'That's better,' she muttered.

Neala peered through a crack. She could see exactly where she'd been with Johnny. She looked up, saw the Krulls still wandering beyond the stakes, and lowered her eyes again to the spot where she'd made love to Johnny.

'Why'd you do it?' she whispered.

'What does it matter?'

'It matters to me.'

'Look, I said I'm sorry.'

'I know. I don't want another apology. I want to know why. You're my best friend, Sherri. How could you stand here and spy on me?'

'We're all going to die here. You know that, don't you?'

'No, I don't.'

'You think your Johnny will wave a magic wand and – *Presto!* – we're home again?'

'Hardly.'

'Those people out there – those *things* – they're going to get us sooner or later. And it won't make a damn bit of difference why I watched you, will it?'

'It makes a difference to me now.'

'Suit yourself,' Sherri said.

'Tell me.'

'Just let it go.'

'I can't. Not if we're going to stay friends.'

'Shit.'

'Okay. If that's all I mean to you . . .'

'You have no idea what you mean to me. Not the slightest.'

The words frightened Neala.

'I love you.'

She looked at Sherri, stunned. 'What do you mean?'

'You know what I mean. And when I saw you, this morning, standing there in the sunlight . . . I just couldn't help myself. I couldn't stop watching.' She made a sour laugh. 'You probably thought I was hankering after Johnny, huh? Surprise, surprise.'

'I can't believe this.'

'Believe it, Neala.'

'But those guys you're always talking about – Jack and Larry. Wesley . . .'

'Men are okay. But you – I *love* you.'

Neala shook her head. She felt disgusted and afraid.

'I'd hoped we might . . . Never mind.'

'What were you going to do, seduce me?'

'Have I ever? Have I ever *tried*?'

'No,' Neala admitted.

'I'd never do anything unless you were willing.'

'Boy.'

'I'm sorry.'

'All these months . . .'

'Sorry,' Sherri said. She stepped away from the wall. 'This would be a great time for an exit, but I think I'll pass on it.'

Neala watched her move across the room and lie down in a corner. Turning again to the wall, she peered out the crack.

*I love you.*

The words were like a heavy stone in Neala's stomach. She

felt betrayed. As if her friendship with Sherri had been a nasty trick. Not a friendship, at all, but a game Sherri had played to stay close to her. To sneak intimate moments: a glimpse of her body, a casual touch, sometimes a quick, happy hug.

Her face felt on fire as she remembered their weekend in San Diego, last month. After a day at Sea World, the motel room. Calling to Sherri from the shower because she'd forgotten her shampoo. Sherri's little joke. 'If I was a guy, I'd climb in and lend you a hand.' Not such a joke, after all. A suggestion.

She must've prayed I'd ask her to come in, anyway.

It must've been torture for Sherri.

The whole weekend. Being so close to me but never close enough.

She remembered other scenes from that weekend, now. The times they changed clothes in the same room. The night Sherri gave herself a breast examination.

If she'd offered to perform the examination on Neala, it would've been suspicious. Sherri'd been too smart for that. She'd played the game well.

She hadn't been subtle that weekend, but she'd misdirected Neala like a skillful magician.

'Get a load of this number,' she'd said, pulling a sheer, black negligee from her suitcase. 'Wesley picked it up at Frederick's. Horniest son of a bitch I've ever met.' She'd dropped her bathrobe onto the bed, and slipped into the negligee. 'Cute, huh?'

'What there is of it.'

'Well, it's the only nightgown I've got, kiddo. I just brought it along in deference to your modesty. I usually sleep in the raw.'

'Don't let me stop you.'

Sherri did a lot in the raw, that weekend. Neala just assumed she liked the free, natural feel of it. Now it didn't seem that way at all. Sherri'd been displaying herself, trying to entice her.

Well, she hadn't been enticed.

That must have been terrible for Sherri. The weekend must have been a torment. All the time they spent together, for nearly a year, was obviously filled with pain and frustrated desire and hope. Constant, unfulfilled hope that Neala would finally respond.

God, the misery Sherri had put herself through!

Neala looked across the dark room. She saw Sherri in the corner, lying on her back, an arm over her face.

She went to her.

She sat down beside her.

'My turn on watch?' Sherri asked.

'No.'

'What're they doing out there?'

'Just waiting.'

'Gonna starve us out.'

'Hey, Sherri.'

'Huh?'

'I'm sorry.'

'You?'

'I'm just sorry I couldn't be what you need.'

'Yeah. Me too.'

Neala reached down, and took Sherri's hand.

# Chapter Twenty-four

They stripped Cordie. Then two boys held her to the ground while another tried to mount her. She twisted and kicked. He battered her legs away, got between them, and clutched her thighs to hold her still. He thrust against her. The head of his erection prodded, missing, missing, then finding the split of her vagina and plunging in. She cringed and closed her eyes tightly.

'Look at him,' Lily said. 'They don't like it when you shut your eyes.'

She kept them shut. The boy pounded into her with quick, hard strokes.

'You'll be sorry,' Lily warned. 'It's an insult, shutting your eyes. You want 'em to kill you?'

Cordie opened her eyes. The boy's face was above her. He watched her with narrow eyes. His bloody lips were drawn back, baring his teeth. He grunted loudly with each thrust, blowing putrid breath into her face.

She turned away. Lily was squatting beside her, next to the boy who kept her right arm pinned. Another girl, this one chubby but small-breasted, stood behind them. As she watched Cordie, she rubbed herself with the knobby end of a bone. The bone appeared slippery and fresh. Cordie quickly looked away, back to the boy gasping above her, then away from him.

The boy pinning her left hand was younger than the others. He watched her with eager, wild eyes. Behind him stood a slender girl with a stump where her elbow should have been. A small, dried hand hung round her neck on a thong, its brown fingers curled as if about to clutch something.

The boy was pumping harder now.

Cordie stared at the girl's withered hand. She tried hard to concentrate on it, to figure out whether it was a left hand or a right hand, to keep herself from thinking about the boy grunting and sweating on top of her dirtying her insides . . .

A left hand.

The girl's left arm had the stump.

Therefore . . .

The dried-up thing dangling between her breasts – was it her *own* severed hand?

The boy suddenly thrust deep and stayed, tight against her, head thrown back and mouth wide, his body twitching as he throbbed inside her. Cordie was sickened by the feel of his jerking penis, his spilling seed. She gagged.

The boy pulled out of her. He stood, pointing at his shiny erection and making a comment in a language Cordie didn't know. Then he stepped back, hands on hips.

The boy on her right let go of her arm.

Cordie whimpered.

'It's part of the test,' Lily said.

When he was on top of Cordie, about to enter her, she clenched her fist.

'Hit him,' Lily whispered, 'and you're dead meat.'

So she lay beneath him, her free arm tense but motionless at her side, as he rode her to a climax.

He stood, said something to the group, and stepped away. He stood at the side of the first boy, and folded his arms.

The one at her left released her other arm. Cordie glanced at Lily, kneeling close by. Lily was flushed and breathing hard. The girl behind her was writhing on the bone she held in both hands. The one-armed girl stood motionless, her bare skin glossy with sweat, her fierce eyes meeting Cordie's.

*Jealous?*

She's jealous, Cordie thought. Of me!

The young one climbed onto her. He pushed his penis into her. It was smaller than the others. His mouth went to one of her breasts. Sucked the nipple. Gnawed it. Wincing with pain, Cordie clutched the grass. Then the pain streaked through her. She grabbed the boy's hair and jerked his head away.

He snarled like a raging dog.

Cordie heard a sharp laugh. She glanced at the one-armed girl, and saw a vicious smile on her face.

'You blew it,' Lily said.

The words struck Cordie with sudden, cramping fear. She pulled the boy's face down to her mouth and kissed it. She darted her tongue into his mouth. She stroked his back. She clenched his buttocks, digging into his smooth flesh, pressing him more deeply into her. The boy moaned with pleasure. She eased his head away from her face, and pushed his mouth to her breast. His teeth clamped it, chewed it. She cried out with pain, but kept thrusting against him, kept squeezing his buttocks, and finally pushed a finger into his tight sphincter. He shook with spasms, moaning and gasping as he came.

He looked haggard and pleased when he climbed off her. He pointed to his erection, spoke, and joined the other two boys.

Cordie sat up.

The three boys began to talk. They nodded. They pointed at her.

The one-armed girl suddenly shouted. She jerked her knife out of her skin belt and flung it to the ground. Strange words spat from her mouth.

The boys nodded.

'Tough,' Lily said.

'What's going on?'

'Kigit says you're shit. She doesn't want 'em to let you in. She says you're weak and yellow. Says she wants to fight you.'

'*Fight* me?'

The boys were nodding, agreeing with Kigit. She turned away from them and walked toward Cordie.

'You'd better stand up.'

'I have to fight her?'

'You better try.'

Cordie got to her feet as the girl approached. Her legs felt very tired and weak. She hurt inside from the assaults. Wetness spilled from her, rolling like syrup down her thighs.

She backed away from Kigit. She moved past the side of the thicket, wondering if she dared to turn and run.

Kigit smiled strangely. She pointed behind Cordie.

Cordie didn't look. She wouldn't be tricked. She continued to step backwards until her bare foot slipped on a patch of wetness. She took a quick step, trying to catch her balance, and tripped on an obstruction.

She fell onto her back. Sitting up quickly, she found herself in the midst of severed human limbs. They were scattered all around – arms, legs, two mauled torsos.

Kigit picked up a glob of loose meat and tossed it underhand at Cordie.

She screamed as it landed on her belly. Then she scrambled to her feet.

Kigit picked up a severed arm. She held it to her own stump and waved it in a parody of her own missing arm.

Cordie turned and ran. She heard the girl behind her, drawing closer. She lunged sideways. Leaped over a dead trunk. Darted through bushes that flailed her skin. But Kigit kept getting closer.

Where were the others? The boys? If it's just this girl, this one-armed girl . . .

Cordie plunged forward as Kigit shoved her from behind. She landed hard, facedown, twigs and thorns tearing her flesh. As she started to get up, Kigit pounded onto her back. The weight drove her down. Kigit's arm cross her throat, choking off her wind. Using both hands, Cordie forced the arm away.

They rolled, but Kigit came up on top. Straddling Cordie's chest, the girl shot a punch between her upraised arms. The fist felt like a hammer smashing Cordie's nose. Her arms dropped heavily. Kigit's knees pinned them to the ground. One blow after another crashed against her face. Finally, they stopped.

Though she kept her eyes open, Cordie was too dazed to struggle. She watched the girl above her, grinning down, then leaning forward so the withered hand dangled above her face. The hand lowered. It's dry fingers dragged across her forehead.

Cordie whimpered at the touch of the clawlike hand. She felt the scrape of its fingernails along her cheek. Kigit used her living hand to guide it toward Cordie's mouth. The fingers hooked her lips. They tore. She tasted blood. She felt the nails against her front teeth.

Lily knelt beside her, and she suddenly realized that the others had caught up. They stood in a close circle around her, watching in silence.

Suddenly, Kigit jabbed the dead hand at Cordie's right eye. She jerked her head sideways. The fingers raked the side of her face. Twisting frantically, she worked her arm out from under the girl's knee. She grabbed a breast and wrung it.

Kigit cried out, falling sideways as Cordie pulled. Cordie kept her grip. She climbed onto the writhing girl, whose single hand battered her arm, trying to free the tortured breast.

Turning, she dug her elbow into Kigit's throat. She put her weight on it. Something crushed, and her elbow punched deeper. The girl bucked, eyes bugging out, mouth agape, arm swinging

124

wildly. Cordie blocked it. She crawled off the convulsing body and got to her knees.

Everyone watched Kigit until she died.

Then a boy, the one who'd been first to assault Cordie, spoke. She turned to Lily for an explanation.

'He say's you're okay, but you've got to pick up Kigit and bring her along.'

'Where?'

'To the village.'

# Chapter Twenty-five

Willis Hogue threw a leg over the counter stool as if he were mounting a horse. 'Give me a coffee, Terk.'

'Where's your trout hat, Hogue?' Terk tapped his own hat, a billowing chef's cap of spotless white.

'Wife's got me over a barrel,' Hogue told him. 'She bought herself a fancy antique mirror, and guess who's hired to hang it up?'

'Ain't me.' Terk poured steaming coffee into a white plastic cup in front of Hogue. 'Must be you.'

'Must be.' Hogue blew on the steam. 'A real tragedy, last night.'

'Yes and no.'

'I was mighty sorry to hear about young Fielding. He was a decent sort. Went to school with my Roger.'

125

'Can't say I was sorry to hear about Shaw and his brat,' Terk said. 'Or Hank Stover, either.'

'Well now, I'm not one to piss on the dead. And Fielding was a decent sort. It's a shame.'

'Hear about John Robbins?'

'Hear what?'

'Bob Rath stopped in for a Danish; he said Robbins flew the coop. They went over by his house there on Olive Street, last night – looking to find the ladies, you see. Well, Robbins weren't there. His car, neither. They're thinking he took up with them.'

Hogue blew on his coffee, and took a sip. 'Well, I suspect they'll turn up. Can't get by the roadblocks, and they for sure won't try walking out.'

'Rath, he said they've got a house-to-house search going on.'

'I wouldn't mind being the one that finds 'em.'

'Maybe you can get in on it.'

'I suspect the wife wouldn't approve. She's mighty hot to get that mirror up.'

Hogue left the diner, and stood beside the highway while a Volkswagen whirred past. The young man and woman inside were strangers. Hogue grinned. Probably on vacation thinking, *My oh my, what a quaint little town.*

Hogue rushed across the highway, hanging onto the belt of his drooping trousers. At the other side, he hitched them up and tightened the belt a notch.

'Mornin' Roy,' he called.

Roy, carrying two suitcases toward the motel office, grinned. 'How're you today, Willis?'

'Can't complain. How's the wife?'

'Oh, Rose Petal's as chipper as ever.'

'That's good, that's good.' Hogue continued on his way, walking along the highway's gravel shoulder.

Why a fella'd take up with a gal that old . . . Well, she hadn't been that old when they got married eighteen or twenty years ago. She must've been sixty, though. A retired hooker, that's what everyone said. Well, one man's meat . . .

Hogue reached the door of Phillips' Hardware. Through its glass, the store looked dim and deserted. Hogue tried the knob.

'Damnation,' he mumbled.

A decal on the glass gave the store hours: Mon–Sat 10 am.–6 pm.' Well, this is Saturday and it's after ten. He checked his wristwatch. Right. Ten forty-five.

He knocked on the door, and waited. Then he knocked again.

'Come on, come on,' he muttered.

'What's the trouble?' Roy called. He was standing beneath his motel sign, still holding the suitcases.

'You know anyplace else that carries Molly bolts?'

'Not off hand. I'm positive Phillips has them.'

'He's not open.'

'Oh, he *must* be.'

'If he's open, he's got a funny way to show it. Door's locked tight as a gnat's asshole.'

'That so?'

'Does he usually open on time?'

'Like clockwork.' Roy set down the suitcases, and approached. His jowls quivered with each step. Houge wondered where Roy picked up his flowered Hawaiian shirt. Probably from one of his more flamboyant guests.

Roy tried the doorknob, as if he thought Hogue incapable. 'You're right,' he said.

'That comes as no surprise.'

Roy pressed his face to the glass. 'Doesn't look like he's in

127

there.' He pounded on the door, then kicked it twice, shaking it in its frame. The exertion worked up a sweat. He plucked out a handkerchief and mopped his brow. He ran the cloth over his shiny pate.

'You know what this means?' Roy asked.

'Means I can't get my Molly bolts.'

'It means Phillips didn't get here.'

'Maybe he caught a bug.'

'Or a bug caught him.' Roy widened his bulging eyes. 'Maybe a *lady*-bug.'

'What're you getting at, Roy?'

'I happen to know that Art Phillips was seeing Peg Stover on the sly.'

'By George, that's right!'

'Now you take me, I think it's kind of funny he didn't open up today, when you consider what happened last night.'

'You've got a point.'

'I think I'll just take a run over to Phillips' place, and see what I can see.'

'I was about to head over that way, myself.'

Roy's eyes narrowed. 'Were you?'

'Why don't we pool our efforts? If we can find the gals, we'll split fifty-fifty.'

'Come along, then. We'll take my van. And Rose Petal. She wouldn't want to miss out on this.'

Hogue waited in the motel office. He fidgeted while the minutes passed, worried that the house to house search would beat them to Phillips' place. If that happened, he would be out a thousand dollars – half the standard bounty for two defectors.

The door behind the registration desk swung open. Roy came out, lifting the Hawaiian shirt above the white paunch of his belly and pushing the barrel of a revolver into his belt.

'You wouldn't have a spare sidearm, would you?' Hogue asked. 'I'd pay you for the loan of one.'

'This babe's all I've got.'

'I'll want to stop by my place, then.'

'You go on ahead in your car. We'll meet you at Phillips'.'

'Well, never mind, then.' He didn't want to give them a headstart.

Rose Petal came out. She clacked her false teeth at Hogue, and winked a lid bright blue with eye shadow.

'Good morning,' he said.

She saluted by touching the head of a claw hammer to the bill of her Dodger cap, knocking the cap askew. She didn't bother to adjust it.

As she followed Roy around the end of the desk, Hogue noticed how her breasts dangled inside her loose T-shirt. Printed on the shirt front was the word BABY with an arrow pointing down.

Sick, Hogue thought.

When she came around the corner, he thought for an instant that she was naked below the waist. Then he saw that she wore pink bikini pants.

Wait'll tell Terk about this, he thought.

Hogue tried not to look at her as they left the office and went to Roy's van. She climbed in ahead of him, presenting him with a full view of her scantily clad bottom – intentionally, Hogue suspected. He turned his eyes away.

Inside the van, Rose Petal disappeared. Hogue took the passenger seat.

'It'll still be fifty-fifty,' Hogue said. 'Regardless of Rose Petal.'

'A deal's a deal.'

'Good enough.'

As the van crossed the highway, Rose Petal reappeared. She

held a crowbar out to Hogue. 'Skull buster,' she said. Her breath smelled like Listerene.

'Why, thank you.'

Little more than a minute later, Roy parked at the end of a block and shut off the engine.

'Phillips' place is three doors up,' he said.

'I don't think we should just go up and ring the doorbell, do you?'

'That wouldn't get us far,' Roy agreed. 'We need a plan.'

# Chapter Twenty-six

Robbins woke up and found Neala asleep beside him on the bed of fur. He raised his head. Sherri was at the front wall, keeping watch.

He gently removed Neala's hand from his belly, and got up. He went to Sherri. 'What're they doing?' he asked.

'Just standing there.'

He peered out. 'What the hell are they waiting for?'

'Maybe they plan to starve us out. Beats getting their heads shot off.'

'Yeah.' He stepped away from the wall, and lifted his T-shirt to wipe the sweat off his face. Then he picked up his rifle. He went to the door and opened it. The air from outside gave no relief; it felt even hotter than the air inside.

'Actually,' said Sherri, 'I think we'll die of thirst long before we starve.'

'We're not gonna do either.'

'What do you plan, mass suicide?'

'I plan to get us out of here.'

'Rotsa ruck.'

He stepped into the sunlight. Squinting he looked through the weirdly tilted crosses and mounted heads.

Must be two dozen Krulls out there. Not doing a damn thing. Just lounging around, like it's a picnic.

Picnic.

Robbins made a grim laugh.

A few of the Krulls perked up when they noticed him. Some pointed. One young fellow ran forward, stopping at the edge of the pikes, and hurled a spear. Robbins watched it soar, knowing it would fall short. It did. It tore half the face off an impaled head. The head twirled, its black hair swinging behind it.

Angry voices broke the silence.

Two Krulls attacked the boy. They threw him down. They stomped and kicked him.

Because he flung his spear at an impossible target?

Or because he damaged one of the heads?

Maybe the area's sacred, Robbins thought. It would explain why the Krulls hadn't entered.

He walked along the front of the cabin to its corner. More Krulls along the side. He counted eight. They could be re-enforced quickly, though, by some from the front.

He moved to the rear. More there. Thirteen or fourteen wandering idly beyond the barrier of heads.

He gasped at a noise behind him. Swung around. Found his rifle muzzle inches from Neala's belly.

For an instant, she looked terrified. Then a smile came to her face. 'Don't shoot,' she said.

'Wouldn't think of it. What're you doing up?'

131

She shrugged. 'Too hot in there.'

'It's hotter out here.'

'But you're here. What are you doing?'

'Looking for a way out.'

'Any luck?'

'Not yet.'

She squinted across the field. Wet hair clung to her forehead. Her face was sweaty. The tiny, moist specks below her eyes glinted sunlight. A drop rolled down toward a corner of her mouth. She licked it away, then dried her face with the front of her shirt. She let the shirt hang open.

'Why don't they come for us?' she asked.

'I'm not certain. I think we might be in the middle of a sacred area, or something. They always stop at the edge of the heads.'

'I would've, too, if I'd had a choice.'

'It's more than just revulsion. Has to be. These Krulls think nothing of tearing people limb from limb. They must have a damn good reason for staying out.'

'Like if these are their ancestors?'

'Yeah.'

'That'd be nice for us.'

'Except.'

Neala nodded. 'Except how do we get out.' She leaned against the wall and hooked her thumbs into the pockets of her corduroys. Her throat and chest and belly were glossy with sweat. 'We gonna make a run for it?' she asked.

'I guess we'll have to. We'll wait till after dark, and sneak out. This way, I guess. The crosses aren't quite so close together, back here. If we can manage to crawl through without knocking any down . . .'

'Everybody decent?' came Sherri's voice.

Neala quickly pulled her shirt together and tucked in its front. 'Yeah,' she called.

Sherri stepped around the corner. 'What's cooking?' she asked.

'We are,' said Neala.

'Maybe that's what they're waiting for.'

Robbins didn't smile. 'We're planning to get out of here tonight,' he said.

'How do we pull that off?'

Robbins explained. As he talked, he saw Sherri look toward the heads. She, gazed at them. She seemed lost in her own grim thoughts. 'I know it won't be easy,' he said. 'I don't want to go out there, either. We can't stay here forever, though.'

'I think I will,' Sherri said. She tried to laugh. It sounded more like a sob.

'It won't be so bad,' Neala said.

'What it'll be,' said Sherri, 'it'll be fuckin' ghastly.'

'We'll leave as soon as it's dark,' Robbins said. Sherri nodded. 'Which gives us all day to look forward to it.'

# Chapter Twenty-seven

'The car's in the garage,' Hogue reported when they regrouped in the alley. 'I couldn't see in any windows, though.'

'Funny Phillips would keep his curtains all shut, like that. But do you know what's even funnier?' Roy asked. 'His doors are locked. Front *and* back. I tried them both. With great stealth, of course.'

'What's wrong with locking the doors?'

133

'Just this,' Roy said. 'Phillips doesn't lock his house. Never. Doesn't believe in it.'

Hogue nodded. Strange, all right. He let his eyes roam over to Rose Petal. She winked at him.

'Should we go in?' Hogue asked.

'I'm ready if you are.' Roy glanced at Rose Petal. 'How about it, sweets?'

She licked the palm of her left hand, then smacked the hammer against the wet spot.

'What've you got to lose?' Art asked. 'If I don't drive you out, they'll catch you anyway. You've got nothing to lose by trusting me.'

Jenny took a long drink of milk, and set down the glass. 'I don't trust him, Mom. Once he's got us in the trunk, we're at his mercy.'

'How else can we get out of here?'

'Maybe I could hide in the back seat, under a blanket or something so I'm out of sight. That way, I can keep him covered and blast him if he tries any funny stuff.'

'They'd see you at the roadblock,' Art said.

'Maybe or maybe not. If we wait till after dark . . .'

The doorbell rang.

For a breathless moment, Jenny felt the same panic she'd experienced not long ago, when she lost her footing high in a tree and nearly fell.

Her mother looked gray and sick.

Jenny forced herself to take a deep breath. 'Who is it?' she whispered.

'How should I know?' Art said.

She grabbed the damp, wadded handkerchief. 'Open up.'

Art smirked.

The doorbell rang again.

Jenny picked up the shiny automatic and pressed its muzzle to his lips. She saw fear in his eyes. He *knew* she would shoot – she'd done it before.

He opened his mouth, and Jenny stuffed it with the rag.

'Mom, tape his mouth.'

The doorbell rang again as she rushed into the living room. She glanced at the door. It had no peep-hole, no way to look out.

The curtains were drawn across the picture window. She wondered if she dare lift a corner and try to see who was at the door.

No. Better just wait, and keep the front covered.

The person would probably leave.

She flinched as the knob rattled.

*What if he's got a key!*

From the kitchen came a crash of bursting glass.

*'Jenny!'*

The curtain above the sink puffed inward as the spray of glass hit it. Then the curtain bunched – a hand was gripping it from the other side. It went taut, and the rod clattered down. The curtain dropped into the sink.

A bald, chubby man pushed his arm through the hole in the window. Roy from the motel. He aimed a dark revolver at Peg.

'Nobody move,' he said. His sweaty face was smiling.

Something crashed into the kitchen door. The door shook, but stayed shut.

'Mom!'

Roy's eyes shifted away from Peg and widened. His revolver started to move.

Peg dropped to the floor. She heard two quick flat cracks, then a single heavy *caroom*.

'Mom quick!'

She scurried under the table, and crawled.

The door crashed again.

She shoved a chair out of her way and crawled toward the hallway entrance, where Jenny crouched with the automatic.

The girl fired again.

'It's okay,' Jenny gasped.

Peg scrambled the rest of the way. She dropped onto the hallway carpet. Looking back, she saw nobody in the window.

Then the kitchen door burst open.

Willis Hogue stumbled in, looking surprised. He back-pedaled. Roy, behind him, shoved him forward.

Jenny fired. Hogue's mouth made a tight O. He dropped onto his rump, and stared down at the hole in his stomach.

Roy, standing behind him, aimed hastily and shot.

Jenny cried out.

Peg whirled around, aghast. Jenny's hand was empty. The outstretched fingers trembled violently. The shiny automatic lay on the carpet a yard away, its slide dented and half torn off.

'Reach for the sky!' Roy announced. He stepped over Hogue's squirming body and came toward them, chuckling quietly.

# Chapter Twenty-eight

Cordie had little chance to see the village before she was pushed into a hut of branches. 'Stay here,' Lily said. 'Grar has to see you.'

Then she was alone. She sat cross-legged in the center of the hut. The floor was specked with sunlight from the leafy roof. She sighed. It felt good to be rid of the body. But later . . .

She didn't want to think about later.

At least for the moment, she didn't seem to be in danger.

They'd accepted her.

They'd fucked her raw. Kigit had tried to kill her. But she'd done everything right, so far. She was almost one of them.

With both hands, she wiped the dripping sweat from her face. From her shoulders and breasts.

Once they trusted her, she could find a way to escape.

It might take a while. A few days, a week . . .

The pelt over the hut's entrance flapped open, and a creature swung in on hairy arms. Cordie caught her breath. She gripped her thighs, digging fingernails into her wet skin, fighting her urges to flee or scream.

The creature, she realized, was a man. A man of hideous deformity, legless and bloated. His mouth twitched into a mockery of a grin.

'Grar?'

The monster swung closer.

Cordie squeezed her thighs harder. Her fingernails pierced her skin.

Inches from her knees, he stopped. His eyes roamed her body.

*No!*

*Not him!*

Watching his gummy eyes, she knew she would die before letting him take her. She crossed her arms over her breasts.

The creature growled.

'No,' she whispered.

Then the fur swung away from the entrance, and a man came into the hut. An old, lean man. He spoke, and the creature scuttled away from Cordie.

'I am Grar,' he said. 'Our companion is Heth. 'Your name is?'

'Cordelia.'

The man came forward on hands and knees; the hut was too small for standing. He wore a skirt of hair that hung to the ground as he crawled. It was many colors: brown, red, blond, and raven black.

He sat in front of Cordie and crossed his legs.

'You are one who escaped the trees, last night.'

'Yes.'

'I understand that you wish to become one of us.'

'Yes.'

'Why?'

Was the question a trick? She saw no malice in Grar's eyes. 'So I won't be killed,' she said.

'Joining us is no guarantee of that. We have dangers unknown to you.'

She nodded.

'You must give us children,' he said. 'Children to replace the many who have fallen. And you will give us fresh blood to mix with the blood of our fathers. Without new blood, the children come forth weak and crooked, like Heth.' He nodded toward the deformed man in the corner. 'The blood of his parents was bad.'

Too much inbreeding? Cordie wondered. She didn't realize it could create such monstrosities.

'You will give yourself to any man until you are with child. After your firstborn, you may accept those you wish, rejecting others.'

'Okay,' she said.

'Now we must go.'

Her heart slammed. 'Where?'

'To your friends.'

'I don't . . . Who?'

'Those who escaped with you from the trees. You will go to them.'

'I don't know where they are.'

'They have taken shelter in the house of The Devil. You must go to them, and bring them out.'

She stared at him, perplexed and frightened.

'Only you, among us, may enter the land of the dead.'

'Oh Jesus, I don't . . .'

'The women are young. Like you, they will give us many children. We must have them.'

'But there's a guy.'

'You will take his life.'

'Me? Kill him?'

'You have killed others. You killed Kigit.'

'This guy's got a gun.'

'You are a woman.'

'That's not . . .' She stopped herself. Defiance would do her no good – and might get her killed. 'Okay,' she said. 'I'll do whatever you say.'

'I hear deceit in your voice.'

'No. I'll do it, honest. I'll kill the guy. I really will. Then I'll make the women come out.'

'If you betray us, your death will be horrible beyond nightmares.'

In a dry voice, she said, 'I won't betray you.'

'Heth.'

The creature scuttled forward.

'Your hand, girl.'

She raised her left arm.

The old man lightly took her wrist. He guided her hand toward Heth. She made a fist.

'Open your hand.'

Her fingers fluttered open.

'Please,' she whispered.

'You must learn a lesson in obedience,' Grar said, and moved her little finger toward Heth's mouth. The dry lips sucked it in. She felt the edges of his teeth. The tongue stroked the length of her finger.

Then he bit.

She saw her bleeding stump.

She saw Heth chewing. The ceiling of the hut tilted strangely, and went dark.

# Chapter Twenty-nine

'What time do you think it is?' Neala asked, staring through the doorway.

Sherri shrugged. 'Cordelia's the one with the watch.'

'I'd guess it's past noon,' Johnny said. 'Maybe one.'

'It gets dark around eight?'

'Yeah,' said Sherri. 'That gives us seven hours. Can you die of thirst in seven hours?'

'I doubt it,' Johnny said.

Neala wiped her face. 'I wish night would get here.'

'It will,' Johnny told her.

'And then,' said Sherri, 'the real fun starts.' She lay down on her back, folded her hands beneath her head, and stared at the ceiling. 'Hide and seek with the boogy-men.'

'We can't stay here,' Neala said.

'If we had water, we could.'

'But we don't.'

'Maybe just one of us should go out, tonight, and bring some back. He could fill that pot . . .'

'You volunteering me?' Johnny asked.

'Sure.' She grinned at him. 'You game?'

'Not hardly. By the time I could make it to water, I'd be home free. I might as well keep going.'

'Right! Great idea! Keep going, and get help. Bring in the cavalry. Get us out of here in a chopper, and blow these fuckers to hell.'

Johnny was silent. Neala turned to him, alarmed. 'You're not seriously considering it?'

'Well . . .'

'Damn it, Sherri!'

'Hey, it was only a suggestion.'

'It has some merits,' Johnny said.

'No!'

'I probably could get help. Search and Rescue over in Melville, has a copter. If I get to them, they could set down right outside the door. Only thing is, it would take a while. I'd have to make it to the road and get my hands on a car. My car, if it's working. Then I'd have to make it through Barlow.'

'What's the problem with that?' Sherri asked.

'Barlow? Everyone knows me. If I'm spotted, they'd try to stop me. But Melville's only half an hour past Barlow, so I could get there pretty fast if nothing goes wrong.'

'Yeah,' Neala said. 'If nothing goes wrong. In the meantime, we'd be sitting here alone. No food, no water, no way of knowing if you made it.'

'The thing is, you'd probably be safe here. Out beyond the heads, you'd be vulnerable.'

'Just like you.'

'I can move fast, alone. If I make it, I'd be back by morning with that copter.'

'And if you don't make it?'

'You're no worse off than if you'd been with me.'

'It's a good idea,' Sherri said.

'Hold it. Just a minute, damn it. Johnny, didn't you say it's twenty miles to get out of Krull territory?'

He nodded, 'That's if you head east.'

'What's this *if*? That's the way you led us, last night. East.'

'If I go out alone, I'll head west.'

'Back the way we came?'

'I'll try to get back to my car. If I can get it started . . .'

142

'The place was *crawling* with Krulls!'

'Last night,' Sherri added.

'Okay, last night. So do you think they just vanished since then?'

Sherri smirked. 'They're right outside.'

'That's right,' Johnny said. 'Right outside. Must be fifty of them surrounding this cabin. That's fifty who aren't prowling the woods. If I can just sneak past the ones right here, the rest of the way should be a cinch.'

'If it's a cinch,' Neala said, 'let's all go together.'

# Chapter Thirty

'You've got to believe me,' Art whined. 'I was lying to them. Once I got them in the car, I was going to drive them straight out to the Trees,'

'Aw shut up, you old kickee.' Rose petal squinted at him through the dim light of the van.

'Honest. You've got to believe me.'

'You rat,' Peg muttered.

'It isn't fair!'

'I knew he was lying,' Jenny said.

'The van lurched sideways. Peg rolled, her back pressing against Jenny. When it straightened, she rolled away.

She lay on her side, lengthwise on the floor of the van, her head toward the rear doors.' Her hands, behind her, were cuffed to Jenny.

Two men had come to the house after Roy called. They'd been rough. They'd jammed on the handcuffs tightly, cutting off Peg's circulation.

They hadn't believed Art.

'I heard Phillips talking,' Roy had told them. 'He said he would drive the gals out tonight, hiding in his trunk.'

It was the one bright spot.

Peg flexed her hands. The numb fingers felt like sausages. She could barely bend them.

'Please, honey,' Art said to the old woman.

Rose Petal glanced toward the front of the van. Roy's bald head was visible above the back of the driver's seat. She looked again at Art.

He was siting upright on the floor, not far from Peg's feet, his hands cuffed overhead to the handle of the side door.

'I'll give you whatever you want,' he said.

'Money, do you want money? Anything. *Jesus* just don't take me to the Trees!'

Rose Petal crawled toward him.

Peg could see sweat sliding down his face and chest. He blinked it out of his eyes.

'A key!' he whispered. 'Have you got a key for the cuffs?'

Rose Petal got up on her knees. She turned her ballcap backwards, like a catcher. Then she raised the hammer.

Art gaped.

She took a quick glance toward Roy, then swung. The hammer thunked, knocking Art's head sideways. His eyes rolled.

'Mom? What's going on?'

Peg couldn't speak. If she opened her mouth, she might scream. She watched Rose Petal toss the hammer into her left hand, and hit Roy's mouth. The hammer broke through his upper teeth. Blood and white chunks of tooth slid down his chin.

Rose Petal swung again. His right cheekbone collapsed.

As if suddenly regaining enough consciousness to know what was happening, Art screamed. He bucked and twisted wildly. Rose Petal slammed the hammer against his forehead.

He slumped.

The van stopped. Roy swiveled his seat around. 'Oh, for Pete's sake,' he muttered. Rose Petal shrugged.

'Why'd you have to do that, sweets?'

She pointed her hammer at Art's face. 'Asked for a blow job.'

Roy laughed. 'Well, I guess the damage is already done. It's up to you to clean the van, though.' Then he turned forward and the van started to move again.

Rose Petal pounded into Art's skull with the hammer claws. When she started to hack at his eyes, Peg shut her eyes tightly.

She heard pounding, and wet slapping sounds, and sometimes a squeal of surprise and delight from the old woman.

Finally, the van stopped again.

The rear doors opened.

'Holy mother of God!' a man gasped.

Peg kept her eyes shut.

'Get over here, Burt. Look what she done to Phillips.'

'Fuckin' A,' muttered the second man.

'Well, let's get on with it.'

Hands clutched Peg under the arms, and dragged her.

'*You* take Phillips out.'

'Queasy?' Roy? asked.

'She's your wife, bud.'

Then Peg was outside the van, a man holding her up. He let go, and she stumbled backward against Jenny. They both fell down.

She opened her eyes. The clearing was brilliant with sunlight. The six dead trees stood in a row. They were taller than she'd imagined. And more ghastly. They looked too much like arms reaching out of the soil, arms picked clean of flesh, their bones smoldering under the sun.

Though birds swooped and fluttered in the bright sky, none went near the Killing Trees.

She and Jenny were pulled to their feet.

A man unlocked the cuff on Peg's left hand. 'Don't make any trouble,' he said in a hushed voice.

At the nearest of the trees, the man fastened the cuff again, securing Peg and Jenny back to back. Without a word, both men walked away. They said nothing as they passed Roy and Rose Petal, who were dragging Art by the feet. They ducked into their car and shut the doors. Then they sat motionless, apparently waiting.

'Well, ladies,' Roy called cheerfully, 'Guess you've met your Waterloo.'

'Sit on it,' Jenny yelled.

'Quiet,' Peg muttered. She didn't want Rose Petal coming at them with the hammer.

They dragged Art's body to the closest tree, and propped his back against it, the crushed pulp of his face toward Peg.

'Have a good time,' Roy said.

Rose Petal waved good bye with her hammer.

Then Roy lifted a shiny whistle to his mouth and blew a high, shrill blast.

As they hurried away, Art's body tipped over. Rose Petal started to come back, but Roy gripped her scrawny arm and pulled her to the van.

The two men in the car followed the van from the clearing.

Peg and Jenny were alone.

146

Peg shut her eyes. She heard the distant engine, the singing birds, the buzz of flies or bees.

'We'd better get out of here,' Jenny said.

'How?'

'I've still got a knife. The one in my sock.'

'Will it cut steel?'

'Won't have to,' Jenny said. 'Somebody'll come by, pretty soon, and uncuff us.'

'I'm not looking forward to it.'

# Chapter Thirty-one

A giant chased Cordie over a barren, glaring landscape of dunes. She whimpered as she ran.

Oh, if he caught her!

His shadow blocked the sun from her body. Such a cold shadow. She tried to run harder, but the sand clutched her feet, slowing her down.

The arms of the shadow reached out.

A monstrous hand gripped her shoulder. Its fingers felt dry as bone.

She bit off its little finger.

Roaring in pain, the giant released her. She ran on, out of the cold shadow, leaving the giant far behind. But she was lost and the dunes were strange. She didn't want to be here, after dark.

Where were Mom and Dad?

They must be nearby. They wouldn't leave her all alone in this horrible place.

She tried to yell, but the giant's finger was still inside her mouth. She pulled it out. How odd! It was just her size.

She stuck the giant's finger onto her stump. A perfect fit.

She began running again, but the finger fell off and disappeared in the sand. Dropping to her knees, she raked through the sand trying to find it.

Ah, here it is!

She pulled, but it was stuck. She pulled harder. Out of the sand came an entire hand, an arm . . .

She staggered back, suddenly afraid.

Someone buried in the sand was rising!

He sat up, sand spilling from his body, and grinned at her. 'Hi, Cordie.'

'Ben? I thought you were dead.'

'Not me,' he said, and brushed sand out of his hair.

No, not sand. Ants.

'Ben!'

He brushed harder His head tumbled off and dropped to his lap and Cordie sat up screaming.

She was in the hut.

Lily sat at her side. 'Nightmare?' the girl asked.

Cordie raised her hand. It was wrapped in a bloody rag. The hand pulsed with pain. 'My finger,' she said.

'Yeah. Well, you're lucky that's all you lost. Grar doesn't trust you much.'

'I told him I'd do it. What does he want! Christ, my *finger*!'

'We've gotta get going. Come on.'

She crawled behind Lily, keeping her injured hand off the ground. The sunlight outside hurt her eyes. Squinting, she got to her feet.

Grar came forward, his skirt of hair floating over his legs. He held a sword. It looked, to Cordie, like a saber from a Civil War movie. He handed it to Lily, and spoke in the other language.

Lily nodded. She turned to Cordie. 'Okay. This way.'

The group of Krulls parted, and Cordie faced the landscape of pikes and heads. She jerked her arm free of Lily's grip.

'Your friends are in the cabin.'

She shook her head. She felt numb.

'Here. This is for you.' Lily held out the saber, hilt first.

'Use it on the guy.' She raised her arm. Saw her hand close around the hilt. The weight of the sword dragged her arm down like an anchor.

'Get going,' Lily said. 'The quicker you get it done, the quicker we can get our asses out of here.' She saw fear in Lily's eyes. 'We don't want to be around when *he* comes back.'

Cordie couldn't move.

Lily pushed her, and she began to walk. The heads seemed to bob and sway in her vision. A bird fluttered down. A black bird. It perched on the nearest head, and pecked a gash in the forehead. The skin split, but no blood flowed.

Something familiar . . .

That face.

*Ben!*

# Chapter Thirty-two

'One's coming through!' Neala said.

Robbins hurried to the doorway. He grabbed his rifle. Dropping to one knee, he took aim. He watched the girl stagger among the crosses, bumping into some.

'She drunk?' Sherri asked.

'Something's sure wrong with her,' Neala said.

Robbins lowered his rifle.

'Well shoot her, for Christsake!'

'None of the others are coming,' he said.

'So What?'

'She looks crazy,' Neala said.

Robbins stood up. He stepped into the sunlight.

'What're you doing?' Sherri asked.

'Just a second.' He ran to the corner of the cabin and checked the Krulls at the side. None were approaching.

'Johnny, what . . .?'

He ran to the rear, looked beyond the barrier, and returned to the front. 'It's okay,' he said. 'She's the only one.'

'You aren't just gonna let her come, are you? Look at that fuckin' sword!'

'That's just what I'm looking at,' Robbins told her. 'I want it.'

The girl tripped, smashing through half a dozen crosses before she sprawled facedown. She raised her head. She got to her hands and knees. Bracing herself on the sword, she stood. She looked back as if to see how far she'd come. Then she faced the cabin. She squinted, and raised an arm to wipe sweat from her forehead.

The motion lured Robbins' eyes to her breasts. They were

large for such a slim girl, and shiny with sweat. Robbins felt a warm rush of arousal. He lowered his gaze to her belly, to her dark wedge of pubic hair.

'Look at that,' Sherri said. 'She's got bathing suit lines.'

Sherri was right. The girl's breasts and pubic area were pale.

'That's Cordelia!' Neala gasped.

Robbins studied the face. It was swollen and bruised and marked with cuts, but it did resemble the girl who'd been with them last night.

'Cordelia!' he called.

Her head nodded slightly.

'Holy shit,' Sherri muttered.

Cordelia staggered forward. She stepped high over fallen pikes, then ducked to pass under the cross-bars of those ahead.

'God, what've they done to her?'

'I think she's in shock,' Robbins said.

She stumbled again, and fell to her knees.

Robbins slung the rifle across his back. He started forward.

'Johnny, it might be a trick.'

'Maybe,' he admitted. He pushed his way through the crosses until he reached her. She was still on her knees. She stared up at him. Her eyes looked wide and blank. He slipped his hands under her armpits, and lifted her.

'It's all right,' he said softly.

She raised the sword high.

'Johnny!' Neala cried.

His hand slid up and gripped her feeble arm.

'It's all right,' he said again.

His other arm circled her back, and he pulled her against him. Pressing her tightly to his body and still clutching her arm, he swung her around and carried her through the fallen crosses.

In front of the cabin, Neala took the sword from her hand.

Robbins carried her inside. He lowered her to the floor. Rolling onto her side, she drew her legs up to her breasts. She held them there. Her mouth sucked on her knee.

'Cordelia?'

She didn't respond.

Robbins turned to Neala and Sherri. 'Maybe we'd better just leave her alone for a while.'

He went toward the doorway, Neala at his side.

'I'll stay with her,' Sherri offered. 'she might need someone.'

'Finc.'

They left Sherri beside the girl, and went outside. They found shade at the rear of the cabin. There, they sat together. They held hands, and talked softly. Neala lay on her back, and rested her head on Johnny's lap. He stroked her hair. When she yawned, Robbins told her to sleep. She shook her head. Her eyes were full of sorrow. 'We have so little time,' she said.

'We'll have years,' he told her.

Tears came. He brushed them from the corners of her eyes.

# Chapter Thirty-three

A burly, red-haired man ran out of the timber, a knife held high, its blade flashing in the sun.

Peg pressed herself hard against the tree, as if hoping the dead trunk would envelope and hide her. 'One's coming,' she whimpered.

'Just one?' Jenny asked.

'So far.'

He wore only a belt and an empty knife sheath. His penis swung wildly as he ran.

'My God!' Peg gasped.

'What?'

'It's Chief Murdoch.'

'Lois's dad?'

'What's *he* doing here?' Far behind him two more figures came out of the trees. One was a woman – a pregnant woman, her belly stretched and bulging. The lean, blond man beside her held a spear. 'Two more,' Peg said.

'Four coming my way,' Jenny said. 'Oh Mom. Oh geez, Mom!'

Murdoch stopped in front of Peg. He pressed the knife point to her throat.

'Don't get many townies,' he said.

'Charlie . . .'

'Always glad when we do, though. I love seeing their faces.' His other hand began to unbutton her dress. 'Always, so shocked. What's Charlie Murdoch doing out here with the Krulls?'

'Don't.'

'They started Barlow, you know. Needed a civilized front. Speaking of fronts . . .' He chuckled softly, drew the knife down her chest, and cut through her bra. He pushed the cups aside. 'Nice.' He lowered the knife. As he sheathed it, Peg saw his penis rising stiff. Then she felt his hands.

'No, please.'

'What's he doing?' Jenny demanded.

'Shut up,' Murdoch said. Then he spoke softly to Peg. 'Know what we're gonna do to you?'

'No.'

'Thought everybody knew.' His hands left her breasts. They opened her belt. Then tugged the dress. The cloth split down to the hem. Crouching, he gripped both sides of the strip, and tugged. The hem popped apart.

The two Krulls stood just behind him, watching. The man was naked, his eyes fixed on her body, one hand stroking his erect penis. The pregnant woman wore something like a bikini on her swollen breasts. Only not of cloth.

Of skin.

Peg felt Charlie's hands slide up her legs. They hooked her panties and dragged them down.

Faces!

The rags of flesh on her breasts were faces. Small, oval faces. The faces of children!

Peg shut her eyes tightly.

She gagged, but stopped when Charlie yanked her legs out from under her. The tree scraped her back. She thought her arms would tear from their sockets. But she didn't fall far. She opened her eyes only long enough to see her legs hooked over Charlie's shoulders. She felt his mouth, his flicking tongue.

'*No!*'


'What are you doing to my mother!' Jenny cried. 'Stop it! Damn you, I'll kill you!'

Then a fat, female Krull hurled a spear at her. It thunked the trunk above her head.

She watched the four approach. Among them, only one looked normal: a boy no older than herself. He was blond and naked. For an instant, she thought he was Timmy. Then she remembered what she'd done to Timmy. She was glad. If she got a chance, she would do the same to this kid.

The others, though . . .

The fat one who'd thrown the spear was hairless and white. Her dead-white skin was shiny and slug-like.

Another woman hurried along behind them. She hobbled, bent low at the waist like a speed skater, one arm twisted behind her back. Her young face was distorted as if fingers were pulling it to one side. Her long breasts hung low. Her knees bumped them as she rushed forward.

The last, a wild-haired man, skittered through the tall grass like a lizard, powerful arms driving him forward, his legs dragging behind him.

Jenny cringed as her mother shrieked 'No! NO!'

Then the boy reached Jenny. He slipped the knife into the neck of her blouse, edge outward, and jerked. The blouse ripped open.

'Oooo,' moaned the fat one. She shoved the boy aside, and spread the blouse, and pressed herself against Jenny. Her skin was slick and sticky. She licked Jenny's mouth. Her hands opened Jenny's pants.

Jenny drove her knee into the soft belly. The girl fell away, gasping. The boy laughed at her.

Now the bent woman came in close. She nuzzled Jenny's belly with her face.

Jenny tried to knee her, but the lizard man had her ankles.

The bent woman sighed, licking Jenny's belly. Then she bit.

The lizard man bit her thigh.

The fat slimy girl, up again, kissed her and squeezed her breasts.

She screamed into the fat girl's mouth.

# Chapter Thirty-four

Neala opened her eyes. She was lying on her side, her body against Johnny, her face touching his bare chest. She felt as if she'd been asleep for a long time. A breeze moved over her skin in warm, fluttery waves.

There had been no breeze, earlier. With a start, she rolled onto her back. The cabin's shadow stretched along distance. 'Oh God,' she moaned. She turned to Johnny. 'It's so late, she said.

'We've got a couple more hours.'

'I don't want you to go. Not without me.'

'You'll be safe here.'

'I don't care if I'm safe. I want to be with you.'

'Well, we'll see. I just . . .'

'Hey guys!' Sherri called through the wall. 'You'd better get in here.'

'Right in,' Johnny said.

Neala sat up. She didn't look toward the wall. All afternoon, she had kept her eyes away from it. If Sherri was spying again, she didn't want to know.

She and Johnny got dressed. They hurried to the front of the cabin and entered its open door.

Cordelia was sitting up.

'She wants to tell us something,' Sherri explained.

'Yeah,' she said. 'It's what they sent me in here for. You're supposed to come out.'

'Surprise, surprise.'

'They won't kill you if you come out.'

'Sure,' said Sherri. 'I'll just bet.'

'No, it's true. They'll take you in. You can join with them. They won't kill you.'

'Why not?' Neala asked.

'They need you . . . They've got too much inbreeding.'

'They want us for making babies?'

'Yeah.'

'What about Johnny? He's hardly capable . . .'

'He can come, too.'

'Stick to the truth,' Johnny warned.

Sherri turned to him. 'You know what she's talking about?'

'I know they'll accept women, sometimes. Young ones. Pretty ones. For recreation. And for breeding, I suppose. That may be why they don't want the Barlow people fooling with them. They don't take men, though.'

'Is that true?' Sherri asked Cordelia.

The girl nodded.

'You mean they'd kill Johnny?' Neala asked.

'I suppose.'

'You bitch! What're you lying for!'

'I'm sorry,' Cordelia whispered. She held up her left hand and plucked a filthy rag away from it. 'See what they did?'

Neala glimpsed the stump, and looked away.

'One of them bit it off. As a lesson. To show what they'd do to me if I didn't get you two to come out.'

Sherri laughed once, harshly. 'This sounds like a great outfit. First they fuck us, then they bite off our fingers.'

'And they kill Johnny,' Neala added.

'Thanks, but I'll pass,' Sherri said.

Cordelia looked up at each of them. 'If you don't come with me, you'll all get killed.'

'They can't get to us here,' Johnny told her. 'If they could, they wouldn't have sent you to talk us out.'

'It's not them. It's ... someone else.' The fear in her eyes chilled Neala. 'I saw him last night,' she said. Her voice lowered to a hoarse whisper. 'He killed Ben. He put Ben's head on a pole. He put all these heads on poles. They call him The Devil, and they won't come to get you because this is his cabin, and he's coming back.'

'When?' Johnny asked.

'Maybe tonight.'

'She's trying to trick us again,' Sherri said.

'No, honest. He's real and he's – horrible!'

'We were here last night,' Johnny said. 'He didn't come then.'

'He was out killing. He killed Ben. He would've killed me, but I hid.'

'If he comes,' said Sherri, 'we'll just hide.'

'You're crazy. He'll kill you all.' She pushed herself to her feet. 'I'm going back. I'll tell 'em you aren't coming out.'

'Don't go back,' Johnny said. 'Stay here. We'll all get out.'

'Oh no you won't. I've seen ... I've seen *him*. I'm going back.'

She stepped unsteadily toward the open door.

'Cordelia, don't.'

'You're fools,' she said. She pointed through the doorway. 'Your heads'll be out there by morning.'

Her sword was propped beside the door. She reached for it.

'Leave that here,' Johnny said.

'Okay,' she said.

Then she grabbed it, whirled around and attacked.

# Chapter Thirty-five

She drove the blade toward Robbins' chest. He was sitting on the floor. It should have been easy.

But in the few steps she took to reach him, Neala dived at her legs, Sherri scurried toward the fireplace, and Robbins dropped backward. She kicked through Neala's arms and lunged at Robbins. His leg swung up. It caught the blade. Crying out with pain, he threw himself sideways. The leg of his jeans held the blade. She lost the sword.

Sherri swung the fire poker at her head. She blocked it with her forearm. Neala sprawled on the floor, grabbed her left leg and bit into her calf. As she tore loose from Neala, Sherri swung again. The poker's black point whipped past her eyes, just missing. She turned and ran. At the door, the poker slashed. It ripped down her back. She raced for the forest of pikes, Sherri close behind. The poker *whushed*. Missed. A skull leered at her. She ducked under the cross-bar. Falling to her knees, she scrambled forward.

She looked over her shoulder. Sherri had stopped.

Neala appeared in the doorway with the rifle. She aimed and fired. Dirt and twigs exploded from the ground beside Cordie.

She lurched forward, plowing through a dozen crosses before another shot blasted the stillness. She threw herself down.

Something under her belly. She knew, without looking, what it had to be. With a gasp, she rolled off it. Her back hit a pole. She froze.

Nothing fell.

Lying on her side, panting, she could still feel the touch of what she had fallen on. She shut her eyes tightly, and reached down. With the back of her hand, she knocked it away.

Then she lay down flat again, and waited for the next shot.

It didn't come.

Finally, she looked back. Sherri and Neala were gone.

She pushed herself to her hands and knees. Ahead, through the tilting bars of many pikes, the Krulls waited. They were silent. All seemed to be watching her.

She remembered Grar's warning. *If you betray us, your death will be horrible beyond nightmares.*

They can't get me here, she thought.

She lowered herself to the ground. She cushioned her face on an arm bruised by the poker, and shut her eyes. The ground felt good beneath her, in spite of the scratchy twigs and weeds.

She would stay here.

Though the breeze was mild, the sun baked her back. Sweat slid down her skin. Sometimes, she felt the tickle of insects. But she didn't move. It would hurt to move. And it would do no good, because there was no way to escape the heat or bugs.

No way to escape the pain.

Or the Krulls.

No, this is how to escape the Krulls.

This is how.

This . . .

Then the terrible heat was gone. She opened her eyes, and saw that dusk had fallen.

Many of the Krulls were gone. Many remained.

Maybe when darkness comes . . .

No.

If she left, they would find her.

Do unspeakable things. *Your death will be horrible beyond nightmares.*

She lowered her head, and closed her eyes.

This is a good place to be.

A good place.

# Chapter Thirty-six

'Johnny, no.'

'Here, give me the rifle.'

'You can't make it.'

'I can try. You two hold out as long as you can. If I don't get back with help, go on out to the Krulls and make the best of it.'

Sherri handed the rifle to him.

Using it as a brace, Johnny pushed himself to his feet. He hobbled across the candle-lit room. Sweat poured down his back. Neala saw that he was putting no weight on his bandaged leg.

'Johnny . . .'

'Once I get to the car, I'll be okay. It'll just take longer than . . . the rifle slipped in his grip. He winced and fell.

Neala rushed to him.

'It's okay, it's okay,' he said.

'No, it's not.'

He planted his rifle butt and started to push himself up. He gritted his teeth. He blinked sweat out of his eyes. His body trembled.

Neala took hold of his arm. 'Wait. Just sit down and rest for a minute. Please.'

He lowered himself.

'Here, I'll take the rifle.'

He gripped it.

'I need to go out for a second.'

'Again?' Sherri asked.

She sighed. 'Must be something I ate. Or didn't eat.'

'I'll go with you,' Sherri said.

'Christ, I don't need a guard.'

'Okay. Well, hurry.'

'Be right back.' She kissed Johnny lightly on the mouth. Then she went out the open door. She walked quickly to the rear of the cabin. The gibbous moon hung low over the distant trees. She wished it weren't so bright.

Propping the rifle against the cabin wall, she stepped out of her corduroys. She took Johnny's key case from a pocket and slipped it into the front of her panties. Then she took off her shirt.

The breeze had died soon after dark, leaving the air still and warm. In spite of the warmth, she shivered as she picked up the rifle. She put the sling over her head. The rifle sapped against her back. The sling tugged at her shoulder. It crossed her body, its wide leather strap digging into her right breast. She adjusted it so it passed between her breasts. Then, crouching, she made her way toward the pikes.

'Neala!'

Sherri's voice. Glancing back, she saw her friend run at her.

She rushed for the crosses, but Sherri grabbed her by the hair, yanked her to the ground, and dropped onto her. She grunted in pain as the rifle rammed her back. Sherri clutched her wrists and pressed them down.

'Let go of me, damn it!'

'You want to go off and get yourself killed!'

162

'Get off me!'

'No. I can't. I can't let you do it, Neala.'

'If I don't go, Johnny will try.'

'We can stop him. Between the two of us . . .'

'Sherri, for Godsake, don't you realize? We can't stay in this cabin. We'll all die. Even if the Krulls stay away, even if this *devil* never comes, we'll just die in there.'

'We could give up, and live with the Krulls.'

'Sure. Only what happens to Johnny?'

'Yeah, I know.' She stared into Neala's eyes. 'You love him, don't you?'

'Yes.'

She let go of Neala's wrists and gently stroked her face. 'Oh Neala,' she whispered 'Oh Goddamn it, Neala. Don't forget me, huh?'

'Wha . . .?'

Sherri's fist swung down. It struck the side of Neala's head. She saw the other fist come down, and tried to block it, but she couldn't get her arm up fast enough. The fist hit, rocking her head.

The weight of Sherri's body left. She tried to raise her head, but couldn't. She felt drunk, powerless to control her movements.

Sherri pulled the rifle sling away from her breasts. Rolled her. Pulled the rifle away. She flopped onto her back again. The ground felt much better without the hardness of the rifle.

Sherri, standing like a giant above her, quickly stripped.

'Don'.'

Sherri slung the rifle onto her back.

Neala raised her head. 'Don',' she said again.

'Oh Neala.' Sherri crouched beside her.

Neala concentrated on her arms. They felt heavy, as if she

163

held a large stone in each hand. But she forced herself to lift them. She felt the girl's big hands slide under her and raise her off the ground. She felt the breasts brush lightly against her breasts, the mouth push against her mouth. She hugged Sherri as hard as she could. Then Sherri forced her down.

'You and Johnny stay put,' she whispered, 'till I get back with the cavalry.'

Her fist smashed down.

Neala tried to open her eyes, but couldn't. She tried to lift her head, but the muscles of her neck wouldn't work.

Not even when she heard Johnny calling.

Then he was above her.

'Neala? Neala, what happened? Where's Sherri?'

She found that she could open her eyes. 'Gone,' she managed. 'Went . . . for cavalry.'

A minute passed before she was able to get up. She put on her shirt. 'I was going to go,' she said. 'I stripped, you know, so I'd look more like one of *them*. But Sherri stopped me. She . . . Oh my God!' Neala pushed her hand into the front of her panties. 'No! Oh Johnny!' She pulled out the leather case.

'My keys.'

'I took them while we were bandaging you. I forgot . . . When she . . . She just *attacked* me, Johnny. I couldn't . . . Oh God, what'll she do, now?'

He shook his head. 'If she makes it that far – well, she'll be fairly close to the road. She can hitch a ride. As long as she doesn't get picked up by Barlow people . . .'

'She hasn't got a chance.'

'Sure she does. She's got as good a chance . . .' He didn't finish.

'As we do,' Neala finished for him.

'Let's get back inside.'

164

She fastened her pants. Johnny struggled to stand, using the fire poker as a staff. Neala helped him up. He leaned on her, and they slowly made their way to the front of the cabin.

As Neala shut the door, a single gunshot blasted in the distance.

Her eyes met Johnny's.

He said nothing.

# Chapter Thirty-seven

Peg clenched her teeth, determined not to cry out as she burned with the boy's penetration. Jenny, suspended from a tripod beside her, was still unconscious – had been since the ordeal at the Trees. Peg wanted her to stay that way.

Didn't want her to see all this.

The way the men took turns.

The other things . . .

She shut her eyes tightly, squeezing tears from the corners as the boy thrust harden. His cock felt like a fiery log. They all did, now, all burned her as they plunged and battered.

So far, only four had used Jenny. Thank God the girl was unconscious, except for the first – the boy at the Trees.

Jenny sucked in a sharp breath as the boy tugged at her madly and throbbed.

Then he left her alone.

She swung by her tied hands, her legs too weak to hold her

up. She looked down. Her legs shimmered in the firelight, dark with blood.

She looked again at Jenny. The girl's head was still down. Her body hung limp from the rope, swaying slightly. This time, the blood was her own. From half a dozen bites. Her screams . . .

But she wasn't dead. Peg could see the slight rise and fall of her chest. Unconscious, but not dead. Maybe it would be best if she never woke up.

'The ghoul-haunted woodland.'

Peg swung sideways, and looked at the man suspended from the tripod to her right. Until now, she'd thought him dead.

'Beasts,' he said. 'Foul, loathsome beasts.'

'I wish they'd kill us,' Peg said.

'Oh, they will. But first they'll have their sport. Last night . . .' He lowered his head.

'What?'

'They had my . . . my Ruth. They . . . oh what they did! *Bastards!*' he cried out. '*Bastards!*'

Several Krulls near the main fire looked back at him. A big man stood up. Peg recognized him as Murdoch.

'Problem?' Murdoch asked through a mouthful of food.

'You bastards!'

Murdoch came toward them. He took another bite from the forearm he carried.

'Bastard!'

Murdoch grinned. 'I know your problem, bud. You're hungry. Well, we've got plenty to go around.' He pushed the severed arm toward the man's face. 'Help yourself.'

The man kicked wildly, but Murdoch spun away.

'How about you, Peg?'

'Go to hell.'

166

'Don't worry, it's no one you know.' He raised the hand to her breast. She cringed at its touch.

'Get away!'

'It's tender and tasty. The best meat of all. The Krulls, they've always known that. Been eating it for generations.'

'Yeah, and look at them.'

'Oh, that's not their diet's fault. That's from their pet. Just a little radiation. Mixed up their genes a bit.'

She watched him bite the arm and rip a chunk from it. He smiled as he chewed. 'Delicious,' he said, the food muffling his voice.

Then he spit it in her face turned away, laughing.

'Ghouls,' the man muttered. 'They . . . last night . . . my Ruth. They . . . they *ate* her! Ate her! Right in front of me! Forced me . . . Pinched my nose so I had to open up, and . . . OH!'

The man began to croon softly and mumble.

Peg glanced at Jenny.

Still out, thank God.

'They left the head,' the man muttered, suddenly intelligible again. 'Don't eat the heads. Save 'em for the pit. Oh, the pit! Wait'll you . . .'

'Shut up,' Peg snapped. 'Goddamn it, just shut up!'

'It lives in the pit,' he mumbled. 'You'll see.'

'Shut *up*!'

He went silent.

Peg stared at the patch of darkness. It wasn't far away. A dozen yards, maybe less. Before night had come, she'd seen that it was a hole in the ground. A wide hole. She'd noticed that the Krulls stayed far from its edge. She'd seen them throw in bones.

'That's why they're here, you know.'

'I don't want to know!'

'To feed it. One told me so. To feed it. To keep it happy.'

167

# Chapter Thirty-eight

Cordie, lying belly-down among the impaled heads, heard the insane roar. The same roar she had heard last night. It came from far in the distance.

But she knew he would soon arrive.

Bringing new heads.

And he would find her.

She raised her head. Beyond the pikes, the open field looked deserted. The others must have run when they heard him.

My chance!

They'll all be hiding!

But if they catch me . . . Better *they* get me.

At least she'd stand a chance, out in the woods. Maybe she could find Mom and Dad, and they'd escape together.

She glanced back at the cabin.

They might let her in, if she begged.

No. That's the worst place to be, even worse than here in the heads.

The door couldn't keep him out.

And they didn't have the rifle, anymore. The big girl, Sherri, must have taken it. She'd seen Robbins and Neala come back to the door without her. Then, she'd heard a gunshot far away.

Somebody got Sherri.

Good.

The bitch had really hurt her with that poker – would have killed her if she could.

Good riddance.

The bitches deserve whatever they get. If they'd only come along with her, they'd all be safe now.

She looked again at the moonlit clearing. Again, she saw no Krulls. She'd better not go that way, though. The roar had come from that direction.

So she turned to her left, and began to crawl. She moved slowly, careful not to bump the poles. When she reached a pair too close together, she squeezed through on her side, her back rubbing one stick, her breasts brushing the other.

There were so many! They seemed endless.

But she kept moving, kept crawling, kept dragging herself forward.

Until a quiet sound stopped her.

The pop of a breaking stick.

She dropped to her side and looked back.

*Him!*

Stabbing across into the ground near the place where she'd entered, so long ago.

How long had he been there?

As she watched, he raised a head high and rammed it down. It made a wet sound.

Then he entered the field of crosses.

He glided through them, turning silently, never bumping a single cross.

Cordie watched, afraid to move.

How could he travel so fast, and not knock the heads off?

He *is* the Devil!

Suddenly, he turned toward Cordie.

He'd seen her!

She heard a tiny whine in her throat. Warm liquid spurted down her thigh.

Then he turned away.

She moaned, and watched him move through the last of the heads.

His awful voice bellowed, 'Krull!'

He kicked open the cabin door.

# Chapter Thirty-nine

Neala flinched as the door crashed open. She pressed her face tightly against the deerskin beneath her, and wished she could burrow in.

Heavy footfalls came toward her.

*No!*

She gritted her teeth, trying not to scream.

*'Krull!'*

Her body quaked, shaken by terror.

Oh Christ, we should've run!

Any moment, he would fling aside the skins that covered her.

*Hail, Mary, full of grace; the Lord is with thee; blessed art thou among women . . .*

From his hiding place behind a draping deerskin, Robbins watched the tall dark shape stride toward the far corner.

Across its back, a rifle hung by a sling.

*My rifle?*

Poor Sherri . . .

The sword clacked against the wall.

The creature swung around. It stood motionless. Robbins held his breath. He gazed at the thing, and shuddered.

Its wide, leathery face looked red in the candle light. One eye was gone, its socket a dark slit as if the lid had been torn away. The remaining eye seemed to glare at Robbins with contempt.

Then it lowered to the stack of skins near Robbins' feet. Robbins looked. He saw Neala's hair. Inches of it curled from beneath one of the skins, glossy in the golden light.

The creature lunged. It grabbed Neala's hair and jerked.

The head came free.

It swung slowly as the single eye studied it.

Robbins staggered from behind the deerskin. With both hands, he swung the saber. Its blade struck, lopping off the outstretched arm. The arm dropped to the floor, Neala's hair still gripped in its hand.

He swung again, this time hitting the neck. The saber hacked through. The head tipped sideways, blood spouting. It toppled. A strip of muscle and flesh stopped its fall, and it hung at the chest, swinging slightly.

The body dropped backwards.

Neala, hidden in the far corner, heard the struggle. Thrusting aside the deerskins, she saw the thing standing headless in front of Johnny. She saw it fall.

Later, Robbins unknotted Neala's long, soft hair. He pulled it from the jawbone of the old head, and tossed the head outside.

Among the crosses in front of the cabin, he found one more sturdy than the others. On it, he impaled the head of The Devil. He propped it near the cabin door.

'Robbins!'

171

Turning, he saw a man moving through the barrier. The thin, pale man casually pushed aside the pikes as he came forward.

Neala took hold of Robbins' arm. He saw that she held the rifle.

'I come in peace,' said the man.

He stepped out of the crosses. A skirt of hair floated about his legs as he moved. He stopped in front of Robbins.

Robbins stared at the moonlit face.

'August?' he muttered.

The old man nodded.

'It's August Hayer,' Robbins said to Neala. 'He's . . . he's the mayor.'

'In the woods, I am called Grar. I am chieftain of the Krulls.'

'Jesus H. Christ.'

'You have slain the devil Weiss.'

'Weiss!' Robbins whirled around. He studied the face of the grim, severed head. 'Can't be.'

'Oh, it is. He's been marauding for years, slaughtering us without mercy. All these heads . . .' Hayer swept a hand across the landscape of impaled heads. 'He was responsible. Our people are primitive and filled with superstition. They called him The Devil, and shunned his cabin. He might have killed many more of us, but for you. With his death, you have purchased your salvation. You shall come with me to the village, and become one with us.'

'That's not good enough,' Robbins said. 'We want out.'

'I'm afraid that's impossible.'

'Is it?'

'We cannot have you leave the woods.'

'Afraid we'd spill the beans? Tell the world about your game?'

'It's hardly a game, Robbins. If you knew the reason we're out here, why the Krulls are here . . .'

'I don't give a damn about reasons.'

'Perhaps you should. If you knew what's at stake . . .'

'I'll tell you what's at stake. Your ass.' He grabbed the rifle from Neala and jammed its muzzle against Hayer's chest, knocking the old man backwards. 'You're gonna lead us out of here. We're going to my car. You know where that is? Good. Any trouble from you or any of your goddamn Neanderthals, and I'll blow a hole through you so big you can drive a bus through it!'

'You're a fool, Robbins. I'm offering you . . .'

'I know what you're offering. I'm not buying.'

'What about your friend?' He nodded toward Neala.

She glanced at Robbins. Her eyes were still raw from crying over the death of Sherri. She looked dazed and weary.

'I don't think Neala would go for it, either.'

'For what?' she asked in a monotone.

'Total freedom,' Hayer said. 'A life of idle pleasure, at one with nature . . .'

'You've seen those freaks,' Robbins said. 'Do you want to live with them?'

'I'd rather die.'

'There it is, Hayer. Get moving.'

'One more item. You have a sister named Peg, and a niece – Jenny, I believe.'

Robbins' stomach went cold and tight.

'You wouldn't want to leave the woods without them.'

'Where are they?'

'In the village, of course. Eagerly awaiting your arrival.' Hayer removed a ring from his little finger and held it out.

Robbins took the ring. He looked at it in the moonlight and touched the smooth oval of its jade. 'Peg's,' he muttered.

'We'd better go with him,' Neala said.

'Yeah.' Helpless rage suddenly shook him. 'Yeah, take us to the village.' He rammed the muzzle into Hayer's belly. The man doubled, clutching himself and wheezing. 'Take us to the village,' Robbins muttered. He slammed the rifle butt into Hayer's shoulder, knocking him to his knees. 'Take us to the village,' he said, and drove his boot into Hayer's face.

# Chapter Forty

'Cordelia!'

She lay facedown among the crosses, watching. She didn't move or reply.

'Cordelia!' Robbins yelled again. 'I know you're out there. Get your ass over here.'

She shook her head, and said nothing.

'I'm not going to hurt you. Now come on. This is your only chance. Weiss – that Devil of yours – he's dead. That means the Krulls aren't scared of this place, anymore. They'll come right in after you.'

She got up on her knees.

'We have a hostage here. We're going to the Krull village. Your parents might be there. We're going to the village, then we're getting out of here. So come on!'

'Do you promise,' she called, 'not to hurt me?'

'If I wanted to hurt you, I'd leave you here.'

'Okay. Okay, I'm coming.'

# Chapter Forty-one

Jenny heard a terrible scream. Mom? No, this time it sounded like a man. She raised her head.

Krulls all around. Moving silently in the firelight. The lizard man. The bent woman. An awful thing without legs. And others. So many, many others. Most were gathered around the big hole.

The man kept screaming. He was among them, somewhere. She couldn't see him.

She looked sideways. Her mother still hung there.

But the man who'd been on the other side of Mom was gone. It must be him.

The screaming stopped. A bunch of Krulls broke away from the group. They carried arms and legs toward the high, blazing fire. One big man – Chief Murdoch – carried the man's middle. Near the fire, he threw it down among the arms and legs. No head was there.

The Krulls stepped back from the hole. They all seemed to be watching it. In the space between two of them, she could see part of the hole.

And she saw the man's head on the ground near its edge. It wobbled for a moment. Then a dark thing squirmed in its hair and snatched it into the hole.

The Krulls all stared.

Nobody made a sound.

Then she heard Murdoch's voice. 'Shall we give it another?' He was talking to Mom!

He turned to the Krulls and spoke in their language. Then he turned again to Jenny's mother. Pulling out his knife, he took a step toward her.

A gunshot blasted the stillness. Murdoch's legs collapsed, and he fell facedown.

Jenny spun herself around. Near a hut, she saw four people standing in the darkness.

'Okay Hayer, tell them all to stay put. The ones behind us, too.'

The old man spoke in the same strange language Neala had heard him use in the woods to keep the Krulls from attacking. As he spoke, Johnny glanced from Cordelia to Neala. 'Go on,' he muttered. 'Hurry.'

Though breathless and shaking with fear, Neala didn't hesitate. She ran forward with the saber. She tried to keep her eyes on the girl suspended inside the tripod, but she couldn't stop herself from looking toward the Krulls. Some were moving, now, as if recovering from the surprise of the gunshot.

Hayer continued to talk, but she heard mumbling among the Krulls.

'Quick!' the girl called.

With a sideways glance, she saw Cordelia running toward the tripod where the woman hung.

She saw a legless thing swinging its torso through the mob. The one she'd seen on the road, so long ago. It had a knife clamped in its teeth.

She reached the tripod.

Someone yelled.

Jerking her head sideways, she saw a spear punch through Cordelia.

Neala swung the saber high, severing the rope. The girl fell.

* * *

'Fucking bastard!' Robbins shoved the muzzle against Hayer's neck and pulled the trigger.

Pivoting, he flicked the lever action and shot the nearest Krull.

Then he limped toward Peg.

Toward the attacking crowd.

Jenny, on hands and knees, glanced toward her mother. She saw a dozen Krulls scurrying toward her. Saw Uncle John staggering toward them, shooting. But a bunch were coming up behind him.

'Uncle John!'

She looked around. The woman who'd cut her down was already running away, running toward Uncle John with the sword high.

Jenny got to her feet, and ran the other way.

A boy with a knife leaped onto Johnny's back. Raised a hatchet. Neala slashed, knocking off his hand.

She swung the saber into a woman's face, whirled, and split the head of a crawling man.

A knife seared her side. She drove her elbow into the face of the girl who'd done it. The girl fell backwards. Neala drove the sword down into her belly.

Someone jumped onto her back. She sprawled onto the girl's body. Felt a blade at her throat.

Robbins punched his rifle to the man's ear and fired. Then he dragged the body off Neala.

He glanced toward Peg. A legless creature, at her feet, was taking a knife from its mouth.

He aimed and pulled the trigger.

*Click!*

* * *

Peg kicked. Her foot caught the legless thing in its face. Flapping its arms wildly, it fell backwards.

But there were so many more!

She twisted and kicked as they approached.

Then she saw her daughter.

'Jenny!' she cried.

The nearest Krulls looked. Turning away from Peg, they began to shriek with alarm.

Jenny ran.

A slithering Krull grabbed for her feet, but missed.

Others reached for her. She was too quick.

A spear nicked her leg, but she kept running. Just a scratch. It barely hurt. Nothing hurt except her hands.

Only one Krull still stood in her way.

Blocked her way.

The fat, slimy one from the Trees. And she looked scared. She tried to duck out of the way.

Jenny shoved the fiery branch into her face. The girl screamed and fell backwards into the pit.

The huge, blazing branch followed her down.

It started with a deafening shriek.

Neala pulled her saber from the chest of a Krull and pivoted, ready to strike at another – but every Krull stood motionless, gaping toward the pit.

Those nearest the pit started to run. Dark cords whipped around the feet of some, and jerked the savages screaming into the hole.

Then every Krull was hurrying away – most running, others dragging themselves along, some scuttling through the village like giant, clumsy spiders.

* * *

Jenny stomped on the wrist of a big, legless Krull on the ground in front of Mom. He growled in pain, and his hand opened. Jenny reached for the knife.

Her charred right hand wouldn't work.

She grabbed it with her left, and shoved it into the creature's eye.

A hand clasped her shoulder.

She swung around, slashing, but missed.

'Uncle John!'

'Give me that.'

He took the knife. Reaching high, he sawed through the rope that held Mom.

Both fell.

But the other woman came. The one with the sword.

Something lashed Jenny's foot. Yelping, she jerked away and saw a dark, snakelike thing curl around the throat of the legless Krull and drag his body toward the hole.

The ground near the hole's edge seemed alive with shimmery tentacles.

'Let's go, let's go!' Uncle John yelled.

Then they were all rushing away.

At the edge of the village, before entering the forest, Jenny turned around. 'Look!' she cried. 'It's out!'

'My God,' gasped the woman with the sword. 'What *is* it!'

The four of them stared. 'What have we done?' the woman whispered.

'Survived,' Uncle John said. 'Let's get out of here.'


They hurried through the woods – swam across the stream. Along the way, they rushed past many Krulls. Some cowered in bushes, others scurried up trees as if to seek safety in the high, hidden branches. None attacked.

They ran past several bodies. At first, Robbins didn't understand. He crouched to inspect one. The woman's throat had been slashed. She still gripped the bloody knife.

'Suicide,' he said.

As they crossed the open field, he looked toward the Killing Trees. He saw movement along their pale, bare branches.

Neala stopped and pointed.

'I see 'em.'

Three dark shapes suddenly dropped from the trees, crashing through limbs, slamming into the ground.

'Come on,' Robbins said. 'We're almost there.'

Neala gazed into the darkness around the car, and saw no Krulls.

None inside the car, either.

She sat in the front seat.

Peg and Jenny climbed into the back.

Johnny slid the key into the ignition – the key that Sherri had forgotten to take, couldn't have used, anyway, because . . . He turned it, and the car started.

Later, on the highway, Neala flung her sword from the window. She watched it curve through the darkness and disappear into the foliage along the roadside. Then she slid across to Johnny. He put an arm across her shoulders, and smiled.

# Out are the Lights

# And Other Tales

# Contents

Out – out are the lights – out all!
   And, over each quivering form,
The curtain, a funeral pall
   Comes down with the rush of a storm,
While the angels, all pallid and wan,
   Uprising, unveiling, affirm
That the play is the tragedy 'Man'.
   And its hero the Conqueror Worm.

Edgar Allan Poe. *The Conqueror Worm*

# Prologue

'You sure it's not haunted?' Ray asked.

The weathered, Victorian house cast a shadow over its weedy yard and Ray's Trans Am.

'Wouldn't that be rich?' Tina said. 'I've never seen a ghost.'

'This may be your big opportunity.' Ray reached for the door handle, but hesitated and looked again out the windshield. He gnawed his lower lip.

'Would you rather not stay here?' Tina asked. 'I mean, just because Todd offered to let us use it, we aren't *obliged* to stay. We could go someplace else if you want. A motel or something.'

'I guess this is all right,' Ray said.

'It's just old. He told me not to expect too much. He bought it as a fixer-upper.'

'When's he planning to start?'

Tina smiled. 'It might be wonderful, once we get inside.'

'I don't like those bars in the windows.'

'He's had a few problems with vandals. So remote, out here . . .'

'I hope there's not a fire. An old place like this, it'd go up like paper. And those bars . . . I don't know, Tina. The place rubs me wrong.'

'You've seen too many movies, that's your problem.'

'Think so?'

'Let's at least have a look inside.'

'Why not.'

183

They climbed from the car. In the shade, the breeze from the ocean felt chilly on Tina's bare skin. She pulled the back of the seat forward, and leaned into the car.

'Let's just leave the groceries and stuff till we've had a chance to look around.'

'I'm getting my blouse,' Tina said. She found it wadded behind the picnic basket they used at the beach, and tugged it free.

Ray made a mocking pout as she put it on.

She grinned. 'I don't want the ghosts to see me in my bikini,' she said.

'Nothing worse than a horny ghost,' Ray agreed.

As she buttoned the blouse, Ray slipped a hand inside the seat of her bikini shorts. Her skin was moist from the damp swimsuit. His warm, dry hand felt good.

He started to take it out.

'Oooo, don't stop.'

He removed his hand, and patted her rump. 'Tempis is fugiting. Let's have that look inside, and get going. It's a long drive to the nearest motel.'

'Maybe you'll just love it here.'

'Well, the price is certainly right. Have you got the key?'

'Right here.' She lifted her handbag off the car floor, and slung the strap over her shoulder.

They started across the overgrown yard.

'I think it's rather quaint,' Tina said.

'It is that, I suppose.'

They climbed half a dozen stairs to a roofed porch that extended along the entire front of the house. As Tina reached into her handbag, she saw the door's heavy brass knocker – a skull.

'That's Todd for you,' she said, grinning. 'It's no wonder he bought the place. It's so *him*.'

Ray didn't look amused. 'What's Todd; a ghoul?'

'He's really rather nice.'

'Is he?'

She hunted for the key, face toward the door to hide her grin. Ray could be so childish, sometimes. It was fun to bait him, but she knew she'd better back off. If she went too far, he might start his silent treatment.

She found the key. 'Ready?'

'As I'll ever be.'

She pushed it into the keyhole, and turned it. A bolt clacked back. She pushed the door open, enjoying the groan of its hinges.

'Naturally they squeak,' Ray muttered.

'We oughtta spray this sucker with WD-40 before we go. That's fix his wagon.'

That brought a grin from Ray.

It's all right now, she thought.

She stepped into the dim foyer, glimpsed someone beside her, and lurched back. She collided with Ray.

Laughing, he caught her in his arms. 'So who's the nervous one?' he asked, and nodded toward the wall mirror. 'Jumping at your own reflection.'

She snapped the waistband of his swimming trunks.

'Big deal,' she said. Then she turned away from him, and looked around. 'The place is rather dismal,' she admitted.

Ray flicked a switch. A ceiling light came on. 'At least there's electricity.'

Tina moved to the front of the staircase. The steps were narrow and steep. At a landing, halfway up, they angled to the right and vanished. 'The bedroom's probably up there,' she said.

'You go ahead, I'll wait here.'

'Ha, ha, ha.'

'Do you want me to lead the way?'

'If you please.'

He shut the front door, and started up the stairs ahead of her. 'Watch out,' he warned. 'Mirror ahead.'

She yanked his trunks.

'Don't!' He grabbed them at his knees. 'Want me to trip?'

'Then don't be such a wiseguy.'

'Sorry, sorry,' he said, pulling them up.

'Nice ass,' Tina remarked.

'Thank you.'

'Cracked, though.'

At the top of the stairs, they came to a narrow hallway. The only windows, at each end, were hung with heavy red drapes.

'Charming,' Tina said.

'Your friend's a great decorator.' Ray found a light switch. Dim bulbs came alive in sconces along the walls.

He tried a door. It was locked. 'Great,' he muttered.

'Hope that isn't the John.'

He tried a door on the other side of the hall, and glanced at Tina as the knob turned. He pushed the door open. The room was bare.

Tina shrugged. 'He's got an austere taste in furniture.'

'I'll say.'

They found two more empty rooms, then the bathroom.

'We're in luck,' Tina said.

They stepped inside. When she saw the enormous tub, she smiled with delight. 'Oh, this is great.'

'No shower.'

'But look at the size of that! Look, it's even got legs. Must be a real antique. Boy, I can't wait!'

'You don't really want to *stay* here!'

'Let's see if there's a bedroom.'

186

'If there's no bedroom, can we leave?'

'Then we can leave.'

They left the bathroom. Tina hurried ahead of Ray, and opened the last door on the right. '*Voila!*'

'Shit,' Ray muttered. He came up the hall, and looked in.

'Now this isn't so shabby, is it?'

'It's all right,' Ray admitted.

Tina kicked off her sandals and walked across the soft thickness of the carpet. 'Ain't shabby at all.' She hopped onto the king-sized bed and marched on its mattress, surveying the long dresser, the armoire, and her own image in the big wall mirrors.

Ray watched her, a grin slowly coming to his face.

'I think this'll do just fine.' she said. 'Don't you?'

'It's not bad.'

'Better than some dippy motel, right?'

'Right.'

She flopped backwards and sprawled on the mattress.

Smiling languidly, she opened the buttons of her blouse.

'Maybe we'd better take a look downstairs,' Ray said.

'Right now?' Slipping off the blouse, she rolled onto her belly. She pressed herself against the soft quilt. Reaching back, she untied her bikini top.

'Right this moment?' she drawled.

And grinned at the warm touch of Ray's hands.

Tina eased away from Ray's warm, sleeping body. She was reluctant to leave the bed, but the room was nearly dark and she was hungry. Ray would probably wake up famished. It'd be nice if she had supper on the stove when he got up.

If there *is* a stove.

She slipped out of bed, picked up her blouse, and stepped

silently over to a window. Through the grill-work, she looked down at Ray's car. She could just bring in the grocery bags, and let the luggage wait.

They'd better bring in the suitcases soon, though.

A thick, gray bank of fog was rolling in from the coast. It already hung in the trees near the highway. When it got here, they would want heavier clothes.

She stepped away from the window and glanced at Ray. He was still asleep, his tanned back dark against the white sheets. She slipped into her sandals. Carrying her blouse, she went to the door.

Before stepping into the hallway, she looked both ways. She caught herself doing it, and rolled her eyes. What'd she expect, for Christsake. *traffic?*

She started down the hall toward the stairs. Ray had left the lights on. The candle-like bulbs in the wall sconces weren't very bright. They made a menagerie of dim shadows as she walked down the hall, shadows within shadows, overlapping and chasing one another along both walls. Watching them, she flapped her arms and twirled. The shadows went crazy. She kicked and spun, swinging her blouse wildly overhead.

A low, moaning sound jerked her to a stop. She stood motionless near the stairway, listening.

The sound, she thought, had come from behind the door – the first door at the top of the stairs, the one they'd found locked.

Feeling suddenly timid and vulnerable, she put on her blouse. She buttoned it, her eyes fixed on the door.

Her hand tightened around the knob.

*What if it's not locked now?* she thought.

She pulled her hand away.

She backed up, watching the door, a tightness clutching her

stomach as she half expected it to swing open. Then she turned from it and rushed to the bedroom.

'Ray?' she called into the darkness. Her hand searched the inside wall for a light. 'Ray!'

'Huh?'

She found it, and snapped it. A bright light came on above the bed. Ray sat up, squinting.

'What're you doing?' he asked.

She hurried forward. 'Let's get out of here.'

'I thought . . .'

'I heard something.'

He threw aside the sheet, sat on the edge of the bed, and reached for his swimming trunks on the floor. 'What'd you hear?' he asked, pulling them on.

'Sounded like a moan.'

'Jesus!'

'Could've been my imagination, I guess.'

'But what if it wasn't?'

'I know.' Flinging through the sheets and blankets, she found her bikini. She climbed off the bed and stepped quickly into the brief pants. She stuffed the top into her handbag, and hurried after Ray.

He stopped in the doorway.

'Where'd you hear it?' he asked.

'The end of the hall. By the stairs. I think it's in the room with the locked door.'

'Christ, that means we've gotta go *past* it!'

'Maybe it was nothing.'

'Let's run. We'll run right by, and down the stairs, and out.' He took his car keys from the small, side pocket of his trunks. 'Ready?'

'I guess.'

189

'Okay, let's *go!*'

He burst ahead of her into the hallway. Tina ran hard, trying to catch up, but Ray was a dozen feet in front of her when the door near the stairway flew open.

A man leaped out, black cape billowing, fangs bared.

# Chapter One

'*Heads, You Lose.* It's playing at the Haunted Palace, over near Lincoln. You know, the theater that was closed for so long. It used to be the Elsinore.'

Connie nodded. She remembered the Elsinore. She'd gone there many times, before it closed. It was an old place, built in the days long before they made theaters like lecture halls – long and low and sterile, three or six to a building. This one's interior had ivy covered walls like a castle, battlements and turrets, and a high blue ceiling speckled with stars. It had been well named. The Elsinore. Hamlet's castle.

'Can I go with you?' Connie asked.

'If you want,' Dal said. 'It's not the kind of movie you like, though. I've heard it's awfully gory.'

'Well . . .' He wants to go alone, she thought. She forced herself to smile. 'You're probably right. You go on ahead.'

'You sure?' he asked.

He wants it definite. His conscience must be bothering him, though not enough to make a difference. 'Yeah,' she said. 'I'm sure. I wanted to wash my hair tonight, anyway.'

'Well, okay,' he said, sounding reluctant.

'What time's it over?'

'I ought to be home by midnight. It's a double feature.'

He kissed her quickly, and she smelled the scent of the cologne she'd given him for his birthday. 'You'll be the bestsmelling guy at the movies,' she told him.

For an instant, he looked flustered. 'Oh yeah, that.'

'Bring me some candy?'

'Sure.'

'Good 'n Plenty.'

'Okay, if they have it. See you later.'

'Have fun. And don't get too scared.'

'Me?' He winked, and left.

Connie stood by the door, disappointed and wondering what to do with herself. It seemed strange, having to face a night alone. Strange and sad, almost like the times before Dal.

Which hadn't been so long ago, really. They'd met only six months before, and he'd moved in two months after that. They'd been together almost every night since then.

Well, he deserved a night on his own. She shouldn't mind. It's healthy to be alone sometimes.

He's with people all day long, at work. Forced to be polite to everyone, including the creeps who come into the store from time to time – creeps he told her about through taut lips, his eyes narrow with anger.

Connie had none of that. Alone in her apartment all day with her typewriter, she met only creeps of her own devising. She dealt with them ruthlessly, and enjoyed it. By three o'clock, though, she was used up. The next three hours, she spent in solitary waiting.

Waiting to see the face of another human being, the only face that mattered much in her life anymore.

She crossed the apartment to her bedroom, and began to undress for a bath.

I spend my days in solitary, she mused, while Dal's among the madding crowd. At night, we each need a different cure. I shouldn't hold it against him if he wants time by himself. I shouldn't feel rejected.

But I do.

Her satin robe felt soft on her bare skin. She tied its belt, and went into the bathroom. As the tub filled, she let the robe fall away. She stepped into the water. It wrapped around her ankles, almost too hot. It stung, at first, when she sat down.

The tub filled. She turned off the faucets. With a sigh, she eased herself backwards. The water rose over her, hot and soothing, until only her face and upthrust knees remained above the surface.

This is not so bad, she thought.

She shut her eyes.

Better than sitting in a cramped, stuffy movie theater. A lot better than that.


Dal drove past the Haunted Palace, and kept on driving. The steering wheel was slick in his sweaty hands. The armpits of his shirt were soaked.

Well damn, she was worth sweating over! He'd never seen a woman he wanted so much.

When she strolled into Lane Brothers that afternoon, Dal couldn't take his eyes off her. She walked toward him, a creamy, pleated skirt caressing her legs, her breasts obviously bare under a loose, velour top that trembled, just slightly, as she moved. Lush, brown hair swung at her shoulders. It brushed the sides of a face so striking that Dal ached.

She stopped in front of him. He stared into her green, clear eyes.

'May I help you?' he asked.

'Yes,' she said, and paused as if to let him savour the liquid whisper of her voice. 'I want a man's cologne.'

'Anything in particular?' he asked.

'I want it masculine, but subtle.'

He nodded. 'Would you like to step over this way?'

Moving sideways towards the counter, he let his eyes drop to the woman's hands. She wore no wedding ring.

'We have a new fragrance called Ram. It's quite popular.'

'I like what you're wearing.'

He smiled and blood rushed to his face. 'My cologne?'

'Yes.'

'It's . . .' He cleared his throat 'It's called Rawhide. It's new from . . .'

'Let me,' she said. Fingertips lightly touching his chest, she leaned toward him. Her face moved close to his neck. He felt her breath. 'Yes,' she said. 'This is just what I want.'

He licked his dry lips. 'Will there be anything else?' he asked. 'Yes.'

Her lips brushed his neck, and she whispered, 'You.'

Thinking back as he drove toward her house, Dal could hardly believe it had happened. It was almost like a dream.

Damn lucky I didn't faint, he thought. He laughed nervously.

All day long, he'd relived those moments with her, analyzed them, wondered at times if it was only a hideous, cruel joke. But who would pull a stunt like that?

No, it couldn't be a joke. It had to be real.

*Had* to be!

Please God, let it be real.

Waiting at a stop light, he took out his wallet and found the slip of paper with her name and address; Elizabeth Lassin, 522 Altina. He put it back.

Altina Road was halfway up a wooded hillside of the Highland Estates, a plush area north of town, an area way out of his financial range.

Not necessarily out of Connie's, though. She could easily afford one now. If her next steamy historical romance ('rape epics', she called them) sold like the others, she'd start looking in this vicinity.

Dal had planned to stick with her – marry her, if necessary.

Until today.

Until Elizabeth.

Lovely Elizabeth. For her, he would gladly give up Connie. God, what *wouldn't* he give up, for her?

For even one night with her.

For even one hour!

He found the address, and swung into a long, circular driveway. As he drove toward the lighted veranda, he gazed at the house. It looked like a southern plantation house – scaled down a bit, but nonetheless elegant. A fitting home for a woman like Elizabeth.

He parked. He climbed from his car. He walked toward the door. He reached toward the lighted doorbell button.

And stopped.

Bet she doesn't live here, he thought. Gave me the address as a joke. Get the guy worked up, toy with him, lots of laughs.

Damn her! If she did a shitty thing like that . . .!

He jabbed the doorbell.

It rang.

God, this probably *is* her house!

He rubbed his sweaty hands on his pants legs.

She'll probably laugh at me.

194

Christ, why didn't I bring her something? Flowers, wine . . .

'Cause I'm a klutz.

Oh shit, why didn't I . . .?

The door opened and she stood in the dimly lighted foyer. her bare feet on the marble floor, her body draped in a white chiffon dress that hung on her like a wispy veil, the mild breezes shifting it against her skin. Her lips were moist and slightly open, her eyes intense, almost fierce.

'Kiss me,' she said.

I'm dreaming, Dal thought, and stepped across the threshold.

# Chapter Two

The line in front of the Haunted Palace moved swiftly once the box office opened. Pete Harvey shuffled forward. Brit stuck close, a hand inside the back pocket of his jeans, a breast pushing softly against his arm.

She was a bit clingy for Pete's taste, but he let her. If a gal clings, she has a reason. She's just more afraid, than some, of getting left behind.

At the ticket window, he bought two tickets from a teenaged girl with straight black hair and white make-up. Supposed to look like a vampire, he supposed. She wore a black T-shirt with the logo, BEWARE OF SCHRECK.

'Your hairdresser?' Pete asked.

The girl laughed. 'It's a wig, and itchy as hell.'

Pete moved along. He gave the tickets to a fat man in red-stained pants and undershirt, a nylon stocking over his head. His face, pale and weirdly mashed, looked grotesque enough to make Pete uneasy.

'Isn't he a charmer?' Brit whispered.

'I think he's overdoing it.'

She hugged Pete's arm. 'Scared you, didn't he?'

'He looks like someone I used to know.'

'Oh?'

Pete nodded, and wished he hadn't brought it up. 'How about some popcorn, or Bon Bons, or something?'

'Do you think I dare?'

'You're skin and bones.'

She leaned against him, nudging him again with that breast. 'Do you prefer your women plump?'

'Plump and juicy. I'm having popcorn and a Pepsi, how about you?'

'I'll have a hot dog.'

Pete laughed. 'Are you serious?'

'A plump, juicy hot dog.' She licked her lips. 'I can almost taste it now.'

He bought the snacks from another pale girl in a Schreck T-shirt.

The auditorium was dimly lit.

'Hey, it looks like a castle,' Brit said.

'The Haunted Palace.'

'Pretty neat.'

'Where do you want to sit?' Pete asked.

'A little closer, I think.'

'An aisle seat all right? I like to stretch out my legs.' He switched to his W.C. Fields voice. 'Trip the little bastards as they toddle by.'

'Oh, you're terrible!'

'It's better than my Bogart.'

'That's not . . .' Laughing, she shook him by the arm.

'Don't rip it off.'

'Come on.' She pulled him toward a seat.

He went along with her, amused but irritated. If he saw more of her, after tonight, he would have to straighten her out on a few items. For now, though, he wouldn't try to criticize her unless she got unbearable. Dragging him like a leashed dog nearly qualified, but he held off.

'Are these all right?' she asked, once they were seated.

'Fine.'

She unwrapped her hot dog. 'Now, tell me. Who did the fat man remind you of?'

'He reminded me of the bird. The black bird, and a beautiful dame, and . . .'

'Right, your Bogart stinks.'

The lights dimmed, saving Pete from a reply.

On the screen, he saw a fog-shrouded forest. A terrible scream brought silence to the theater. Something moved among the trees. Slowly, the dim figure of a man appeared. He limped forward through the fog.

The fat man who'd taken the tickets.

He wore the same tan slacks, the same sleeveless T-shirt. They streamed with blood. In his right hand, he held a hatchet dripping gore. A nylon stocking distorted his face.

'Good evening,' he said. 'Welcome to the Haunted Palace.'

'Freaky,' Brit whispered.

'I am your host, Bruno Blood.'

Laughter in the audience.

'Each night, I shall bring you a feast of hideous delights, tales of horror to make you cringe and scream. You'll see all the best in grisly entertainment. Not only the latest gems of satanic. morbidity, but also the great classics of the past.

'In weeks to come, I shall bring you such fare as *Halloween, Freaks. The Hills Have Eyes, Rabid. The Texas Chain Saw Massacre*, and *The Night of the Living Dead*.'

Whistles and applause greeted his announcement. He held up his bloody hatchet for silence, as if he foresaw the audience reaction.

'Plus!' he bellowed. In a soft and menacing voice, he continued. 'Plus a special treat available *only* at the Haunted Palace. Each night, in addition to the regular features, you'll witness the evil, delicious exploits of Otto Schreck. the madman – a new depravity each and every week.'

The audience roared with yells, whistles, and applause, A lot of regulars, Pete figured.

'Schreck must be quite a guy,' Brit whispered in his ear.

Pete shrugged.

'And now,' Bruno said, 'prepare yourself for tonight's show. Sit back, take hold of a friendly hand, and . . .' He grinned. 'Don't look to see who is sitting behind you.'

The audience went wild as Bruno turned, and slowly limped away until he vanished in the fog.

The screen went dark.

'Is Schreck first?' asked a girl behind Pete.

'It's after the feature,' a boy whispered. '*Heads, You Lose* first, then Schreck, then *Nightcrawlers*.'

'Three?'

'Schreck's a short. Ten, fifteen minutes. Just wait, though. It'll be fabulous.'

The first movie started. Brit tossed her hot dog wrapper to the floor, grinned at Pete, and squeezed his thigh.

# Chapter Three

Taking Dal's hand, Elizabeth led him down the hallway to a bedroom. She pushed the door shut.

The room was dark except for lights from the pool in back.

'Isn't it lovely?' she said. 'We'll go swimming later, if you like.'

He watched her walk across the carpet and open the sliding glass door. A breeze entered the room, stirring her gown. The lights from the pool passed through it, making the material nearly transparent. Breathless, Dal gazed at the dark, slender shape of her legs and buttocks.

'You're beautiful,' he whispered.

She looked over her shoulder, turning slightly, her breasts visible through the veil of fabric. 'Come here,' she said.

He stepped toward her.

She turned to him. 'Don't move,' she said. Slowly, her fingers opened the buttons of his shirt. Her hands slipped inside, and lightly caressed his chest.

She drew the shirt off him. Her mouth brushed his chest, kissing, licking his nipples, as her hands unfastened his pants. When they were loose, she reached inside.

Dal moaned at the cool touch.

'You're so big,' Elizabeth murmured. 'So big and hard.' She knelt, sliding the pants down his legs. Her tongue stroked the underside of his shaft. Its touch nearly set him off.

He stepped back.

'What's wrong?'

'Nothing,' he gasped. 'Nothing. It's just . . . too much. I don't want to . . . not so fast.'

'There'll be more,' she said. Reaching out, she clutched his buttocks. She pulled him forward, and licked, and sucked him deeply into her mouth.

Connie, alone in her apartment, felt restless. After bathing, she washed her hair and put it in curlers. That took little more than an hour.

She heated up coffee, carried it into the living-room, and tried to read. Though her eyes moved over the words, her mind kept wandering.

To Dal.

She felt cheated, being left alone this way. Especially on a Friday night.

Ever since high school, Friday nights had been a time for dating and fun, a time for football games, dances in the gym, parties, bowling, movies, or just bumming around with her friends on the lookout for a good time. Friday nights brought a terrible urgency for freedom after a week of confinement, a need to get out and *do* something.

Here I am, she thought.

Alone, at home, hair in curlers – stuck here on Friday night with nothing to do but bemoan my outcast fate.

She would never allow Sandra Dane such a miserable situation. Sandra Dane, the beautiful raven-haired mistress of White Oak plantation, wouldn't sit here grumbling. She'd rush out to the stables, and mount her stallion, and ride wildly through the moonlit countryside, the wind in her face.

She wouldn't go out in curlers, though.

Connie got up from the couch. Taking off her robe, she went into the bedroom.

Where'll I go? she wondered. Since I don't have a stallion . . .

A nice, long walk.

She opened a dresser drawer, and pulled out her blue warmup suit.

Seven-Eleven's open all night.

She stepped into her pants. They felt soft and snug.

It's pretty far away, she thought, but right on Pico. A heavily travelled boulevard like Pico shouldn't be very dangerous, even at night.

She put on the jacket of her warm-up suit, zipped it halfway up, and regarded herself in the mirror.

That's how Sandra Dane would wear it, she thought.

Sandra, of course, is rape-prone.

Rape-prone. Shit. Not funny at all.

Bending down to tie her shoes, she saw her jacket bulge open, revealing her entire left breast.

No way.

She zipped it to her throat, and headed for the door. With her handbag slung over her shoulder, she stepped outside.

From the balcony, she saw that someone on the ground floor was having a party. All the other apartments, she imagined, were deserted.

People out enjoying themselves.

As she trotted down the stairs, she pulled up the hood of her jacket to hide her curlers.

Fine way to spend a Friday night, she thought.

I should've gone with Dal, whether he wanted me or not.


Elizabeth bent over the bed, and pulled back the covers. She lay down on the white sheet, her arms and legs outstretched.

'This time,' she said, 'I want to look at you.'

One of her arms curled toward the headboard. Directly over the bed, a light came on – a low-hanging light like those Dal had seen over pool tables. Though it left the rest of the room in shadow, it cast soft light on the bed, and on Elizabeth.

Dal climbed onto the end of the bed. He crawled slowly, sliding his hands up the smoothness of her spread legs as he looked at her. At her solemn, intense eyes, at the painful beauty of her face. At her slim neck, and the hollows above the bows of her collar bones. At breasts, so full when she was upright, now low against her chest, pulled by gravity and her arms stretched overhead. The nipples looked almost brown. He fingered the firm, rumpled skin. Elizabeth squirmed. He moved his fingers down the softness of her breasts and along her ribs, and over a pale ridge of skin.

A scar.

Six inches long, running diagonally down her belly.

Dal drew his finger gently along it.

'Operation?' he asked.

'Without the benefit of a surgeon,' she said.

'What do you mean?'

'My husband, bless his heart, opened me up with a carving knife.'

'My God,' Dal muttered.

'He thought I'd been unfaithful.' She folded her hands behind her head, and frowned toward the ceiling. 'He was such a jealous man. He was far older than me, and incredibly wealthy, so he concluded that I'd only married him for his money. Which wasn't true at all. I loved him, I truly did, even when he made my life unbearable.

'The harder I tried to convince him of that, though, the more certain he grew of my infidelity. He followed me, he eavesdropped. He saw proof everywhere, in everything I did. At one point, he hired a private investigator, then accused the investigator of having an affair with me.'

'It must've been horrible,' Dal said.

'It wasn't pleasant. He beat me constantly. With fists, with his belt. His favourite whip was an extension cord.'

'Why didn't you leave him?'

'I loved him. I always believed that someday, somehow, he would finally come to realize he had no reason for his jealousy. But it didn't work out that way.'

She propped herself up on her elbows, and stared into the darkness.

'One night, he tried to kill me. It was our sixth anniversary. I'd given the housekeeper the day off, so we could be alone. I expected him home at seven. He was a lawyer, and very successful, as you can see from all this.

'I realized, sometime around six, that we had no champagne. So I threw on some old clothes and drove over to Vendome. On the way, I saw an ambulance in my rearview mirror. I pulled off the road to let it pass. The shoulder was rough and littered with debris, and I think that's where I picked up the nail.

'I drove on to Vendome, and bought the champagne. But when I returned to the parking lot, my front right tire was flat.

'One of the clerks changed it for me. By the time I got here, though, Herbert was already waiting in a rage.

'Here it was, our anniversary, and I only went out to do something nice for him, and he had the gall to accuse me of adultery.

' "Who were you fucking?" '

'I'd had it. I threw down the champagne bottles so they shattered all over the foyer. Herbert slapped me, and kept yelling, "Who? Who were you fucking!" '

' "I didn't catch his name," I said. "But he was young and handsome and hung like a horse." '

'Herbert turned away. I knew I'd hurt him, and I was glad.

He'd finally gone too far. Then I heard him crying. He was in the kitchen, sobbing like his heart was broken. I went to him. His back was toward me. I put my hands on his shoulders. Before I could say a word, he turned around and slashed me with a knife.'

Dal saw her eyes lower to the scar on her belly. She stared at it as she continued.

'I ran. He chased me upstairs with that knife, but we had pictures on the wall. Framed portraits. At the top, I jerked one down and swung it at him. The corner of the frame hit him in the face, and he fell down the stairs.

'I want to him, but he didn't move. He just lay there, staring up at me. The fall – it broke his neck.'

'Did he die?' Dal asked.

Reaching out, she took Dal's hand. She guided it to the slick wetness between her legs. 'Don't talk. Fuck me. Fuck me, now. Put your cock in me, and fuck me till I scream.'


Connie enjoyed the long walk to the Seven-Eleven. It felt good to be out in the night air, walking briskly, sometimes slowing down to look at the window display of a closed store. At times, she forgot about Dal, forgot that he had abandoned her for a couple of horror movies.

In the Seven-Eleven store, she stepped over to the rack of paperback books. She spun it, glancing at covers, until she found *Barbary Rage*, 'a lusty tale of passion on the high seas.' She flipped the front book forward, and saw only one behind it. Two left. Last week, there'd been four.

Not bad, not bad.

Someone tapped her shoulder. She swung around.

'Oh, I'm sorry,' the young man said. He had a friendly smile and a pale, almost invisible moustache.

'It's all right,' Connie said.

'I thought you were somebody else.'

'No, I'm just me.'

He laughed. 'From the back you looked . . . well, I thought you were an old girlfriend.'

'Sorry,' Connie said.

The boy shrugged.

She turned again to the book rack, and studied paperbacks for a minute. When she looked around, the boy was standing at the end of a long line, a six-pack of Michelob at his side.

Must be older than he looks, she thought.

He was still in line when she left the store. She crossed the street, and looked back. A girl in shorts and a halter top came out, a small sack in her hand.

Connie walked away.

Had the boy, she wondered, been trying to pick her up? If so, he hadn't been very persistent.

Should've tried harder, pal.

Tonight, I might have been willing. Serve Dal right.

She kept walking. Farther and farther from the apartment. With no destination in mind until she remembered the liquor store next to Safeway. She might as well stop in there, see if they'd got her book in yet.

She walked for blocks. Finally, she reached the liquor store. But she didn't go in. She stood on the sidewalk, staring across the intersection and down the next block at the lighted marquee of a movie theater.

The Haunted Palace.

Dal thrust and thrust, driving into her. She was wild under him, gasping, shoving up to meet his thrusts, fingers digging into his back. Their sweaty bodies slapped together.

They rolled. and she was on top. He clutched her breasts, squeezed and mauled them. Her face was sweaty and contorted above him. She twisted, writhed as if trying to grind his spike deeper into her slick tightness, impale herself on it, ream out her hugging sheath.

Connie glanced at the movie posters, at the grim, coloured stills above them. The girl in the ticket window was reading a paperback.

Clever, Connie thought, dressing her up like a vampire.

She looked at the posted showtimes.

A *triple* feature?

No, the one in the middle, *Schreck the Vampire*, was only a short.

She glanced at her wristwatch.

*Schreck the Vampire* should be starting soon.

Wouldn't Dal be surprised if she went in, and sat down beside him?

He might be pissed, though.

*What if he's not alone, if he's sitting with his arm around a girl . . .?*

No. He wouldn't.

But the fear of it was enough to keep her from entering.

She looked again at the showtimes. *Nightcrawlers* would be next, after the vampire thing. Then *Heads, You Lose* came on again, at 11:20.

Give him five minutes to drive home.

So she could expect him by 11:25 or so.

As she walked away, she wondered if he would remember the Good 'n Plenty.

'Shall we go for a swim?' Elizabeth asked.

'That'd be great. I think I'll hit the john, first.'

Elizabeth smiled strangely. She sat up, and pointed into the shadows across the room.

'See the doorway?'

'I think so.'

'It's right through there.'

Dal climbed from the bed. He walked over the thick, soft carpet toward a patch of darkness deeper than the shadows.

'Don't trip,' Elizabeth said.

He looked back at her. The bed and Elizabeth were closer than he expected, so bright and starkly clear in the overhead lamp that he could see the red marks his mouth had left on her skin.

'I'll try not to,' he said.

He stepped into the doorway, bumped a dark shape, and lurched backwards. 'What the hell!'

'Here, let me get it out of your way.'

Elizabeth leaped from the bed. She rushed to Dal's side, patted him on the rump, and stepped past him. Leaning into the doorway, she pulled something forward.

Then she turned on the bright, fluorescent lights of the bathroom.

'*Jesus!*' Dal gasped.

The withered, bald man in the wheelchair blinked his eyes.

Elizabeth grinned. 'Dal, I'd like you to meet my husband, Herbert. He likes to watch. I know he must enjoy it.' She patted the old man's cheek. Patted it hard. 'You *do* enjoy watching us, don't you, Herbert?'

## SCREAM GEMS PRESENTS OTTO SCHRECK in
## SCHRECK THE VAMPIRE

Near the head of the coffin, two black candles burn. They are in a statue's stone hands. Only blunt stubs remain of the candles. The hands of the statue are clotted with black. The mouth gapes with silent agony. They eye holes are empty.

Bones litter the dirt floor of the cellar. The small, fragile bones of rodents. Bigger bones. Of dogs and cats. Of humans.

In a shadowy corner of the cellar, a human rib cage trembles. A rat, inside it, waddles up the spinal column. It squeezes underneath a collar bone, pauses, then moves up the neck and climbs onto the pale, hanging jaw.

The jawbone breaks loose. The rat tumbles. It starts towards the skull again, but stops and raises its head at the faint, rumbling sound of an engine.

The engine goes silent.

In front of the house, a woman climbs the porch steps. She is young and cute, her blonde hair windblown, her legs bare under the tails of a plaid blouse.

A slim, dark-haired man follows her up the stairs.

Smiling, the woman searches her handbag and takes out a key. 'Ready?' She opens the door, enters, and leaps back against the man. He hugs her, laughing.

'So who's the horny one?' he asks.

She tugs open the waistband of his swimming trunks. 'Aren't you?'

The woman turns toward the stairway. 'The bedroom's probably up there.'

She follows him up the stairs. As they climb, she suddenly jerks his swimming trunks. They drop from his pale buttocks.

'Don't!' He clutches them. 'Want me to trip?'

'Then don't be so damned handsome.'

'Sorry, Mary.' He pulls up his trunks, and continues to climb.

'Nice ass.'

'Thank you.'

'Cracked, though.'

At the end of the upstairs hall way, she pushes open a door. *Voila!*

He hurries to join her.

'Now this isn't so shabby, is it?'

'It's all right,' he says.

Leaving her sandals on the carpet, she says, 'Ain't so shabby at all,' and leaps onto the bed. She walks on the mattress, hands on hips, turning to look at the room. 'I think this'll do just fine, don't you?'

The man grins.

Mary falls backwards, bouncing slightly as she hits the mattress. With a seductive smile, she opens her blouse.

The man steps toward her.

Out of the blouse, she rolls over and unties the back of her bikini.

The man bends over her. He strokes her back. He kisses her between the shoulder blades.

In the cellar, black gummy wax drips from the hands of the statue. The candles are nearly spent. Their flames waver and stretch, as if struggling not to die.

The rat crouches beside the coffin, nibbling a bit of raw meat.

Fingers curl around the edge of the coffin lid, lift it, and slide it aside.

The rat pauses at the sound of scraping wood.

A hand snatches it from the ground. It squeals as Schreck, sitting upright in the coffin, raises it toward his pallid face.

'The blood is the life,' he whispers.

He bites off the rat's head, and spits it out. He raises the rat above him like a wine bottle, the blood splashing his face, spilling into his wide mouth, running in dark rivulets down his cheeks and chin.

In the dark bedroom, Mary lies awake beside the sleeping man.

The wooden steps of the cellar stairway groan as Schreck slowly climbs. At the top, he pushes open a door. His hand leaves a bloody print on the wood.

Mary climbs from bed, and steps silently across the carpet to a window. She stares out.

Schreck climbs the main stairway. When he reaches the top, he looks up the long, dimly lit hall.

Mary crosses the bedroom. She pauses in the doorway, and glances to her right.

Schreck, seeing her, slips through a door. For a moment, he watches her. She is naked. She skips and twirls, dancing down the hallway, waving her arms overhead.

Schreck silently closes the door. Leaning against it, he stares at the ceiling and runs his tongue over his dry lips. He moans.

Mary stops. She gazes at the door. Quickly, she puts on her blouse and fastens it. She reaches for the knob, then jerks her hand away and runs. She runs up the long, dim hall, bare legs flying, the tail of her blouse flapping above her buttocks.

She lunges through the bedroom door. 'Hey! Hey!'

'What?'

The light comes on. The man sits up, shading his eyes against the brightness. 'What're you doing?'

'Let's get out of here.'

'I thought . . .'

'I heard something.'

'What'd you hear?' he asks, pulling on his trunks.

'Sounded like a moan.'

'Jesus!'

'Could've been my imagination, Arthur.'

'But what if it wasn't?'

As he rushes toward the door, Mary retrieves her bikini from the mussed bed. She steps into the shorts, and stuffs the top into her handbag.

'Where'd you hear it?'

'The end of the hall. By the stairs.'

'Christ, that means we've gotta go *past* it!'

'Maybe it was nothing.'

Schreck, in the dark room, grins at the sound of rushing footsteps. He jerks open the door. Leaping into the hallway, he grabs the throat of the running man and flings him against a wall.

The terrified woman halts. She simply watches, aghast, as Schreck picks up the man and throws him over the railing.

With a smile, he walks toward her. 'You will be my bride.'

'No. Come *on!*'

'We shall wander the nights together, you and I – all the nights of eternity – feasting on the blood of the innocents.'

As he reaches for her, she throws herself through a doorway. She tries to shut the door, but Schreck blocks it with his arm. Then he punches through the frail wood, and clutches her throat. He thrusts her away. He rushes into the room for her.

He pulls her into the hallway. He tears open her blouse. Fingers plying her full breasts, he lowers his head. He licks the blood from her splinter-torn face.

He kisses the side of her neck.

He bites. Blood spurts from the torn vein, painting his face, spraying the nearby wall. He presses his mouth tightly to the wound, and swallows furiously.

211

Breathless, he raises his head. The blood, no longer shooting, throbs out. He cups his hands to catch the flow.

When the hands are full, he raises them high. 'The blood is the life,' he says. He washes his face in it.

Then he is carrying the woman's naked body down the cellar steps. Her skin is pale in the dim light.

He lowers her into his coffin.

He lights two black candles, and fixes them upright in the hands of the statue. As the eyeless, stone face looks on, Schreck climbs into his coffin. On his knees above the corpse, he whispers, 'My bride.'

The End

# Chapter Four

The audience hissed, booed, clapped and cheered. The theater lights came on.

Pete turned to Brit. 'What'd you think?'

'Gross-out. You know what's funny though? That girl who played Mary looks just like my best friend. Best *girl* friend,' she corrected.

'Was it?'

'Guess not. The credits said her name was Wilma Payne. The voice wasn't like Tina's, either.'

'Well, they say we all have a double somewhere.'

'This was really uncanny, though. I mean, she's identical.

Even the way she walked and acted – you know, her mannerisms. And the things she said, like the cracked ass. She says that kind of stuff. It was kind of spooky, if you ask me.'

'Tina isn't an actress, is she?'

'She's a history teacher at Pacifica Coast University. That's where I went, you know. We were roomies there, and she went back, after grad school, and got a job. You know, what I ought to do is give her a call, tomorrow. She'd probably get a kick out of this thing.'

'Bruno said it's only shown here.'

Brit shrugged. 'Well, maybe she could drive down, or something. PCU's only a couple of hours up the coast.'

'If she looks like the gal in the movie, I wouldn't mind seeing her, myself.'

'*You!*' Brit pounded his knee. 'Why don't you get me some Milk Duds before the intermission's over?'

# Chapter Five

Elizabeth rolled the wheelchair toward the bed. 'Help me put him in.'

'In *that?*' Dal asked.

'It's his bed.'

Dal shook his head. He felt as if he might throw up. 'We did it in *his* bed, with him watching?'

'Don't blame yourself, dear. You had no way of knowing.'

'It's sick.'

'But doesn't it excite you, now that you know?'

'I think I'd better leave.'

She smiled as if amused by his timidity. 'Won't you help me, first? You wouldn't want poor Herbert to spend the night in his wheelchair, would you?'

'You can move him alone,' he said. The words sounded nasty, and he immediately regretted them.

'Certainly I can,' Elizabeth said. 'I don't think I *shall*, however. If you want to be responsible for the poor man spending the entire night . . .'

'I'll help.'

'Herbert thanks you.'

'Where are the sheets?'

'On the bed.'

'But they're a mess! They're all wet and ucky. We can't put him down on those.'

Elizabeth patted a shoulder of the motionless man. 'Certainly we can. Herbert understands, don't you dear?'

A car slowed down, and drove alongside Connie. Heart suddenly racing, she walked more quickly. The car kept pace.

This is what I get, she thought, angry with herself in spite of her fear.

She glanced at the car. A light-colored Mustang. Its passenger window was rolled down. She saw the dark shapes, inside, of two men.

An arm beckoned to her from the window.

'Not interested,' she said.

The car sped up. At the end of the block, it turned right and vanished.

'Oh shit,' she muttered.

They'd be waiting for her. She knew. It had happened once before. On a summer night five years ago, in Tucson.

Only then, she hadn't been alone.

Tears suddenly stung her eyes, making the streetlights streak and blur.

Those bastards.

Those goddamn punk bastards.

She would never again find a man like Dave, and they . . . Two of the three had knives. She could still hear the sound as one of the boys jammed a blade into Dave's belly, a sound like a punch, then Dave's breath blasting out. It was the last sound she heard before the third punk, the one with the tire iron, knocked her senseless.

Wiping the tears from her face, she crossed the street in the middle of the block.

If they want me, she thought, they'll have to work for it.


'Now can I go?' Dal asked, stepping away from the bed.

'Now you may.' Elizabeth moved close to him. Her nipples brushed his chest. She fingered his limp penis. 'Wouldn't you prefer, however, to join me in the shower? Unless you would rather take your incriminating odors home with you. Your darling Connie might be suspicious, if you do.'

'I suppose. I can't get my hair wet, though.'

'My blow-drier will take care of that.'


Connie looked at the corner across the street. A car was parked there. A light-colored Mustang. Its lights off.

With any luck . . .

She started to cross the intersection. The Mustang swung around in a U-turn and shot toward her. She ran down the street, leaping onto the curb as the Mustang bore down.

Its passenger door flew open. A teenaged boy jumped out.

Connie backed away, staring at him. At his white T-shirt, his tan work-pants, his black hair and nervous grin.

215

Just like the others. Like a fucking clone of the ones who killed Dave, who beat and raped her.

'Get away from me,' she said.

The other man came up behind him. This one was heavier than the first, but he wore the same uniform. 'Come on for a . . .' She couldn't make out the rest of it.

'Yeah,' said the first. 'I'm hungry. Feel like eating some pussy.'

'Your mother,' Connie snapped.

'*Puto!*' He pulled out a switchblade knife.

Connie backed into the entry way of a shoe store.

'My mother, you don't talk about her that way!'

She stopped, back to the door.

'Not here, Joe,' said the other. 'Too much traffic, man.'

'My mother, she's no whore!'

'No more than your sister,' Connie said.

Joe snarled and stabbed. Sidestepping, Connie grabbed his wrist and elbow. Her knee shot up, snapping his forearm. As he fell, she swung around and kicked. Her foot caught the other man in the groin. He dropped to his knees, clutching himself. Her next kick hammered his forehead. He fell facedown.

Connie picked up the knife.

'Who'd you steal the car from?' she asked Joe.

'Nobody! Check the registration, cunt.'

She kicked his broken arm.

He was still sobbing as she walked over to the Mustang. She climbed in, and drove away.

'Almost dry,' Elizabeth said, running her fingers through Dal's hair as she stroked it with the hot air of the blower. 'Your girlfriend will never suspect you've been copulating behind her back.'

'I hope not.'

'What would she do?'

'Ask me to leave, I suppose.'

'That would be a pity.'

'It'd be a disaster. Do you have any idea what I'd have to pay for an apartment in this city?'

'Considerable, I should imagine. If that's the worst you have to fear, however, you've little to fear.'

'Well, I don't think she's the type to stab me, if that's what you mean.'

'Does she love you?'

'Who knows? I guess so.'

'Then you'd best be careful. A woman's vengeance is often remarkably savage.'

'I noticed.'

She laughed. 'Herbert is getting no worse than he deserves. Save your sympathy.'


Connie drove the Mustang to the Seven-Eleven store. She couldn't pass the book rack without checking on *Barbary Rage*. After seeing that nobody had bought a copy in the last half-hour, she hurried on.

She bought a screwdriver, a single can of Budweiser, a quart can of charcoal lighter, and a pack of Marlboros.

The clerk dropped two books of matches into her sack.

Connie drank the beer as she drove. Illegal, she knew. For tonight, though, she was making her own laws.

'I hereby legalize the consumption of alcoholic beverages in stolen motor vehicles,' she said.

It tasted very good.

She parked in the lot of the Safeway supermarket. The store was closed, the lot deserted except for a lone VW near the far side. It looked empty.

Connie left the engine running. With the screwdriver, she punched holes into the top of the charcoal lighter can. She emptied the can, shaking fluid onto the back seat, the floor, the front seat.

Outside the car, she took a quick look around. Nobody nearby.

She ripped the cardboard flap off a book of matches. Striking a match, she touched it to the exposed heads. They flared. She tossed the flaming pack onto the front seat.

Slowly, the fire spread.

She shut the door and walked away, sipping her beer.

Red lights flashed in Dal's rearview mirror. A siren screamed.

No. please!

Jesus, a ticket. That's just what he needed. They write down the date and time. If Connie sees it, she'll know he wasn't at the movies.

Then he saw that the lights belonged to a fire truck.

Thank God.

He pulled over and let it pass. Still shaking, he drove several more blocks. He parked on a sidestreet, and walked to the Haunted Palace.

'*Nightcrawlers* just started,' said the girl in the ticket window. She looked awful. It took a moment for Dal to realize she was supposed to look that way.

He gave his ticket to a fat man in bloody clothes. The man's face was twisted horribly under a nylon stocking.

'You missed tonight's Schreck,' said the man.

Dal shrugged. 'I'll catch it another time.'

At the candy counter, he bought a pack of Good 'n Plenty.

# Chapter Six

Connie was in bed when Dal got home. She breathed slowly and heavily, pretending to be asleep. She didn't want to tell him what she had done.

She didn't want to tell anyone, ever.

She felt rotten about hurting the kids. Maybe they deserved it, but what if she'd injured them permanently? Or killed one? That guy she'd kicked in the head . . .

What if a fireman got hurt trying to put out the Mustang? If the tank blew up . . .

Dal climbed into bed. He lightly kissed her cheek. She moaned as if disturbed in her sleep. Dal rolled away.

Connie lay awake for a long time. She shifted to her stomach, to her back, to her side. Her pillow was sweaty so she turned it over. She flung the top sheet aside, pulled off her damp nightgown, and stared at the ceiling.

When she awoke in the sunlight of morning, she was vaguely surprised to realize she had fallen asleep.

She eased herself carefully out of bed, hoping to avoid waking Dal. She found her nightgown on the floor. A gift from him.

A 'moving in present' he'd called it. The gown reflected his taste: it was short, low-cut, and transparent. She couldn't step outside in it, not even for a moment to grab the newspaper. She put it on, anyway. Before leaving the room, she took her robe from the closet.

As she slipped into the robe, she saw a box of Good 'n Plenty on the dining-room table.

Dal hadn't forgotten.

She felt a warm rush of affection for him. It only lasted a moment. Then, her anxiety came back. She hurried to the front door, and opened it.

The newspaper lay on the Welcome mat. She quickly picked it up. She rushed inside, tugging the plastic band off the paper.

Dropping to her knees, she spread the paper on the carpet. She leaned over it, her eyes moving swiftly over the front page.

Nothing there.

Nothing about the two kids.

Nothing about the burning Mustang.

She turned the page. Another and another. She searched the first and second sections. Section three was sports and financial. She skipped that. Wouldn't be in the entertainment section, either. Only the classified remained. Feeling light with relief, she put the paper together and flung it onto the couch.

No mention of what she had done.

The kids had probably kept the incident to themselves. If they went to a hospital – which they must've done – they gave a false story to explain their injuries.

The Mustang fire must've been too routine to report. No injuries there. It hadn't blown up in someone's face, after all.

Off the hook.

With a sigh, she got to her feet. She went into the kitchen, and began to prepare a pot of coffee.

Off the hook unless she ran into those kids again.

She took the open can of Yuban from the refrigerator, and peeled off its plastic cover. Carrying it to the counter, she raised it close to her nose and sniffed. Such a wonderful odor.

She'd always loved that smell. It reminded her of being a

child, of lying in bed early in the morning listening to the rhythmic slurp of coffee perking in the kitchen. She wished she could hear that sound again. Nobody hears it now. Nobody uses a percolator. Drip machines are so much quicker, more efficient. Progress.

At least coffee still smells like coffee.

She scooped it into a paper filter.

A hand patted her fanny. She jumped, spilling grounds.

'Dal!'

He grinned. 'Morning.' He pulled her into his arms, and kissed her.

'How were the movies?' she asked.

'Not bad. I've seen better, but they were okay. What'd you do last night?'

Connie shrugged. 'Washed my hair, and read.'

'Doesn't sound very exciting.'

She shrugged. 'Well, my old friend Joe dropped by and banged me a few times.'

'Oh really?' Dal asked. Though grinning, deep red filled his face.

'Hey, only kidding!'

'I know, I know.' He turned away.

# Chapter Seven

Freya pushed the button of the remote control box, and watched the television screen flash from channel to channel.

Nothing on but shit.

*Daffy Duck, Scooby and Scrappy-Doo*, an ancient rerun of *The Lone Ranger*.

Roller Derby, for Christsake.

She lifted her teacup off the *TV Guide*, took a sip, and checked the listings. Okay, not bad. Ten more minutes of crap, and something called *Monster Walks* comes on. A 1932 thriller. Rex Lease, Vera Reynolds, and Sheldon Lewis.

Might be good.

She'd rather be at the beach on a fantastic, sunny Saturday like this. So many of the mornings had been overcast, lately. Typical June weather for Pacifica Coast. But business is business. She'd be spending plenty more weekends inside if she didn't get lucky and find a new roommate.

It wasn't that easy, summer in a university town.

A glut of vacancies.

And of those gals who'd inquired during the past three weeks, so many had been unsuitable.

The doorbell rang.

Christ, you'd think they'd have the decency to phone, first.

She got up from the couch. Walking to the door, she tugged at her tight, binding shorts and adjusted her slipping tube-top. She forced a smile onto her face, and pulled the door open.

'Greetings!' the girl said. She had carrot-red hair, and freckles to match. She wore thick, wire-rimmed glasses. Her blotchy cheeks bulged as if each carried an uneaten plum. She had a figure like a potato, and wore clothes to emphasize it: tight jeans and a T-shirt. The T-shirt was decorated with a leering vulture. It read, 'Patience my ass – I'm going out and kill something.' Incredibly, she wore no bra. Her breasts hung inside the T-shirt like bulging water balloons.

'Can I help you?' Freya asked.

'I'm here about the apartment. Are you the one looking for a roommate?'

'No,' said Freya. 'I'm the new roommate.'

'But this morning's paper . . .'

'I took the place last night. She didn't have time to get the ad pulled.'

The girl shrugged. 'Those are the breaks, I guess.'

'Yep. Sorry. You should've got here sooner.' Freya closed the door.

She stared at the television. Slim Claymore was on, Stetson tipped back, grinning like a moron. 'If you're in the market for a used car, come on down to Slim's Chevrolet, where you'll get courteous service and the best deal . . .'

The telephone clamored. Freya hurried into the kitchen and picked it up. 'Hello?'

'Hello.' A young woman's voice. 'Is Tina there?'

'No, she's not. Would you like to leave her a message?'

'When do you expect her back?'

'Who is this, please?'

'I'm Brit Anderson. I'm a friend of Tina's. We were roomies at PCU'

'Oh yes, she's spoken of you.'

'I guess you must be her present roommate, huh?'

'We've been sharing this apartment for the past couple months.'

'Well . . . Do you have any idea when she might get back?'

223

'She's probably gone for the weekend.'

'Oh, that figures.' Brit laughed. 'Tina was always off somewhere.'

'Do you want me to have her call you when she gets back?'

'Please. I'd appreciate it.' She gave Freya her phone number. Freya copied it down. 'That's Brit what?'

'Anderson.'

'Okay. I'll be sure to give her the message. Nice talking to you.'

'Thanks. Good-bye, now.'

'Good-bye.'

Freya hung up. She hurried into the living-room. *Monster Walks* had already started. 'Damn,' she muttered, and dropped to the couch. The screen went blank for a moment.

'Howdy friends! Slim Claymore here to invite you to come on down to . . .' She changed the channel. '. . . here to invite you to come on down . . .' Same commercial, slightly different timing.

She switched again, this time to Bugs Bunny. Bugs was preferable to Slim. She watched the hare outsmart Elmer, then she turned back to the movie station.

'. . . where prices are so low you'll have a slim chance of finding a better deal.'

The movie came on.

It was nearly over, an hour later, when the telephone rang again.

'Hello?' she asked.

'Hello. I'm calling about the apartment. I saw the ad, this morning, and I'm wondering if you're still in the market for a roommate.'

'I sure am,' Freya said. 'Would you like to stop by and have a look around?'

'I'd love to. When would be a convenient time for you?'

'The sooner, the better.'

'Fine. I'll be there in about fifteen minutes. My name's Nancy.'

'Very good. See you then.'

Exactly fifteen minutes passed before the doorbell rang. Freya opened the door.

'Hi, I'm Nancy.'

Nancy wore sunglasses on top of her head, resting lightly in a tuft of blonde curls. Her eyes were bright, her skin clear, her nose slightly upturned.

A cute girl, Freya thought.

She wore a short sleeved jumpsuit of pale blue. Its zipper, open several inches, showed a long V of pale throat and chest.

'I'm Freya. Come on in.'

'Thank you.'

'Are you new to Pacifica Coast?'

'I've been here a few days. I'm staying at the Travel Inn till I find a more permanent place.'

'Well, maybe this is it.'

'Maybe so.'

She showed Nancy the living-room, then the kitchen.

'Are you a student?' she asked.

'I feel like I've always been a student.'

'What field?'

'Psych.'

'Gonna be a shrink, huh?'

Nancy laughed. 'I hope so.'

'You seem . . . too mature for a freshman.'

'Oh, I'm transferring from Santa Monica College. I have to pick up three credits this summer, and I'll start as a junior.'

'Is this your first time away from home, Nancy?'

'Oh, I've gone off to camp, and stuff. You know. But I've never lived on my own before, if that's what you mean.'

'You lived with your parents in Santa Monica?'

She nodded.

'This would be your bedroom, here.'

They entered the sunlit room.

'It comes furnished, as you can see.'

Nancy wandered the room, looking into the closet, pushing down on the mattress, glancing out the windows. 'This is very nice.'

'So are you,' Freya said in a low voice. 'You're . . . very nice.' She reached out for the tab of Nancy's zipper.

'Hey!' Nancy knocked her hand away. 'No thanks. Jeez!' She shook her head. 'I'm not into that kind of stuff.'

'Ever try it?'

Blushing, Nancy shook her head.

Freya drew down her tube-top. Her breasts popped free.

'No!'

'Come on, darling, touch.'

'No!' Nancy rushed past her.

The front door slammed.

The last of Nancy.

Freya pulled up her top, returned to the living-room, and picked up the *TV Guide*.

She sighed.

Christ, she was getting tired of this.

If it's not one thing, it's another.

Sooner or later, though, the right girl would show up. A girl perfect in every way. A girl with no close family. A girl like Tina.

# Chapter Eight

Brit phoned Pete and got a recording.

'Pete Harvey, Private Investigations. I'm speaking to you, but I'm not here. If you leave a message. I'll get back to you as soon as possible. At the sound of the tone, have at it.'

The tone beeped.

'Forget it,' Brit said, and hung up.

She didn't want to wait around for him to call back. She wanted him now. She had no idea where he might be, though. So forget it. She would go alone.

Might be better, that way. If she asked Pete to go along, he might think she was getting too serious about him. He seemed a bit wary about getting involved.

With her, anyway.

Three dates already, and he hadn't slept with her yet. Well, some guys like to take it slow.

She threw a few things into her suitcase, and went down to the car.

As she drove up the coast, she had second thoughts about going without Pete. He'd be a good man to have around, if she ran into trouble. Something definitely fishy about Tina and the movie. *And* the roommate.

The farther she drove, the more nervous she grew. Finally, she stopped at a Denny's, and used a pay phone. Pete's recording answered.

'Damn it!'

She banged the phone down.

The hell with him.

She shoved through the door and rushed across the lot to her car. She started the engine. For a moment, she considered heading back home.

That'd be chickenshit.

Besides, she was almost to Pacifica Coast. In half an hour, she'd be there.

God, she'd spent four years in that little town. Nothing to be afraid of.

Probably wasn't even Tina, in that movie. And if it *was* her, so what? It was just a movie.

They're supposed to look real, for Godsake. Look at *The Exorcist*, how they made Linda Blair's head spin around. That looked real. Look at *The Omen*, how that sheet of glass chopped off David Warner's head. That looked real too. Just as real as Tina's blood spurting all over the place.

She'd seen Linda Blair in plenty of films after *The Exorcist*. Same with David Warner. She knew, for a fact, they'd lived through those shots. Hell, it's only special effects.

*Tina was different.*

Only because I know her.

Brit left the parking lot, and headed for Pacifica Coast.

Only because I know Tina, she thought. And because the theater was creepy. And because the film had an amateur, grainy look that made it all seem rather cheap and sleazy like some of those porno films she used to see with Willy.

Weird Willy.

Liked to practice what he saw on the screen. She went along with it. too. until he got too rough. The whip was the last straw.

Weird Willy. His great ambition in life was to see a 'snuff movie'.

God have mercy on his girlfriend, if he ever saw one of . . .

*Snuff movies?*

228

The thought hit her like a punch in the stomach.

'Ridiculous,' she said aloud.

But she realised that the idea had been in her mind for a long time, lurking there, whispering its warning. That's why she phoned Tina, this morning.

That's why the voice of the roommate, Freya, had given her a chill of dread. Because, even on the telephone, she'd recognized the voice.

The voice of Mary in the film.

Tina's voice.

Brit drove through downtown Pacifica Coast, and parked in front of the police station.

Her stomach churned.

What will I tell them?

I saw my friend killed in a movie, and I think it might've been real. Oh, why's that? Because they didn't use her real name in the credits, and it wasn't her voice. Are you sure it *was*, indeed, your friend? I'm almost positive. She's missing, and . . . (Freya said she'd gone off with a boyfriend – but Freya must be in on it.) Can't we check?

And the police would drive her out to Tina's apartment, and Tina would open the door.

She'd better make sure.

She left the car, and walked to a service station on the next block. She dropped a dime into the public telephone, and dialed.

Her heart raced. The black phone was slippery in her hand.

'Hello?'

'Hello, Freya.'

'Who is this, please?'

'Brit Anderson. I called this morning.'

'Oh yes.'

'Is Tina there?'

'Yes, she is. Just a moment, please.'

Brit shut her eyes and sighed. She wiped her trembling hands on her slacks.

Thank God.

The whole thing *had* been a figment of her imagination. It *was* someone else in the movie. Not Tina, at all. A look-alike with a voice like Freya.

'Hello?' Freya's voice.

'Yes?'

'Tina's in the shower, just now. Could she call you when she's out?'

'Well . . . I'm calling from a public phone. I'm here in town, though. Maybe I could just drop over in about ten minutes.'

'Fine. I'll tell her.'

Brit parked across the street from the apartment house. She climbed from the car. The afternoon sun was hot on her face, but she felt a cool breeze from the ocean.

She walked across the street on weak legs. God, what a day! She felt exhausted, emotionally drained, but elated.

She'd felt like this, all day, after the quake of '72.

Disaster over. Friends, loved ones, and self miraculously intact.

She passed through a squeaking gate, walked alongside the deserted, glistening pool, and climbed the stairs to the balcony.

Apartment 210.

She knocked on the door.

It was opened by a lean, dishwater blonde wearing tight shorts and a tube-top. 'Brit?' the woman asked.

'Yes.'

'I'm Freya. Come on in.'

She entered. The curtains were shut.

'I'll tell Tina you're here.'

230

Freya crossed the room. Her shorts were too small. Pale crescents of buttock showed beneath the pockets. She disappeared. Brit heard her knock. 'Tina, your friend's here.'

Freya came back. 'She'll be out in a minute. Christ, she takes forever in there. Can I get you something to drink? Some wine, maybe?'

'That'd be great.'

'Red or white?'

'White, please.'

She sat on the couch. Moments later, Freya returned with two glasses of white wine.

'So, you're Tina's old roommate from college days?'

'Yeah.' The wine was cold and fruity, and not too sweet.

'Do you live near here?'

'Los Angeles.'

'Oh? I used to live there. How do you like it?'

'Too many people. That's the only trouble. But lots of things to do.' Her cheeks felt numb. 'I like movies.'

'Oh, so do I. Especially thrillers.'

'Me too. That . . . That's partly why I'm here.' She heard a strange sound, like a distant roar. But it came from inside her head. 'Thought I saw Tina . . . in a film.'

Freya grinned. 'At the Haunted Palace?'

'Yeah.' She tried to set down her empty glass, but dropped it.

'Oh, you did.'

'Schreg da . . . Sch . . .'

'*Schreck the Vampire.*'

Brit realized, vaguely, that her face was about to hit the coffee table.

Then it did.

# Chapter Nine

On Wednesday morning, Connie went to the main branch of the Santa Monica public library. She took the bus.

Though she hated driving near buses and considered their drivers madmen intent on cutting off every car nearby, she found that she enjoyed riding inside them. Inside the bus, she could relax. She didn't have to watch the road, or dodge maniacal bus drivers.

When it reached her stop, she moved up the aisle toward the front. The aisle was clear except for a boy with a bushy Afro. On top of his shoulder, he held a radio as big as an attaché case. He grinned and turned sideways to let her by.

On the sidewalk, she watched the bus pull forward and ease to the left, ignoring the car beside it. The car's brake-lights flashed on. It stopped abruptly to make way for the bus, and was nearly rear-ended by a station wagon.

'Nice,' Connie muttered.

In the library, she found four books about Mississippi paddle-wheel boats. She checked them out, not bothering to browse the fiction or even to check for her own books. At other times, she'd done both. Disappointing results. Now, she used the library only for research.

With the four books in her shoulder bag, she walked down Santa Monica Boulevard to the small mall. She spent a long time in a paperback bookstore. They carried both of her titles. After gloating, she moved on. She bought five books, and left the store.

She stared across the sunny mall at Lane Brothers, then checked her wristwatch. A quarter till twelve.

Why not?

Making a wide circle to avoid contact with a grimy pan-handler, she walked to the entrance of the clothing store. She stepped inside. She spotted three young, well-dressed men among the racks, but not Dal.

One of them approached. 'How can I help you, this morning?'

'Is Dal here?'

'No, but I am. I'm Ken.'

She'd heard tales of Ken. He looked as slick and artificial as Dal described him.

'Has Dal already gone to lunch?' she asked.

'No. As a matter of fact, he didn't come in today. He's down with a bug, as they say. I'm sure that I can be of service, though.'

'Thank you,' she said, and turned away.

Outside, she walked. She gazed straight ahead. Her stomach hurt. She felt like curling up, and hugging her belly, and shutting her eyes tightly. She wanted to close out everything – the whole damn world.

First Dave.

Now Dal. She'd lost him. She knew she'd lost him because why else would he call in sick to work, and keep it a secret from her?

God, she thought they'd been happy together.

Someone grabbed her arm, jerked her backwards. A car flashed past, inches away. She turned to the man, who still held her arm.

'Are you okay?' he asked. His blue eyes looked gentle and concerned.

'Guess I'd better watch where I'm going, huh?'

'Unless you've got ambitions to be a hood ornament.'

She laughed. 'Well, I owe you one.'

'I'm ready to collect.'

'Oh?'

'What did you have in mind?' he asked. 'One what?'

'How about a Bloody Mary?'

'Accepted.'

'I'm Connie,' she said, and offered her hand.

He shook it. 'I'm Pete.'

'Come on Wednesday,' Elizabeth had told him, Friday night.

'I don't know,' Dal had said.

'Wednesday,' she repeated. 'That will give us time to miss one another.'

'But there's Connie. I can't just take off, Wednesday night, without some kind of excuse.'

'If you don't wish to arouse her suspicion, come during the day when you're supposed to be at work.'

'I only get an hour for lunch.'

'Take the whole day off. Spend it with me.'

He shook his head. 'I don't know, Elizabeth. That's . . . it's taking a big chance.'

'If you don't wish to come, don't come.' She kissed him lightly on the mouth. 'I'll be here Wednesday, waiting.'

For days, he'd thought about her offer. He didn't want to go. He had a decent job, and a good set-up with Connie. He could lose both, if he kept on with Elizabeth.

Also, she frightened him.

If a woman could enjoy screwing men in front of her paralyzed husband . . . God, no telling what else she might do, no telling what she might want *Dal* to do.

He decided, finally, to stay away. He would be much better off if he never saw Elizabeth again.

He was pleased with his decision. He felt clean and honest and relieved.

He was halfway to work, Wednesday morning, when he changed his mind. He called Lane Brothers from Elizabeth's house. When Ken answered, he explained that he'd come down with a bad case of diarrhea.

'Don't give me that shit,' Ken had said, and laughed outrageously.

'I should be able to make it in tomorrow,' he said.

Elizabeth unzipped him.

'Have yourself a nice vacation,' Ken said.

Her hand reached in and fondled him. 'Vacation, my ass.'

More laughter from Ken.

Elizabeth freed his penis. 'Okay, see you tomorrow, Ken.' She put it in her mouth.

'See you then, buddy. Keep your shit together.'

Dal hung up. 'Mission accomplished,' he said with a trembling voice. Elizabeth moaned. As she sucked and licked, Dal stroked her soft hair. 'No audience?' he asked.

She didn't answer. Her mouth worked. Her hands unfastened his pants, and pulled them down, and clutched his bare buttocks.

He saw Herbert off to the right. Outside by the pool. Wheelchair against the glass door. Watching him with shiny, wide eyes.

Dal didn't care. Too late to care. Only Elizabeth mattered: her probing fingers, the slick tight hole of her mouth.

Herbert didn't matter till afterward.

'Does he *have* to watch?' Dal asked.

'Of course.'

'It's sick, Elizabeth.'

She smiled. 'I know. Isn't it delicious?'

They sat by the pool, Herbert facing them, and drank

Burgundy. Dal wore his boxer shorts. Elizabeth wore nothing.

'Can he hear what we say?'

'Indeed he can. He hears, sees, and thinks. He breathes, swallows, and defecates. And that's about the extent of his achievements. Isn't it, Herbert?' She pinched his cheek. Her fingers left white marks that turned red.

'Could he feel that?'

'Could you, Herbert? Don't be shy, speak right up. Aw, what's the matter? Cat got your tongue?'

'Doesn't he have a nurse, or anything?'

'Heavens no. He has me. I see to his needs. It's a terrible burden, sometimes, but I feel it's the least I can do for him.'

'You ought to get him a nurse.'

'*Ought* I? Oh, I don't think so. We don't want to fritter away our fortune on such luxuries, do we? There won't be nearly as much left for me, if we do that. Herbert, after all, is not going to live forever. I hate to say this in front of the poor dear, but I think his time is limited. No, I don't imagine Herbert will be with us much longer.' She finished her glass of wine. 'Let's go in for a dip. And for Godsake, take off those silly shorts.'

'How long have you been deaf?' Pete asked.

'You noticed.'

'Is it supposed to be a secret?'

Connie swirled her Bloody Mary with the celery stalk. 'Not exactly,' she said. 'I don't broadcast it to everyone I bump into, but I get around to it pretty quickly. I can't pick up everything that's said. If people don't know I'm deaf, they might think I'm just stupid.'

'I wondered which it was.'

Connie laughed.

'It isn't every day you see a woman walk out in front of a honking car.'

'It was honking? I'm surprised I didn't notice.'

'You're not completely deaf?'

'Just about. There's still some conductive hearing. You pick up vibrations of sounds, at least if they're loud enough. Something like a car horn, definitely.'

'I suspected you didn't hear it,' Pete said. 'As we walked over here, I said a couple of things with my head turned away.'

'You ought to be a detective.'

'I am.'

'You're kidding.'

He took a business card from his wallet.

Connie sipped her drink. It was heavy on the tabasco sauce, and made her eyes water. Blinking, she read his card. 'Pete Harvey, Private Investigations.' It gave his address and phone number. 'Can I keep it?' she asked.

'Sure.'

'Never know when I might need a private eye.'

'Let's hope you don't. Not in my professional capacity, at least.'

She tucked the card into her pocket book, briefly considered giving one of her cards to Pete, and decided not to. She didn't want to start talking about her work. Not right now.

'When did you lose your hearing?' he asked.

'It's been five years.'

'An illness?'

'Accident.'

'Tough break.'

'Could've been a lot worse.'

'How'd it happen?' he asked.

'A knock on the head.'

'Some knock.'

'I'll say. I was in a coma for three weeks.'

Pete shook his head.

'Well, I came out lucky. Even being deaf – it's not as bad as it could be. At least I had twenty-one years of hearing. I know how the world sounds, and I can talk.'

'You talk just fine.'

'Thank you.'

'And you read lips like a pro. I could use a gal like you on my staff, except for one thing.'

'What's that?'

'I have a strict rule: I don't get involved with people who work for me.'

'What?' she asked, feeling heat rush to her face.

'I don't want this to end when we walk out of here.'

'Oh.' She grinned. 'Neither do I.'


SCREAM GEMS
PRESENTS
OTTO SCHRECK
in
SCHRECK THE INQUISITOR


She is strapped to a chair in the center of a bare room, squinting into the brilliant light as if trying to see who is behind it.

Her young face is frightened.

'Who's there?' she asks. 'Please, I know someone's there. Who are you? What do you want with me?'

'I am the Grand Inquisitor. I wish to ask you a few questions.'

She groans. 'Please, what's going on?'

'You have information I need.'

'Who are you?'

He steps from behind the light. He wears a black, hooded robe.

'Oh Jesus.'

'Take not the name of the Lord in vain, heretic.'

She cranes her neck, trying to look past him. 'Ted, are you here someplace? Ted? Is this some kind of . . .'

'Who is this Ted? One of your heretic friends?'

'What's this heretic stuff?'

'Tell me about the Coven.'

'Oh God . . .'

His hand flashes out. It smacks her cheek, the heavy blow knocking her head to the side. She begins to cry. 'Tears will do you no good, witch.' Grabbing her hair, he jerks her head backwards. 'Tell me about the Coven.'

'*What* Coven?' she cries out, her voice shrill.

'Ah, you will play your games.' He raises a handful of her long, black hair. 'Do you wish to lose your precious hair?'

'No!'

He removes shears from his robe pocket. 'The names, then, of those in your Coven.'

'I don't know anything about a Coven.'

She screams, as if in pain, when he cuts through the hair. He cuts close to her scalp, and tosses great handsful into the darkness beyond the small area of light. Though she yells and pleads and flings her head about, he works feverishly and doesn't stop until nothing remains but short, choppy bristle.

Schreck steps back, and nods with approval. 'Are you prepared, now, to give me the information?'

'You *bastard!*' she shrieks. 'Goddamn you to hell, you goddamn fucking bastard!'

'You dare speak to me of Hell and damnation? You? A sister of the Devil?'

'Fucking pervert!'

A grin curls his lips.

The rage suddenly leaves her face. 'I'm sorry,' she mumbles. 'Please, I'm sorry. I'll do what you want. I'll tell you anything. Just don't hurt me. Please.'

'Tell me the names.'

'John Brown, and . . .'

'You take me for a fool?'

'No!'

'I could tear off your fingernails. Would you like that?'

'No,' she sobs.

'Perhaps you would prefer me to burn out your eyes, or snip your nipples off.'

She shakes her head, crying softly.

'There are so many ways to make you speak of your hellish brethren: breaking bones, burning holes in your tender flesh, slicing it with a knife, shredding it with a whip, tearing it off inch by inch with my teeth. I've done it all. Crude methods, but effective. What shall we do with you?'

'Let me go,' she pleads. 'I promise, I'll never tell anybody anything.'

'You must tell *me* something, first.'

'I don't know about any Coven. If I knew, I'd tell you. Honest! I don't know anything about Covens or witches or here tics . . .'

'Then you shall suffer.'

She is on the floor, naked and spread eagled, her wrists and ankles bound to nails in the hardwood.

Schreck crouches beside her. 'See my little friends?' He holds a jar in his hand. 'Yes, they are spiders. Three dozen spiders. Do you like spiders, my little witch?'

'Please, don't.'

He slowly unscrews the lid. 'Tell me what I need to know, and I shall spare you the discomfort.'

'I don't know anything!'

'Unfortunate.'

Schreck removes the lid. He shakes out spiders. The girl shuts her eyes tightly and shakes her head as they drop onto her face. They fall, floating down like dark flakes, dotting her pale throat, her breasts, her belly. They creep over her tangle of pubic hair. They scurry on her thighs.

The girl screams and writhes.

Schreck, crouching beside her, watches with bulging, wet eyes.

'I shall leave you now, and give you a few hours to enjoy your playmates.'

'*No!* Get them *off* me! Get them *off*!'

He leaves the room.

A small, black spider crawls along the girl's forehead. It climbs the ridge of her eyebrow. She shakes her head wildly, trying to dislodge it. It halts as if to hang on. When she stops shaking her head, it moves down onto her eyelid.

Her scream is interrupted by the crack of a gunshot.

A man rushes into the room. He drops to his knees beside her. 'My God, Susan.'

'*Get them off!*'

The man sets his revolver on the floor. His hands work quickly, flicking and brushing the spiders away.

When they are off her face, she opens her eyes. 'Oh, thank God. I thought I'd . . .'

'It's all right. Schreck's dead. You're safe, now.' Taking out a pocket knife, he begins to cut the cords.

'Oh Ted, how did . . . how did you find me?'

'I'll tell you later.' He finishes cutting her loose, and helps her up. 'Here, take this.' He removes his shirt.

Susan puts it on.

'Did you talk?' he asks.

'About what?'

'The Coven.'

'I don't *know* anything about any Coven. I kept trying to tell him that, but he wouldn't listen. I don't know what's going on. How did I get here? Who is that awful man? He . . . oh Ted, take me out of here! Please!'

'You didn't tell him the members of the Coven?'

'Damn it, I don't know about a Coven! If I knew, I would've told him right away, before he . . . Look what he did to my hair! And those . . . those *spiders!* I'd have told him anything.'

The man turns away from her.

Schreck enters the room.

'She doesn't know,' Ted tells Schreck. 'I'm sure of it.'

Dropping to her knees, Susan grabs the revolver. She aims at Schreck and fires. The roar of the blast fills the room, but Schreck doesn't fall. Instead, he walks toward her. His lean, bony face wears a terrible smile. Susan shoots again and again.

'Blanks, heretic.'

She looks to Ted, who grins at her and shrugs. 'I'm afraid he's right.' Ted walks slowly from the room, leaving her alone with Schreck.

'I have no more use for you,' Schreck says. He holds a leather switch. He flicks it, cutting the air with a sound like a whistle. 'We shall make your death slow and agonizing, as befits a foul toad such as you.'

Whirling away, Susan rushes to a window. She hammers it with the revolver. The glass bursts. She grabs a long, jagged shard. 'Stay back! I'll kill you!'

Schreck laughs with disdain as he approaches. 'If you're so fond of glass, perhaps you would like to eat some. I can arrange that. I can arrange many delights featuring glass.'

With both hands, she suddenly presses the shard to her throat and tugs it sideways, ripping a deep gash across her skin.

Schreck steps closer. Her blood sprays his face and robe. 'I had such plans for you.'

He stomps his foot, splashing blood.

'You spoiled them!'

He raises the switch.

Before he has a chance to strike, Susan drops to her knees. Schreck steps out of the way as she falls forward. Her face thuds the floor.

'Spoiled them!' Schreck yells.

## The End

# Chapter Ten

On Friday, Connie waited in agony for Dal to come home from work. She had wanted to tell him before, but couldn't. Now, time was running out.

No more delays.

God, if only there was some way out of it!

Finally, the front door opened.

She went to Dal. 'How was your day?' she asked.

'Not bad, not bad.' He tossed his sport coat onto the couch and turned to her, expecting a kiss.

She kissed him quickly.

'How'd you do today?' he asked.

'Not as well as I'd like.' Her writing had gone badly because of her worries. Rather than let the day go to waste, she spent most of her time typing without trying to force herself to concentrate.

She followed Dal into the kitchen. He mixed a batch of martinis for himself. While he worked on that, Connie made a vodka gimlet. 'Want some potato chips?' she asked.

'Sure. What's for dinner?'

It's *coming*!

She breathed deeply. She felt numb. 'I thawed out a steak for you.'

'Yeah? What are you having?'

'I'm . . . going out for dinner.'

Dal looked confused.

'I have a date,' she explained.

His face went red. 'A *date*?'

'I'm sorry, Dal. I meant to bring it up earlier . . .'

'With a man?'

She nodded.

'What are you talking about?'

'I met him Wednesday. At the library. He asked me to have dinner with him tonight.'

'Well *Jesus Christ*!'

'I'm sorry, Dal.'

'What am I supposed to do?'

'Have the steak.'

'Oh, that's what I need, funny answers. You think this is funny?'

'Not at all.'

'Boy, I thought . . . Never mind. *Jesus!* Well, go out and have a ball. Want to bring him back here, later, for a little slap 'n tickle?'

'Dal, please.'

'It's a little short notice for an eviction, don't you think?'

'You don't have to go.'

'But it'd be nice if I would.'

'I didn't say that.'

'Well just exactly what *are* you saying?'

'I don't know. It's just a date, Dal.'

'Yeah, my ass.' He turned away.

'Dal!'

Ignoring her, he picked up the martini pitcher and left the kitchen. She followed him into the living-room. He opened the front door.

'Dal. don't run off.'

He glanced back at her. 'Have a ball,' he said.

'Where are you going? Dal!'

He stepped outside, and jerked the door shut.

Connie felt the impact of its slam.

The door opened. Elizabeth looked up at him with deep, green eyes, and smiled.

'Martinis, anyone? asked Dal.

She pulled the glass pitcher down to her lips, and sipped.

'Mmmm. We must have olives, though. Come along. Herbert's out by the pool. Why don't you join him? I'll get glasses and olives.'

He watched her walk toward the kitchen. Her feet were bare. He could see through the thin, white fabric of her caftan. She wore nothing under it. For a moment, he considered following her into the kitchen, raising the caftan above her waist, and stroking the firm smooth curves of her buttocks.

But she had asked him to join Herbert at the pool. Best do as she asked. Plenty of time, later on, for the other.

He went out to the pool. Herbert's wheelchair faced the table, almost as if it hadn't been moved since Wednesday. He wore a different shirt, though. A bright red, flowered shirt. It made him look like a Hawaii vacationer.

A withered, paralyzed tourist. More corpse than man.

Dal turned away from the staring eyes. The pool was still in sunlight. He thought back to Wednesday, and the slick feel of Elizabeth's skin as they grappled under water.

'Having a nice chat?' she asked, coming out with a tray. On the tray were two long-stemmed glasses, a jar of green olives, and a cheese board with Brie and crackers. Her breasts jiggled slightly as she walked. Their tips were dark through the fabric. She sat down beside Herbert.

'So,' she said, 'how did you slip away from Connie?'

'We had a little quarrel.'

'How clever. You picked a fight, and walked off in a huff.'

'Something like that.'

'Nothing too drastic, I hope. You didn't tell her about us?'

'No.'

'That's fortunate. You wouldn't want to spoil such a fine opportunity.' She plucked olives from the jar, and dropped them into the empty glasses.

Dal poured the martinis.

They picked up the glasses.

'To you and Connie,' said Elizabeth.

'Why should we drink to that?'

'Because you're going to marry her, of course.'

'I am?'

'Certainly.'

'You're joking.'

'My dear, I have expensive tastes, you would be completely incapable of satisfying on the meager salary of a sales clerk. If you're interested in pursuing this relationship, you simply must be able to afford me.'

'But you're rich.'

'Herbert is. I'll be rich when, alas, he passes on. That, however, doesn't relieve you from the necessity of seeing to my needs, once we're together.'

'But marrying Connie . . . Her money wouldn't be mine.'

'Half of it would, I believe. Think it over.' She again raised her glass. 'To you and Connie, and wealth.'

'I don't know . . .'

'You want me, don't you?'

'More than anything.'

'In that case, your decision shouldn't be difficult.'

Dal hesitated, then clicked his glass against Elizabeth's.

They drank.

'So, how did you get to be a private eye?' Connie asked.

'I started out with the L.A.P.D.'

'I should've guessed.'

'How's that?' Pete, across the table from her at Victoria Station, grinned as he sliced into his prime rib.

'Oh, you all have that clean-cut, Steve Garvey look.'

'Just like Reed and Molloy.' He took a bite of beef.

'When did you leave the force?'

He chewed for a moment, and started to answer.

'I can't hear you,' Connie said. 'If you talk and chew at the same time, it comes out gobble-dee-gook.'

Pete laughed. After swallowing, he said, 'How's this?'

'Just fine. I'll eat while you talk.'

'Thanks!'

'So, how come you left the police?'

'We had a disagreement. Well, no, not really. My beef wasn't with the department. More with the public. We'd been under a lot of pressure about officer-involved shootings. This was a couple of years ago. I was cruising along Sunset, one fine night, and saw this black woman running up the middle of the street with a knife. She was chasing a kid. My first thought was that the kid had snatched her purse, or something. But he came right to my car, yelling for help. I got out, and the kid sort of ducked behind me. "She crazy, man," he says. And the gal is yelling too, about cutting off the kid's private parts. I'm between the gal and the kid, though, and she keeps coming. She doesn't obey my command to stop. It's this wicked-looking hunting knife, you see. So I draw down on her, and she ignores it and keeps coming, and I'm thinking about all the heavy times I'll get from the bleeding hearts if! drop this gal. I mean, she's black, she's female, and she's unarmed except for a harmless little knife. So I hold off firing. And in the meantime, she throws the knife. I dodge it, and it kills the kid. The kid, it turns out, is her homosexual son.'

'*You're* the one,' Connie said.

'I'm him.'

'You cuffed the gal to the body . . .'

'Yeah.' He grinned. 'I cuffed both her hands to both the dead guy's hands, and walked away.'

'I wondered what kind of a man would do that.'

'Now you know. Here he is. Dirty Pete in the flesh.'

'Pleased to meet you, Dirty Pete.' She reached a hand over the table and shook his. 'Better eat, now, before your dinner gets cold.'

'Okay. I'll eat and you do the talking. How did you get to be an author?'

'It all began with a rotten social life.'

* * *

'It's quite simple, really,' said Elizabeth. 'Haven't you ever proposed before?'

'No.'

'That surprises me, I must say. You seem so impulsive. Be a dear, and push me off.'

Her air mattress had drifted, footfirst, against a side of the pool.

Dal, sitting on the end of the diving board, got to, his feet. He turned around carefully, and walked, the board springy under his feet. He climbed down. The concrete was still warm, though the sun no longer hit it. He liked the feel of the breeze.

And he liked what it did to Elizabeth. It was the breeze, he assumed, that made her nipples stand rigid.

He glanced at the martini glass she balanced on her belly.

'Would you like a refill, while you're beached?'

'I would adore one.' She lifted the glass, tipped it to her mouth, and sucked in the olive.

Dal pulled her mattress alongside the wall, and took the glass from her. He retrieved his glass from the end of the diving board, and carried them to the table. 'Fix you one, Herbie?' he asked.

He smiled, realizing that the man's silent presence no longer unnerved him.

'Herbie,' he said, 'you're a good fellow.'

'He was never that,' Elizabeth called.

Dal finished pouring the drinks. He returned to the pool. He climbed down the tile steps at the shallow end, and waded out to Elizabeth.

He placed the glass on her belly. 'Thank you. dear,' she said.

'Think little of it.'

'Now, pretend I'm Connie.'

'Why'd I do that?'

'You're going to propose to me.'

'Huh?'

'You said you've never proposed before. Here's your chance.'

'Oh,I don't know.'

Elizabeth raised her head slightly off the inflated pillow, sipped her martini without spilling, and rested the glass on her belly. 'You start by taking her to a nice restaurant. Have a few drinks.'

'Ply her with liquor.'

'Precisely. Have a marvelous meal. Lobster, perhaps.'

'I can't eat seafood.'

'Then steak. Châteaubriant would do nicely. When you're done, order after-dinner drinks. Cognac . . .'

'Connie likes Irish Coffee.'

'Fine. Have that. And now, it's time. You're both full, slightly high, and happy.'

'Okay.'

'I'm Connie.'

She started to drift away. Dal caught her by the foot, and pulled her back to him. 'Connie, I want to marry you.'

'Marry me? Oh, Dal! Are you sure? Why would you want to marry someone like me?'

' 'Cause Elizabeth told me to.'

'That won't do at all.'

# Chapter Eleven

They stepped out of the restaurant. 'That was very nice.' Connie said. 'Thank you.' She took Pete's hand.

'The night's young. Anything special you'd like to do?'

'Yes, as a matter of fact.'

'Shoot.'

'Let's go to a movie.'

'A *movie*?' He looked at her, grinning, as if he thought it a fine, rather childlike idea. 'Anything in particular?'

She shrugged. 'I don't care. Just so it's dark.'

'Do you like scary films?'

'Do you?'

'They're my favorite. I know just the place. I don't know what's playing there tonight, but it'll probably be good.'

'Bet I can guess. The Haunted Palace.'

'You've been there?'

'Not since it changed hands. It used to be the Elsinore.'

'It's a far cry from that, now.'

In the darkness of the car, they didn't try to talk.

Connie fastened her seatbelt. She thought it would be nice to open it, and scoot across the seat, and snuggle with Pete. She hadn't done anything like that in years. Tonight, though, she felt as eager and daring and uncertain as a teenager. She hesitated. Pete might think she was acting silly, or possessive. On the other hand, she felt so far away from him, strapped into the seat way over on this side of the car.

With a trembling hand, she unfastened the safety harness. Pete looked at her, and smiled. She slid across the seat. He put

251

an arm around her. Connie snuggled against him, and rested a hand on his thigh.

A block from the Haunted Palace, Pete eased his car to the curb. They walked to the theater, holding hands.

On the marquee, Connie saw that *Dracula, Down Under* was showing with *The Town that Dreaded Sundown*.

The girl in the ticket window smiled at Pete. 'How are you, tonight?' she asked.

'Not bad. I see you haven't found a new hairdresser.' He handed her the money.

'*The Town that Dreaded Sundown* is just starting,' she said. 'Too bad you didn't get here half an hour sooner. You missed tonight's Schreck.'

'He's a little tacky for my taste.'

The girl laughed. 'Oh, you'd have *loved* this one, *Schreck the Inquisitor*.'

'Sounds charming.'

Inside, Pete gave the tickets to a fat man in bloody clothes.

'Evening, Bruno.'

Bruno growled through the nylon stocking he wore over his face.

'Do you hang out here?' Connie asked.

'Only been here once,' Pete said. 'Last week.'

'It *is* a little tacky.'

'So are most of the movies. Fun, though.'

'Yeah. Like a carnival.'

'Popcorn?'

'I couldn't eat a thing, at the moment. Maybe a drink, though.'

The auditorium of the theater was just as Connie remembered it: the castle walls, the battlements and turrets, the ceiling like a starlit sky.

252

She had spent a lot of time in movie theaters, after the Tucson incident. Too much time. First in Tucson, then in Los Angeles.

Hardly a day passed that she didn't find herself alone in a dark theater, eating popcorn and hot dogs and Good 'n Plenty, staring at a screen where silent people struggled through tragedy, fought to survive, laughed, and fell in love.

She went to the movies, though she knew she shouldn't. She should be writing more pages than the two or three she managed daily. She should be reading. Most of all, she should be out in the world, *doing* something, meeting people, not hiding in the darkness of a movie house.

One day, two years ago, she went to a noon showing of *The Island*. When it was over, she stayed in her seat and watched *Jaws II*, though she had seen it before. When that ended, she went out to the lobby to leave. Beyond the glass doors, the afternoon looked sunny. A young couple strolled by, holding hands and happy.

Her throat tightened. Her eyes filled with tears.

After buying a Pepsi and a fresh bucket of popcorn, she returned to her seat. She watched *The Island* again. She watched *Jaws II* again. When *The Island* started for a third time, she stayed in her seat.

She felt sick with herself. Cowardly and self-destructive. But she couldn't force herself to walk out.

Finally, a man sat down beside her. He smelted strongly of sweat and onions. He put a hand on her knee.

She was wearing a skirt.

The hand moved under its hem.

She lifted the hand. The man smiled at her. His lips moved, blowing stench into her face.

She broke his forefinger, and walked out of the theater.

The next day, she didn't go to a movie. Nor the next day. She was certain, if she went back even once, she would fall again into the pattern. She was like an alcoholic, afraid to take a single drink because it would lead to another and another.

She read voraciously.

She finished her novel, *Bayou Bride*, in three months.

She took a course in self-defense from a tough, scarred ex-Marine who claimed to be a mercenary – and proved it to Connie's satisfaction by disappearing one day. She assumed he'd gone to Rhodesia. She never saw him again.

One of the men in the class dated her, and she found that she could go to movies safely as long as she didn't go alone.

Then she met Dal. He took her often. He knew how she loved movies, though she never told him about her bad years as an addict.

It was really mean of him, leaving her home last week when . . . She didn't want to think about Dal.

Not tonight.

She could worry about him later – how to tell him . . .

She took Pete's hand, and didn't let go.

When *The Town that Dreaded Sundown* ended, the lights came on.

'How'd you like it?' Pete asked.

'I'll probably have nightmares,'

He smiled. 'You up for another one?'

She glanced at the clock. Nearly eleven. Dal was probably back at the apartment, waiting for her. She didn't want to face him. She wanted to stay here with Pete, holding his hand, and never leave.

'Sure. let's stay,' she said.

'Ready for some popcorn now?'

'That'd be great.'

*Dracula, Down Under* began soon after Pete's return.

It was an Italian film about a vampire among the Australian aborigines.

'Oh no,' Connie said.

Pete looked at her.

She shook her head. 'Nothing,' she whispered, and took a handful of popcorn from the tub on his lap.

It was enough, being with him.

It didn't matter that the movie made no sense. She ate popcorn, and drank her Pepsi, and paid little attention to the screen.

She leaned closer to Pete.

He put his arm across her shoulders.


'Could we see each other tomorrow?' Pete asked outside her apartment door.

'I'd like that.'

'We could go to the beach.'

'Great. I'll make a picnic lunch.'

'I'll bring the beer. Or would you prefer wine?'

'Beer.'

They held each other tightly, and kissed.

'I had a wonderful time,' Connie said.

'Me too.'

'I'd ask you in, but Dal . . .'

Pete shook his head. 'On the first date, I only kiss.'

'That so?'

'It's a lie, actually.' He pulled her close, and kissed her again. His hand gently went to her breast.

She sucked in a sharp breath. 'Oh God, Pete.'

'Goodnight'

'Goodnight. See you tomorrow.'

'Around ten?' he asked.

'Great.'

'Goodnight.' He kissed her once more.

'Goodnight.'

They didn't part for a long time.

Then Connie went inside, alone. She leaned against the door, too weak to move, hurting in a strange way that made her want to cry and laugh.

A long time later, she searched the apartment. Dal wasn't there, thank God.

She put the guard chain on the door.

Then, feeling guilty, she took it off.

Then she put it on again. If Dal came back in the middle of the night, she didn't want him crawling into bed with her.

Not tonight.

Not ever again.

Pete Harvey had her now.

Dirty Pete.

With a squeal of delight, she hugged herself and twirled across the room.

# Chapter Twelve

Another Saturday going to pot. Freya sat in front of the television with her tea, and stared at Popeye.

The pits.

Sunday, for Christsake, was better than this.

Ha! Sunday, for Christsake. A funny.

But it was true. Sunday morning TV had a parade of weirdos.

A real circus. Some of those evangelists put on a better show than Loony Tunes. Especially the healers. Christ, the way they slapped folks around, and grabbed canes out from under cripples, and stuck their fingers in deaf people's ears! *Out, you devils! Out, Satan!* Be a kick, some morning, if the guy's finger came out of an ear with a big yellow glob of wax.

Well, shit, nothing good like that on Saturday morning. Just a bunch of feeb cartoons and reruns of crap she saw twenty years ago.

Nothing decent till 10:30. *Phantom of the Opera*. The Claude Rains version from '43. Nowhere near as good as the Lon Chaney, with those boobs trotting around the tunnels with their fingers in the air so the phantom couldn't drop nooses around their necks. 'The phantom's loops are quick!' they kept saying. What a gas! Well, the Rains version couldn't hold a candle to that, but it sure beat watching *Heckle and Jeckle*.

The N-double A-C-P must've got down on Heckle and Jeckle. She'd swear those magpies used to talk like Amos and Andy.

The doorbell rang, startling Freya so she slopped tea onto her bare leg. She brushed it away with her hand, and got up. Her leg was still wet as she crossed the room. She rubbed it again. She adjusted her tube-top, and opened the door.

'Greetings.'

'Oh, hello.' Freya said. She forced a smile.

'Remember me?'

'I remember. I see you changed your shirt.' The vulture T-shirt had been replaced by one that read. 'Don't get mad, get even.'

'I saw the ad in the paper.' she said. 'I thought I'd come back.'

Like a bad penny, Freya thought. 'Well, I'm afraid the apartment is still not available.'

257

'Why not?'

'It's already taken.'

'That's the story you gave me, last week.'

'It's just as true, today.'

'Then why was there an ad in today's paper?'

'It must be an error.' Freya said.

'No, I don't think so. I think you just decided you don't want me for a roommate. Isn't that right?'

'That's right.'

'Because I'm a gross slob, right?'

'That's right.'

'Suppose I make it two-fifty.'

'You're awfully eager.'

'This place is only a block from campus. Besides, I like your style.' She gave Freya a brash grin. 'Now, how about showing me around?'

'I admire your persistence.' Freya said, loathing the girl more each second. 'What's your name?'

'Chelsea.'

'I'm Freya. Come on in.'

The girl entered, and wrinkled her nose. 'You need some light in here,' she said, and opened the curtains. 'That's better.'

Freya cringed.

'Are you from around this area?' she asked.

'No.'

'Where are you from?'

'What does it matter?'

'I'm just curious. If we're going to live together, don't you think we should know more about each other?'

'Does that mean you'll take me?'

'I'm thinking about it.'

'Well, if you really want to know, I'm from Oakland.'

'Ah. Home of the Hell's Angels. Did you live with your folks?'

'What are they?'

'You don't have parents?'

'No, I was hatched. Can't you tell?'

'I was only wondering.'

'Well don't. Just show me the apartment, okay? If I wanted a third degree, I'd set myself on fire.'

'As you wish,' said Freya. She showed Chelsea the kitchen, the bathroom, and the spare room.

'When can I move in?'

'As soon as you pay me.'

'Two-fifty.'

'Six hundred,' Freya said.

'Come again?'

'First and last month's rent. That's five hundred.'

'I can count.'

'Plus a hundred deposit for breakage.'

'You're a doozy.'

'I'm only protecting myself.'

'You think I can't come up with six hundred, right?'

'Oh, I hope you can,' Freya said.

She meant it.

'Is a check okay?'

'Cash.'

'This is Saturday.'

'Then you can move in Monday after the banks open.'

'You're trying to pull something.'

'Not at all. If you can come up with the cash today, you can move in today.'

'How about fifty down, and the rest Monday morning?'

'And you move in today?'

'Yep.'

'No thanks. Monday will be plenty soon enough.'

'You're a pal.'

'Shall we plan to see each other Monday morning, then?'

'We shall count on it.' Chelsea said, mimicking her.

When she was gone, Freya made a telephone call.

'Hello?'

'Good morning, darling.'

'Princess!'

'I have one for you,' she said.

'Marvelous!'

'This one's a bit different,'

'How so?'

'She's a pig.'

'A pig?' he asked, the lightness leaving his voice.

'I know you want beauties, darling, but this gal's wonderful. She's ugly, gross, and obnoxious.'

'This wasn't part of our plan, princess.'

'Wait'll you see her.'

'She's disgusting and repulsive?'

'Very.'

'Hmm.' He paused for several seconds. 'Perhaps we *can* fit her in. Let me work on it, and get back to you.'

'Great.'

'In the meantime, keep looking for a beauty. Tina was absolutely marvelous. Someone like her.'

'I'll keep the ad in the paper.'

'Yes. Do that. And come over tonight, if you can.'

'You got another one?'

'Oh, indeed I did. Unfortunately, it has two female voices. I'm not quite sure how to handle the dubbing of that, but I'll try to think of something before you arrive.'

'What time?'
'Oh, eight o'clock.'
'Great. See you then, Todd.'

# Chapter Thirteen

Dal stopped at Conroy's, and bought a dozen red roses in a vase. He carried the vase out to his car. Holding it in place on the passenger seat, he headed for the apartment.

The roses had been Elizabeth's idea.

'She'll be touched by your thoughtfulness and generosity.' Elizabeth had told him. 'She'll forget all about your little spat.'

Naturally, he hadn't explained the real cause of his trouble with Connie. It was too humiliating. Not only that, but Elizabeth would recognize Connie's date for what it was – a sign that she had lost interest in Dal, a sign that marriage was probably out of the question. He didn't want Elizabeth to know that, so he made up a story to satisfy her curiosity.

'She burnt dinner,' he'd said. 'We had these two beautiful sirloin steaks, and she left them in the broiler too long. Completely forgot about them. By the time she remembered, they were charcoal black. I said, "You don't expect me to eat this, do you?" Then I chewed her out. I told her I'd been working my tail off, all day, and how I came home looking forward to a nice meal, and the least she could do is not fuck it up.'

261

'You sound positively abhorrent.'

'She pissed me off.'

'Will you yell at me, that way, if I burn your food?'

'Never.'

'Why not?'

'Because I love you.'

'And you don't love Connie?'

'She's all right. I don't love her, though.'

'You must learn to act as if you do. Make her feel that she is the whole world to you, that your life would be a pit of ashes without her.'

'I'll try.'

'You must do better than try. You must succeed. I want you to marry her within the month.'

'My God, that's only three weeks away!'

'I'm sure you'll find a way.'

That was the time to mention Connie's new boyfriend. He couldn't force himself to tell her, though. Not enough nerve.

Three weeks. Impossible.

Unless . . . Who knows, maybe she ended up hating the guy who took her to dinner, last night.

Not much chance of that.

He drove up the alley behind the apartment house, and carefully parked the car in its stall. He carried the vase of roses into the courtyard, and up the stairs to the door of the apartment.

He unlocked the door.

The guard chain snapped taut.

'Shit!'

He kicked the door. The chain flung it back at him, slamming it with a bang. Embarrassed, he looked around to see if he was being watched. He saw no one.

He felt like kicking the door down.

That would get him inside, but further from his real goal.

So he pushed the doorbell, instead. It didn't ring; it lit bulbs in every room. He jabbed the button, again and again, to make the bulbs flash.

The chain rattled. The door opened.

'Dal.'

Though she smiled, her eyes looked troubled.

'These are for you.'

'Oh, they're beautiful. Thank you.'

'May I come in?'

'Of course.'

Of course? Then why the chain? 'Are you alone?' he asked.

'Sure I am.' Connie took the flowers, and set them on the dining-room table.

Dal watched in silence. She wore a wrap-around skirt. Her white blouse was tied in front, leaving her midriff bare. Her beach outfit.

She came back to him.

'About last night,' he said. 'I want to apologize. I acted like an ass.'

'You had a right to be upset, Dal.'

She stepped toward the bright window, and he turned to face her. She wants the light on my lips, he realized. She's always maneuvering for that.

'I should have been more reasonable,' he said. 'I mean, I don't own you. You have every right to go on a date. It's just that I was . . . hurt, I guess. The thought of you being with another man . . . It was just unbearable.'

'I'm sorry,' she said.

'Forgive me?'

'There's nothing that needs forgiving. You wouldn't have felt badly, if you didn't care for me. I can hardly fault you for that.'

'I more than care for you, Connie. I love you.'

She blinked as if slapped. 'No you don't.'

'I do. I've loved you since the first moment I saw you.' He reached for Connie. Shaking her head, she grabbed his wrists, and pushed his arms down.

'Don't.'

'Connie!'

'I'm sorry, but . . . We've had . . . I do like you, Dal, and I'll always be grateful for the times we've had. But I think they're over, now.'

'No.'

'Yes. I want you to find a place of your own, now. You don't have to move out today, or anything, but the sooner you get your own apartment, the better off we'll both be.'

'Connie, you can't mean it.'

'I do mean it.'

'You must've had a damn good time, last night.'

She looked up from his lips, and met his eyes. 'If things had been better between you and me, I never would've accepted the date. In fact, I would never have *met* him. I stopped by Lane Brothers, Wednesday morning.'

The words made his bowels suddenly ache.

'I thought we might have lunch together, but you weren't there.'

'I . . .'

'You don't have to tell me where you were. I know.'

'What?'

'You were with a woman.'

'I was *not*.'

'You don't have to lie. It doesn't matter anymore.'

'I was not with a woman.'

'You were with her last Friday night at the movies, and all day Wednesday, and probably last night.'

'That's a lie!'

*How could she know?*

'It's the truth. I walked out to the theater, Friday night. I thought I'd surprise you. But I was the one who got the surprise. I saw you sitting with her, with your arm around her.'

*It's all a bluff,* he realized. She doesn't know anything. She's only guessing.

'That was a good trick,' Dal said. 'If I was sitting with a girl, it's news to me. If you want to believe it, though, go ahead. I'm sure your conscience feels better if you can convince yourself that I'm the one at fault. I was alone in that theater. I was alone Wednesday, unless you want to count the clerks I talked to while I was shopping for this.'

He reached into his pocket, and pulled out a small jewelry box. He opened it.

Connie stared at the diamond ring. Tears filled her eyes. 'Oh Dal,' she muttered.

'I was planning to . . . last night . . .'

'Oh Dal, I'm sorry.'

He took the ring from the box, and held it out to her. 'Try it on.'

She shook her head. 'I can't. I'm sorry. I . . .' She sobbed and turned away.

Dal put a hand on her shoulder.

She shrugged it off, and faced him. 'It's over, Dal. It's over. I'm sorry. I still want you to move out.'

'But why?'

'It's Pete.'

'The guy you were with last night?'

She nodded.

265

'I've been aced out, huh?'

'I'm sorry.'

'Okay. I'll move out, like you want. I don't want to pressure you. In case this Pete doesn't . . . Well, the ring will still be waiting.'

Nodding, Connie wiped the tears from her face.

'Guess I'd better go apartment-hunting.'

'I'm sorry.'

Dal turned from her. He stopped outside. The door shut.

He slipped Elizabeth's engagement ring into its box, and headed for the stairs.

# Chapter Fourteen

Freya hated driving this time of the evening. The sun hung low over the Pacific, blinding her. Sunglasses helped, but not nearly enough. Most of the time, she could barely see the road ahead of her. She blocked the sun with her hand. That wasn't easy, though. After a few minutes, her upraised arm felt as if it were being dragged down with lead weights.

The stretch along the Coast Highway seemed endless. Finally, she came to the turnoff. She didn't notice the unmarked road until she was beside it. She hit her brakes, swung onto the highway's shoulder, and backed up.

She read the sign. PRIVATE ROAD. KEEP OUT.

She drove forward. The road curved into a thickly wooded

area. She stopped at a metal gate, opened its padlock, and swung the gate wide. After driving through, she shut the gate and snapped its lock into place.

The one-lane road left the pine trees behind, and snaked across low hills to the house.

Freya gazed at the house as she drove toward it. She loved the house. She loved its weathered siding, its bay windows, its gables, its single, peaked tower.

So marvelously creepy!

It looked like dozens of other old, dark houses in dozens of old, spooky movies.

Soon, it would belong to her.

She could hardly wait!

She had such visions of how it would be, of wandering its halls on stormy nights, candle flames throwing weird shadows on the walls. No electric lights. She would get rid of all those, and use electricity only for the television and refrigerator and such.

It would be glorious.

So incredibly creepy, the greatest spook-house of all time – and *hers*.

She climbed the porch steps. As she aimed her key at the lock, the door groaned open.

'Todd.'

'Princess.' He kissed her cheek. 'You're looking lovely tonight, as usual.'

'Thank you.'

He gestured for her to follow, and started upstairs. 'I hope you had a pleasant drive.'

'I survived it.'

'Traffic wasn't too bad?'

'No. Traffic was fine. It was the damn sun that nearly killed me.'

'I'm sorry to hear that. I have some news to cheer you, though. I found a solution to our problem.'

'Another woman?'

'Yes. She's waiting in the control room.'

'What did you tell her?'

'I explained that she would be perfect for a voice-over in a short suspense show I'm producing.'

'Is she safe?'

'She's a streetwalker.'

'Can she read?'

'Oh, I do hope so.'

Todd opened a door at the top of the stairs. A slim, black woman was sitting on a bench at the control booth, leaning back, her elbows resting on the blank screens of two video monitors. Her ankles were crossed. She wore boots, and tight shorts, and a vest held loosely together in front by laces.

'Freya, this is Tango.'

'Pleased to meet you,' Freya said, staring at the girl's glossy, dark skin. The vest was open wide enough to expose much of her breasts.

'Pleasure's mine,' Tango said. Leaning forward, she held out a hand to Freya.

The hand was warm. It lingered in hers, and slid away.

'All set?' Todd asked. 'Let's run through the tape once with the audio, then I'll give you some time to familiarize yourselves with the scripts before we do the dubbing.'

Freya nodded.

'Whatever you say,' said Tango. 'You're the bossman.'

They turned to the main television screen.

'Get the lights, Freya, if you please.'

Reluctantly, she reached for the light switch. Darkness wasn't necessary for viewing, but Todd always insisted on it. For atmosphere, he said.

Maybe it's best, Freya thought. With the lights on, she wouldn't see much of the tape. Her eyes, she knew, would be on Tango.

'I believe I'll call this *Schreck the Ax-man*.'

'Why not *The Ax-man Cometh*?' Tango suggested.

Todd laughed politely. 'I'm afraid not, darling. Too much levity spoils the soup.'

The two young women sit close to their campfire, as if they believe its bright flames will keep them from harm.

The one in the plaid flannel skirt tilts her head back, and squirts a stream of wine into her mouth from a leather bota.

'Don't you ever miss?' asked her friend, who has obviously missed often. The front of her gray sweatshirt is wet and redstained.

'Takes practice, Lynn.'

She passes the bota to Lynn, who raises its spout to her lips and starts to squirt.

'Hello, young ladies.'

They both jump. Lynn shoots the stream off into her nose and eyes, and the man laughs. 'Sorry,' he says. 'I didn't mean to startle you. I saw your fire.' He walks close to it. He is a stout, red-bearded man. 'My name's Jim.'

'I'm Kristi. This is Lynn.'

'Mind if I join you?'

Kristi glances at Lynn, then smiles at the man and says, 'Help yourself.'

He steps closer to the fire, where the girls are sitting beside each other on a six-foot log. 'You can use our table,' Kristi suggests, sweeping her arm toward the stump standing upright beside her.

'Thanks,' he says, and sits on it.

He wears tight, faded jeans. The sleeves have been cut off his denim jacket at the shoulders, and his tanned arms look thick and powerful. 'Can I have a taste of that?'

Lynn shrugs, smiling nervously. She glances at Kristi, as if for permission. When Kristi nods, Lynn passes the bota to her, and she hands it to the man. He squirts a long stream of wine into his mouth, and doesn't spill a drop. He gives the bota back to Kristi. 'Where you girls from?' he asks.

'San Diego.'

'Long way from home.'

'Are you from around here?' Kristi asks.

'Me? I'm from Scottsdale.'

'Arizona?'

'California. She's a little burg just the other side of Sunny Lake.'

'Where's that?'

'Just the other side of Loon.'

'And that's just the other side of *this* lake,' Kristi adds, nodding her head toward the shoreline down the slope from the campsite.

'I canoed in, saw your fire.'

'Probably the whole world can see our fire,' Lynn says, and laughs nervously.

'Pretty near. Can I have another taste of that? It's Zinfandel, right?'

Kristi laughs. 'Fantastic! A wine connoisseur in the middle of the forest primeval!'

'Not a connoisseur, just a drinker.' He tips back his head, and squeezes the sides of the bota. When he is done, he passes the leather sack to Kristi.

'I wanted to talk to you about this fire,' he says. 'It's a warm night. You don't really need one.'

'We like it,' Kristi says.

'Sure. I know how you feel. She's bright and cheery, and keeps the darkness at arm's-length. Gives you a good feeling. Helps you forget you're alone in the woods, with god-knows-what prowling around and watching you.'

'You're not helping the situation,' Kristi says, and contorts her face in an exaggerated expression of fear. Lynn grimaces, looking very nervous.

'I'm serious, now. You ought to douse your fire. After dark, it's like a neon sign, tells folks you're here. If they're the wrong kind of folks, and come snooping, you could be in big trouble.'

'We can take care of ourselves,' Kristi tells him.

Lynn, who doesn't look so sure of that, chews her lower lip.

'Even if you have guns, which I doubt, it's still no guarantee. The way you're dressed, Kristi, I can see you're unarmed unless you've got some dinky thing way down in one of your jeans pockets.' He aims a finger at Lynn. 'You might have a pistol concealed under that bulky sweatshirt, but I'd bet you don't.' Smiling, he pulls a knife from the sheath on his belt. 'Now, I'm sitting here with a knife. You're there without guns. What're you gonna do?'

'Why don't you put that away?' Kristi says. Her voice, so confident before, is trembling slightly.

'Scared?' Jim asks.

'Put it away, all right?'

'I just want to put a little fear into you. You need it. You're both vulnerable as hell, and don't seem to realize it.' He slides the knife into its sheath.

'I'll bet you haven't heard about our murders. If you'd heard, you wouldn't be out here at all, much less with a roaring fire.'

Kristi and Lynn glance at each other. Lynn shakes her head.

'That's what I thought,' Jim says.

'You want to tell us?' asks Kristi.

271

'Five murders in the past two months, all of them within a few miles of here. The first was a fourteen-year-old girl. She went out alone on Sunny Lake to do some night fishing, and never came back. They found most of her body a week later in an abandoned boat house. Someone had used an ax on her.'

Lynn groans.

'Is this really true?' asks Kristi. 'Or are you just trying to scare us?'

'It's true, all right. The next two victims, just a month ago, were Randy Wilson and his wife. Randy owned the hardware store in Scottsdale. He and Mary used to do a lot of hiking. They were camped about a mile from here the night they were killed.'

'With an ax?' Lynn wants to know.

'Same as the girl. Same as the two teachers we found last week. Those gals were camping over by Loon. Chopped up like cordwood.'

'You don't have to be so graphic.'

'I just want you to understand the danger you're in.'

Lynn makes a sickly smile.

'We're here now,' Kristi says. 'What do you want us to do? Just pack up, right now, and pull out?'

'Wouldn't be a bad idea.'

'Except for one thing. Our car's about seven miles from here. We're not about to hike seven miles in the dark. We'd probably break our necks.'

'I can give you a lift in my canoe,' Jim offers.

'Our car's *away* from the lake.'

'I don't mean to your car. I'll take you over to Scottsdale. We can drive over and pick up your car in the morning. What do you think?'

'I don't know,' Kristi says, and gets to her feet. She gestures. Lynn stands up. 'Give us a couple minutes to talk it over.'

Jim nods. He picks up the bota, and begins shooting a stream of wine into his mouth.

Kristi walks away from the fire, twigs and pine cones snapping under her white sneakers. Lynn follows. They stop in the darkness just beyond the area of light cast by the fire.

'Should we go with him?' Kristi asks.

Lynn shrugs.

Kristi brushes hair away from her eyes. 'What about these murders?' she asks. 'Have you heard anything about them?'

'Not a word,' Lynn says.

'Me neither. Of course, I don't read the papers.'

'Neither do I. Five murders, though. Wouldn't something like that make the six o'clock news?'

'You'd think so,' Kristi says. 'This is really boondocks, though. Maybe they're keeping it quiet.'

'I don't know.' Lynn steps close to Kristi. 'I think . . .'

'Whew! Didn't you bring any deodorant?'

Lynn sniffs the armpits of her sweatshirt. 'Isn't me: Anyway, look. Maybe this Jim-guy made it all up.'

'What for?' Kristi asks.

'Who knows? Maybe he wants to get us dependent on him, so we'll let our guard down. Maybe he wants to get our equipment in his canoe, and steal it. Hell, maybe he gets his kicks drowning campers . . .'

'You've got a wild imagination, Lynn.'

'I'm just thinking of the possibilities.'

'Look, we've got to make up our minds.'

'You decide for us.'

'No! You can't put it all on me. Give me a yes or no. Come on, Lynn. Do you want to pack up and go with him in his canoe, or not?'

'A yes or no?'

'Right.'

Lynn shakes her head, and pushes a hand through her short, bristly hair. Turning, she looks for a long time at Jim. He is drinking more wine. 'Okay,' she says, her voice whiny with defeat. 'No.'

'Are you sure?'

'I'm sure,' she says reluctantly. 'Maybe he's telling the truth, but I don't want to go with him. Not in a canoe, I can't even swim.'

'All right, it's settled.' Kristi turns away.

'Wait.'

'Yeah?'

'What if he won't leave?'

Kristi frowns. 'Did you have to say that?'

Then they both return to the fire. Kristi makes it brief. 'We decided to stay here.'

'I was afraid of that.'

'Thank you for the offer, and for warning us, but . . .' She shrugs.

'You decided to take your chances,' he finishes for her.

'That's about it.'

'Well, thanks for the wine.' He stands. 'I'd better be on my way. I saw another fire, down at the south end. I'd better let *them* know. Good luck, ladies.'

Without another word, he walks into the darkness. Kristi and Lynn wait for a few seconds, then quietly follow him. They stand close together. Looking down the slope, they watch him climb into his canoe, and shove off. They watch for a long time, until the sound of his paddle dipping into the water disappears in a whisper of wind.

Then they return to the fire, and sit down.

'Maybe we ought to put it out,' Lynn says, looking tense.

Kristi shrugs. 'Why bother? If the ax-man's around, he already knows where to find us.'

'Don't say that!'

'Let's have some more wine, and forget about it, okay? That guy was probably just some kook who gets his laughs scaring people.'

'Geez, I hope so.'

Kristi lifts the bota and squeezes a long, thin stream of wine into her mouth. As she passes the leather bag to Lynn, a shape moves silently among the trees behind them.

Lynn raises the bota. She squirts into her mouth.

The shape moves into the shimmering light of the fire. It is a man. He wears black, leather pants. His bare chest is shiny in the firelight. A black hood covers his head. His eyes glisten through holes in the hood. In his hands, he holds a double-bit ax.

'I think I'm ready to hit the sack,' Kristi says. 'One more for the road.' She reaches out for the wine bag.

Lynn holds it out to her.

With a grunt, the man swings the ax in a swift, sideways blow. It chops through Lynn's neck. Her head flies, tumbling. It rolls into the campfire.

For an instant, she sits there headless, still holding out the bota to Kristi as blood spouts from her neck stump and rains down.

Kristi screams.

The bota drops. The body topples forward, shouldering into the campfire, scattering flaming branches across the ground.

Kristi screams and screams as she jumps to her feet and tries to run. The man grabs her shirt collar. He throws her to the ground.

On her back, Kristi gazes up at him.

275

He laughs, and pulls away his hood. His face is gaunt, his wet eyes bulging, his mouth writhing with a terrible grin.

'I am Schreck,' he says.

He raises the ax high overhead, and brings it down.

It knocks through Kristi's upthrust hands, and splits her face.

Todd turned off the machine.

Freya flicked on the lights, and saw his wide grin. She turned to Tango, who wore a smirk.

'Well ladies, what do you think?'

'That's one baaad dude,' said Tango. 'Wouldn't want to mess with him.' She laughs. 'No sir, no way.'

Todd looked amused. 'What about you, Freya?'

'Fantastic!'

'I thought you might enjoy it.'

'How'd you do that?' Tango asked. 'I mean, how'd you do that with the head?'

'Just chopped it off.'

Tango laughed. 'I know, it's a trade secret. I'll lay odds you used a dummy.'

'Very astute, young lady.'

'Sure looked real.'

'I appreciate the compliment.' Todd removed three scripts from a manila folder, and passed them out. 'I've underlined your parts. Tango, you're Kristi. Freya, you're Lynn. I, of course, will play myself. Take a few minutes to look them over.'

After glancing through her script, Freya spent the remaining time looking over Tango. The girl knew she was being watched, and seemed to approve. As she read, she casually loosened her vest. She twisted in such a way that a nipple appeared in the laces.

Todd paid no attention.

She was doing it for Freya alone.

'Ready?' Todd asked.

'Ready when you are,' Tango said. 'How come we're doing this? You know what I mean? I'm just curious, is all.' She fluttered the script. 'This looks like just what they said except for their names and a couple things. Maybe I'm just ignorant, but it seems kind of funny to me.'

'Their voices simply aren't what I want,' said Todd.

She shrugged. 'It's your dime, honey.'

'Let's begin.'

# Chapter Fifteen

They walked along the balcony to the door of Connie's apartment. She pushed her key toward the lock, but Pete stopped her hand.

'Let me,' he said.

'I didn't catch that,' said Connie. 'The light's off.'

Pete shook his head. He took the key from her, and opened the apartment door. No lights were on inside, either, so he didn't bother to speak. He stepped into the room, ahead of her, and found a light switch on the wall. A lamp beside the couch came on.

'You're certainly acting mysterious,' she said.

'Just careful. Some guys, when they're dumped, they do crazy things.'

'Dal's never been violent,' she said.

'That you know of.'

'I don't think he'd do anything to hurt me.'

Pete shrugged. 'If he bought an engagement ring, he's serious enough to be a threat. I ran into a guy once, he threw his fiancée out a fourteenth-story window because some fellow sent her flowers for her birthday. Turned out, they came from her brother.'

'You're full of grim stories,' Connie said, smiling as if she wanted more. 'Would you like a drink?'

'Ah, a libation,' he said, doing his Fields voice. 'Nothing I'd rather partake of, my dear.' It was out of his mouth before he realized she probably wouldn't understand his distorted lip movements. He didn't have time for embarrassment to set in, though.

'Come up and see me sometime,' she said.

He laughed. 'You're remarkable.'

'When I'm bad, I'm better.'

He took hold of her hands. 'Very true,' he said. 'You were very, very bad this afternoon.'

Her face, still flushed from a day in the sun, turned a deeper red. 'You were pretty bad, yourself. Now, what would you like, a beer?'

'Great.'

They went into the kitchen and Connie took two bottles of Budweiser from the refrigerator. 'Want a glass?' she asked.

'The bottle's fine. I think I'll use the facilities first, though.'

'Right through there.' She pointed.

Pete used the toilet, but didn't return immediately to the living room. First, he stepped into another room and turned on the light. Connie's office. He stepped past cluttered, metal bookshelves and opened a closet door.

'What're you doing?'

He turned to Connie. She stood in the doorway, frowning slightly.

'Just snooping.'

'You're looking for Dal. You think he's hiding somewhere, just waiting for you to leave so he can jump out and cut my throat.'

'It happens.'

'You worry me, Pete, you know that?'

'Can't be too careful.'

'I think you *can* be too careful. If you have to spend your life looking over your shoulder, always afraid there might be some terrible villain back there just waiting for you to let your guard down so he can jump you ... Yeah, I think you can be too careful. Where's the fun, if you're always on your toes for disaster to strike?'

'Oh, I have my share.'

'Shall I show you the bedroom, or have you already checked it out?'

'Not yet.'

He followed her into the bedroom, and grinned as she rushed to the bed, dropped to her knees, and peered under the draping coverlet. 'What on *earth?*' She reached into the space beneath the bed. 'I wonder what that ... *aaah!*' Her body lurched forward. Belly down, she twisted and kicked. She clutched the bedframe as if to keep herself from being pulled under.

Pete ran to her side. He reached down for the bedframe, ready to fling it aside, when Connie grabbed his hand.

He saw her smile.

'That wasn't funny,' he said.

'Yes it was.'

She pulled him down to her, and kissed him.

When his hand slid under her blouse, he was surprised to feel the smooth, bare skin of her breast. She must've taken her bikini off while he was in the bathroom. He pulled the blouse up. The nipple was rigid in his mouth, and had a slightly salty taste.

He moved a hand under her skirt. Up her thigh. Her bikini pants were also gone.

'You're a darling.' he said.

She didn't answer. Of course not. His mouth was on her breast.

He raised his head. Connie's eyes lowered to his lips.

'You're a darling,' he repeated.

With a smile, she reached both hands inside his shorts, and held him.

'Would you like your beer now?' Connie asked.

'It's probably warm.'

'We'll make believe we're in Ireland, drinking lukewarm Guinness in a pub.'

'I'd rather be here,' Pete said.

'Back in a jiffy.' As she climbed off the bed, Pete patted her bare rump. She walked to the bedroom door and looked back at him. He lay on the sheets, hands folded under his head, his limp penis lying against his thigh. 'Have you no modesty?' she asked.

'A little late for that.'

'True,' she said.

There'd been plenty of modesty, that afternoon, when he took her into his house near Venice beach. A lot of drinking on the couch, a lot of talking until the right moment came and he took her into his arms. They wore only their swimsuits. Hands stroked exposed skin, moved hesitantly over the fabric, and finally explored beneath the swimsuits. At last, they were naked against each other, slick from suntan oil and sweat, gritty with sand, and they made love on the couch.

They showered together.

They ate hamburgers.

They made love again, this time on the fresh sheets of Pete's bed.

After all that, Connie realized, she still felt modest in front of him. To go for the drinks, stark naked, seemed slightly daring, slightly naughty, as if she were flaunting her nudity to arouse him.

Still in the doorway, she stared at his penis. She lowered her hands, and caressed her thighs.

Pete shook his head, grinning. 'What're you up to?' he asked.

'Oh, nothing.'

Her thumbs slid against her groin, and she watched his penis rise.

'Forget the beer,' he said.

'Can't. We've got to replenish our vital fluids.'

She turned from him. She felt sexy and silly and bold – and happier than she'd been since . . . No, don't think about Dave.

Too late.

But the memory didn't hurt, the way it always had. Strange. Very strange.

She stepped into the living-room.

'Having fun?' Dal asked. He was on the couch, sitting with both feet on the floor and his back straight.

Connie slapped her hands to her breasts and spun away. She hurried into the bedroom.

Pete was already up.

281

'Stay here,' Connie said. 'I'll take care of it.' She jerked her robe from its closet hook, and put it on as she rushed into the hallway.

Dal still sat on the couch. 'You couldn't even wait for me to move out,' he said.

'I . . . I didn't expect you.'

'Where'd you think I'd be – at my *girlfriend's* house?'

'Dal, please.'

'Our bed.'

'It's my bed.'

'Christ, you should've heard yourselves carrying on.'

'You shouldn't have listened.'

'You're my girl, Connie.'

'Not anymore.'

'You'll always be my girl. I love you. Just remember that, when he dumps you. He will, you know. Once he's tired of you, he'll dump you. I've seen his type. Jaguar, beach house, rugged good looks. I give you about a week.'

'Get out of here.'

'A week, and you'll come running to me, you'll come begging.'

'Come back at noon tomorrow. Your belongings will be outside the door waiting for you.'

'You'll come begging,' he said again. Then he left.

# Chapter Sixteen

'Okay, ladies, that wraps it up.' Todd took out his wallet, and paid Tango with twenty-dollar bills – ten of them.

'Don't you get paid?' she asked Freya.

'I'm a partner.'

'Ah, so.'

'You go on ahead, Todd, I'll drive Tango home.'

'Far be it from me to stand in the way of true romance. Be sure to lock up when you leave.'

'I will.'

When Todd was gone, they left the control room. Freya led Tango by the hand. They entered a room at the end of the hall, and Freya turned on the lights.

'You're so beautiful,' she said. She reached for the laces of Tango's vest.

'Ah-ah. No freebies, honey.'

'How much?'

'Depends what you want.'

Freya opened her purse. Her hands shook as she drew out her billfold. She counted the cash. To her dismay, she found only a ten-dollar bill, and three ones.

'For that, honey, you get diddle-shit.'

'I . . . I have plenty more at home. I thought I had . . .'

Tango smiled. 'That's all right. You just take me to where the money is. This old house is a bit too haunty for my taste, anyhow.'

'I want you here, Tango.'

'No money, no fuckee.'

Freya sighed. 'Well, let's go to my apartment, then.'

They left the bedroom, and walked down the narrow hallway. Freya watched their strange, faint shadows on the walls. She remembered how Tina had danced and twirled as if fascinated by those shadows. Oh, how she would love to see Tango doing that . . . If only she had brought more cash along. Another night, maybe.

They descended the stairway. Neither spoke. The wood creaked under their weight.

They crossed the foyer.

Freya reached for the doorknob.

It didn't turn. Alarmed, she glanced at Tango.

'Let me try.' Tango struggled with the latch and knob. 'Shit, lady, that sucker's locked.'

'There's a back way out,' Freya said.

'There better be.'

She led the way, turning on lights as she went. They passed through a dining-room with a chandelier hanging over a large, mahogany table. Crystal goblets glimmered on the shelves of the highboy. Freya paused to admire them. Someday, they would all belong to her.

'Move,' Tango said. 'I want *outa* here.'

Freya pushed through a swinging door to the kitchen. She turned on the light, and stopped so abruptly that Tango bumped her.

She stumbled forward.

The man in the white apron and chef's hat clutched her arm. and flung her aside.

'I want dark meat,' Schreck said.

Swinging around, Tango threw herself at the door. She wasn't quick enough. He grabbed her hair and jerked her toward him. Hooking an arm around her throat, he lifted her.

Tango squirmed and kicked. Her boot heels thudded against Schreck's shins, but had no effect. Veins stood out on her face and her eyes bulged from the pressure of his grip. Her struggles, frantic at first, became feeble.

She was carried to a counter.

Freya got to her feet, watching.

'Stay out of the shot,' Schreck muttered.

He lifted Tango onto the counter.

Freya spotted the camera on a swivel mount near the ceiling. Todd had made no attempt to hide this one. He must've installed it this afternoon. It was directly above the counter where Schreck had placed Tango.

'Cut the laces,' Freya said.

'Shut up.'

'Come on, do it.'

'Leave,' said Schreck.

'I want to watch.'

'You want to watch?' He picked up a meat cleaver and swung around. 'Out!' he roared.

'It's all right with Todd if I . . .'

Schreck suddenly grinned. 'Come here.'

Her skin pricked. She shook her head.

'Come here! You want to watch.'

'No. That's . . .'

'Come here, or I kill you.'

She hesitated, wondering if she should try to run. She didn't dare. With slow, unsteady steps, she approached Schreck.

She watched his eyes. They were wet and bulging. They were somehow like spiders. They gave her goose-bumps, and nauseated her.

He gripped her arm.

'Watch,' he said.

Tango moaned.

Schreck put down the cleaver.

'Watch, but don't touch.'

'Help me,' Tango whispered.

Schreck picked up a knife and two-pronged carving fork.

Freya's fear turned to excitement as he sliced through the laces and opened Tango's vest.

The woman raised her head. She looked at Freya. 'Please . . .'

'Head down,' said Schreck, and plunged the fork into her eye.

Freya spun away. She doubled over, vomiting. Before she was done, Schreck jerked her upright by the hair.

'You want to watch,' he explained. 'Mustn't miss a moment.'

# Chapter Seventeen

After Connie insisted he leave, Dal headed for Elizabeth's house. Halfway there, he changed his mind. If he went to her, he would have to admit defeat; a temporary set-back, at least. Elizabeth wouldn't like that.

He might lose her.

Rather than chance that, he decided to spend the night in a motel. He found a room at the Palm Court, just off Pico. It was a tiny room, but clean.

The television picture had shadows.

The bed had Magic Fingers, but Dal had no quarter.

He felt very depressed as he climbed into bed. For a long time, he couldn't sleep. All so damned complicated. He only wanted Elizabeth. To get her, though – to keep her – he had to marry Connie.

Not necessarily.

He only had to get rich.

*Only.*

If it were easy to get rich, he'd have done it long before now.

He could think of only one way to do it: marry money. Must be plenty of rich gals around town. But he only knew one.

Damn, he was halfway to home base before this Peter stuck his nose into the picture.

Sure, his nose. Stuck in more than that, the bastard.

Look on the bright side, though: maybe he *will* dump Connie. Could happen.

Especially with a little help.

Dal lay with his eyes shut, oblivious to the noise of cars passing just outside his window, and thought about ways to help.

In the morning, he woke up feeling good. He took a long, hot shower. Then he went for a walk. He ate a breakfast of sausage and eggs at Sambos. At a Drug Mart down the street, he brought an injector razor, a can of shaving cream, and roll-on deodorant.

Couldn't face Elizabeth looking like a bum.

Grinning, he returned to his motel room. He shaved, rubbed the sticky ball on his armpits, and checked out.

He practiced his story as he drove to Elizabeth's house.

She opened the door, looking as radiant as Dal felt. She wore a silken robe that matched her green eyes. It was belted loosely shut. It barely hung low enough to cover her groin.

'You look beautiful this morning,' Dal said.

'Don't stand there gawking. Get in here and kiss me.'

He gladly obeyed. As he kissed her, his hands roamed down the slick robe and under it. He squeezed the cool skin of her rump. He pressed her tightly against him.

'I don't have much time,' he said. 'Connie's at church. I just had to stop by, though.'

'Did it go well?'

'It went great. Unbelievable.'

'Tell me.'

'Later,' he said, grinding his hardness against her.

'Now,' she said. She pushed herself away, and walked ahead of him into the living-room. She sat on a white davenport. and put her feet up.

Dal sat by her feet. 'I did just as you suggested. I bought her flowers, on my way home yesterday.'

'And did she like them?'

'She loved them. Absolutely loved them. She cried, and apologized for the way she burnt dinner, and wanted to know where I'd spent the night.'

'What did you tell her?'

'That I'd spent most of it just driving around aimlessly, in a daze. And that I'd finally parked on a quiet street, somewhere, and gone to sleep on the backseat.'

'Lovely,' Elizabeth said. Her foot patted his thigh.

'Oh, Connie ate it up. I've never seen her look more guilty.'

'I hope you quickly moved in for the kill.'

'You'd have been proud of me.'

'Would I?'

'While Connie was crying and full of remorse, I took her into my arms and said, "Why don't I take you out for dinner, tonight, and we'll have a good time and forget all about our little quarrel."'

'And did you?'

'We did.'

'Bravo.'

Dal patted the lightly tanned top of her foot, and moved his hand up her shin. 'We went to a quiet, French restaurant . . .'

'Which one?'

'Henri's.'

'Ah, lovely.'

'And I proposed to her.'

'Did she accept?'

'How could she refuse?'

Dal slipped his hand beneath her upraised leg, and caressed the smoothness of her calf.

'She did accept?'

'Of course. And I gave her the ring.'

'Did it fit?'

'It was a bit tight. We'll take it to a jeweler, next week, and have it expanded.'

'She liked the ring?'

'She was flabbergasted. She said, "It's magnificent." I think she was a bit shocked to think I would spend that kind of money, but I didn't hear her complain.'

'So, you are now an engaged man.'

'Yep.'

'When's the big day?'

'July thirty-first.'

Elizabeth grinned. She swung her leg upward, and propped it on the back of the couch. 'Let me be the first to congratulate you, dear.'

'I don't want to,' Connie said.

'It won't take long,' Pete told her. 'I'll give you a hand. Both hands, if you prefer.'

'I'd really rather not. Let's just go somewhere. He can come in and get the stuff, himself. If I put it outside, I'd be worried someone might take it.'

'That'd be too bad.'

'I'm the one who'd feel guilty about it.'

'You aren't afraid he'll come in and tear the place up?'

'Dal? No. He's basically pretty timid.'

'Those are the kind who go haywire when things get rough.'

'Really, Pete, you worry too much.'

'You keep telling me.'

'Because it's true.'

'Even paranoiacs have enemies.'

She smiled. 'I know. And a broken clock is right twice a day. More coffee?'

'I'll get it.'

Pete left her. Alone on the private, rear balcony, she moved her lawn chair closer to the railing so her face would be in the sunlight. She sat back, and took a deep breath. The morning breeze was cool, the sun hot. She wondered if she had ever felt this good before.

Sure. Yesterday. And Friday night.

Being with Pete.

It was like being reborn – young and fresh and happy, the day ahead full of promise.

He came back, and handed her the coffee mug. He sat down on the chair facing her.

'How about going to the Marina for a champagne brunch?' he asked.

'Great!'

# Chapter Eighteen

Freya stayed home from work Monday morning. She called in sick. Though she felt fine as she dialed, her heart began to race and her stomach suddenly hurt when Dr Eginton answered the phone.

Sheila Eginton, Dean of Women, the condescending bitch.

'I do hope it's nothing serious,' she said.

'I do too,' said Freya, making her voice tight as if holding back a groan of pain. 'I . . . I'm going to the doctor this morning.'

'I see. We'll do our best to forge along without you.'

'Fine.'

'Do take care of yourself.'

'I will.' She hung up.

Well, she wouldn't have to put up with bitch Eginton much longer. If everything went as planned, she'd be kissing the job good-bye at the end of the summer quarter.

Too bad she couldn't get Edgy out to Todd's house. She'd love to see her in Schreck's hands. The dean was too big, though; her disappearance would cause a stink.

So far, their caution had paid off.

Only the disappearance of the camping girls got any play in the news. Todd had been a bit careless there. Overconfident, maybe. But he assured Freya that he would hang onto that tape, not even send it to the lab for conversion to 35mm, until the thing had blown over.

Then there was the business with Tina. That should've worked perfectly; neither Tina nor her boyfriend had living parents to miss them. Tina moved out, ran off with the guy, and left no forwarding address. That was supposed to be the story if anyone asked. Freya should've stuck to it when the roommate called. That'd been a dumb mistake. But who would think the gal'd keep pushing it?

Well, they took care of that little problem. Nobody had popped up, yet, asking about her. A good sign. Maybe she hadn't even been missed. Could be trouble, though, when they showed the film.

Good old Brit might have friends who frequent the Haunted Palace.

Shit, why worry? With the over-dub and dyed hair, who would recognize her?

Should've dyed Tina's hair. Couldn't, of course, the way it was shot. Probably wouldn't be able to do it with Chelsea, either. The gal has to be under control, for that. Like what's-her-face in the *Inquisitor* film. Or that moronic hitchhiker Todd picked up for his first one, *Schreck the Executioner*.

A small change of appearance, like that, was probably enough to keep folks from recognizing their friends.

If she could think of a way to disguise Chelsea . . . What the shit, Chelsea's from Oakland. That's a long, long way from L.A.

Freya poured herself a cup of tea, and glanced at the kitchen clock. Seven-thirty.

Banks open at ten.

Chelsea the Pig should arrive by eleven.

Plenty of time to kill. She went into the living room, turned on the television, and switched the channel to *Good Morning, America*.

At 10:32, the doorbell rang. Freya got up, tugging at her tight shorts, and opened the door.

Chelsea, a cheerless smile spreading her cheeks, waved a

handful of green in Freya's face. 'Six hundred bucks,' she said. 'Didn't think I'd be here, did you?'

'I never doubted for a moment.'

Today, her T-shirt read, 'Save a tree – eat a beaver'.

Freya took the money. She stood in the doorway, counting it. Six hundred dollars, in fifties.

'Receipt, please.'

'Of course. Come on in.' As she filled out a receipt, she said, 'Are you always this obnoxious, Chelsea?'

'When it suits me.'

'Suppose we call a truce? I'll help you bring your stuff up, and I'll even take you out to dinner, tonight, to celebrate.'

'You'll pay?'

'Of course.' She waved the six hundred at Chelsea. 'I just came into a lot of money.'

'You're a doozy.'

They went down to the street. Freya saw a dull, gray van plastered with bumper stickers: NUKE IRAN; PLEASE TAIL-GATE – I NEED THE MONEY; I NEVER HAD IT; I BRAKE FOR MIDGETS; STILLBORNS HAVE MORE FUN, and half a dozen others.

'Your van, I presume.'

'How'd you guess?'

As they unloaded it, Freya appraised the goods. Not much looked promising. The stereo, portable television, and type-writer might bring in a few bucks, but everything else looked like junk.

'Where you taking me for dinner?'

'It's a lovely restaurant up the coast.'

'Up the coast? How *far* up the coast?

'Only about fifteen minutes,' Freya said.

'There's gotta be someplace closer.'

'Nothing this nice. It has a lovely view of the ocean.'

'Do I have to dress up?'

'Is it possible?'

'Now who's obnoxious?'

'You look very nice,' Freya said when Chelsea came out of the bedroom in a dress that looked like an old table cloth.

'I pass inspection?'

'With flying colors.'

They went down to Freya's car.

'Fifteen minutes?'

'About that. Maybe a little longer. The place is worth it, though. Best food you've ever tasted.'

'Hope they serve plenty,' Chelsea said. 'I could eat a horse.'

'They don't serve horses.'


'You said fifteen minutes.'

'We're almost there,' Freya said. The sun was higher above the ocean than last time, and made the driving easier.

'Lot of trouble to go through for a dinner.'

'This place is special.'

'So you say.'

'Wait till you see it.'

When Freya swung onto the turnoff, Chelsea said, 'You've got to be kidding. There's no restaurant up there.'

Fortunately, Todd had remembered to leave the gate open. That would've really aroused Chelsea's suspicion. So far, she didn't seem worried – only curious.

When Chelsea saw the house, she shook her head. 'That's it?'

'That's it.'

'Is this a joke?'

'It's a restaurant. The finest restaurant for miles.'

'I'll believe it when I see it.'

294

A single car, a blue Plymouth, was parked in front. Freya pulled alongside it.

'If this place is so great,' Chelsea said, 'why's there only one car?'

'It's very exclusive.'

Freya climbed from the car. Chelsea opened her door against the Plymouth, and squeezed out. 'Couldn't park any closer to it, could you?'

Freya smiled. 'Don't be a spoilsport.'

'This is sport?'

They headed for the porch stairs. As they started up, the front door opened. Todd stepped out, wearing a tux. He held the door wide.

'Ah,' he said. 'Young ladies, we've been expecting you. Welcome to Hillside Manor. I am Clarence, the maitre d'.'

They followed him into the foyer.

'As you see, young ladies, Hillside Manor is a most unusual restaurant. It is the home of Rudolph Webb, noted chef and author of *Webb's Cuisine*. He opened his home to the public, fifteen years ago, as a – shall we say – testing ground for his recipes.'

They entered the dining-room. The long, mahogany table was set for three. Todd seated Freya and Chelsea across from each other near the head of the table.

'As diners here,' he continued, 'you shall be partners in the creation of an original dish. Would you care for a cocktail before dinner is served?'

'Gin and tonic,' Chelsea said.

'I'll have white wine. The house wine, please.'

'Splendid.'

Todd turned away, and disappeared through the swinging door to the kitchen.

'This is weird,' Chelsea said. 'We're guinea pigs for this chef, huh?'

'Guinea pigs never had it so good.'

'How did you find this joint?'

'A date brought me here. I was awfully nervous, at first. I didn't really believe it was a restaurant. I thought he'd tricked me, and brought me here for some kind of mischief. It is a rather creepy old house. But I was in for a pleasant shock. We had duck in some kind of marvelous wine sauce. Probably the best meal I'd ever had.'

Todd returned with the drinks. Freya raised her glass of wine. 'Here's blood in your eye.'

'Mud,' Chelsea corrected.

'Whatever.'

They drank.

Chelsea nodded toward the place setting at the head of the table. 'Is somebody going to join us?'

'Oh yes. The chef himself. He'll come out, after the food is prepared.'

'Wonderful,' Chelsea muttered.

'You'll enjoy it. He really is quite a fascinating guy.'

'The food better be good. I'd hate to barf in front of the chef.'

'Young ladies – your host, Rudolph Webb.'

Todd held open the kitchen door, and Schreck entered the dining-room. He walked stiffly to the table, his lean face solemn, and held out a hand toward Chelsea.

The girl made a sickly smile, but shook the offered hand.

'Welcome,' said Schreck. 'You are?'

'Chelsea.'

He stopped around the table. Freya shuddered as he took her hand. In his black tuxedo, he looked to Freya like an undertaker.

A pallid, gaunt undertaker who spent too much time with his corpses.

'I'm Freya,' she said.

'Yes, I remember. Welcome again to my home.'

He sat. Todd poured red wine into his glass. He raised it to his thin lips. As he drank, a trickle slid from one corner of his mouth and dripped from his chin. He didn't seem to notice. When he emptied the glass, Todd filled it again.

'Refresh the ladies' drinks,' Schreck commanded. 'Then serve the soup.'

Todd took their glasses away.

'The first course,' said Schreck, 'will be a delicate soup of meat and herbs. I'm certain you will find it most unusual, rather like the Mexican albondigas, but more hearty.' He grinned, his lips drawing back to reveal crooked, dark teeth and pale gums.

Todd brought the drinks. Freya found her hand shaking as she raised the glass. Chelsea met her eyes, and glared.

'I eat with my guests,' said Schreck, 'so that I might have the opportunity to savour their reactions as they savour my cuisine. It is an indulgence on my part, but I believe we should permit ourselves to enjoy the effects of our creative efforts. I am, if you please, the playwright attending the opening night performance of his drama – gauging audience reaction, thrilling to the laughter and tension and applause, noting lapses where, perhaps, the script might require an adjustment.'

Todd entered, pushing a serving cart. He set a bowl of soup at each place, and returned to the kitchen.

Freya eyed the brown, lumpy liquid in her bowl. It looked identical to the soup in front of Chelsea and Schreck. Todd had assured her, though . . .

'*Bon appetit*,' said Schreck.

He dipped a spoon deep into his bowl, and brought up bits of meat along with onions and other limp vegetables. The spoon dripped as he raised it to his mouth. He chewed slowly, as if probing the mixture for its subtle flavors. Then he swallowed, and sighed with pleasure.

Freya, fighting to control her nausea, took a sip of wine.

She picked up her spoon, slid it into her soup, and stirred as she watched Chelsea take her first taste.

The girl's spoon shimmered with broth. She sipped it, nodded, and smiled nervously at Schreck. 'Delicious,' she said.

Freya continued to stir. Mine's only Iamb, she told herself. But she couldn't bring herself to try it. She watched Chelsea bring up a spoonful from the bottom. It was laden with vegetables and chunks of meat. It vanished into Chelsea's mouth. The girl chewed, and nodded.

Freya's stomach convulsed. Vomit came to her throat. She swallowed hard, and finished her wine.

'It's great,' Chelsea said. 'Best soup I've ever had.'

Schreck grinned and nodded.

'I normally don't care much for soup,' she continued. 'It's usually so bland.' She shoveled in another spoonful. And another. 'Have you tried it?' she asked Freya.

Freya nodded. 'Excellent.'

'Will this be in your next cookbook?'

'Most certainly,' said Schreck.

'I'd really like the recipe.' She spooned more into her mouth. As she chewed, she said, 'What kind of meat is it?'

'Can you guess?'

'I don't know. Pork?'

'No.'

She raised a spoonful, and gazed at it. With her teeth, she picked out a chunk of meat and ate it separately. She shrugged. 'What is it, rabbit or something?'

Schreck grinned. 'You're getting warm.'

She finished the spoonful, dredged the bottom of her dish, and came up with a larger piece. She studied it. 'Hey, this one's still got the bone.' With her free hand, she lifted it from the spoon and turned it over. Freya glanced at the small, shiny shield of nail.

Chelsea dropped the piece as if it burnt her. It splashed into her soup. She shoved her chair back, but Schreck grabbed her arm.

'What was it?' he asked.

'A . . . a *toe*!'

'Oh dear, you guessed correctly.' Schreck chuckled.

Chelsea gagged. She tried to struggle free from Schreck's grip, but couldn't. She threw up on herself, and began to cry.

Todd entered with the white wine. 'I hope you're enjoying your meal,' he said, smiling.

'Yes,' said Schreck. 'I believe we're ready for the next course.'

'Very good.'

'Leave the bottle,' Freya said. She filled her glass, quickly drank it all, and filled it again.

Chelsea continued to cry.

'I don't understand,' said Schreck, 'why you're so upset. Only moments ago, you were raving about its flavor.'

'You're *crazy*!' Chelsea sobbed.

'I'm sure you'll appreciate the next course even more.'

Todd brought in a platter and set it down in front of Chelsea.

Chelsea began to scream.

'A true delicacy. Lightly simmered visage over steaming linguini, topped with a delicate tomato sauce. I call it Face Marinara.'

Freya watched, disgusted and fascinated, as Schreck threw Chelsea to the floor and forced her to eat.

He pinched her nostrils shut so she had to open her mouth.

He snapped her fingers.

He tore open her dress and stabbed her with a fork.

At last, she choked on a mouthful of scorched flesh. She kicked and convulsed and turned blue and died.

Todd entered the room, clapping. 'Bravo, bravo!'

He slapped Schreck on the back.

'Satisfied?' he asked Freya.

She nodded. 'Thanks,' she said.

'Well, shall we retire to the control room, and see what Bruno got for us?'

'Todd,' Schreck said, and nodded towards the corpse.

'Certainly. She's all yours.'

As Schreck picked up the body, Freya followed Todd from the room. She grabbed his arm. 'Mine *was* lamb, wasn't it?'

'Princess,' he said, 'what kind of beast do you think I am?'

# Chapter Nineteen

Connie did a lot of good work, Tuesday. The scenes filled her head as if she had become Sandra Dane. She could smell the sour breath of Sandra's stepfather as he fell upon her. She could feel his weight, and his rough hands tearing her crinoline – hear his yelp of pain as she kneed him in the groin.

The warm night air. The smell of the stable. The feel of her stallion, Thunder, between her legs as she rode him bareback over the fields. Her sudden fear as Thunder leaped a fence, and stumbled, and she flew head over heels.

The Union soldier, one of Sherman's hateful marauders, coming to help her. He had Pete's smile, and Pete's eyes. Though she'd heard dreadful tales of Sherman's army, this man seemed different. She knew she had nothing to fear from him.

A light flashed on her desk.

Damn!

She dropped her pen on the spiral notebook, and got up. Her muscles felt stiff. She stretched as she made her way to the front door.

She half expected to find Dal outside, returning for something he would claim to have forgotten when he moved out, Sunday.

But it wasn't Dal.

It was a young woman with troubled eyes.

'Yes?'

'You're Connie, aren't you?'

'Yes.'

'May I come in, please? I have to talk with you about Pete.'

'About Pete? What's . . .?'

'I'm his wife – Sandra.'

Connie grabbed the doorknob to steady herself. 'His wife?'

'Yes.'

'That's impossible.'

The woman shook her head. 'It's quite possible, I'm afraid.'

'He would've told me.'

'Would he?'

'I've been to his house. There was no . . . He *can't* be married!'

'He took you to his beach house in Venice. That's where he always takes his . . . his women. May I come in?'

'No! You're lying! This is a trick or something.'

'I want you to stop seeing Pete. I know he . . . he can be quite overwhelming and perhaps you think you love him. He always has that effect. I've . . . I've put up with it for quite a while. God knows how many times I've thought about divorcing him. But I love him, Connie, and . . . and I've just found out that I'm pregnant. I'm going to have Pete's baby.'

'No!'

'I'm sorry. I know this must be awful for you – but think what it's like for me. My husband . . . He didn't come home, the whole weekend. He said he was on a case, but I knew it was a lie. The same old lie. So I went to the beach house, Saturday. I went in. I have a key, of course. I went in, and heard you both, and . . .' Her chin trembled. She bit down on her lower lip, and took a deep breath. 'I want my husband back, Connie. I want the father of my baby. Please. You seem like a decent person, Connie. Don't . . . don't keep my husband away from me.' She wiped tears from her eyes, and walked away.

Dal threw his necktie onto the couch, and stepped into the small kitchen area of his new apartment. He took his gin bottle from a carton on the breakfast bar. After a short search in the crowded box, he found his vermouth. He slipped a plastic cup off the end of a stack, and made himself a martini.

No olives.

Well, shit.

He opened his freezer compartment, eyed the stack of frozen dinners, and decided to eat out. No reason to eat that stuff, cramped up in this tiny apartment.

He'd taken the first furnished one-bedroom apartment he could find, on Sunday. After Connie's spacious, open place, this cubicle was enough to give him claustrophobia. Didn't even have direct access to the outside. Instead, you walk down a hallway and downstairs to get out.

He'd known, even as he carried in his few possessions, that he would hate this place.

He just had to keep reminding himself – it's not for long.

Then he met Etta, the girl across the hall, an actress, the solution to his problem.

He wondered if she'd returned yet.

Martini in hand, he crossed over to her apartment and knocked. He heard footsteps. He smiled at the peephole, and the door opened.

'Loverboy. Come on in.'

He entered admiring Etta. She was gorgeous, with a deep tan and thick blonde hair, and curves that never quit. Of course, she couldn't compare to Elizabeth.

'Did you do it?' he asked.

'Sure did, honey. Give a sip.' She took the martini from his hand, drank some, and handed it back. 'I was fabulous. You should've seen me. You? Bite my tongue. Darryl Zanuck should've seen me. Give this a listen.'

She turned on a small, cassette recorder.

For a few seconds, Dal heard the buzz of blank tape. Then came Etta's voice.

'Testing, testing, *uno, dos, tres.*'

More blank tape.

'Yes?' Connie's voice.

'You're Connie, aren't you?'

'Yes.'

He listened to all the tape. At first, the sound of Connie's voice made him ache. He wondered why he'd let himself lose her. But her shock pleased him. She really took it hard. Good. She deserved it for cheating on him. He sipped his martini. His power thrilled him – to tear apart all that trust and love by such a simple deception!

'What do you think?' Etta asked when the tape ended.

'I think you deserve an Oscar.'

'Right on.'

Dal took out his wallet. He gave her a hundred dollars, in twenties.

'If you ever need me again,' she said, 'I'll be here.'

'We'll see how this turns out.'

'Yeah, well, good luck.'

'The ring.'

'Oh! You mean I don't get to keep it?' With a laugh, she slipped it off her finger and gave it to Dal.

Briefly, he considered asking Etta to join him for supper. He decided against it, though. He didn't feel like risking a refusal. Besides, if Elizabeth found out . . .

Connie felt desolate. She took a long bath, but that didn't help. Her mind replayed the conversation, went over every minute of her times with Pete, seeking unknown answers.

She wished she'd asked the woman for proof. A driver's license. Some kind of evidence to back up her awful words.

But Connie didn't want proof.

She wanted, so much, to disbelieve the woman. She clinged to the hope that it was a mistake, or a prank, or a vicious lie.

Maybe Dal put the woman up to it. For vengeance. Or to make her drop Pete.

But she knew, even as she thought such things, that she was clutching desperately at straws.

The woman had told the truth.

Pete's married.

He'd been lying to her, twisting her emotions, encouraging her to fall in love. Trickery to get her into bed.

No, she couldn't believe that.

She didn't know what to believe.

She fell onto her bed, and stared at the ceiling. Her mind was a helpless tangle.

She looked at the clock. Nearly seven. Pete should be here by now. Unless he knows. Maybe his wife confronted him today, and he'll never come again.

She covered her eyes with a pillow, then quickly flung the pillow aside. If her eyes were covered, she wouldn't see the doorbell light.

It began to flash.

Her stomach knotted. She felt as if she might vomit.

*Please, let it be Pete.*

She left the bedroom.

*Let him tell me it's a lie. Please, make it not be true.*

She opened the door, and it was Pete. He smiled, and stepped toward her. She held out a hand to stop him.

'Don't,' she said.

'What's wrong?'

'You're married.'

His face turned ashen.

'Admit it. You're married!'

'How . . . How did you find out?'

# Chapter Twenty

Pete swung his foot into the doorway. The door hit it, stopped against his shoe. With his shoulder, he forced the gap wider. 'Connie, let me in. Let me in, damn it.'

She said nothing. She made whimpery, grunting sounds as she tried to hold the door shut.

Then it was open. She stepped back, shaking her head and crying.

'Listen to me. I love you, Connie. Listen to me.'

'Oh Pete, how could you? How could you do this to me, to Sandra?'

'Who's Sandra?'

'Your wife, for Christsake! She was here today. She knows all about us.'

'My wife's name is Barbara. She knows nothing about us, and couldn't give a damn what I do.'

'That's impossible.'

'It's true.' Pete took hold of Connie's shoulders. 'She left me. We were only married for two years. We lived in the beach house: Barbara and me and her brother. He was a college student. He paid a third of the monthly mortgage, and . . . the thing is, he and my wife were lovers. Apparently, it had been going on for years. It's still going on, for all I know. The only reason she married me, in the first place, was to make her arrangement with her brother look innocent. I just happened to stumble over them, one day. They thought I was going to kill them, or something, so they both lit out. That's the last I ever saw of my wife.'

'Oh Pete.' She hugged him tightly. 'I thought . . . I was so afraid . . .'

He stroked her hair, then moved back so she could see his lips. 'I haven't seen or heard from my wife in nearly a year.'

'Then who . . .? A woman came here this afternoon, Pete. She said she's your wife, Sandra, and that she's pregnant, and wants me to stop seeing you.'

'What did she look like?' he asked.

'She was about my height, blonde, very attractive.'

Brit Anderson? That hardly seemed likely. Their relationship hadn't been serious enough to warrant such a drastic maneuver. He'd only gone out with her a few times, they'd never had sex, and he hadn't seen her for nearly two weeks. If she were so upset by his neglect, she would've been in touch with him.

Well, she did make those two calls the day after their last date. Strange calls. She'd sounded upset. He phoned her back, several times, but no one ever answered. After meeting Connie, that Wednesday, he stopped trying to get in touch with her.

'Did you notice anything unusual about her?'

'Like scars?' Connie shook her head. 'Nothing I can think of.'

'Any jewelry?' Brit, he remembered, wore a gold chain necklace with a star.

'Not that I . . . oh, a diamond ring. I did notice that. A diamond wedding ring. It looked . . .' Her face hardened. 'It looked like the ring Dal had for me.'

'Well, wedding rings all look pretty much alike, don't they?'

'This had a Marquise diamond. You know, one that's cut so it's kind of long and pointed at both ends. They're not as common as round solitaires.'

'You think Dal might've put her up to it?'

'Who else would want to? He must be trying to break us up.'

'He'll have to do better than that,' Pete said.

'A lot better,' said Connie. She moved into his arms, and pressed herself close against him. 'A lot better,' she whispered.


Pete spent the next day in his van, keeping watch on the employee parking lot of the Masters Hardware warehouse. According to a tip received by the general manager, a guy named Jesse Cook was the culprit. Every worker in the warehouse knew it, apparently, but only one had been willing to blow the whistle – anonymously, at that.

A simple operation. Cook would walk out, during lunch, and put a case of Schlage locks into his trunk. Or an electric heater, or a food processor, or whatever happened to strike his fancy.

Pete had been hired to catch Cook in the act. This was his third day on the job. So far, Cook had tried nothing.

At quitting time, the wiry little guy came out to his Firebird empty-handed, and left.

Pete reported his lack of progress to the general manager.

'Let's give it till the end of the week,' the man said. 'If he hasn't tipped his hand by then, we'll try a new tack.'

Immediately after leaving, Pete drove into Santa Monica. He left his van in a parking structure on Fourth Street, and walked to the old mall.

Lane Brothers was still open. He entered, and stepped toward the counter. There were half a dozen people in the small, quiet store. Three of the young men looked like sales clerks. One glanced at him, and quickly looked away.

Had to be Dal.

Pete ignored him. At the counter, he asked for the manager.

An older man was called from a back room. 'I'm Owen Lane. May I help you?'

'Yes.' Pete handed the man a business card for Ronald Watts, Special Assistant for Attorney General George Deukmajian. 'I'd like to question one of your employees about an investigation we're conducting.'

Owen Lane blushed. 'Of course. Who do you want to see?'

'Dal Richards.'

'Is it . . . something serious?'

'May I speak to Mr Richards, please?'

'Of course.' He turned away. 'Dal?'

Dal came forward, fastening the center button of his blazer, smiling bravely. His eyes flicked toward Pete, and quickly looked away. 'Yes, Mr Lane?'

'This gentleman is Mr Watts from the Justice Department.' To Pete, he said. 'Would you prefer to talk in my office?'

'Thank you.'

They left Owen Lane outside the door. Pete shut it, and Dal's smile fell away.

'What do you want?' he snapped.

'I'm Pete Harvey.'

'I know.'

'Yes. I figured you might. I've never met you, though. I decided, since we're both interested in Connie, that we should get acquainted.'

'Okay, we're acquainted. Good-bye.'

Pete shook his head.

'Look, I've got a customer out there . . .'

'He can wait.'

'What do you want?'

'That was a nasty trick you pulled on Connie.'

'I don't know what . . .'

'Sending my "wife" over.'

309

'You're nuts.'

'If I'm wrong, I'm sure you'll forgive me.'

'Forgive you for what?'

'Turn around, and put your hands behind your back.'

'No you . . .'

'Yes I do.' Pete spun him around and slapped a handcuff onto his left wrist.

'Hey!'

He grabbed the right hand, and cuffed it.

'Now we're walking out of here.'

'Hey, this is . . .'

'You have the right to remain silent. If you choose to give up that right, everyone in the store is going to notice you.'

'You can't do this!'

'Oh, I think I can.'

Pushing Dal ahead of him, he left the office. Owen Lane looked stunned, his face red, his mouth and eyes gaping.

'Mr Lane . . .' Dal started.

Pete shoved him forward. 'Thank you for your co-operation, Mr Lane.'

'Is he . . . under arrest?'

'I'm afraid so. Good day, sir.'

Pete steered Dal down the mall. Shoppers stared. Children on skateboards stopped and pointed. A gray-whiskered wino limped close, eyed Dal, and said, 'Trow da book at'm.'

When they reached Santa Monica Boulevard, Pete took off the cuffs.

Dal was crying softly. 'You bastard,' he said, 'I'll get you for this.'

'Have a nice day,' Pete said, and walked away.

SCREAM GEMS
PRESENTS
OTTO SCHRECK
in
SCHRECK THE MAD DOCTOR

'It won't be long now, my darling,' Schreck says, kneeling beside a bed. 'I have found the perfect specimen. She is so young, so vital. Soon, if the operation succeeds, you shall be heir to her vitality. You shall rise from your bed and walk as you once did, with the buoyancy of youth in your step. Once again, I shall take you into my arms.'

He lifts her hand. It is brown and withered as if the skin has been stretched over bare bones.

'Oh my darling Beatrice, we shall dance through the long, joyous hours of the night. Soon. Oh so soon.'

Leaning forward, he stares down at the face of the corpse. Its mouth is open, its teeth bared in a mirthless grin. He kisses its sunken cheek.

'Goodnight now, my love.'


A young woman lies on an operating table. Her body is covered by a white sheet. Her shoulders are bare.

Opening her eyes, she lifts her head and looks down at herself. She squirms, but can't raise her arms or legs.

The door swings open. Schreck enters, dressed in a green operating smock and cap. As he approaches, he ties a paper mask across his nose and mouth.

'How are you feeling?' he asks.

'Confused.'

'That's quite understandable, Miss Thatcher. Do you recall anything of the accident?'

'Accident?'

'The crash.'

'No, I . . .' She pauses, frowning. 'I remember *El Sombrero*. The Happy Hour. I went there after work and . . . Oh, the pier. A guy was going to take me to the Santa Monica pier. The carousel. You know, the famous carousel there? We were going to . . . He crashed?'

'Apparently, he'd been drinking heavily. He hit a telephone pole.'

She shakes her head. 'I don't feel . . . Was I hurt?'

'I'm afraid so, Miss Thatcher.'

'But . . .'

'You've been unconscious since they brought you in.'

'Wha . . . what's *wrong* with me?'

'Your legs.'

She strains to raise her head higher.

'We'll be operating shortly.'

'No!'

'We must. Otherwise, you may lose them.'

He takes a syringe from a tray of implements beside her bed.

'What's that?'

'It will help you relax.'

'But I feel fine!'

He peels back the sheet, uncovering her right arm. It is strapped to the table.

'No, don't!'

'This won't hurt at all,' he says, and sinks the needle into her upper arm.

'You . . . You can't operate without my permission. I don't give it. You can't have my permission.'

'I'm afraid you're in no condition to make such a decision,' he says, and removes the empty syringe from her arm. 'Relax now, Miss Thatcher.'

She wakes up screaming. Her head strains upward. She is naked on the table. Schreck stands beside her, arm pumping a saw buried deep in her thigh.

'Hurt?' he asks.

She keeps on screaming.

Below the tourniquet, Schreck continues to saw until the bone parts. Then he takes a long-bladed scalpel from the tray, and slices through the remaining muscle and flesh.'Ah-ha!' he says.

He lifts the severed leg off the table, and holds it high.

'Clean as a whistle,' he says.

The woman passes out.

Her eyelids flutter open. She is lying on a bed, no longer in the stark, bare operating room.

Groaning, she raises an arm.

She pulls the sheet off her body and gazes down at two bandaged stumps where her legs should be.

She lowers her head to the pillow, and weeps.

Soon, Schreck enters the room. 'And how are we today?' he asks.

'My . . . My legs,' she says in a weak voice.

'They had to go, I'm afraid.'

'You're . . . no doctor.'

'Oh, but I am. I must say, the operation was a great success. Now, if we're as successful with the next stage . . .'

Her chin trembles. 'No,' she says.

'Oh yes.' He pats her shoulder. 'Buck up. I'm sure we have nothing to worry about. You're young and strong. With any luck at all, you'll pull through just fine.'

After he leaves, she rolls onto her belly, whimpering with pain. She drags herself to the edge of the mattress. She reaches down to the carpet, and tries to lower herself.

Her torso drops.

Her bandaged stumps pound the floor, and she faints.

She wakes up in the operating room.

'Ah, Miss Thatcher, just in time to observe the procedure.'

Her right arm is strapped to a board beside her body. A tourniquet of surgical tubing is already tied in place.

Schreck places a scalpel against the skin of her upper arms.

'No!' she shrieks.

'We came through stage two like champs,' says Schreck, grinning down at her.

She raises her head.

No arms, no legs.

She lays her head back, and her eyelids tremble shut.

Schreck slaps her awake. 'Miss Thatcher, the procedure is complete. The artificial limbs may seem a bit awkward and painful, at the outset. But you are a very lucky young lady, very lucky indeed.'

As he pulls her to a sitting position, the sheet slides away. She begins to gasp wildly. Schreck tosses the sheet to the floor.

From the bandaged stumps of her arms hang arms. Legs protrude from her bandaged thighs.

Their brown, withered skin looks as if it has been stretched over bare bones.

A waltz is playing. Schreck, in a tuxedo, dances across the floor with Beatrice in his arms. 'You have never danced better, my darling. You seem so young, so vital tonight, as if her very essence has flowed into your veins.

'Nor have you ever looked more lovely, my Beatrice. What do you ask? Why didn't I give you a new face? How could I. This is the face that I love.' He kisses her twisted, gaping mouth.

The music changes to a tango.

'Shall we, my darling?'

Lifting one of her pale, youthful arms, he begins to dance. Her bare feet swing above the carpet, her dress billows out. Schreck spins her wildly, laughing.

He laughs, even as one of her legs drops to the floor.

'We shall dance until dawn,' he says. 'We shall dance as we have never danced before.'

The End

# Chapter Twenty-one

'Dal, what's wrong?'

He shook his head, afraid he might cry if he tried to talk. He stepped into Elizabeth's arms. He put his hands under her loose blouse and caressed the smoothness of her back.

'You didn't break up with Connie?'

'No.'

'Why aren't you with her?'

On the way over, he'd anticipated such a question. He had an answer ready. 'She thinks I'm in San Diego. On a buying trip.'

'What's wrong, then?'

'Later.' He lifted her blouse. He took her breasts in his hands, squeezed them, pressed his face between them, kissed them, licked a nipple until it was slippery and rigid, and sucked it deep into his mouth.

Elizabeth moaned and stroked his hair.

He pulled her shorts down her legs. Squeezing her buttocks, he licked a trail down her belly. He found that she had shaved her pubic hair. He licked the smooth mound. His tongue went lower. She trembled, and her fingers clenched his hair.

'Now?'

'Okay.' Dal sat up in bed and crossed his legs. Elizabeth lay in front of him, hands folded behind her head. Hair clung to her forehead with sweat. She was still breathing heavily.

Herbert, in his wheelchair a yard away, stared at her with shiny eyes.

'Well?'

'I got fired.'

'How?'

'Pete came into the store. He was furious, apparently, because Connie told him about our engagement.'

'He didn't take the rebuff kindly?'

'He had a phony police i.d. or something, and he pretended to arrest me. He handcuffed me and marched me right out of the store.'

'Subtle bastard.'

'When I got back, Mr Lane took me into his office and fired me.'

'Didn't you explain to him?'

'Yeah, of course. I don't know if he believed me or not, but he said it didn't matter. Goddamn self-righteous bastard.

He said even if I was telling the truth, that he didn't want an employee whose personal life interfered with the job.'

Elizabeth reached down and stroked his knee. 'I'm sure you can find something else.'

'Yeah. But what's to keep Pete from doing it again? He could pull that stunt every time I land a job.'

'If he posed as a cop, you might get him arrested.'

'Great. That'd *really* get him pissed at me.'

Elizabeth rolled onto her side. Her hand glided over his thigh, sending a shiver up his back. She raked the hair of his scrotum. 'Let me shave you,' she said.

Dal moaned and smiled.

'Then we'll go out and kill the bastard.'

'Pete?'

'Who else?'

'You're joking.'

'Am I? It would have to look like an accident, of course.'

'Are you serious?'

'Don't you want to?'

'I'd like him dead, that's for sure.'

'Then it's settled. Stay here. I'll get the shaving cream and razor.' She swung out of bed, patted Herbert on the cheek, and trotted into the bathroom. She returned, soon, with a wet towel, a can of Rapid Shave, and a straight razor.

'Haven't you got a safety razor?'

'Of course. But it wouldn't be half the fun.'

'Do you know how to use that?'

She knelt on the bed and looked down at her own smooth crotch. 'Does it look like it?'

'It looks great.'

'Now, we have to decide on a method that's perfectly safe. Lie back. There. How about a car accident?'

* * *

They sat in a booth at Savilli's, an Italian restaurant chosen by Connie because, in addition to good food, it catered to Santa Monica's senior citizens. For their sake, it abandoned the semi-darkness common to better restaurants and kept the place well-lit. This made it less difficult to read Pete's lips.

'I know it was a nasty trick,' he said. 'I was feeling pretty nasty when I did it'

'That sort of thing could get him fired.'

'I hope so.'

The waitress came. Pete asked for another round of margaritas.

'What if Dal reports you?'

Pete grinned. 'Hell, he could sue me, get me busted, get my ticket pulled.'

'Your what?'

'Ticket. My private investigator's license.'

'My God, Pete.'

'Oh, I'm not too worried. From what I've seen of Dal, he's basically a sneak and a coward. If he wants revenge, he won't go through the legal system. He's more the type to burn down my house or poison my dog – if I had one – or maybe bribe a couple of punks to rough me up.'

Connie saw the waitress approach with fresh drinks. She finished her first margarita, tipping the glass high and sucking up the remaining froth. Pete laughed. She licked the foamy mustache off her upper lip. The waitress took her glass, and set down a full one.

When she left, Pete said, 'I'm a little worried, though, that he might try something with you.'

'I can handle him.'

'Can you?'

'My hands are deadly weapons.'

They both laughed. Then she remembered breaking the arm of the guy who attacked her, kicking the other one in the face, burning their car. Her face turned hot.

'What's the matter?' Pete asked.

'I wasn't exactly joking about my hands.'

His eyes narrowed. He looked intrigued.

'I got attacked a couple of weeks ago. Two guys jumped me, and I had to bust them up pretty badly. I sort of – I don't want to say I enjoyed it, but – at the time it was kind of exciting. I felt so *powerful*. Like I could take on the world. But later on, I just felt sick about the whole incident. I still do when I think about it.'

'You feel dirty inside.'

'Exactly.'

'You should try killing someone.'

'Thanks, I'll pass on that.'

Pete lifted his bell-shaped glass, and drank, and backhanded the foam off his mouth. 'At any rate, I think we should stay together for the next few nights. Until Dal's had a chance to cool down.'

'Do you think it's necessary?'

'It couldn't hurt,' he said.

'Couldn't hurt at all,' Connie agreed. 'Your place or mine?'

'Which would you prefer?'

'Yours. It's so rustic and romantic.'

'How would you like to move in? Just for a few days,' he quickly added.

'I'd like that. Just for a few days.'

'Or as long as you'd like.'

'When do we start?'

'How about tonight?'

When the waitress returned, Pete asked for the clams in the half shell as an appetizer. Connie, who'd never eaten them before, expected the clams to be served fried and crispy.

She stared at the wet, slimy-looking things and said, 'This isn't the way Howard Johnson does it.'

'Try one.'

'I'll try anything once.' She scooped a clam out of its shell and slipped it Into her mouth. She bit into it once. Unlady-like to spit it out, she thought. So she swallowed it and managed not to gag.

'What do you think?' Pete asked.

'It's not for nothing they're called clams.'

She took a long drink of margarita. Amused, she watched Pete finish off the serving. 'I guess we don't have as much in common as I'd thought,' she said.

Pete grinned and chewed.

The rest of dinner, Connie found delicious. She ate a side dish of linguini in a delicate sauce of oil and garlic, then a full plate of veal parmesan, sipping the house rosé between bites.

'Great stuff,' Pete said as he finished.

He paid the bill. Outside, Connie thanked him for dinner and kissed him. They walked to his car, holding hands.

Dal waited in the passenger seat of Elizabeth's Mercedes. She was gone for two minutes. Then she stepped out of the shadows near the house, and started across the street.

She wore white shorts and a white halter top. By contrast, her skin looked very dark. Beautiful, Dal thought.

The car light came on when she opened the door. She smiled and climbed in and shut the door. The car went dark.

'Not home,' she said.

'What should we do?'

'Wait.'

'That could take hours.'

'What's your hurry?'

'I just want to get it over with, that's all.'

'Someone's coming. Kiss me.'

'Huh?'

'We want them to think we're lovers.'

'Aren't we?'

'Of course we are.'

He pressed his lips to her open mouth.

Pete drove Connie to her apartment house. He entered first, and had a quick look around while Connie waited in the doorway. 'It's okay,' he said.

They went into her bedroom. She knelt beside her bed. 'Did you check under here?'

'If he grabs you this time, I'll let him have you.'

'The little girl who cried wolf,' she said, and reached under the bed. As she gripped her suitcase, a hand patted her rump. 'My God, he's attacking from the rear!' She didn't move. The hand pressed against her skirt, slid lower and rubbed between her legs. 'You'd better stop him, Pete. He's getting fresh. Next thing you know, he'll be pulling up my skirt and . . .'

He did. And then he slipped her panties down.

She felt his touch. Her hand went limp on the suitcase. 'I guess I can get it later,' she said.

An hour later, wearing fresh panties and nothing else, she again knelt beside the bed. She dragged the suitcase out, and threw it onto the bed beside Pete. He took a sip of beer, and grinned.

'You look pleased with yourself,' Connie said.

'I am.'

'You ought to be.'

He drank his beer and watched her pack. She didn't pack much: toilet articles, a few changes of clothes, her swimming suit, half a dozen paperback novels, and her manuscript. 'All set,' she announced, and shut the suitcase. 'You just gonna sit there?'

'It's the best seat in the house.'

'But the show's over.' She stepped into her corduroys, and pulled a blue velour top over her head.

'Just an intermission,' Pete said. He climbed off the bed and got dressed.

He carried her suitcase to the door.

'I'd better take my own car,' Connie said. 'I'll want to come back for my mail and stuff.'

'I can bring you by.'

'Every day?'

'Is your mail that urgent?'

'You don't know much about writers, do you?'

'I'll never know enough about this one.'

She kissed him. Then they went outside, and down the stairway to the courtyard. They went through the gate. Pete put the suitcase into Connie's car, then patted her rump and went to his own car.

'There he is!' Dal said as a Jaguar turned onto the road.

'Down.'

They both ducked. The low grumble of the engine grew louder, and suddenly died. Dal raised himself enough to peer out the windshield. He saw the Jaguar in the driveway of Pete's house. As Pete bent over to raise the garage door, another car appeared at the end of the block. Dal hunched down. He heard the Jaguar engine start again. When he looked out, he saw a different car in Pete's driveway.

Connie's Plymouth Fury.

'Oh shit,' he muttered.

Elizabeth pushed herself up, and looked out. Across the street Pete lowered the garage door and met Connie beside her car. He took her suitcase. They walked together across the yard, and disappeared into the shadows near the front door.

'Who do you suppose *she* is?' Elizabeth asked.

Dal suddenly realized she didn't know what Connie looked like. Good thing. What would Connie, his fiancée, be doing at Pete's house – with a suitcase? 'I don't know who she is.'

'I suppose it doesn't matter unless she sees me.'

'What if she *does* see you?' Dal asked.

'Do you want to call the whole thing off?'

'You mean if she sees you?'

'I mean right now. We can't kill this guy without taking chances. A hundred things could go wrong. You've got to want it bad, even enough to cut down anybody who gets in our way.'

'But she's innocent.'

'Not if she sees me.'

'I don't know.' Dal shook his head, thinking. If they killed Connie, tomorrow's newspaper would certainly identify her. That'd finish him with Elizabeth. She'd see all his lies, know that he wouldn't be getting rich, and dump him.

By then, however, they would've committed two murders together. Maybe he should threaten to turn himself in – and tell all – unless she continued the relationship.

'What'll it be?' Elizabeth asked.

'Let's get him.'

Soon, the lights in the front windows of the house went out.

'Let's give them an hour,' Elizabeth said.

'A whole hour?'

'I don't want to kill anyone we don't have to. Give them an hour, and perhaps the lady will stay in bed.'

Dal hoped it would work that way. It just might. Connie, after all, wouldn't hear the doorbell.

Pete thought, at first, that the ringing doorbell was only part of his dream. Then he opened his eyes in the darkness and heard it again.

He glanced at the alarm clock. Nearly midnight.

Who the hell would be ringing the doorbell at this hour?

It frightened him.

Heart thudding wildly, he rolled away from the warmth of Connie's sleeping body. The room was chilly. He stepped through the darkness to the closet, and pulled his bathrobe off its hook. The doorbell rang again as he rushed down the long hallway.

Standing in darkness by the door, he turned on the outside light. His door had no peephole.

'Who's there?' he called.

'Please,' said a woman's voice. 'My car broke down.'

Pete opened the door. The woman on the front stoop looked beautiful and frightened.

'I'm awfully sorry to disturb you,' she said. She glanced at his robe, and smiled as if embarrassed, as if she knew he was naked beneath it. 'I just didn't know what to do.'

'That's all right,' Pete said. 'Would you like to use the phone?'

She looked behind him into the darkness. 'I don't know if I should. Are you alone?'

'I'm harmless.'

'Well . . . Who would I call?'

'Triple A, I suppose.'

'I don't belong.'

'You don't have to. They'll just charge you a service fee.'

'You mean money?'

Pete nodded.

The woman chewed her lower lip. 'But I only have about three dollars.'

'What's wrong with your car, do you know?'

'I've got a flat.'

'Do you have a spare?'

'Sure. I've got a real nice one. It's right in my trunk'

'Okay. Hang on a minute while I get dressed, then we'll see if I can't change it for you.'

'Oh, would you?'

'Come on in, if you'd like.'

'Well, thank you. I'll just wait here, though, if it's all the same.'

'Whatever,' he said. Did she think he'd attack her?

He didn't want to shut the door in her face, so he left it open and returned to the bedroom. As he shed his robe in the darkness, light filled the room. He saw Connie sitting up, her arm raised to the bedside lamp. She squinted and yawned. 'What's up?' she asked.

Pete stepped into his jeans. 'I have got to go out for a minute. Some gal has a flat.'

'Gonna change a tire?'

'Yep.' He put on a gray sweatshirt, and slipped his bare feet into sneakers.

'Want me to help?' Connie asked.

'Just keep the bed warm.'

'Mmm. I'll leave the light on for you,' she said. She lowered herself onto the bed, and pulled the blanket up to her bare shoulders.

Pete went down the hall to the open front door.

'I sure do appreciate your helping me like this,' said the woman.'

'Glad to help.'

'My car's right across the street here.' She walked ahead of him, pointing to a pale Datsun. Its left front tire was flat.

Connie, warm and drowsy beneath the blanket, suddenly came wide awake.

Too damned bizarre!

In all her life, nobody ever came to the door at midnight with a story about a flat tire. And if it ever *had* happened, she would've been too suspicious to fall for it.

A set-up?

Dal!

She scurried off the bed, grabbed Pete's robe and pulled it on as she ran down the dark hallway. She jerked open the front door.

A woman in the street, Pete close behind her.

Connie looked both ways.

To the right, a car shot away from the curb. No headlights on.

'Pete! Look out!'

He jerked around, and tried to leap out of the way. The speeding car caught him in the legs and Connie screamed as she watched Pete cartwheel over the car and crumple onto the pavement behind it.

The car stopped.

The woman climbed in.

It sped away.

Connie raced to the telephone. She picked it up and dialed 0. She waited five seconds, then said, 'Hello, hello. Operator? I'm deaf. If you're there, send an ambulance to 186 Seafront Lane in Venice. A man's been hit by a car. It's a hit and run, so send the police, too.' She repeated the address, and hung up.

She ran outside crying.

* * *

'She saw it,' Elizabeth gasped. 'She was in the doorway. She saw it.'

'Oh Jesus!'

'Turn around. You've got to go back.'

'Did she see you?'

'Not close up. But she saw the car. Do it!'

'This city has thousands of gray Mercedes. We covered the license plate. There's no way . . .'

'Go back.'

He'd already turned the corner onto Pacific, but there were no other cars nearby. He made a U-turn and headed back toward Seafront. As he slowed for the turn, he saw several people down the lane. He drove on by. 'Forget it,' he said. 'We can't get them all.' With a shaking hand, he turned on the windshield wipers to clear off the spattered blood.

# Chapter Twenty-two

A doorbell startled Freya awake. She sat up in bed, shaking, and flinched as the doorbell rang again.

She looked at her alarm clock. Twelve-twenty.

Who the hell . . .?

The *police*?

She cringed as it rang again. Swinging herself out of bed, she turned on a lamp. She crouched at her dresser, wiped her cold wet hands on her thighs, and pulled open a drawer. The bell rang again, again.

Jesus, it had to be cops! Who else would come at this hour? They're rounding us up. Oh Jesus!

She jerked a nightgown out of the drawer, and put it on as she rushed through the apartment. The bell kept ringing. She turned on a lamp in the living-room. Turned on the porch light. Opened the door.

The chubby girl's T-shirt read, 'Save a tree – eat a beaver'. She smiled up at Freya and said, 'Greetings.'

Freya opened her mouth to scream.

She fainted, instead.

# Chapter Twenty-three

In Elizabeth's garage, Dal inspected the car. The only damage seemed to be a couple of small dents in the hood. There wasn't as much blood as he expected. Elizabeth filled a bucket, and he sponged the car clean. He dumped the bucket of pink water into a flower bed behind the pool.

They went into the house. Dal flopped on the sofa. He was still shaking, his heart racing.

'I'll stir up a batch of martinis,' Elizabeth said.

She left him alone. He rubbed his face. He saw Pete in front of the car, heard the thud of the impact, saw Pete tumble toward him. He shook his head sharply. He didn't want to think about it. Getting up, he went into the kitchen to be with Elizabeth.

She stood at the counter pouring gin into a beaker. Dal pressed his face to the back of her head. Her hair felt thick and soft, with a fresh outdoor smell. Reaching around, he held her breasts. They were bare under the halter top. The nipples pushed against his hands through the fabric.

'Does it excite you?' she asked.

'You always excite me.'

'Not me. What we did.'

'I don't know,' Dal said. He didn't want to admit that he felt dizzy and confused. But holding Elizabeth helped.

'I feel absolutely grand,' she said.

'It doesn't bother you?'

'Only that we let the girl live. Unless she's a complete fool, she'll know it wasn't an accident. You may find yourself a suspect when the police start snooping.'

Dal dropped his hands. He stepped away from her, and leaned back against the counter.

'They'll find out, quickly enough, about your rivalry over Connie. A little more digging, and they'll learn how you got fired.'

'My God,' he muttered.

Elizabeth poured the martinis into a pair of glasses. 'None of this would've come up, of course, if the girl hadn't seen us.'

'What'll we do?'

She handed a glass to him. 'Cheer up, darling.' She clinked the rim of her glass against his, and took a sip. Dal drank. The martini was cool in his mouth, and made a hot trail down him as he swallowed. 'I'm your accomplice, remember? I certainly can't allow the police to arrest you.'

'What'll we do?' he asked again.

'An alibi would help, of course. You told Connie you were going to San Diego?'

'Yes,' he said, though he'd told her no such thing.

'Did you say which hotel?'

He shook his head.

'That's fortunate. At least they can't catch you in an outright lie.'

'What'll I tell them?'

Elizabeth leaned against the counter beside him. She frowned at the clear surface of her drink. She took a sip. Then she smiled. 'If they ask where you were tonight, you explain – reluctantly of course – that San Diego was a lie to appease Connie. Actually, you picked up a prostitute on Sunset. You went to a motel with her. You're not sure which one, but she signed in and you spent the night together. Voila! You have an alibi that can't be disproved. The cops don't have any physical evidence connecting you to the crime. You're home free.'

'Why would I go to a prostitute, though, if I'm engaged to Connie?'

Elizabeth shrugged. 'Perhaps you can say she's an old-fashioned girl who won't let you touch her before the wedding night?'

'Nobody'd believe that.'

'You're probably right. Ah! I have it! She's an old-fashioned girl who won't give head.'

'Good. That's good.'

'Okay, you have your story. They've got no evidence. We're home free.'

'Good, I hope so.'

'There's just one more thing.'

'What?'

'We'll have to stay away from each other. If they connect us, they've got the car.'

'But . . .'

'It won't be forever.' Elizabeth drew her fingers over his cheek.

'How long?'

'A few weeks, I suppose.'

'I don't want to be away from you.'

'I don't like it either, darling.' She opened the top button of his shirt. 'This will be our last time together for a long while. Let's make it memorable.'

She led him into the bedroom. They took off each other's clothes. Under the bright light and the staring eyes of Herbert, they made love.

When they were done, Elizabeth straddled him and rubbed his chest. 'I have a surprise,' she said.

'Mmm.'

'Back in a minute.' She climbed off, and left the room.

Dal folded his hands behind his head, and looked at Herbert sitting motionless in his wheelchair beside the bed. The man's steady gaze made him uneasy. He pulled up the sheet to cover himself, and wished Elizabeth would hurry back. He didn't like being alone with Herbert.

Finally, she came in. She walked silently through the darkness, and into the pool of light near the bed. A dish towel covered her hands. She stepped behind Herbert, and licked her lips.

'Took you long enough.'

'I had a lot to do.'

'What's under the towel?'

'The surprise.'

She lifted the towel away.

Dal jerked upright. 'My God, don't!'

'It's time,' she said. She wrapped her hand in the towel and gripped the butcher knife and swung it down. It plunged into

Herbert's throat. A spray of blood hit Dal. He rolled backwards, out of the way, as Elizabeth jerked out the knife and stabbed again.

'Oh my God,' he gasped. 'Jesus!' He scrambled off the bed.

Elizabeth, with a half smile on her face, rammed the blade again into Herbert's throat.

'My God, *stop*! For Godsake!'

She pulled out the knife. She was breathing hard. She wiped its handle with the dish towel, and stepped around the end of the bed.

Dal backed away. 'No,' he muttered.

'An . . . an intruder broke in,' she said, walking toward him. Hair hung in her face. Her skin was slick with sweat. 'Took a knife from the kitchen. Killed poor Herbert. Beat up poor Elizabeth, raped her.'

'You're nuts!'

'Am I?'

'You can't get away with it.'

'Of course I can.'

She backed him against the sliding door. 'And you'll help me. You, darling, are the intruder.'

He thrust out his hands to ward off the knife.

Elizabeth laughed softly. She turned the handle toward him. 'Take it,' she said.

'Huh?'

'Take it. Don't worry about prints. You can wipe them off with the towel. I'll tell the police you wore gloves.'

She pressed the knife into his hand.

Dal stared at the dripping blade.

'When you're done, go outside and smash a hole in the glass. It'll look like you broke in.'

'My . . . my fingerprints are everywhere.'

'I got most of them.' She grinned. 'That's what took me so long, out there. When I tell the cops you wore gloves, though, they might not even bother to check.'

'My God, Elizabeth.'

'Don't worry. They'll never even suspect you . . . or me.' She took his wrist, and pulled him toward the bed. She sat on the mattress. Still holding his hand, she lay down. She guided his hand lower, until the knife touched her belly.

Dal jerked his hand away. 'What're you doing!'

'Cut me.'

'*Cut* you?'

'It has to look real.'

'I can't *cut* you!'

'Can you punch me?'

'I . . . I don't know.'

'Try.'

'Where?'

She tapped her cheek.

'God, Elizabeth.'

'Do it!' she snapped.

He climbed onto the bed and straddled her. He set the knife on the sheet. He raised his fist.

'Go ahead.'

'I can't.'

'You have to.'

His arm trembled. Then he was crying. 'I can't. Don't ask me to. Please.'

'Okay then.'

'I'm sorry.'

'It's all right, darling. I guess I should be flattered, huh?'

'I'm sorry.' He climbed off her.

'Go ahead and get dressed. Then break that window.'

He picked up his clothes.

Elizabeth picked up the butcher knife. She pressed its blade to her throat.

'What . . .!'

'Shhhh.'

He saw the blade slide on her skin, saw a line of blood spill out.

*'Elizabeth!'*

She carved a second cut onto her throat. She cut her right cheek, her forehead. Dal stared, cold and numb. The blade went to her right breast.

'No!' Dropping his clothes, he ran to her and grabbed her hand.

'Then hit me,' she said. 'Beat me up. Hurt me.'

Pinning her knife-hand to the sheet, he punched her face.

'Again,' she muttered.

He hit her again.

'Scratch me. Bruise me.'

Dal did as he was told, reluctantly at first. She sobbed and writhed under him, and urged him on. He punched her, raked her with fingernails, squeezed and twisted her slippery skin. Then he was hard and aching. He shoved himself into her, pounded, and burst with quick release.

He climbed off her, exhausted. She lay on the bed, torn and sheathed in blood. She raised her head to see herself.

'This'll do nicely,' she moaned. 'Now get dressed . . . Break that window and get the hell out of here . . . so I can call the cops.'

'Are you all right?'

'Do I . . . look all right?'

Dal started to get dressed. He was wet with blood. His

clothes stuck to him. 'When will we see each other again?' he asked.

'I'll . . . phone.'

# Chapter Twenty-four

'Greetings again.'

Freya raised her head off the couch. She looked at the girl on the nearby chair, and shut her eyes. Her head hurt.

'You okay?'

'Yeah.'

'I was starting to worry. You bashed hell out of your head when you fell. Hit the bookcase. You been out for a goddamn hour. You always go around fainting?'

'I . . . I've been sick.'

'Yeah? You too? I just got over a case of the trots, myself. Something I ate.'

Freya opened here eyes. She sat up slowly, feeling dizzy, and touched the back of her head. A big lump. She looked at the girl. 'Who are you, anyway?'

'Who do you think?'

'Chelsea?'

The girl grinned.

'Can't be.'

'Can't?'

'She's . . .' Freya caught herself. 'She's out of town.'

'Oh shit. Where?'

'Up north.'

'Damn it, she knew I was coming. What's she trying to pull?'

'You're her twin?'

'Right on the money. Name's Grenich.' She spelled it.

'I'm Freya.' She spelled it.

'When's *el grosso* coming back?'

'She didn't say.'

'When'd she leave?'

'Today.'

'Just in time to miss me.'

'She said it was an emergency.'

'I'll bet. Hey look, you mind if I flop here tonight?'

'No. That'd be fine.'


# Chapter Twenty-five


Someone touched Connie's shoulder, startling her awake. She was in the hospital waiting room, slumped in a plastic chair. She looked up at the doctor beside her.

'Mr Harvey's out of surgery,' he said.

'How is he?'

'He's stable, Miss Brent. His vital signs look good. That's about the best we can offer at this point.'

'But he will survive?'

'We can't promise anything, but I think there's a good chance of it.'

'May I see him?'

The doctor shook his head. 'Later, perhaps. Visiting hours are from four to five, and eight to nine. He'll be on the third floor, once he's out of intensive care. Now, I'd suggest you go home and try to get some sleep.'

The sun came up while she was driving home. She thought about heading over to Pete's house for her suitcase, but she didn't want to go there. Maybe later today, if she felt better.

Her neck was stiff from the hours in the waiting room. Her eyes were raw and burning. She felt tired and hollow and sick.

When she got to her apartment, she lay on her bed and covered her face with a pillow. Images twisted through her mind: Pete on the bed, grinning and sipping beer; Pete broken on the pavement; jerking her out of a car's way the day they met; tumbling through the night and crumbling to the street; Dal grinning as he aimed the car; the doctor shaking his head – 'I'm sorry, Miss Brent, but he didn't make it'; a preacher beside the grave – 'Earth to earth, ashes to ashes'; the casket slowly lowering . . .

She flung the pillow aside and sat up. She sat motionless, wondering what to do with herself. She felt like doing nothing. If she could just sleep, just shut off her mind and sleep and not wake up until it was all over . . . A bath might help.

She turned on the faucet and took off her clothes and sat in the hot shallow water, hugging her knees to her breasts as the tub filled. When the water was deep, she lay back. Her shoulders touched the cold porcelain. She flinched and quickly slid lower, sighing as she was wrapped in heat. The warmth was soothing. The water's gentle motion caressed her. She shut her eyes.

After the bath, she would make sausages and fried eggs. A

whole bunch of them. Then she would go to Westwood and browse bookstores and buy a dozen books, at least. And then she would buy herself a dress, a lovely new dress for visiting Pete tonight. Maybe get him a gift. A special gift . . .

She was chilly. She sat up, the cool water sluicing down her chest. She realized she'd been asleep. She unplugged the drain, thinking she might refill the tub with hot water. Except for the cold, she felt good. If she could just return to the cozy warmth . . . But her hands were pale and shriveled. She certainly didn't need another doze in the tub.

But she was so cold.

She slid the glass door shut. Kneeling, she reached for the faucet. Moments later, hot water was raining onto her head, pelting her shoulders and streaming down her chilled skin, sheeting her in warmth. She raised her face into the shower. It tapped her eyelids, filled her mouth. She swallowed some, and let the rest spill down her chin.

Standing, she picked up the soap and remembered the day at the beach house – only a few days ago – showering with Pete, his hands rubbing her soapy body everywhere. Then she soaping him, his skin slippery under her hands.

She started to cry. Sobs shook her body. She dropped the soap and covered her face. The water pounded on her back. It began to turn cold. She shut it off. She shoved open the shower door and climbed from the tub. She pressed her warm dry towel to her face and fell to her knees, crying harshly.

Later, she found herself lying on the bathroom rug. She'd been asleep. Sun from the window was warm on her back. She got up, feeling weak. Except for her hair, she was nearly dry.

She felt very hungry.

Rubbing her hair dry, she went into the bedroom. She put on fresh clothes, then went into the kitchen. She took a pack of sausages from the refrigerator. As she poked at its plastic wrapper, the lights flashed on and off.

Someone at the door.

She went to it and opened it.

'I thought I'd drop by and see how you are.'

She stared at Dal in disbelief. His face was somber. He looked haggard.

'I read about it in the paper,' he said.

'That's the first you knew about it, I suppose.'

He nodded. 'I was afraid you might feel that way. That's another reason I came by. I want you to know I had nothing to do with it.'

'Is that so?'

'Can I come in for a minute?'

She stepped away from the door and let him enter. She shut the door. She faced him.

'The article said the police are looking for a suspect. I suppose that's me.'

'That's right.'

He turned away and walked toward a chair. Connie opened the draperies to fill the room with light. Then she sat across from him, watching his mouth.

'You have every reason to think I was involved. I mean, after everything Pete's done to me. I lost my job, you know.'

'I didn't know.'

'Yeah. Because of that stunt he pulled. But Christ, I wouldn't try to run a guy over, no matter what he did.'

'Tell that to the police.'

'I intend to.'

'Why don't you call them now?'

He looked shocked. 'Now?'

'I know they're looking for you. It'll save time. You can use my phone, and I'll keep you company till they arrive.'

'I can't.'

'Why not? They'll find you anyway, sooner or later. You might as well get it over with.'

'I have a job interview in half an hour.'

'Do you indeed.'

'I didn't come over here to argue, Connie. I came over to offer my sympathy.'

'I don't need your sympathy.'

'How *is* Pete?'

'He'll live,' she said, praying she was right. 'And if he saw the face of the driver, you'll be in deep trouble.'

Dal grinned. The corners of his mouth trembled. 'I hope he did see the driver. Then maybe you'll believe me.'

'I know you did it, Dal.'

'Then why don't *you* call the police?'

'Last night I called for an ambulance.' The memory almost brought fresh tears. She paused, trying to regain control. 'I called and thought I was talking to an operator . . . but I wasn't, apparently. I was talking to no one, to a ringing phone, probably . . . and I didn't even know it. If someone else hadn't called for an ambulance . . .'

'I'm sorry.'

'So I don't think I'll call the police. What I might do, I might disable you and go next door and ask a neighbour to call.'

'You're crazy.'

'Maybe. I'll tell you why I won't do it.'

He smirked. 'Tell me.'

'Because if I attack you, I won't be able to stop. I'll kill you.'

'That so?' he asked, looking pale.

'And I don't want to kill you, because then it'll be hard to find out who the woman is.'

'What woman?'

'Your friend with the Mercedes.'

He shook his head. 'You're not making any sense.'

'Yes I am.'

'I don't know any woman with a Mercedes. That's a bit out of my league.'

'That's true.'

'Look, I don't need this. I just came by . . .'

'I know. To offer your sympathy. Well, thanks anyway. But you're the one who'll need sympathy, Dal. You and your girlfriend. Something bad is gonna happen to you both.'

'Connie, for . . .'

'You tried to kill my man.'

He got up. 'I'm leaving.'

She walked to the door and opened it. Dal stepped outside.

As soon as she shut the door, she rushed across the room, grabbed her purse, and ran back to it. She opened it a crack and peered out. Dal was halfway down the stairs. She waited until he reached the bottom. When he was out of sight, she stepped onto the balcony and looked over the railing. Dal, at the end of the courtyard, was nearly to the rear gate. He'd parked in the alley: Connie's car was in front. She ran down the stairs, and out the front gate to her car.

She glanced both ways. Dal could exit the alley at either end of the block; if she chose wrong, she might lose him. She decided on the south end because it was closer.

She backed onto the road, and hit the gas pedal. With a quick spurt, the car shot to the corner. She stopped. As her eyes sought the alley's opening, she saw Dal's red VW already heading down the road. Away from her, thank God. If he'd come this way, he couldn't have missed her.

While she was stopped, a car passed. Great. It would run interference for her. She pulled out and followed it, sometimes veering to the left for a glimpse past it. They were gaining on Dal.

He turned right and disappeared around the side of an apartment house.

Approaching the corner, Connie eased off the gas. She took the turn slowly. Dal's car had almost reached the end of the block. It stopped at an intersection, then continued straight ahead. Connie sped up.

On the next block, his VW turned into the driveway of an apartment complex. Connie drove by, squinting into the darkness of the subterranean parking lot. She glimpsed his brake lights, and drove on.

If Dal knew he was being followed, he might've ducked in to lose his tail. That, Connie knew, was one possibility.

The other two were more intriguing.

She stopped near the corner. In her side mirror, she could see the driveway. She waited for Dal's car to appear.

Nearly two minutes passed. Then a station wagon came up the road behind Connie. She turned the corner to let it pass, then drove slowly along to an empty stretch of curb. She parked, and leaned her forehead against the steering wheel.

Dal, she realized, hadn't ducked into the lot to lose her. He was too impatient to wait inside for more than half a minute. So, unless he'd gone out a rear exit – if there was one – he'd entered the lot to park.

The apartment complex was his destination.

He lived there.

Or the woman did.

Connie climbed from her car and walked back to the driveway she'd seen Dal enter. Its pavement sloped into shadows. She stepped down it.

The parking lot was cool, and dark after the brightness

outside. She took off her sunglasses. There were only half a dozen cars down here. She didn't see Dal's VW. She saw a dark brown Mercedes, but not a gray one.

Maybe around the corner . . .

The concrete felt slippery, as if it had been waxed. Poor footing if she was attacked.

Who would attack her, Dal?

'Those parking structures are bitches,' her self-defense instructor had warned. 'Great places to get mugged or raped. And where do you think the creep's waiting for you? He's crouched there between the parked cars. So always walk right up the middle of the driveway, so you'll have plenty of time to see him coming.'

Connie walked up the middle, her glance darting from car to car. Several times, she looked behind her. Then she came to the curve. She stepped over to the concrete wall, and peered around it.

Her heart flip-flopped.

She ducked.

Had Dal seen her? She didn't think so. He was still sitting in his car. My God, why? She'd expected him to be in a room by now.

Maybe he did know that he'd been tailed.

If that were true, he'd drive right past her once he thought it was safe to leave. She looked around. The nearest car to hide behind was yards away. Should she dash for it? Or maybe break for the sunlit entrance and try to get back to her car while Dal was still waiting?

Standing, she chanced another glance at Dal. He opened his door. She pressed herself to the wall and looked to the right at the nearby elevator.

If he walked straight to the elevator, the wall would conceal her. She could watch him in safety, as long as he didn't turn around.

She looked for floor numbers above the elevator door.

None.

Damn! She could've watched them to see where Dal got off. Without them, she'd have no idea which floor to check.

She'd have to look in the lobby. Maybe his mailbox or buzzer . . .

He walked by, moving slowly, head down, and the idea barely had time to form in Connie's mind before she rushed out. He started to turn. Her stiff open hand chopped the side of his neck. He dropped to his knees. Connie tensed, ready to kick the back of his head, but the single blow had been enough. He fell forward. His face hit the concrete.

The keys were in his hand. Connie took them. She found one with a room number. 316. She threw down the keys and jerked the wallet from his rear pocket. Should she just take the money? No. a real mugger might want the credit cards, the license, the works.

She stuffed the wallet into her handbag.

Then she ran from the parking lot.

In the heat and brightness outside, she put on her sunglasses. She walked quickly to her car and drove home.

# Chapter Twenty-six

'Sure you don't want to come along?' Grenich asked.

'No, really. I can't look food in the face before noon.'

'I was counting on you driving. Haven't got a car, myself.'

'How did you get here?'

She held up her thumb.

'Want to take my car?'

'Can I?'

'Sure.' Freya took her keys from her handbag, and gave them to the girl.

'You sure it's okay?'

'No problem. Have fun.'

'Want me to bring you something back?'

'No. Thanks.'

'Okay. Back in a jiff.'

The moment she was gone, Freya raced to the telephone and dialed. She waited nervously as it rang.

'Hello?'

'Todd.'

'Princess.'

'We've got troubles.'

'With a capital T?'

'Sure, make jokes. That's just what I need.'

'What *do* you need?'

'Help. My God! You know who's here – who dropped in last night? Chelsea's twin sister. Her *identical* twin. I tell you, I nearly dropped dead.'

'Ho! I should think so! Thought the delightful lady'd come back from the grave, eh?'

'That's exactly what I thought. And it's not funny. What'll we do?'

'What did you tell her about Chelsea?'

'I said she'd gone on a trip.'

'And so she did – a trip from whose bourne no traveler returns.'

'Todd!'

'You'll have to bring her out to the house, I think.'

'And how do I manage that?'

'Where is this lovely specimen now?'

'She headed over to the Box for a Breakfast Jack.'

'Marvelous. When she returns, simply explain that Chelsea called while she was out. She wants the two of you to meet her at a fabulous old house on the coast.'

'What if she doesn't buy it?'

'Oh, she'll buy it. You underestimate yourself, princess. You are a master of duplicity – or should I say mistress?'

'Well, I'll try.'

'We'll be waiting for you. Perhaps we can work the twin angle into the story-line. Wonderful potential. See you soon.'

'Sure.'

He hung up.

Freya heated water. She took her tea into the living-room, sat on the couch, and stared at the blank screen of the television.

'Look, I admit I ran the light. Okay? But I did not steal the car.'

'The registration . . .'

'I know,' Grenich said. 'She let me borrow it. Look officer, her apartment's only a block from here. Can't we just go back and *ask* her? Please?'

\* \* \*

The doorbell rang. My God, back already? Must've changed her mind.

Freya got off the couch and went to the door.

*Guess who phoned while you were out.*

'Miss Jones . . .' the cop started.

She sprang through the doorway, shoved Grenich against him, and ran.

'Hey!'

Her bare feet slapped the painted concrete as she raced along the balcony. At the top of the stairs, she glanced back. The cop was running toward her.

'Stop!' he shouted.

She lunged down the stairs. Missed one. Tumbled headlong.

Like a nightmare when she falls down a long flight of stairs, and endless flight, and always wakes up before she hits.

But Freya wasn't asleep and she didn't wake up and she hit with a quick blast of pain as if she'd been smashed in the face with a sledge hammer.

'Is she dead?'

The cop nodded.

'Christ on a crutch!'

Richard Laymon

# Chapter Twenty-seven

Back in her apartment, Connie finished unwrapping the sausages
she'd planned for breakfast. They were still cool from the
refrigerator; she supposed they would be all right. She put them
in a skillet and turned the burner on low.

Then she made coffee. She stared at its dark stream as it
slowly filled the pot.

Now what? she wondered, watching it. Give Dal's address to
the police? That's what she'd half-planned to do when she got
the idea of following him. A good reasonable justification. Find
out where he lives so the cops can arrest him. But that had only
been half her plan. Not really what she wanted to do. Just an
excuse.

So what's your *real* plan, kiddo?

Bust into his place tonight and murder him? Hell, she
could've finished him off this morning, if that's what she wanted.

Stake him out, that's it. Follow him. Sooner or later, he would
lead her to the woman with the gray Mercedes.

*Then* go to the police.

Maybe.

The coffee stopped steaming. It dripped a few times. She
picked up the pot and filled her mug. She poked the sausages
with a fork, turned them. They'd take a good deal longer.

She sipped her coffee, and went to the kitchen table. She
opened her handbag. Reaching in, she pulled out Dal's wallet.

Another good reason to stay away from the cops; they might
not look fondly on her methods.

Sitting at the table, she emptied Dal's wallet. Twenty-eight

348

dollars in the bill compartment, along with assorted cards and papers. She set them aside. The wallet had slots for six credit cards. She pulled out the cards and stacked them neatly. Then she emptied the clear plastic picture holders, taking out his driver's license, Social Security card, a Red Cross card with his blood type, his high school graduation photo, and a Polaroid shot of Connie, herself, in a bikini.

He used to beg her to pose nude. She never allowed it, but one night he caught her in the shower. She chased him and tore up the photo and then they made love.

To think she used to . . .

She ripped the photo into tiny bits. She dropped the pieces onto the table. They made a nice little pile. She tore up the photo of Dal, and added it to the pile. Then his Red Cross card, his Social Security card, his driver's license.

She drank some coffee, and remembered the sausages. She got up to check them. She rolled them over. They were doing fine. She added more coffee to her mug, then took scissors from a drawer and returned to the table.

The plastic was easy to cut. She snipped up his Shell card, his Chevron card, his automobile club card, his Visa and Master Card, his Sears card. The pile of debris was growing.

Nothing left to add but the odds and ends she'd found in his bill compartment. She got up to check her sausages, then sat down again. She took a long drink of coffee. Then she tore up a post office receipt, a plumber's business card, and an old envelope corner on which he'd written Connie's address the day they met.

She wished she'd never given it to him.

She found four postage stamps. She set them aside to keep, then tore up three nondescript receipts and added them to the pile. She picked up a piece of tissue paper, the kind used at Dal's store – correction, former store – to wrap clothes before boxing them. She ripped it in half, the split nicely dividing a woman's first name from her last, her address number from her street, and dropped the pieces into the pile.

She picked them up again.

She held the pieces together.

The words were in Dal's handwriting: Elizabeth Lassin, 522, Altina.

Could be anything.

Could be *her*.

Altina, she knew, was up in the Highland Estates. A plush area where she wouldn't mind living herself someday.

Lots of fancy cars. Cadillacs, Rolls Royces, Mercedes.

'My God,' she muttered.

Then she smelled burning sausage.


Connie looked up the circular driveway. The door of the two-car garage was shut. Somehow, she had to see inside.

She walked up the driveway. The house seemed deserted, but she kept her eyes on the windows. If anyone looked out, she planned to go to the front door with a story.

*I'm a new neighbor, thought I'd drop by to get acquainted . . .* Sounded perfectly plausible.

Of course, it wouldn't work if the woman recognized her. If it's the gal who posed as Pete's wife . . . But Connie didn't think it was her. The woman last night had seemed older. Her hair was different, too: darker and longer.

She reached the garage. Standing close to its door, she couldn't see the house windows – or be seen from them. Bending down, she gripped the handle and pulled. The door didn't budge.

A pathway led around the corner of the garage. She went to it, and looked along the side. No window.

But maybe in back.

She walked up the path, stepping lightly from one flagstone to the next. The ground was covered with redwood chips like the school playground when she was a kid. Their sweet aroma was the same. She remembered the squeak of swing chains, the yelling of kids on the monkey bars, the smell of her lunch box. All so vivid. If she closed her eyes, she could . . .

She had to keep them open.

She came to the end of the garage, and stopped. Crouching, she peered around the corner.

A swimming pool. Plenty of outdoor furniture. No people.

She took a step forward, and looked at the back wall of the garage. It had a window. Sidestepping between the wall and a row of oleander bushes, she made her way to the window. She cupped her hands around her eyes, and looked through the glass.

Except for light from the single window, the garage was dark. Off to the right, she saw the vague form of a car. Maybe a Mercedes. Maybe not. To be certain, she would need a better look.

She had to break in.

The idea made her stomach go tight and cold.

I can do it, she told herself. After a mugging, what's a little breaking and entering?

She stayed close to the garage wall, and sidestepped toward the house. As she was about to step out from behind an oleander, a movement caught her eye.

At the far end of the pool was a woman.

Connie stared, holding her breath.

The woman was walking slowly away, taking small steps, holding herself rigid as if in pain. She had long, dark hair like the woman last night. In the sun, it was a rich, red-brown. She wore a white, string bikini. When she turned at the pool's corner, Connie saw her front. She was matted with bandages: bandages on her face, her neck, her chest and belly, her thighs. Her skin was blotched with bruises, her face swollen and blue.

As Connie watched, she walked along the other side of the pool. She was nearly even with Connie when she stopped at a chaise longue. She untied her bikini and let it fall. Then she eased herself onto the chaise and lay back. Her head turned until she faced the house.

Connie stood motionless behind the oleander.

The woman didn't move her head. She lay on her back, arms at her sides, her skin glistening with moisture.

Asleep?

The sunglasses hid her eyes.

Connie didn't dare move.

Finally, the face turned away.

Connie waited a few seconds, then inched back along the garage wall. The woman's head remained turned. At last, Connie reached the corner. She ducked around it, then looked back once more. Apparently, the woman hadn't seen her. She still lay there, naked except for the bandages, facing the back fence.

Connie circled around to the front of the house. Hoping to God the woman was alone, she tried the front door. Locked. She checked the windows along the front of the house. All were shut.

On the far side of the house, a bathroom window stood open. She looked around. The redwood fence was close behind her; if there were neighbors on the other side, they wouldn't see her.

She struggled with the screen, and finally got it off. She pushed the window high, boosted herself up, and climbed in. She tiptoed across the bathroom. When she looked into the bedroom, she almost screamed. She covered her mouth, and stared at the blood-matted carpet beside the bed.

My God, what had happened here? So much blood! She thought about the woman's bandages. Had all of this come from her? It hardly seemed possible. Even the wall by the bed was splattered with it.

She wanted to get out. Fast. But she'd come this far. She needed to see inside the garage.

She walked swiftly to the sliding glass door. Stepping close to the draperies, she peeked out. The woman was still on her chaise.

Leaving the bedroom, Connie started down a hall-way. She came to other open doors, glanced into the rooms, and saw nobody.

At the rear of the living-room was an enormous picture window with a sliding door at one end. She saw the woman across the pool. On hands and knees, she crept the length of the room, staying behind furniture whenever possible. Then she was in the kitchen. She crawled across its tiles to a door at the far end.

She reached up for the knob. Turned it. Pushed the door open and looked into the dark garage.

She crawled ahead.

The garage was hot and stuffy, and smelled of grease.

She stood up. She pushed the door shut, and walked through the darkness to the car. Feeling along its side, she found a door handle. She opened the door, and the interior light came on.

A Mercedes, all right.

A gray Mercedes.

Leaving the door open for the light, she stepped to the front of the car. She couldn't see the bumper or grill, but the shiny hood showed two small dents. They were enough for her.

She went over to the garage window to see if the woman was

still on her chaise. Even as she looked, the woman flinched and sat upright, frowning toward her.

*What . . .?*

Oh God, an alarm. The car has a burglar alarm! She'd triggered it when she opened the door! She hadn't heard it, of course – but she should've, caught the vibrations!

The woman sprang from the lounger and rushed alongside the pool.

Thoughts darted through Connie's mind. She could make a dash for the front door. Or find the garage door opener and get out that way. Or stand and fight.

That's it. Take the woman out. Bring in the cops. Plenty of evidence now. She knew, from research for an old crime novel, that there'd still be traces of blood on the car.

She shut the car door, pressed her back to the wall by the kitchen door, and waited.

Her heart felt as if it might explode. She blinked sweat out of her eyes.

God, what if I faint?

What if she has a gun?

The door stayed shut.

What's taking her so long?

Connie wiped a hand on her corduroys, and gripped the knob. She slowly turned it. She eased the door open a crack, and looked into the kitchen.

The woman stood at the other end of the kitchen, talking on the telephone.

The telephone. That's what brought her running, not a car alarm.

She stood there naked, dripping sweat, her back to Connie.

Then she turned.

Gazing at her mouth, Connie could almost hear the words formed by her tongue and lips.

'*Dal, you fucking idiot.*'

# Chapter Twenty-eight

'Thanks. That's just what I need after everything I've been through.'

'You weren't supposed to get in touch.'

'What can it hurt to call?' Dal asked, swiveling the seat of his stool. 'They didn't tap your phone, for Christsake.'

'What if a cop had picked it up?'

'I was ready for that. I would've pretended to be a magazine salesman.'

'Brilliant.'

'I know. Hey, look, how did it go?'

'I don't think we should discuss it on the phone.'

'That's ridiculous.'

'I'll just say that everything went as planned.'

'Fantastic! Did they check for fing . . .?'

'Dal!'

'Okay, okay.'

'No, they didn't. By the way, mister.'

'Yeah?'

'I read this morning's paper, did you?'

He knew what was coming. It was the main reason he'd finally decided to call. 'Yes,' he said.

'The woman last night.'

'Yes?'

'Your fiancée.'

'I know.'

'What the fuck was she doing there?'

'I asked her that, myself. This morning, after I read the article. She broke down, said she was lonely with me away and it meant nothing – just a last fling with her old boyfriend.'

'And why'd you lie to me last night? Don't tell me you didn't recognize her.'

'I recognized her. I just . . . couldn't bring myself to tell you. I was in shock. I couldn't believe it was her.'

'You should've told me.'

'I know. I'm sorry.'

'Don't ever lie to me, Dal.'

'I'm sorry.'

'You can lie your head off to the rest of the world, but save the truth for me.'

'I will. I promise.'

'All right. I take it nothing is up?'

'Huh?'

'She didn't suspect anything?'

'No. She thinks it was related to his job. Someone wanted to get even.'

'Very good.'

'So everything's working.'

'Seems to be.'

'We should get together and celebrate.'

'Sure. Don't call again, Dal, unless there's an emergency.'

'When can we get together?'

'A month, maybe.'

'I don't know if I can stand it.'

'You have to. Bye, now.'

'Hey!'

She hung up.

Dal hadn't mentioned the mugging, yet. But he didn't dare call her back. He'd tell her about it another time.

# Chapter Twenty-nine

Connie watched her leave the kitchen. She waited a few seconds, then opened the door wider and looked out. No one. She stepped into the kitchen. Through the window, she saw the woman heading back to her chaise.

She hurried to the front door.

Then she was striding up the driveway, breathing deeply of the fresh warm air. She felt as if she'd spent hours caged in that house. So good to be out and free!

Once her car was running, she felt even better.

She drove down the road away from the house, and tried to piece together what she had learned.

Obviously, the woman was Elizabeth. She was the one who lured Pete out of the house, last night. Dal used her car to run Pete down. But what happened to Elizabeth? Why the bandages? Why the blood in the bedroom? Did Dal attack her? That hardly seemed likely.

The bits she'd caught of the phone conversation, with Elizabeth turned away half the time, didn't make much sense.

As she drove out of the hills, she wondered where to go next. She didn't want to return home and spend the rest of the afternoon worrying about Pete.

Go to the police? Tell them what she'd learned? What's the penalty for attempted murder? Not much. Hell, even a life term for first degree murder never amounted to more than fifteen years. So what would they get, three or four? Unless Pete . . .

No! He's got to live!

She headed for the hospital, getting more nervous with each mile. All the detective work had kept her from dwelling on Pete's condition. Now, she could think of nothing else. Her hands were wet on the steering wheel and she had trouble getting enough breath.

She imagined the worst.

'I'm sorry,' the doctor would say. Just like in the movies. 'We did all we could, but . . .'

No, no, no!

The doctor had said he was stable.

'Complications.'

Finally, she entered the parking lot. She walked into the hospital on shaky legs. The lobby smelled like floor wax. She ignored the reception desk, and went to an elevator. Her hand felt cold and numb as she pushed the up button. She leaned against the wall to steady herself while she waited.

The elevator came. It was deserted. She stepped inside, and pressed the button for the third floor. When the doors slid shut, she wanted to squat down and hug her belly. She leaned on the wall instead. Her teeth were chattering. She clenched her mouth shut.

The doors opened. She stepped out, and walked to the nurses' station.

A pink-faced woman smiled up at her. 'Yes?'

'I'm here to . . . Mr Harvey? Is he . . .?'

'Just a moment, please.' Her eyes lowered to a clipboard.

Connie pressed her knuckles on the desktop to hold herself up.

The nurse smiled. 'Mr Harvey has been taken off the critical list.'

'How is he?'

'He's doing just fine, all things considered.'

'Oh, thank . . .' A sob broke Connie's voice and she covered her face, weeping. She was vaguely aware of the nurse getting up and putting an arm around her and leading her to a couch. The nurse sat down with her, patted her back. When she finally calmed down, the nurse brought her a cup of coffee.

'May I see him?'

'Well now, visiting hour isn't till four, and . . . Just a moment.' The nurse left her and walked down the hall. She looked into a room, then came back. 'I think it'll be all right if you just want a peek. He's sleeping, though. He shouldn't be disturbed.'

'I'll just look.'

The nurse led her to the room and opened its door.

Both legs were in traction. The head and face were bandaged. He was snoring.

Connie smiled. The nurse led her away.

'Can you tell me his injuries?'

'Well, just in general.'

'That's all right.'

'He has compound fractures of both legs, three broken ribs, a concussion, plus a roomful of lacerations and contusions. Doctor was worried most about the concussion, but it isn't real severe, fortunately. Now, you should get on home and climb in bed before you fall down.'

Connie looked at her watch. Nearly three. 'If visiting hour's at four . . .'

'You just forget about visiting hour. Mr Harvey won't be in any condition to appreciate your company. If I were you, I'd just go home and take care of myself, and come back tomorrow.'

'But tonight . . .'

'He won't even know you're here, honey.'

Back at her apartment, Connie climbed into bed. She intended to heed the nurse's advice – but only so far. She would take a little nap, then fix dinner and dress up and head out to the hospital for the eight o'clock visiting hour. Even if Pete wouldn't know she was there, at least she could sit by him, hold his hand. And who knows, maybe he would be awake after all.

She slept.

When she opened her eyes, the room was dim.

'Oh no,' she muttered. She looked at the clock. Five after eight. 'Damn!'

The hospital was a half hour drive. By the time she could get dressed and over there . . .

Forget it. Tomorrow would have to do.

She sat on the corner of the bed and wondered how to spend the evening. She felt very good. And very hungry. Putting on her satin robe, she went into the kitchen. She looked in the refrigerator. Nothing she could make a decent dinner out of. And anything in the freezer would take forever to thaw.

So I'll go out, she thought. How about the Sizzler? Then she had a better idea: she would drive over to the Safeway, buy a fresh slab of tenderloin and some other goodies, come back to the apartment and have a feast.

A regular celebration.

Hoist a few drinks to Pete's health, a few to the imminent downfall of Dal and Elizabeth.

Great idea!

She hurried into her bedroom to change.

As she slowed down for the entrance to the Safeway parking lot, she saw the movie theater on the next block.

The Haunted Palace.

Where she'd gone on her first night out with Pete.

She drove past the Safeway.

Don't do this, she warned herself. Don't get started again. The minute something goes wrong in your life, you head for the movies.

This is different. Not an escape, like the other times. Pete is alive! We'll be together again. This isn't an escape, it's a celebration!

A celebration of my first date with Pete.

As she parked behind the theater, she hoped it had hot dogs.

# Chapter Thirty

Connie paused in front of the ticket window of the Haunted Palace, and checked the show times. *The Howling* had started at 7:15. *Savage Schreck* would come on at 8:55, followed by *City of the Dead* at 9:10. If she wanted to stick around, *The Howling* would show again at 10:50.

She stepped up to the window and bought a ticket from the same white-faced girl with straight black hair who'd sold the tickets to Pete.

Bruno waited inside the door, his face twisted under the nylon stocking. His bloody T-shirt reminded Connie of the carpet at Elizabeth's house.

'Hi, Bruno,' she said, and handed him the ticket. He ripped it in half. Giving back the stub, he touched her hand. She went into the restroom to wash it.

No hurry. The less she saw of *The Howling's* finish, the better. In a different theater – one without Bruno hanging around – she would've waited in the lobby until the movie ended.

In the mirror above the sink, she saw that she didn't look as bad as she expected. A little pale. A little nervous in the eyes. Her hair could use a shampoo.

The top of her warm-up suit was open too much. She raised the zipper a couple of inches. If she'd known she would be out for more than a quick trip to the supermarket, she would've worn a bra. She felt rather exposed without it. Nothing to be done, though. She hiked up her pants and left the restroom.

The girls at the refreshment counter looked like clones of the ticket girl. The nearer one smiled with bright red lips.

'I'll have a hot dog and a large Pepsi,' Connie said. 'Make that two hot dogs.'

While she waited, she looked around. Bruno, standing by the door, was watching her.

Creepy.

Well, he's *supposed* to be creepy.

Turning away, she watched the numbers appear on the cash register. She paid the girl, and took her food to the end of the counter. There, she opened the foil-wrapped hot dogs. Steam drifted up from them. Mouth watering, she squirted mustard onto both hot dogs. She wrapped them up, grabbed a straw and a couple of napkins, and hurried into the dark auditorium.

She found an empty seat at the end of a row, but didn't want to block the man behind it. She took the next seat over.

She ate her hot dogs slowly, trying not to watch the screen. But the action drew her eyes.

What the hell, she decided. So I'll know how it ends.

She watched the rest of the movie, fascinated.

Then the lights came up. Looking around, she saw that the theater was crowded for a weeknight. Must be a couple hundred people, she guessed.

She checked her wristwatch. Ten to nine. If she'd gone to the hospital, she would just be arriving. Ten minutes to spend with Pete.

She should've gone.

Too late now.

Maybe she'd overslept on purpose. Maybe, subconsciously, she didn't want to see Pete tonight. Didn't want to see him lying there broken.

The thought made her burn with guilt. Well, she would make up for it tomorrow. She'd be there waiting at four . . .

The lights dimmed.

Words appeared on the screen, red and dripping like blood: **SCREAM GEMS PRESENTS OTTO SCHRECK IN** . . . flames curled out of **SAVAGE SCHRECK.**

It is daylight. A young woman in a dirty gingham dress makes her way down a slope, glancing nervously over her shoulder. At the bottom of the slope, she crouches by a brook. She dips her hands into the water and drinks.

Knife raised, an Indian rushes down the slope. His body is naked except for a red breechclout. Warpaint streaks his skin.

A goddamn maniac, Connie thought.

The girl continues to drink.

*Get out of there!* Connie wanted to shout.

363

Finally, she looks around. Fright twists her face. She throws herself into the brook, splashes to the surface, and wades through the waist-high water.

The savage leaps from the shore, black hair streaming behind him, knife clamped in his teeth, and drops onto the girl's back.

They crash into the water.

The girl breaks the surface. She is on her back, coughing, kicking, waving her arms. She seems, at first, to be floating. Then she is lifted straight out of the water. The savage raises her overhead and throws her.

She smashes through a bush near shore, hits the ground shoulder-first, and rolls.

She lies there stunned.

The savage strides through the water. Climbing the bank, he takes the knife from his teeth.

The girl is on her hands and knees, trying to get up.

*Run!* Connie thought.

But she can't get to her feet.

The savage kicks her in the belly.

Connie grunted as the impact lifted the girl completely off the ground.

She falls onto her back, clutching her belly, her knees upraised.

The savage crouches at her head. He twists her hair around his hand, and pulls it taut. He presses the knife against her scalp.

'Oh God,' Connie muttered.

A young man in the next row looked around at her, grinning. Connie smiled back, and shrugged.

Blood streams down the girl's face. Her eyes bulge. Her mouth is stretched open so wide she looks as if her cheeks might rip.

At least I can't hear the scream, Connie thought.

Suddenly, a revolver muzzle pushes against the back of the savage's head. He stops trying to scalp the girl.

Connie sighed with relief.

While the girl lies on the ground, crying and clutching her slashed head, a red-haired man in cowboy clothes ties the savage's hands with strips of rawhide.

The scene changes. The savage sits astride a horse beneath an oak tree. A rope hangs from a branch overhead. Its noose is around his neck.

*All right*, Connie thought.

The girl stands nearby, watching. Her head has been bandaged with a strip of fabric torn from her dress.

The cowboy smiles at her. His mouth moves. 'You wanta do the honors?'

She nods, steps to the rear of the horse, and slaps its haunch. The horse lunges away. The rope snaps taut, jerking the savage off the saddle. He swings, kicking and twisting, his face turning purple, his tongue lolling out.

The girl and the cowboy turn away and start walking.

'That's another good Indian,' the cowboy says.

'What are you gonna do to me?' asks the girl, looking frightened.

What's wrong with *her*? Connie wondered. This is the guy who saved her life.

'I'll see you safely back to the settlement,' the cowboy tells her.

They're still walking away, but the savage swinging below the tree is now straining, his arm and chest muscles bulging.

The cowboy says, 'I'm sure your folks will be mighty glad to see you.

'Bullshit,' the girl says. 'You're gonna kill me, just like you killed Tina.'

The savage's hands burst free. With rawhide dangling from both bloody wrists, he reaches overhead and clutches the rope. He climbs it, pulling himself upward hand over hand.

'You're crazy,' says the girl. 'You're all crazy. You don't seriously think you can get away with this? You show this thing on the screen, and people are gonna see me. They'll recognize me, just like I recognized Tina.'

What's all this? Connie wondered.

'Oh, sooner or later I suppose someone will. In a few weeks, though, I'll be long gone. We'll have thirteen *Schrecks* by then. Filmworld is picking up the whole package for an even million – planning to edit them into a feature. Nice, don't you agree? You'll be a star.'

'A dead star.'

'You'll be immortalized on the silver . . .' His mouth springs wide as the savage, behind him, shoves a knife into his back.

The girl tries to run, but the savage grabs her hair and jerks her backwards off her feet. He drags her to the tree. As he props her against it, she scratches his face. He slams a knee into her belly, doubling her. Then he starts tying her to the tree.

Connie watched, totally confused. She'd seen plenty of awful movies before, but this had to be the worst. Not only vicious and gruesome, but the dialogue made no sense at all. This must be one of those crazy film-within-a-film movies that Europeans seemed so fond of making. An artsy-fart movie. Not supposed to make sense.

The savage finishes tying her to the tree.

'You bastards!' she cries. 'Let me go!'

Connie watched the savage wander through the trees, gathering twigs. As she realized what they were for, she muttered, 'Oh no.'

The man in front of her looked around again, smiling. His mouth moved, but the darkness hid his words. He might be saying anything. Connie assumed he was being friendly. Smiling, she nodded agreement with whatever he'd said. He nodded back, and turned away.

OUT ARE THE LIGHTS

Twigs and sticks are piled around the girl's feet. The savage, several yards away, is standing behind a small fire. He slowly wraps cloth around the head of an arrow. When it is secure, he lowers it into the fire. He raises his bow. He aims the flaming arrow at the girl. It streaks through the air.

It hits the tree inches above the girl's head.

'My name if Brit Andersen,' she says. 'I'm not an actress. This is not a movie, it's real. If you can hear me out there . . .'

The savage lights another arrow. 'They'll hear whatever we like, bitch.' He shoots the arrow. It enters the kindling at her feet. Smoke rises out, then flames.

She writhes against the ropes. The hem of her dress catches fire.

*'My name is Brit . . .'*

A flaming arrow plunges into her chest.

# Chapter Thirty-one

Connie grabbed the shoulder of the man in front of her, and he jumped. 'I've got to talk to you,' she whispered. 'In the lobby. I'm deaf. I read lips. I need light to see what you say.'

He nodded.

As they walked up the aisle, Connie glanced back at the screen and saw the girl burning – hair on fire, skin turning black.

She pushed through the door and clutched the man's arm.

367

He frowned at her, looking puzzled. 'That girl ... she was killed.'

'I know, but ...'

'It wasn't fake. They *killed* her.'

'Are you out of your mind?'

'What was she saying there at the end?'

'Hail Marys.'

'No. That must've been dubbed. She was saying her name is Brit Anderson, and she's not an actress, and it's really happening. There's a phone over there. I want you to call the police.'

'The *police*? Hey, that's serious business.'

'She was murdered.'

'Maybe you should talk to the manager.'

'He might be in on it.'

'Oh for ...' He shook his head. 'Is *everyone* in on it?'

'No, but the manager ...'

'I've been coming here since it opened. The man may look awful in that get-up, but he seems to be a perfectly nice guy. Come on.' He crossed the lobby toward the entrance, where Bruno was taking tickets.

Connie hurried after him.

'Could we speak to you in private for a moment?'

Bruno nodded. He called to one of the vampire girls at the refreshment counter, then led the way to an office on the far side.

Connie followed both men inside. She stood near the open door.

Bruno pulled the stocking off his head. Without it, he had a pleasant, chubby face. 'Now,' he said. 'What seems to be the problem?'

Both men looked at Connie.

'The girl in that Schreck film wasn't an actress. Her name is Brit Anderson and she was murdered on camera. Actually murdered.'

Bruno shook his head. 'I'm afraid I don't understand. What leads you to think such a thing?'

'She said so. Her real words were dubbed over, but I read her lips.'

'Are you certain of this?'

'I know what she said, and I believe her.'

Bruno nodded. He picked up the telephone, and dialed O. 'Operator, put me in touch with the police. Yes, this is an emergency.' He covered the mouthpiece and said, 'They'll get to the bottom of this.' Then he took his hand away. 'Yes. I'm calling from the Haunted Palace movie theater at 8424 Pico. Would you send a car over here right away? We have an urgent situation . . . Apparently, murder has been committed . . . Yes. Thank you.' He hung up. 'That should get them here in short order.'

He stood up. 'Shall we go upstairs and seize the evidence?'

They followed him through the lobby. The carpeted stairway was roped off. A sign hung from the plush cordon: BALCONY CLOSED. Bruno unhooked one end of the cordon, and let them through.

At the top of the stairs, he stepped over to a door. He pushed a key into its lock, and opened it. 'Right through here,' he said.

The man and Connie entered.

She saw a pair of movie projectors near the side wall. One was running, its reels turning slowly, flashing pictures through the tiny window in front of it. A miniature image reflected on the pane.

Someone between the projectors.

Bruno talked to him, then picked up a film can and checked

the label. 'It has to be rewound. Only take a minute. I should go down and see if the police are here yet.'

He stepped past the man.

'Excuse me,' he said, and moved past Connie. He shot an elbow into her side, knocking her off balance, and threw the door shut. Connie fell against the wall.

She saw the projectionist leap from between the two big machines. No warpaint, but she knew his face, his mad eyes.

Bruno swept her feet from under her. As her back hit the floor, she saw Schreck punch a screwdriver into the belly of the man who'd come up with her.

She flung up her crossed arms and blocked a kick Bruno aimed at her face.

Someone clutched her ankles.

'No!'

Schreck lifted her feet. He raised her off the floor until she was hanging upside down. In that position, with no leverage and her vision distorted, she was nearly defenseless. Still, she blocked Bruno's first punch to her belly. The second punch got through, knocking her wind out. She clutched her belly, and he kicked her in the head, and when she opened her eyes she was facedown on the backseat floor of a car speeding through the night.

# Chapter Thirty-two

The car drove for a long time. Connie's head throbbed with pain. Her arms, tied behind her back, were tingly and almost numb. Somebody's feet were on her back and rump. When she tried to lift her head, once, they stomped hard. After that, she didn't move.

She had a good idea of what they planned to do with her. She was frightened, but angry too.

Angry at herself. For letting Bruno sucker her that way. Obviously, he hadn't phoned the cops. Was his phone unplugged? She should've been more careful, damn it. And she got that poor man killed: she didn't even know his name.

Now, everything she'd learned about Dal and Elizabeth was useless. She should've gone to the cops with her information. But no, she'd been too damned set on getting her own revenge. Stupid! Now they might just get away with running Pete down.

Should've.

So damned many should'ves.

She should've gone to the hospital, tonight. Now she'd never see Pete again.

It's not over yet, kiddo.

Not over yet. Keep telling yourself that.

The car stopped. Doors opened. She was dragged out by her feet. Schreck lifted her and slung her over his shoulder. He carried her through the darkness. She felt a cool breeze on her back where the jacket of her warm-up suit had pulled up. The air smelled like the ocean.

We're near shore, she thought, and wondered what good that

knowledge would do. What good would any of it do? Her martial arts training sure hadn't helped. Maybe the reverse. If she hadn't been so damned confident, she never would've waltzed into the projection room like an idiot.

Schreck carried her up a few wooden stairs. He waited a moment, then took her through a doorway. They were in darkness. He started up more stairs, his shoulder shoving into her belly with each step he climbed. The stairs seemed to go up forever. Finally, they stopped and he carried her through a long straight way. He turned. Her head brushed a wall or a door-frame. He carried her forward several steps; and bent over.

Connie fell backwards through the darkness. She landed on something soft – a bed? – with her legs hanging over the end.

An overhead light came on. Squinting in its brightness, she saw Schreck above her. He took a screwdriver from a deep pocket of his coveralls. She sucked in her belly. The blade pushed against her navel.

Bruno, behind him, said something.

'Sure, I can wait,' Schreck answered. He took the screwdriver away. He flipped it end over end, caught it by the handle, and slipped it into his pocket.

The two men sat down in chairs across the room.

'Can I sit up?' Connie asked, raising her head to see the response.

Bruno nodded.

She sat up, taking the pressure off her shoulders and numb arms. The men stared at her. 'What are you waiting for?' she asked.

'Todd,' said Bruno. 'The producer. He'll be along soon.'

'The producer?'

'Producer, writer, director.'

'The brains,' Schreck said, and smiled in a way that sent a chill up Connie's back.

'I'm going to star in one of your little productions?'

'I'm the star,' Schreck said.

'But we'd be nowhere,' added Bruno, 'without the little people.'

'I'll be recognized,' Connie said.

Bruno shrugged. 'Maybe. That'll be Filmworld's problem.'

'It'll get back to you.'

'Oh, I doubt that. Todd's the only connection, and he'll be in South America living like a king.'

'Where'll you be?'

'I'll still have the theater – a fairly profitable enterprise. I'm completely ignorant, naturally, of anything unusual about the *Schreck* films. I'm only an innocent exhibitor. And Otto, here, will undergo cosmetic surgery – he can use it, don't you think? With his new face, he'll continue as projectionist and my partner in the theater.'

'I have a lot of money.'

'Do you?'

'How much would it take to get you guys to let me go?'

'More than you have, I assure you.'

'Half a million dollars?'

'Come now.'

'I have that much in my savings account. Just untie me, and . . .'

Another man entered the room. Connie recognized him from tonight's film: he'd played the cowboy. 'Oh, she's a beauty!' he said.

'Look, let me go. I'll keep my mouth shut. You can split up my money among the three of you.'

'Oh, we can't do that,' he told her. 'We have a film to make! The thirteenth and final *Schreck*!' Stepping close to Connie, he brushed a curtain of hair away from the side of her face. 'It's a pity they had to bang you up, but we'll make do.' He patted her bruised cheek. 'You've come as something of a surprise, unfortunately, so we'll have to work out a story-line before we commence shooting. I like to begin with the mode of death, and work backwards from there.'

'Don't strain your brain.'

He slapped her. Then he stepped right away and sat on a dresser. 'Can you see me all right? I don't want you to miss any of this.'

'I can see you.'

'Good. Now, we must find a way of dispatching you that hasn't been done to death – if you'll pardon the pun. We've already used knives, a fork, a scalpel, an axe, arrows, a chain saw. We hanged one. One unfortunate lady choked on human flesh. Schreck bit out the throat of another. Guns are out, naturally. Too mundane.'

'Let me skin her alive,' Schreck suggested.

'We don't want excessive nudity. We're doing horror, after all, not porn.'

'Film it from behind,' Bruno said.

Schreck scowled. 'All the good stuff's in front.'

'Well, we'll keep it in mind. Let's brainstorm for a bit, though.'

'Drown her in the bathtub?' Bruno asked.

'We already drowned one in the stream.'

'I'll pound nails in her.'

'*Schreck the Carpenter*,' Bruno said, and laughed.

'Bury her alive?'

'How would we film it?'

'How about I eat her?'

'*Schreck the Snatch* . . .'

'Too close to *Gourmet Schreck*.'

'Shit,' said Bruno. 'What's left?'

'We'll think of something. Genius, after all, is ninety percent perspiration.' He grinned at Connie. 'Do you have any preferences?'

'Yeah! Suppose I kill Schreck and escape? It'd give your film a nice upbeat finish. Audiences go for that.'

'Good thought, but I don't think we'll run with it.'

'We bury her alive,' Schreck said. 'But shallow. I bash her on the head, and throw the dirt on her. Only she's not dead. She digs her way out and tries to run away. I chase her down. I can take her head right off with the shovel.'

'I like it.'

Connie felt dizzy and faint. She took deep breaths.

'What do you think, Bruno?'

'Who digs the hole?'

'We'll let her do it. Good drama there, digging her own grave.'

'Just so I don't have to do it.'

'I'll take her head off last,' Schreck said. 'Chop her up some, before that.' His hands, gripping an imaginary shovel, jab the air. '*Ram* her in the back. Get her down. Take off one of her hands, maybe. Or both of them. Maybe take off her feet. Then take that shovel and . . .'

Connie threw herself sideways and vomited on the mattress.

Schreck untied her feet. He made a loop at one end of the rope, and dropped it around her neck.

'Struggle a bit,' Todd said. 'You're on *Candid Camera*.' He pointed to a mirror above the dresser. 'Bruno's in the control room getting this down, so make it look good.'

She turned to the mirror. 'My name is Con . . .'

Schreck jerked the rope, yanking her off the end of the bed. She fell to her knees.

'Lovely,' Todd said.

Schreck dragged her by the rope. She kicked and choked. Then he grabbed her hair and pulled her to her feet. 'Walk, bitch,' he said.

Todd left the room first. He pranced ahead of them down the lighted hallway.

Schreck walked behind Connie, keeping the rope taut.

'Pull,' Todd said. 'Try to get free. You're fighting for your life.'

'Fuck you,' Connie said.

The rope jerked her backwards off her feet. She cried out as she landed on her tied arms. Schreck stepped past her. He grabbed her left foot, and dragged her to the end of the hall.

He'll break my arms, she thought. If he takes me down the stairs like this, they'll both . . .

But he stopped at the head of the stairway. He leaned over her, gripped her crotch and the front of her jacket, and hoisted her overhead. He carried her down the stairs that way, holding her high, one fist like a post pounding her chest, the other clutching as if to split the fabric of her warm-up pants and claw into her.

The door at the bottom of the stairs was open. He carried her outside, and stopped.

She expected to be hurled into the night, but he simply swung her down and shoved her against the wall. Todd was standing on the lawn, smiling and nodding.

Then Bruno came out the front door with a video camera on his shoulder as if he were here to capture the event for *Eyewitness News*. He stepped down the porch stairs, turned on a powerful light, and aimed the camera at her.

Schreck punched her in the belly. As she doubled over, choking, he flung her from the porch. She twisted in midair, and landed on her side.

Schreck cut her hands free. He grabbed the back of her

jacket and carried her like a piece of luggage. Her feet dragged the grass, her arms hung numb and useless. Near the back of the house, her zipper popped apart at the bottom. It skidded open, dropping her. Schreck let her fall to the ground.

She didn't try to get up. She lay there on the cool wet grass. Her arms were no longer numb. They hurt and tingled.

She tried to think, but she couldn't concentrate. Her mind seemed blurry.

Schreck jerked her to her feet. She turned her face away from the brightness of Bruno's camera light.

Bruno pushed a shovel at her.

She took it.

He pointed to the ground at her feet.

She could barely grip the shovel. She punched it at the ground. It hardly went in an inch. She jumped on the top edges of its head. Her weight forced it deeper. She pried out a wedge of dirt, and dumped it on the grass. Then she repeated the process. This time, her arms were stronger. She jumped on the shovel with more force. It plunged in deeper. She took out a larger load.

Todd, she saw, was standing close to Bruno. Schreck remained beside her.

She stabbed in the shovel, jumped on it, and removed the dirt. She dumped it onto the growing pile. Then she lunged forward.

Schreck grabbed her. He caught the hanging hood of her warm-up jacket.

Todd's mouth moved. 'Let her go! Run her down!'

Schreck let go.

Connie ran. Glancing back, she saw Schreck close behind her. The others followed. She ran harder, but the shovel weighed her down. If she tossed it, she might outrun Schreck.

Ahead, she saw the tree where they'd burned the girl. Beyond it would be a steep slope, the brook, and a thickly wooded area. If she could make it to the woods . . .'

She glanced back.

Saw Schreck's wild face, his reaching hands.

*Bayonet roll!*

Shovel clutched to her chest, she threw herself head over heels, hit the grass, twisted around and jammed the handle to the ground. Schreck, unable to stop, ran against the shovel blade. The shaft jerked in Connie's hands. She yanked it, throwing Schreck overhead. He hit the ground and rolled. She rushed him. She raised the shovel high and crashed it down on the back of his head.

Looking around, she saw Todd and Bruno racing to catch up.

Schreck rolled onto his back.

Connie punched the shovel blade into his belly. It hardly went in an inch. She jumped on it with both feet, and it plunged in deep.

She jerked it out and whirled around. Shielding her eyes from the camera light, she saw Todd and Bruno a dozen feet away.

'Okay bastards, who's next?'

# Chapter Thirty-three

A nurse pushed the wheelchair out the automatic doors of the hospital. 'We're going to miss you, Pete.'

'Well, we'll be back one of these days. Give us about nine months.'

'Rascal.'

Connie handed him the crutches, and he used them to push himself out of the chair.

'Now watch yourself crossing streets,' the nurse said.

'I'll be careful.'

Connie smiled. 'I don't think he has to worry about any more accidents.'

# Epilogue

## SCREAM GEMS
## PRESENTS
## VENGEANCE!

In the shadows at the head of the cellar stairs, the door opens. A woman in a white nightgown lunges through it. Stumbling off the top stair, she throws herself against the railing. It wobbles, but stops her fall.

The door above her swings shut.

Pushing herself off the railing, she steps up to the door and tries it. Locked.

Slowly, she descends the stairs, moving out of shadows and into light. Her nightgown is grimy and torn, exposing her right breast. Her neck and face and legs are bandaged, her face dark with bruises.

Halfway down the stairs, she stops. She gazes at something below, then hurries to the bottom.

A man lies on the bone-littered floor near a coffin – tied and gagged.

Kneeling beside him, she peels the wide strip of tape off his mouth. His mouth is stuffed with a handkerchief. She pulls it out.

'Untie me,' the man says.

'Not just yet.'

'Please.'

'Tell me what's going on.'

'How do I know?'

'How'd you get here?'

'Some guy rang my doorbell. A fat guy. I opened up, and he stuck a gun in my face.'

'Who was he?'

'Untie me, huh?'

'Who was he?'

'Never seen him before. I figured he was a cop, you know? In fact, I asked him. He grinned and said, "You're under arrest for attempted murder. For hit-and-run." He didn't read me my rights, though. Then, down at the street, he opened the trunk of his car and bashed me on the head.'

'Roll over.'

He rolls onto his side, and the woman picks at the knotted rope behind his wrists.

'That's about what happened to me, too,' she says. 'Mine was a red-headed guy. I knew for sure he wasn't a cop. I saw plenty last night, and they didn't behave like this guy.'

'Did he hurt you?'

'Yeah. The bastard knocked me around, tore my nightgown. He didn't bash my head, though.'

'Did he put you in a car trunk?'

'Fuckin' right he did.' She finishes untying his hands. He rolls over, sits up, and starts to work on the knot at his feet.

'Who do you think they are?' he asks.

'Somebody's figured it out.'

'Huh?'

'Somebody knows we did it.'

'Who?'

'Three guesses.'

He shakes his head and unwraps the rope at his feet. He rubs his ankles. 'Just tell me, okay?'

'Your adorable fiancée.'

'You're kidding.'

'Think about it. She saw us. She put it all together.'

He scowls and shakes his head. 'I guess . . . maybe so. What do you think she's gonna do?'

'I don't know, but we'd better get out of here.' She helps him to his feet. They stand by the coffin, each silently scanning the cellar.

Behind them, the coffin lid is flung off. They whirl around. Inside the coffin, a hooded figure sits up. The hood belongs to a warm-up jacket worn backwards. Ragged holes have been cut for eyes and mouth.

As the figure stands up, the man and woman back away. It steps out of the coffin, bare feet crushing the bones on the cellar's dirt floor.

'It's her,' the woman says.

The man shakes his head. He is pale and trembling.

'What do you want?'

The figure doesn't answer.

'Let's take her,' mutters the woman. 'Now!' She attacks.

Alone.

The hooded one grabs her arms, pivots, slams her to the floor, and steps past her.

'It *is* you,' the man says, moving backwards. 'You think I . . .'

He shrieks as a kick smashes his left knee. He drops sideways, screaming. Before he hits the floor, a second kick shatters his right knee.

The hooded one pivots and shoots knuckles into the face of the attacking woman. The blow slams her backwards. The nape of her neck hits the coffins' edge. Her head snaps back. She jerks and trembles as if a thousand volts are ripping through her body. Then she slumps.

Slender figures press her neck as if seeking a pulse. Then the hooded one straddles her body, grips her beneath the arms, and wrestles her into the coffin.

The man is still on the floor, whimpering.

The hooded one drags him to the coffin.

'No!' he cries. 'No, please! I'll do anything! Whatever you say!'

'Confess.'

'Okay! I did it. We both did it. There!'

'Get in the coffin.'

'No!'

Screaming, he fights as the hooded one struggles to lift him. His hands jerk open the jacket. He pounds the bare back, claws furrows in the skin. He rips at the blonde hair behind the hood. Then he falls into the coffin on top of the woman. Grabbing its edges, he pulls himself up. A fist smashes his nose, and he drops away.

The hooded one places the lid on the coffin.

Muffled screams rage inside the coffin as the lid is nailed down.

## The End

# And Other Tales

# Mess Hall

Jean didn't hear footsteps. She heard only the rush of the nearby stream, her own moaning, Paul's harsh gasps as he thrust into her. The first she heard of the man was his voice.

'Looks to me like fornication in a public park area.'

Her heart slammed.

Oh God, no.

With her left eye, she glimpsed the man's vague shape crouching beside her in the moonlight, less than a yard away. She looked up at Paul. His eyes were wide with alarm.

This can't be happening, Jean told herself.

She felt totally helpless and exposed. Not that the guy could see anything. Just Paul's bare butt. He couldn't see that Jean's blouse was open, her bra bunched around her neck, her skirt rucked up past her waist.

'Do you know it's against the law?' the man asked.

Paul took his tongue out of Jean's mouth. He turned his head toward the man.

Jean could feel his heart drumming, his penis shrinking inside her.

'Not to mention poor taste,' the man added.

'We didn't mean any harm,' Paul said.

And started to get up.

Jean jammed her shoes against his buttocks, tightened her arms around his back.

'What if some *children* had wandered by?' the man asked.

'We're sorry,' Jean told him, keeping her head straight up, not daring to look at the man again, instead staring at Paul. 'We'll leave.'

'Kiss goodbye, now.'

Seemed like a weird request.

But Paul obeyed. He pressed his mouth gently against Jean's lips, and she wondered how she could manage to cover herself because it was quite obvious that, as soon as the kiss was over, Paul would have to climb off her. And there she'd be.

Later, she knew it was a shotgun.

She hadn't seen a shotgun, but she'd only given the man that single, quick glance.

Paul was giving her the goodbye kiss and she was wondering about the best way to keep the man from seeing her when suddenly it didn't matter because the world blew up. Paul's eyes exploded out of their sockets and dropped onto *her* eyes. She jerked her head sideways to get away from them. Jerked it the wrong way. Saw the clotted wetness on the moonlit trunk of a nearby tree, saw his ear cling to the bark for a moment, then fall.

Paul's head dropped heavily onto the side of her face. A torrent of blood blinded her.

She started to scream.

Paul's weight tumbled off. The man stomped her belly. He scooped her up, swung her over his shoulder, and started to run. She wheezed, trying to breathe. His foot had smashed her air out and now his shoulder kept ramming into her. She felt as if she were drowning. Only a dim corner of her mind seemed to work, and she wished it would blink out.

Better total darkness, better no awareness at all.

The man stopped running. He bent over, and Jean flopped backward. She slammed something. Beside her was a windshield plated with moonlight. She'd been dumped across the hood of a car. Her legs dangled over the car's front.

She tried to lift her head. Couldn't. So she lay there, struggling to suck in air.

The man came back.

He'd been away?

Jean felt as if she had missed a chance to save herself.

He leaned over, clutched both sides of her open blouse, and yanked her into a sitting position. He snapped a handcuff around her right wrist, passed the other bracelet beneath her knee, and cuffed her left hand. Then he lifted her off the hood. He swung her into the car's passenger seat and slammed the door.

Through the windshield, Jean saw him rush past the front of the car. She drove her knee up. It bumped her chin, but she managed to slip the handcuff chain down her calf and under the sole of her running shoe. She grabbed the door handle. She levered it up and threw her shoulder against the door and started to tumble out, but her head jerked back with searing pain as if the hair were being torn from her scalp. Her head twisted. Her cheekbone struck the steering wheel. A hand clasped the top of her head. Another clutched her chin. And he rammed the side of her face again and again on the wheel.

When she opened her eyes, her head was on the man's lap. She felt his hand kneading her breast. The car was moving fast. From the engine noise and the hiss of the tires on the pavement, she guessed they were on the Interstate. The highway lights cast a faint, silvery glow on the man's face. He looked down at her and smiled.

The police-artist sketch didn't have him quite right. It had the crewcut right, and the weird crazy eyes, but his nose was a little larger, his lips a lot thicker.

Jean started to lift her head.

'Lie still,' he warned. 'Move a muscle, I'll pound your brains out.' He laughed. 'How about your boyfriend's brains? Did you see how they hit that tree?'

Jean didn't answer.

He pinched her.

She gritted her teeth.

'I asked you a question.'

'I saw,' she said.

'Cool, huh?'

'No.'

'How about his eyes? I've never seen anything like that. Just goes to show what a twelve-gauge can do to a fellow. You know, I've never killed a *guy* before. Just sweet young things like you.'

like me.

It came as no surprise, no shock. She'd seen him murder Paul, and he planned to murder her, too – the same as he'd murdered the others.

Maybe he doesn't kill them all, she thought. Only one body had been found. Everyone talked as if the Reaper had killed the other six, but really they were only *missing*.

Maybe he takes them someplace and keeps them.

But he just now said he kills sweet young things. Plural. He killed them all. But maybe not. Maybe he just wants to keep me and fool with me and not kill me and I'll figure a way out.

'Where are you taking me?' she asked.

'A nice, private place in the hills where nobody will hear you scream.'

The words made a chill crawl over her.

'Oooh, goosebumps. I like that.' His hand glided over her skin like a cold breeze. Jean was tempted to grab his hand and bite it.

If she did that, he would hurt her again.

There'll be a world of hurt later, she thought. He plans to make me scream.

But that was later. Maybe she could get away from him before it came to that. The best thing, for now, was to give him no trouble. Don't fight him. Act docile. Then maybe he'll let his guard down.

'Do you know who I am?' he asked.

'Yes.'

'Tell me.'

'The Reaper.'

'Very good. And I know who you are, too.'

He knows me? How could he? Maybe followed me around on campus, asked someone my name.

'You're Number Eight,' he said. 'Just think about that. You're going to be famous. You'll be in all the newspapers, they'll talk about you on television, you'll even end up being a chapter in a book someday. Have you read any books like that? They'll have a nice little biography of you, quotes from your parents and friends. The bittersweet story of your brief but passionate relationship with that guy. What was his name?'

'Paul,' she murmured.

'Paul. He'll get a good write-up, himself, since he's the first guy to die at the hands of the Reaper. Of course, they'll realize that he was incidental. You were the intended victim, Paul simply an unlucky jerk who got in the way. He got lucky, then he got unlucky. Good one, huh? Maybe I'll write the book myself. He got off and got offed. Or did he? Which came first? Did he go out with a bang?'

'Why don't you shut up?'

'Because I don't want to,' he said, and raked a path up her belly with a single fingernail.

Jean cringed. Air hissed in through her teeth.

'You should be nice to me,' he said. 'After all, I'm the one making you famous. Of course, some of the notoriety may be a trifle embarrassing for you. That book I was telling you about, it'll have a whole lot about today. Your final hours. Who was the last person to see you alive. And of course, it won't neglect the fornication in the park. People read that, a lot of them are going to think you were asking for it. I suppose I'd have to agree with them. Didn't you know any better?'

She *had* known better. 'What about the Reaper?' she'd asked when the movie let out and Paul suggested the park.

'He'll have to find his *own* gal.'

'I mean it. I'm not sure It's such a great idea. Why don't we go to my place?'

'Right. So your demented roommate can listen through the wall and make noises.'

'I told her not to do that anymore.'

'Come on, let's go to the park. It's a neat night. We can find a place by the stream.'

'I don't know.' She squeezed his hand. 'I'd like to, Paul, but . . .'

'Shit. Everybody's got Reaperitis. For Godsake, he's in *Portland.*'

'That's only a half-hour drive.'

'Okay. Forget it. Shit.'

They walked half a block, Paul silent and scowling, before Jean slipped a hand into the rear pocket of his pants and said, 'Hey, pal, how's about a stroll in the park?'

*'Didn't you know any better?'*

His hand smacked her bare skin.

'Yes!'

'Don't you ignore me. I ask you a question, you answer. Got it?'

'Yes.'

The car slowed. The Reaper's left hand eased the steering wheel over and Jean felt the car slip sideways. It tipped upward a bit, pressing her cheek against his belt buckle.

An off-ramp, she thought.

The car stopped, then made a sharp turn.

A cold tremor swept through Jean.

We're getting there, she thought. Wherever he's taking me, we're getting there. Oh, Jesus.

'You thought it couldn't happen to you,' he said. 'Am I right?'

'No.'

'What, then? You were just too horny to care?'

'Paul would've kept on pouting.' Her voice was high, shaky.

'One of those. I hate those sniveling, whiny pouters. Take me, for instance – I never pout. That's for the losers. I never lose, so I've got no reason to pout. I make *other* people lose.'

He slowed the car; turned it again.

'I hate pouters, too,' Jean said, trying to keep her voice steady. 'They stink. They don't deserve to live.'

He looked down at her. His face was a vague blur. There were no more streetlights, Jean realized. Nothing but moonlight, now.

'I bet you and I are a lot alike,' she said.

'Think so, do you?'

'I've never told anyone this before, but . . . I guess it's safe to tell you. I killed a girl once.'

'That so?'

*He doesn't believe me!*

'Yeah. It was just two years ago. I was going with this guy, Jim Smith, and . . . I really loved him. We got engaged. And then all of a sudden he started going with this bitch, Mary Jones.'

'Smith and Jones, huh?' He chuckled.

'I can't help it if they had stupid names,' she said, and wished she'd taken an extra second to think up names that sounded *real*, damn it. 'Anyway, he spent less and less time with me, and I knew he was seeing Mary. So one night I snuck into her room in the sorority and smothered her with a pillow. Killed her. And I enjoyed it. I laughed when she died.'

He patted Jean's belly. 'I guess we are two of a kind. Maybe you'd like to throw in with me. I can see some advantages to an arrangement like that. You could lure the pretty young things into my car, help me subdue them. What do you think?'

She thought that she might start to cry. His offer was just what she had wanted to hear – and he knew it. He knew it, all right.

But she went along, just in case. 'I think I'd like that.'

'That makes it an even fifty percent,' he said.

The front of the car tipped upward. Again, Jean's cheek pressed his belt buckle.

'You're the fourth to try that maneuver. Hey, forget about killing me, I'm just your type, let's be partners. Four out of eight. You're only the second to confess a prior murder, though. The other one said she pushed her kid sister out of the tree house. I sure do pick 'em. Two murderers. What are the chances of that?'

'Coincidence,' Jean muttered.

'Nice try.'

His right hand continued to fondle her. His left hand kept jogging the steering wheel from side to side as he maneuvered up the hill.

She could reach up and grab the wheel and maybe make them crash. But the car didn't seem to be moving very fast. At this speed, the crash might not hurt him at all.

'Let's hear the one about your rich father,' he said.

'Go to hell.'

He laughed. 'Come on, don't ruin the score. You'll make it a hundred percent if you've got a rich father who'll pay me heaps of money to take you back to him unscathed.'

She decided to try for the crash.

But the car stopped. He swung the steering wheel way over and started ahead slowly. The car bumped and rocked. Its tires crunched dirt. Leafy branches whispered and squeaked against its sides.

'We're almost there,' he said.

She knew that.

'Almost time to go into your begging routine. Most of them start about now. Sometimes they hold off till we get out,'

I won't beg, Jean thought. I'll run for it.

He stopped the car and turned off the engine. He didn't take the key from the ignition.

'Okay, honey. Sit up slowly and open the door. I'll be right behind you.'

She sat up and turned toward the door. As she levered the handle, he clutched the collar of her blouse. He held onto it while she climbed out. Then he was standing, still gripping her collar, knuckles shoving at the back of her neck to guide her around the door. The door slammed shut. They passed the front of the car and moved toward a clearing in the forest.

The clearing was milky with moonlight. In the center, near a pale dead tree, was a ring of rocks that someone had stacked up to enclose a campfire. A pile of twigs and broken branches stood near the fire ring.

The Reaper steered Jean toward the dead tree.

She saw wood already piled inside the wall of rocks, ready *for a match*.

And she felt a quick glimmer of hope. *Someone* had laid the fire.

Right. *He* probably did it. He was up here earlier, preparing.
She saw a rectangular box at the foot of the tree.

A toolbox?

She began to whimper. She tried to stop walking, but he
shoved her forward.

'Oh please, please, no! Spare me! I'll do anything!'

'Fuck you,' Jean said.

He laughed.

'I like your guts,' he said. 'In a little while, we may take a
good look at them.'

He turned her around and backed her against the tree.

'I'll have to take off one of the cuffs, now,' he explained. He
took a key from the pocket of his pants and held it in front of
her face. 'You won't try to take advantage of the moment, will
you?'

Jean shook her head.

'No, I didn't think so.' He shot a knee up into her belly. His
forearm caught her under the chin, forcing her back as she
started to double. Her legs gave out. She slid down the trunk,
the barkless wood snagging her blouse and scraping her skin. A
knob of root pounded her rump. She started to tumble forward,
but he was there in front of her upthrust knees, blocking her
fall. She slumped back against the trunk, wheezing, feeling the
cuff go away from her right wrist, knowing this was it, this was
the big moment she'd been waiting for, her one and only chance
to make her break.

But she couldn't move. She was hurting and dazed and
breathless. And even if she hadn't been disabled by the blow, her
position made a struggle pointless. She was folded, back tight
against the tree, legs mashing her breasts, arms streched out
over her knees, toes pinned to the ground by his boots.

She knew she had lost.

Strange, though. It didn't seem to matter much.

Jean felt as if she were outside herself, observing. It was someone else being grabbed under the armpits, someone else being lifted. She was watching a movie and the heroine was being prepared for torture. The girl's arms were being raised overhead. The loose cuff was being passed over the top of a limb. Then, it was snapped around the girl's right hand. The Reaper lifted her off her feet and carried her out away from the trunk. Then he let go. The limb was low enough so she didn't need to stand on tiptoes.

The man walked away from his captive. He crouched on the other side of the ring of rocks and struck a match. Flames climbed the tented sticks. They wrapped thick, broken branches. Pale smoke drifted up. He stood and returned to the girl.

'A little light on the subject,' he said to her. His voice sounded as faint as the snapping of the fire behind him.

This is okay, she thought. It's not me. It's someone else – a stranger.

It stopped being a stranger, very fast, when she saw the knife in the Reaper's hand.

She stood rigid and stared at the dark blade. She tried to hold her breath, but couldn't stop panting. Her heart felt like a hammer trying to smash its way out of her chest.

'No,' she gasped. 'Please.'

He smiled. 'I knew you'd get around to begging.'

'I never did anything to you.'

'But you're about to do something *for* me.'

The knife moved in. She felt its cool blade on her skin, but it didn't hurt. It didn't cut. Not Jean. It cut her clothes instead – *the straps of her* bra, the sleeves of her blouse, the waistband of her skirt.

He took the clothes to the fire.

'No! Don't!'

He smiled and dropped them onto the flames. 'You won't need them. You'll be staying right here. Here in the mess hall.'

Somewhere in the distance, a coyote howled.

'That's my friend. We've got an arrangement. I leave a meal for him and his forest friends, and they do the clean-up for me. None of this "shallow grave" nonsense. I just leave you here, tomorrow you'll be gone. They'll come like the good hungry troops they are, and leave the area neat and tidy for next time. No fuss, no bother. And you, sweet thing, will be spared the embarrassment of returning to campus bare-ass.'

Squatting beside the fire, he opened the toolbox. He took out pliers and a screwdriver. He set the pliers on the flat top of a rock. He picked up the screwdriver. Its shank was black even before he held it over the fire. Jean saw the flames curl around it.

'No!' she cried out. 'Please!'

'No! Please!' he mimicked. Smiling, he rolled the screwdriver in his hand. 'Think it's done yet?' He shook his head. 'Give it a few more minutes. No need to rush. Are you savoring the anticipation?'

'You bastard!'

'Is that any way to talk?'

'HELP!' she shouted. 'HELP! PLEASE, HELP ME!'

'Nobody's going to hear you but the coyotes.'

*'You can't do this!'*

'Sure, I can. Done it plenty of times before.'

'Please! I'll do anything!'

'I know just what you'll do. Scream, twitch, cry, kick, beg, drool . . . bleed. Not necessarily in that order, of course.'

He stood up. Pliers in one hand, screwdriver in the other, he walked slowly toward Jean. Wisps of pale smoke rose off the shank of the screwdriver.

He stopped in front of her. 'Now where oh where shall we begin? So many choice areas to choose from.' He raised the screwdriver toward her left eye. Jean jerked her head aside. The tip moved closer. She shut her eye. Felt heat against its lid. But the heat faded. 'No. I'll save that for later. After all, half the fun for *you* will be watching.'

She shrieked and flinched rigid as something seared her belly. The Reaper laughed.

She looked down. He had simply touched her with the nose of the pliers.

'Power of suggestion,' he said. 'Now, let's see how you like some *real* pain.'

Slowly, he moved the screwdriver toward her left breast. Jean tried to jerk away, but the handcuffs stopped her. She kicked out. He twisted away. As the edge of her shoe glanced off his hip, he stroked her thigh with the screwdriver. She squealed.

He grinned. 'Don't do that again, honey, or I might get mean.'

Sobbing, she watched him inch the screwdriver toward her breast again. 'No. Don't. Pleeease.'

A rock struck the side of the Reaper's head. It knocked his head sideways, bounced off, scraped Jean's armpit and fell. He stood there for a moment, then dropped to his knees and slumped forward, face pressing against Jean's groin. She twisted away and he flopped beside her.

She gazed down at him, hardly able to believe he was actually sprawled there. Maybe she'd passed out and this was no more than a wild fantasy. She was dreaming and pretty soon she would come to with a burst of pain and . . .

No, she thought. It can't be a dream. Please.

A dim corner of her mind whispered, *I knew I'd get out of this.* She looked for the rock thrower.

And spotted a dim shape standing beside a tree on the far side of the clearing.

'You got him!' she shouted. 'Thank God, you got him! Great throw!'

The shape didn't move, didn't call back to her.

It turned away.

'No!' Jean cried out. 'Don't leave! He'll come to and kill me! Please! I'm cuffed here! He's got the key in his pocket. You've gotta unlock the cuffs for me. Please!'

The figure, as indistinct in the darkness as the bushes and trees near its sides, turned again and stepped forward. It limped toward the glow of the fire. From the shape, Jean guessed that her savior was a woman.

Others began to appear across the clearing.

One stepped out from behind a tree. Another rose behind a clump of bushes. Jean glimpsed movement over to the right, looked and saw a fourth woman. She heard a growl behind her, twisted around, and gasped at the sight of someone crawling toward her. Toward the Reaper, she hoped. The top of this one's head was black and hairless in the shimmering firelight. As if she'd been scalped? The flesh had been stripped from one side of her back, and Jean glimpsed pale curving ribs before she whirled away.

Now there were *five* in front of her, closing in and near enough to the fire so she could see them clearly.

She stared at them.

And disconnected again.

Came out of herself, became an observer.

The rock thrower had a black pit where her left eye should've been. The girl cuffed beneath the tree was amazed that a one-eyed girl had been able to throw a rock with such fine aim.

It was even more amazing, since she was obviously dead. Ropes of guts hung from her belly, swaying between her legs like an Indian's loincloth. Little but bone remained of her right leg below the knee – the work of the Reaper's woodland troops?

How can she walk?

That's a good one, the girl thought.

How can *any* of them walk?

One, who must've been up here *a very long time*, was managing to shamble along just fine though both her legs were little more than bare bones. The troops had really feasted on her. One arm was missing entirely. The other arm was bone, and gone from the elbow down. Where she still had flesh, it looked black and lumpy. Some of her torso was intact, but mostly hollowed out. The right-hand side of her ribcage had been broken open. The ribs on the left were still there, and a shriveled lung was visible through the bars. Her face had no eyes, no nose, no lips. She looked as if she might be grinning.

The girl beneath the tree grinned back at her, but she didn't seem to notice.

Of course not, dope. How can she see?

How can she walk?

One of the others still had eyes. They were wide open and glazed. She had a very peculiar stare.

No eyelids, that's the trouble. The Reaper must've cut them off. Her breasts, too. Round, pulpy black discs on her chest where they should've been. Except for a huge gap in her right flank, she didn't look as if she'd been maimed by the troops. She still had most of her skin. But it looked shiny and slick with a coating of white slime.

The girl beside her didn't seem to have any skin at all. Had she been peeled? She was black all over except for the whites of her eyes and teeth – and hundreds of white things as if she had been showered with rice. But the rice moved. The rice was alive. Maggots.

The last of the five girls approaching from the front was also black. She didn't look peeled, she looked burnt. Her body was a crust of char, cracked and leaking fluids that shimmered in the firelight. She bore only a rough resemblance to a human being. She might have been shaped out of mud by a dim-witted child who gave her no fingers or toes or breasts, who couldn't manage a nose or ears, and poked fingers into the mud to make her eyes. Her crust made papery, crackling sounds as she shuffled past the fire, and pieces flaked off.

A motley crew, thought the girl cuffed to the limb.

She wondered if any of them would have enough sense to find the key and unlock the handcuffs.

She doubted it.

In fact, they didn't seem to be aware of her presence at all. They were limping and hobbling straight toward the Reaper.

Whose shriek now shattered whatever fragile force had allowed Jean to stay outside the cuffed stranger. She tried to keep her distance. Couldn't. Was sucked back inside the naked, suspended girl. Felt a sudden rush of horror and revulsion . . . and hope.

Whatever else they might be, they were the victims of the Reaper.

Payback time.

He was still shrieking, and Jean looked down at him. He was on his hands and knees. The scalped girl, also on her knees and facing him, had his head caught between her hands. She was biting the top of his head. Jean heard a wet ripping sound as the girl tore off a patch of hair and flesh.

He flopped and skidded backward, dragged by the rock-thrower and the one with the slimy skin. Each had him by a foot. The scalped girl started to crawl after him, then grunted and stopped and tried to pick up the pliers. Her right hand had no fingers. She pawed at the pliers, whimpering with frustration, then sighed when she succeeded in picking up the tool using the thumb and two remaining fingers of her other hand. Quickly, she crawled along trying to catch up to her prize. She scurried past Jean. One of her buttocks was gone, eaten away to the bone.

She gained on the screaming Reaper, reached out and clamped the pliers to the ridge of his ear and ripped out a chunk.

Halfway between Jean and the fire, the girls released his feet. All six went at him.

He bucked and twisted and writhed, but they turned him onto his back. While some held him down, others tore at his clothes. Others tore at *him*. The scalped one took the pliers to his right eyelid and tore it off. The burnt one snatched up a hand and opened her lipless black mouth and began to chew his fingers off. While this went on, the armless girl capered like a madcap skeleton, her trapped lung bouncing inside her ribcage.

Soon, the Reaper's shirt was in shreds. His pants and boxer shorts were bunched around his cowboy boots. The scalped girl had ripped his other eyelid off, and now was stretching his upper lip as he squealed. The rock-thrower, kneeling beside him, clawed at his belly as if trying to get to his guts. Slime-skin bit off one of his nipples, chewed it and swallowed. The girl who must've been skinned alive knelt beside his head, scraping maggots off her belly and stuffing them by the handful into his mouth. No longer shrieking, he choked and wheezed.

The dancing skeleton dropped to her bare kneecaps, bent over him, and clamped her teeth on his penis. She pulled, stretching it, gnawing. He stopped choking and let out a shrill scream that felt like ice picks sliding into Jean's ears.

The scalped girl tore his lip off. She gave the pliers a snap, and watched the lip fly.

Jean watched it, too. Then felt its soft plop against her thigh. It stuck to her skin like a leech. She gagged: She stomped her foot on the ground, trying to shake it off. It kept clinging.

It's just a lip, she thought.

And then she was throwing up. She leaned forward as far as she could, trying not to vomit on herself. A small part of her mind was amused. She'd been looking at hideous, mutilated corpses, such horrors as she had never seen before, not even in her nightmares. And she had watched the corpses do unspeakable things to the Reaper. With all that, she hadn't tossed her cookies.

A lip sticks to my leg, and I'm barfing my guts out.

At least she was missing herself. Most of it was hitting the ground in front of her shoes, though a little was splashing up and spraying her shins.

Finally, the heaving subsided. She gasped for air and blinked tears out of her eyes.

And saw the scalped girl staring at her.

The others kept working on the Reaper. He wasn't screaming anymore, just gasping and whimpering.

The scalped girl stabbed the pliers down. They crashed through the Reaper's upper teeth. She rammed them deep into his mouth and partway down his throat, left them there, and started to crawl toward Jean.

'Get *him*,' she whispered. '*He's* the one.'

Then Jean thought, maybe she wants to help me.

'Would you get the key? For the handcuffs? It's in his pants pocket.'

The girl didn't seem to hear. She stopped at the puddle of

vomit and lowered her face into it Jean heard lapping sounds, and gagged. The girl raised her head, stared up at Jean, licked her dripping lips, then crawled forward.

'No. Get back.'

Opened her mouth wide.

*Christ*!

Jean smashed her knee up into the girl's forehead. The head snapped back. The girl tumbled away.

A chill spread through Jean. Her skin prickled with goose-bumps. Her heart began to slam.

*It won't stop with him.*

*I'm next*!

The scalped girl, whose torso was an empty husk, rolled over and started to push herself up.

Jean leaped.

She caught the tree limb with both hands, kicked toward the trunk but couldn't come close to reaching it. Her body swept down and backward. As she started forward again, she pumped her legs high.

She swung.

She kicked and swung, making herself a pendulum that strained higher with each sweep.

Her legs hooked over the barkless, dead limb.

She drew herself up against its underside, and hugged it.

Twisting her head sideways, she saw the scalped girl crawling toward her again.

Jean had never seen her stand.

If she can't stand up, I'm okay.

But the *others* could stand.

They were still busy with the Reaper. Digging into him. Biting. Ripping off flesh with their teeth. He choked around the pliers and made high squeaky noises. As Jean watched, the charred girl crouched over the fire and put both hands into the flames. When she straightened up, she had a blazing stick trapped between the fingerless flaps of her hands. She lumbered back to the group, crouched, and set the Reaper's pants on fire.

The pants, pulled down until they were stopped by his boot tops, wrapped him just below the knees.

In seconds, they were ablaze.

The Reaper started screaming again. He squirmed and kicked. Jean was surprised he had that much life left in him.

The key, she thought.

I'll have to go through the ashes.

*If I live that long.*

Jean began to shinny out along the limb. It scraped her thighs and arms, but she kept moving, kept inching her way along. The limb sagged slightly. It groaned. She scooted farther, farther.

Heard a faint crackling sound.

Then was stopped by a bone-white branch that blocked her left arm.

'No!' she gasped.

She thrust herself forward and rammed her arm against the branch. The impact shook it just a bit. A few twigs near the far end of it clattered and fell.

The branch looked three inches thick where it joined the main limb. A little higher up, it seemed thin enough for her to break easily – but she *couldn't* reach that far, not with her wrists joined by the short chain of the handcuffs. The branch barred her way like the arm and hand of a skeleton pleased to keep her treed until its companions finished with the Reaper and came for her.

She clamped it between her teeth, bit down hard on the dry wood, gnashed on it. Her teeth barely seemed to dent it.

She lowered her head. Spat dirt and grit from her mouth. Turned her head.

The Reaper was no longer moving or making any sounds. Pale smoke drifted up from the black area where his pants had been burning. The charred girl who had set them ablaze now held his severed arm over the campfire. The slimy, breastless girl was pulling a boot onto one of her feet. The skinned girl, kneeling by the Reaper's head, had removed the pliers from his mouth. At first, Jean thought she was pinching herself with them. That wasn't it, though. One at a time, she was squashing the maggots that squirmed on her belly. The rock-thrower's head was buried in the Reaper's open torso. She reared up, coils of intestine drooping from her mouth. The rotted and armless girl lay flat between the black remains of the Reaper's legs, tearing at the cavity where his genitals used to be.

Though he was apparently dead, his victims all still seemed contented.

For now.

Straining to look down past her shoulder, Jean saw the scalped girl directly below. On her knees. Reaching up, pawing the air with the remains of her hands.

She can't get me. Jean told herself.

But the others.

Once they're done with the Reaper, they'll see that bitch down there and then they'll see me.

If *she'd* just go away!

GET OUT OF HERE!

Jean wanted to shout it, didn't dare. Could just see the others turning their heads toward the sound of her voice.

If I could just kill her!

Good luck on that one.

*Gotta do something*!

Jean clamped the limb hard with her hands. She gritted her teeth.

Don't try it, She thought. You won't even hurt her. You'll be down where she can get at you.

But maybe a good kick in the head'll discourage her.

Fat chance.

Jean released the limb with her legs. She felt a breeze wash over her sweaty skin as she dropped. She thrashed her feet like a drowning woman hoping to kick to the surface.

A heel of her shoe struck something. She hoped it was the bitch's face.

Then she was swinging upward and saw her. Turning on her knees and reaching high, grinning.

Jean kicked hard as she swept down.

The toe of her shoe caught the bitch in the throat, lifted her off her knees and knocked her sprawling.

*Got her!*

Jean dangled by her hands, swaying slowly back and forth. She bucked and tried to fling her legs up to catch the limb. Missed. Lost her hold and cried out as the steel edges of the bracelets cut into her wrists. Her feet touched the ground.

The scalped girl rolled over and crawled toward her.

Jean leaped. She grabbed the limb. She pulled herself up to it and drove her knees high but not fast enough.

The girl's arms wrapped her ankles, clutched them. She pulled at Jean, stretching her, dragging her down, reaching higher, *climbing* her. Jean twisted and squirmed, but couldn't shake the girl off. Her arms strained Her, grip on the limb started to slip. She squealed as teeth ripped into her thigh.

With a *krrrack!*, the limb burst apart midway between Jean and the trunk.

She dropped straight down.

Falling, she shoved the limb sideways. It hammered her shoulder as she landed, knees first, on the girl. The weight drove Jean forward, smashed her down. Though the girl no longer hugged her legs, she felt the head beneath her thigh shake from side to side. She writhed and bucked under the limb. The teeth kept their savage bite on her.

Then *had* their chunk of flesh and lost their grip.

Clutching the limb, Jean bore it down, her shoulder a fulcrum. She felt the wood rise off her back and rump. Its splintered end pressed into the ground four or five feet in front of her head. Bracing herself on the limb, she scurried forward, knees pounding at the girl beneath her. The girl growled. Hands gripped Jean's calves. But not tightly. Not with the missing fingers. Teeth snapped at her, scraping the skin above her right knee. Jean jerked her leg back and shot it forward. The girl's teeth crashed shut. Then Jean was off her, rising on the crutch of the broken limb.

She stood up straight, hugging the upright limb, lifting its broken end off the ground and staggering forward a few steps to get herself out of the girl's reach.

And saw the others coming. All but the rotted skeletal girl who had no arms and still lay sprawled between the Reaper's legs.

'No!' Jean shouted. 'Leave me alone!'

They lurched toward her.

The charred one held the Reaper's severed arm like a club. The breastless girl with runny skin wore both his boots. Her arms were raised, already reaching for Jean though she was still a few yards away. The rock-thrower had found a rock. The skinned girl aswarm with maggots picked at herself with the pliers as she shambled closer.

'NO!' Jean yelled again.

She ducked, grabbed the limb low, hugged it to her side and whirled as the branchy top of it swept down in front of her. It dropped from its height slashing sideways, its bony fingers of wood clattering and bursting into twigs as it crashed through the cadavers. Three of them were knocked off their feet. A fourth, the charred one, lurched backward to escape the blow, stepped into the Reaper's torso and stumbled. Jean didn't see whether she went down, because the weight of the limb was hurling her around in a full circle. A branch struck the face of the scalped girl crawling toward her, popped and flew off. Then the crawling girl was behind Jean again and the others were still down. All except the rock-thrower. She'd been missed, first time around. Out of range. Now, her arm was cocked back, ready to hurl a small block of stone.

Jean, spinning, released the limb.

Its barkless wood scraped her side and belly.

It flew from her like a mammoth, tined lance.

Free of its pull, Jean twirled. The rock flicked her ear. She fell to her knees. Facing the crawler. Who scurried toward her moaning as if she already knew she had lost.

Driving both fists against the ground, Jean pushed herself up. She took two quick steps toward the crawler and kicked her in the face. Then she staggered backward. Whirled around.

The rock-thrower was down, arms batting through the maze of dead branches above her.

The others were starting to get up.

Jean ran through them, cuffed hands high, twisting and dodging as they scurried for her, lurched at her, grabbed.

Then they were behind her. All but the Reaper and the armless thing sprawled between his legs, chewing on him.

*Gotta get the handcuff key*, she thought.

Charging toward them, she realized the cuffs didn't matter. They couldn't stop her from driving. The car key was in the ignition.

She leaped the Reaper.

And staggered to a stop on the other side of his body.

Gasping, she bent over and lifted a rock from the ring around the fire. Though its heat scorched her hands, she raised it overhead. She turned around.

The corpses were coming, crawling and limping closer.

But they weren't that close.

'HERE'S ONE FOR NUMBER EIGHT!' she shouted, and smashed the rock down onto the remains of the Reaper's face. It struck with a wet crunching sound. It didn't roll off. It stayed on his face as if it had made a nest for itself.

Jean stomped on it once, pounding it in farther.

Then she swung around. She leaped the fire and dashed through the clearing toward the waiting car.

# Dinker's Pond

The prospector's yarn went like this. I just kept mum and listened him out.

From the start, she wouldn't have nothing to do with me. She was Jim's gal from head to toe – and all the goodies in between.

I told him, 'Jim, we don't wanta bring her along.'

'I sure do,' he allowed.

'She ain't good for nothing but spawning trouble and ruination.'

Jim said, 'She's right pretty.'

Well, I knew that, but it was off the point. 'She only just wants to fall in with us 'cause of the strike. She's after our gold, that's all. Why, she likely don't even *like* you.'

Jim got this drifty look in his eyes, and I could see his mind was back on last night when he'd sampled Lucy's wares. She'd met up with us yesterday afternoon when we come strutting out of the assay office, which made me suspicious right away. I guess she kept herself stationed there, just waiting for a couple of prospectors to come out grinning.

Right off the bat, she latched onto Jim.

He's the gullible one. That's how come she sidled up to him, not me. Jim's got less sense than mule flop, and it shows all over his face.

You might say to yourself I'm peddling sour grapes when I tell you that's why she went for him, but it's not so. Jim's no younger than me. He wasn't any more sprucy, and he didn't smell any better, and I'm just as fine a specimen of manhood as him. In addition, we were equal partners, though Lucy couldn't of known that at the start.

Nope. Jim's just a stride short of idiot, whereas I've got a fair parcel of brains and common sense.

I'm not one to be led around by the pecker, but you can't say that for Jim, and Lucy knew it.

Next thing you know, I'm all by my lonesome in the saloon and he's got himself a fine room in the Jamestown Hotel getting convinced he's in love.

Which brings me back to that drifty look in his eyes while we're putting away steak and eggs the morning after.

'I reckon she likes me just fine,' he said. 'She's not real keen on you, though, George.'

'Now, there's a fine state of affairs. How long have you and me been partners?' I asked.

He scrunched up his brow, giving it a shot. 'I reckon it's been a spell.'

'It's been a right *long* spell, and now you're all set to ruin us. A woman at the digs is the worst kind of bad luck, you know that just as well as me. You recall what happened to Placer Bill and Mike Murphy over on the Kern.'

Jim puzzled over that, looking for the answer on the spikes of his fork.

'Let me refresh your memory, then. Why, Bill and Mike, they was thick. They was buddies more years than you got teeth.'

'I got most my teeth.' Jim allowed.

'Well, that's the point. It was a lot of years. You couldn't find better buddies than Bob and Mike . . .'

'Thought you said he was Bill.'

'Robert William, that was his name. Some called him Bob, some Bill. Thing is. Bob and Mike was like brothers till the black day a woman showed up at their digs. She took to Mike, right off, and treated Bob so bad you'd think he had the scabbies. Poor Bob, he was left out cold and lonesome. But did he complain and carry on? No, sir. He. was too big a man for that. He bore his troubles in silence. And you recall what happened then?'

'What was the gal's name?' Jim asked.

'Greta.'

'I recall a Greta Gurney in Bible school. A redhead. Was this Greta that took up with Mike a redhead?'

'I don't believe she was.'

'Didn't you never see her?'

'Let me tell the story, will you? You're enough to drive the patience out of a hospital for the blind and crippled.'

'Well, I just . . .'

411

'This weren't your Greta. This was some other Greta. Now, the point I'm trying to stick you with is this – when she went strolling into the digs, she brought disaster and tragedy down on the luckless heads of Bill and Mike. It wasn't bad enough she spurned Bill and made a shambles of two fast pals. No, sir. That was bad, but it weren't bad enough.

'The way it turns out, she'd run off from her spouse. She didn't let on about that, however. No, she kept mum on the. subject of her spouse. He was Lem Jaspers, a one-eyed smuggler from Frisco. And he went looking for her. And he found her out there on the Kern with Bill and Mike, and massacred the three of them.'

'Killed 'em?'

'He killed 'em mean and slow. I'd tell you all about it, but I don't want to spoil your breakfast. Let me just say it weren't pretty. He put out Mike's eyes with a burning stick to make him suffer for looking at Greta. And he cut off Mike's pecker with a Bowie knife and shoved it up Greta's whatsis. He told her, "You wanted it so bad, now you got it."'

Jim was starting to look a little gray around the lips.

'After they was dead,' I went on, 'he took the skin right off Greta. Peeled her raw. He tossed her face in the campfire. The rest of her skin, he tanned it. I won't tell you about the tobacco pouch. But Lem used some of Greta's hide to fashion himself a new pair of moccasins so he could have the pleasure of walking around on her all the time.'

'Mighty lowdown of him,' Jim allowed.

'That wasn't the lowest of the low, either. Lem didn't let it go with taking out his vengeance on Greta and Mike. He took poor Bill and gutted him like a trout. Here, Bill was just as innocent as a baby, never put a hand to Greta, but Lem slaughtered him just the same.'

'That weren't right.'

'Right or not, Bill met himself a grisly end, and it was all because his buddy turned traitor on him and took up with a gal. Like I said, a woman at the digs is the worst kind of luck.'

'What happened to Lem?'

'Well, I don't know. For all I know, maybe he got tired of being a widower and hitched up with your Lucy.'

Jim spent a long time pondering that, scowling down at his plate and wiping his hand around on it to get up the last of the egg yellow. After he was done licking his hand, he raised his eyes to me. I could see he was grateful for the warning. But what he said was, 'We'll keep our eyes sharp. If this Lem comes along, you and me we'll shoot him dead.'

A man only has so much breath to spare in this life, and I'd just wasted a good parcel of it. I might as well of told my story to the butt end of a mule.

Later on in the morning, just before the three of us headed out, Jim took me aside. 'I had a talk with Lucy,' he whispered. 'She don't know any Lem Jaspers, but she knew a Jasper Wiggens once. She claims she never married him.'

I figured Lucy was bound to warm up to me, once she got to know me better. She got to know me a whole sight better on our travels back to the Stanislaus where we'd made our strike, but she didn't warm up like I hoped.

The way she looked at me, one would think I had nasty stuff hanging out my nose.

The trip took longer than it should've. Every now and again, they'd leave me on the trail so I could keep the mules company, and Lucy'd take Jim off into the woods. She did it mostly just to torment me. Half the time, she'd come back half unfastened to give me a look at regions she never planned to let me scout around in.

Lucy was as cruel and cold-hearted as any woman that ever crossed my path.

Still, I tried to be friends with her. I wanted to get into her good graces, even if not her drawers. And who knows but that the former might lead up the trail to the latter?

No matter what I did, though, she spurned me.

She even spurned my stories. Jim liked to listen to them pretty near as much as I liked the telling. On the first night, she sat there by the cookfire sighing and rolling her eyes around while I told my best rip-snorter about the squaw with the two-headed baby. One head was partial to one of her tits, and the other hankered all the time for the other. Trouble was, the heads didn't match up with the tits they favored, so the squaw had to hold the child upside down at chow time. The little scamp liked that just fine. Only thing was, he got so fond of being upside down he never learned the use of his legs. He grew up walking on his hands with his feet in the air, and drowned himself one day when he tried to wade a stream that weren't even waist deep.

Well, Jim just nearly split his sides while I told that one. Lucy, she just sat there acting like she wished I'd either shut up or die.

Before I could start in with a new story, she said to me, 'George Sawyer, you're about as crude as the day is long. I'd rather be snakebit than listen to another one of your vile whoppers.'

'Why, that was a true story,' Jim said, sticking up for me.

She turned her eyes on him. They were pretty eyes that glimmered in the firelight, but there didn't seem to be much warmth inside them. 'If you believe that was true. Jimmy dear, why you've got dust in your brain pan.'

Jimmy dear looked at me, scowling from the effort of trying to piece a thought together. 'You been telling fibs?'

'A false word has never passed these lips. Why, I was there when the boy drowned, both heads down in the creek and his feet kicking like a hanged man.'

Jim turned to Lucy, raised his eyebrows and said, 'See?'

'All I see,' she opined, 'is one lying fool and one idiot. Makes me wonder why I ever took up with you in the first place, James Bixby.'

That let the air out of his sails something horrible to witness. He sat there, slumped over and speechless, while Lucy flounced her way into the shadows and crawled into her blankets.

I tried to cheer him up. 'How'd you like to hear about the time I got pulled under the quicksand and . . .'

'Never happened at all,' he muttered, looking as if he'd caught me with a fifth ace in my hand. 'You'd of gone down in the quicksand, you'd be dead, George.'

'Well, I *would've* been dead, but there was such a heap of skeletons down there at the bottom that I was able to fashion myself a ladder and . . .'

I could see by his eyes that he was just starting to believe me again. I could see his doubts just melting away. But all of a sudden, Lucy called to him.

'Come on away from that lying, foul-mouthed nogood. Right this minute. I'm cold over here. Come on over and heat me up.'

Jim was mighty quick on his feet after he heard that.

I was left all by my lonesome, listening to the lively crackle and snap of the fire, the wind in the trees, and Lucy grunting and squealing like a sow getting stuck by a hot poker.

My own poker got mighty hot while I heard her carrying on that way.

Lucy weren't a sow, even if she did sound like one.

Sitting there on my rock, I felt like the two-headed boy. One of my heads thought it'd be a nice idea to poke her. The other would just as soon put a bullet in her noggin.

Neither one of my heads done a thing about it.

After that first night on the trail, I didn't tell no more stories. A couple of times, I made the offer. The offer caused Jim to shake his head sadly, and caused Lucy to spit in the fire.

Finally, we got to our digs on the Stanislaus. We got there just after dark. Lucy didn't express any great fondness for our shack. I allowed as how she might rather sleep under the stars, but she asked me to shut my yap.

She spent a good portion of the night bellyaching about how she couldn't properly breathe in such close quarters, and how a woman requires some privacy, and how this was the one and only night she would ever spend beneath the same roof as George Sawyer, a lying man of such vile habits and temperament that he was no better than a plague of worms.

Lucy not only gnashed her teeth and bitterly complained about our 'hovel,' but she refused Jim her favors. 'My modesty won't allow it,' she protested. 'Not with *him* breathing down our necks.'

I considered her remark about modesty to be a joke, but neither Jim or me was happy with her decision, which come as a letdown to both of us. On the trail, I'd grown partial to the sounds she made. I'd started looking forward to the three of us in the shack. She was right about close quarters. If she and Jim went at it in the shack, I was sure to hear more than her wild grunts and groans. I was likely to see more, too. The way I had it figured, that would suit Lucy just fine. The more she could torment me, the better she'd like it.

But maybe she reckoned it'd push me too far and I might join in.

Maybe she was right.

At any rate, she didn't risk it. She just left Jim alone that night.

While I tried to get asleep, I figured up a few of the wrongs she'd done to me and Jim.

She'd stolen my pal. She cheated me and Jim out of the pleasure we took in my stories. Finally, she was holding out, robbing Jim out of the reason he'd brung her along in the first place and keeping me from the pleasures of being a witness when she got herself poked.

Like I said before, I never met a crueler, colder-hearted woman.

Come the next morning, Jim set out with an axe figuring to knock down some forest and put up a mansion for his lady. I figured I'd let him handle that on his own. I was here to dig gold. His lady could sleep in the dirt, for what I cared.

I took my pick out to the mine and set to work. However, I couldn't get the blamed woman out of my head. I kept pondering on her, wondering what she might be up to now that she was all by her lonesome. Pretty soon, I come to figure this'd be a fine chance to visit with her. Without Jim around to muddle up the works, maybe I could set things right with her. Or at least give her my angle on matters.

Well, I went looking for her. Lucy weren't in the shack, and she weren't at the river. I scouted some more, and pretty soon I come upon her.

The gal was down by the shore of Dinker's Pond, slipping off her duds. I ducked behind the big old tree at the top of the slope, and give my eyes a treat. I'd gotten looks at bits and pieces of her along the trail, but now I got to see the whole woman and it weren't any wonder Jim felt obliged to bring her along. She could knock the breath out of a dead man.

Me, I got caught up in looking, and she was up to her knees in the pond before I sung out.

'Get on outa there!' I yelled.

She jumped like I'd jabbed her with a stick. I reckon she forgot to be modest, for she turned herself around and rammed her fists into her hips without even trying to cover nothing. 'George Sawyer!' she railed. 'You son-of-a-bitch! You dirty, rotten, lowdown, leprous, claim-jumpin' son-of-a-whore!'

'I ain't no claim-jumper,' I informed the woman, and started on my way down the slope.

She aimed an arm at me and shook a finger. The finger weren't all the shook. 'Don't you come any closer! Get outa here! You bastard, don't you dare come down here!'

I kept coming, and she started backing up till the water crawled around her waist. About that time, she remembered her modesty and so she hunkered down till she was covered to the neck.

'Wouldn't do that, were I you,' I said. I sat myself down on a stump by the shore. Her clothes were heaped in front of me, but I kept my boots off them. 'You'd better listen to me, gal, and step outa that water pretty lively.'

'I most surely won't.'

'Should've gone over in the river, if you wanted to get yourself wet. Shouldn't of come here.'

'I go where I like. Sides, the river's so cold I'd freeze up solid.'

'You're in Dinker's Pond,' I informed her.

'Well, it's a good pond. It *were* a good pond till you showed up. Go on and get.'

'Used to be a good fishing hole,' I allowed. 'Up till around a year ago. Just ask Jim if you don't believe me. But the fishes, they all petered out after we strung up Clem Dinker.'

Lucy, she squinted her eyes at me. Then her hand come up with a rock. She kind of unsquatted there for a second and let fly. I got distracted, admiring her, or I could've dodged. The rock give me a good clip on the shoulder.

I jumped up, rubbing my hurt.

'Don't you come in here!' Lucy yelled, and fetched up another rock.

'Not me. I ain't a fool like some.'

'I'm a fool, am I?' She pitched the rock, but I ducked it.

'You're a fool for sure, you don't come outa there.'

'Jim, he's gonna shoot you dead.'

'Jim'll be mighty grateful I happened to come on down here and warn you off.'

'You just come here fixing to doodle me.' All of a sudden. she lost her mean glare and found a smile. 'You're scared of the water, George Sawyer. Ha!'

'I'm scared of *that* water. You'd be scared of it, too, if you knew what I know.'

'Oh, dear me, yes. I'd be thrown into such a fright I'd hop right out and be ever so grateful. Oh, George, you're just pitiful.' She eased herself back and started floating, all sprawled out pale and shiny on the water, grinning up at the sky. 'You're just the most pitiful thing.'

'I'm half inclined to leave you to your fate,' I called.

She picked up her head, and the rest of her sank out of sight. 'Did you say something, poor George?'

'Maybe I'll just go off and leave you.'

'You can't leave, George.' She must've found the bottom, for she come up a little. The water was almost up to her shoulders. It was too murky to let me see anything worthwhile, unless you

419

count her smile. That wasn't under water, but I wouldn't count it. It was too smirky and mean. 'Why, you haven't scared me witless yet,' she said. 'I 'spect, once I've heard your whopper, I'll just come out screaming and hurl myself into your manly arms.'

She reckoned I *couldn't* scare her out of the pond.

I took it for a challenge.

So I set myself down on the stump. 'Did you ever hear of a fella named Clem Dinker?'

'Why, no, George. Do tell me all about him.'

'Clem, he was a crazy man that used to live in a tree over across the river. He was so skinny, looked like he never ate nothing. But that weren't so. Clem used to eat everything he could get his teeth on.

'When it come to food, he was just about the most patient, sneaky fella you ever seen. He'd sit so quiet, up in his tree, that birds'd come along and settle on him. When they done that, he'd grab 'em quick and pop 'em right into his mouth. Munched the tweeters up, wings, beaks, eyes and all. We used to hear him off in the distance, coughing up feathers.'

Lucy shook her head and rolled her eyes up at the sky. 'Well, George,' she said, 'I just got goosebumps running all up and down my body. You keep scaring me like this, I might just swoon dead away.'

'If you swoon, you're on your own. Now, do you want to keep on mocking me, or you want to hear about Clem?'

'Oh, I beg your pardon. Please, go on.'

'Clem, he'd eat just about anything. He just weren't particular. If he could get his teeth on it, he'd chow it down. Did I tell you he had pointed teeth?'

Lucy laughed.

'Yes, ma'am. You may not care to believe it, but Clem filed all his front teeth so they come to points. They was so sharp, he couldn't talk much without ruining his lips. You'd be talking to the fella, and he'd no sooner answer back than the blood'd start flying at you. He'd act like he didn't even notice, and you'd be standing there getting rained on. It was enough to make you lose your train of thought.'

'If your mama'd had a lick of sense,' Lucy said, 'she would've strangled you at birth.'

'I'm only just telling you how it was. I ain't making up any of this. You don't believe me, ask Jim. He'll tell you same as me. Why, I laid down for a snooze one day after chatting a spell with that man, and Jim come upon me and I was so bloody he took me for dead and had a grave half dug before I woke up.

'But that's off the point,' I said before Lucy could start in again. 'Thing is, Clem Dinker was crazy mad, and he'd eat anything he could get his pointy teeth into. Not just birds. We seen him eat a beaver, once. And there was a trapper over yonder had a hound till Clem got hold of it. He gobbled up squirrels, coons, coyotes, butterflies, spiders, slugs and worms.'

Lucy wasn't smiling any more. She was giving me a hateful look, and her upper lip had crawled up above her gums. I could see she was ready to start yelling, and I might never have a chance to finish my story. So I got to the point quick.

'Clem finally ate one of our mules. Her name was Jane, and we come upon Clem with his face buried in her innards. So we strung him up.' I twisted around and pointed up the slope at the same tree I'd hidden behind to watch Lucy strip off her duds. 'See that branch there? The one sticks out this way? That's where we hung him from.'

'You didn't hang nobody,' Lucy said. She didn't say it spunky, though. Seemed like she'd lost some of her starch.

'I put the noose around his scrawny little neck, myself. We

stood Clem smack on the edge, up there under the three. The plan was, we'd give Clem a push, and he'd swing out over the bank and strangulate.

'But he was our first hanging. The mistake was, we should've made the rope tight between Clem's neck and the branch. Way it turned out, it had a mite too much slack in it. So when we nudged him off the edge, he didn't swing so much as he dropped. Plucked his noggin right off his shoulders.

'Well, we carted Clem's body off into the woods and planted it. All but his head. Being round like it was, it rolled on downhill and plopped into the pond here. We never could find hide nor hair of it. That's how come we call this place Dinker's Pond. His head's still in there, far as we know.'

Lucy, she just sort of stared at me.

'After a spell, the fish in there started to peter out. Pretty soon, there wasn't none to be caught at all. Oh, you'd get nibbles pretty quick. Bring up your hook, and your bait'd be gone. But you never had a fish for your troubles. Me and Jim went through a whole parcel of worms before we give up on our old fishing hole.'

Lucy, standing real still, slanted her eyes down at the water. Then she jerked them up at me real quick. I could see she was riled that I'd caught her looking at the water. 'Weren't a breath of truth in that yarn, George Sawyer. It didn't tell me nothing I didn't already know – just that you're vile trash that ain't fit for human civilization.'

'I ain't no liar,' I said.

I caught her eyes checking around some more.

Then they darn near popped out and Lucy threw a holler that made my hair stand up. She commenced to thrash around considerable. The water around her churned and bubbled and got kind of red.

I give some thought to splashing in to try and save her. Would've been mighty heroic.

That was the end of George's yarn, and the end of the whisky bottle sitting between us on the saloon table.

'And you didn't even lift a finger to save her?' I asked.

'She didn't amount to much, anyhow,' George said.

'Now you want *me* going out to the digs with you?'

'Gets mighty lonesome out there. It surely does. I reckon I'd risk some bad luck for the company of a sweet thing like you.'

'You've got Jim, don't you?'

'Well, he come at me with his axe when he saw what happened to Lucy. Couldn't talk him outa it. He got it into his head it was me killed Lucy and chewed her up that way. So I had to shoot him.'

'Did you do her that way, George? Was it you?'

'Why, Mabel, bite your tongue. I ain't that kinda man. And you ain't lowdown like Lucy was. That gal was pure poison. She was such poison I run across Dinker's head next morning in the pond there, afloating face up with his lips turned black.'

# Madman Stan

The TV screen went blank.

Billy, sitting on the floor in front of it, felt his mouth sag open. He twisted his head around. Agnes gave him a mean smile from the couch. She had the remote control in her hand, aimed like a gun at the television. 'Hey, that's no fair,' he said. 'The show wasn't even over.'

'It is now,' Agnes said. 'Time for beddy-bye, children.'

Billy turned his eyes to Rich, looking for help.

The boy's arms were folded across his plaid robe. He was frowning. 'We're allowed to stay up until eleven on Saturday nights,' he informed the woman. 'It isn't even ten yet.'

Billy nodded, proud of his older brother.

'Children your age belong in bed at a decent hour,' Agnes said.

'If I may speak my mind,' said Rich, 'that really bites.'

Agnes smiled at him. 'Aren't you the little darling?'

'Well, it does. And Mom and Dad are going to hear about this. *They* let us stay up. So does Linda.'

'Linda isn't here,' Agnes said in her sweet, nasty voice. 'And frankly, I'm more than a little sick of hearing about that twit.'

'Linda isn't a twit,' Billy said, gaining courage from his brother's stand against this dumpy old creep. 'She's a lot nicer than you are. And besides, you don't even know her.'

Agnes peered at her wristwatch. 'I'm losing my patience, children. It's off to bed with you, now.'

'You're a really rotten babysitter,' Rich said.

'Why, thank you. And you, my dear, are a really rotten child.'

Rich's face turned red. He stood up. 'Come on, Billy. Let's get out of here.'

'Yeah.' He got to his feet.

'Don't go away mad,' Agnes said, and chuckled.

They headed for the other end of the living room, glancing at each other. Rich looked steamed.

'No, I mean it,' Agnes called after them. 'Come back here. I've got a little surprise for you. Something to cheer you up.'

They turned to face her. 'What?' Rich asked.

The lamplight gleamed on Agnes's glasses. Her chubby face widened with a grin. 'A bedtime story. A *scary* one.'

Billy felt a quick flutter in his stomach.

He looked at Rich. Rich looked at him.

'I'll just wager your precious Linda never tells you spooky stories.'

'Sure she does,' Rich said, and Billy nodded.

'Not as spooky as mine.'

That wouldn't be too hard, Billy thought. Linda was great, but her stories were just okay. Billy figured *he* could tell scarier stories than Linda.

'You want to hear it, don't you?'

Billy blurted, 'Sure.'

Rich shrugged, 'Yeah, I guess so.'

'Should I . . .?' Billy stopped himself.

'Should you what?' Agnes asked.

'Nothing,' he muttered.

He had almost said 'turn off the lights.' That's what they did when Linda told stories. Made the living room dark and sat on the couch, Linda between them. Even if her stories weren't so hot, it was wonderful. She would put her arms around them. Even in winter, she always seemed to smell like suntan oil.

'Why don't we turn off the lights?' Agnes suggested.

Rich shook his head. 'Billy's afraid of the dark.'

You lying sack, Billy thought, and nodded and tried to look worried.

He wasn't afraid of the dark. Not usually, anyhow. But he certainly did not want to be in a dark room with Agnes.

'Leave the lights on, then.' She patted the cushion on each side of her.

Billy pretended not to see that. He sat down on the carpet,

facing her, and crossed his legs. Rich sank to the floor beside him.

Agnes laughed softly and shook her head. Her cheeks wobbled. 'You're not frightened of *me*, are you?' she asked.

'Huh-uh.' That was the truth, too. He wasn't frightened of Agnes. Not much, anyhow. But the idea of sitting close to her on the couch was revolting. The woman was not only fat and ugly, but she had some kind of sour smell like a washcloth that had sat around damp too long.

For the zillionth time, Billy wished Linda didn't have that date tonight. He sure liked sitting up there with her.

'This is how we always sit,' Rich lied again.

'I didn't relish the idea myself,' she said, 'of you two darlings up here with me.'

'Are you going to tell us the story?' Rich asked. He sounded good and impatient.

'Are you ready for it? Maybe you need to wee-wee first.'

'We'll urinate later,' Rich told her.

Billy almost laughed, but held it in. He didn't want to make Agnes mad, or she might call off the story.

The woman scooted back on the couch. She grunted softly as she brought her legs up and crossed them on the cushion. Billy was surprised she *could* cross them, they were so thick. He was also surprised her pink sweatpants didn't split open. The way they bulged, they looked as if they might burst at any second and let Agnes's flesh flop out all over the couch.

She folded her arms across the front of her sweatshirt in a way that made her look like she was trying to hide a couple of footballs and sneak them past the defensive line.

The idea of that made Billy smile.

'Would you like to tell us what you find amusing, young man?'

He felt his face go hot. 'Nothing. Huh-uh. I was just daydreaming, that's all.'

'Don't daydream during my story.'

'We're both going to fall asleep if you don't get on with it,' Rich said.

'All right.' She cleared her throat. She squirmed a little as if trying to work her fat rump deeper into the cushion. 'This is the story of why nobody goes to bed at night without making sure to lock the house up tight.'

'I know, I know,' Rich said. 'So the boogeyman can't get in.'

'Save your sarcasm for that Linda twat. And don't interrupt me, or I won't let you hear the story.'

'C'mon, Rich,' Billy said. 'Don't interrupt.'

Rich made a quiet huff.

'In some towns,' Agnes said, 'people don't lock their doors at night. But we always do, here in Oakwood. There's a very good reason for that. It's because of the madman.' Agnes bobbed her around head. 'Madman Stan,' she said, her voice lower, almost a whisper. 'Nobody knows where he comes from. But I've heard it said he hangs around the cemetery, especially on hot summer nights when he likes to take off all his clothes and get up against the tombstones. They're cool, you know. They feel good when it's so hot at night you can't sleep. Remember that, come summer.'

Rich glanced at Billy and rolled his eyes, upward.

But Agnes didn't seem to notice. She was gazing straight ahead, swaying gently back and forth.

'Myself,' she said in that same low voice, 'I've never seen him in among the graves. But I've been told by others. I've been told that's where he takes his victims. Nobody'll even whisper what he does with 'em. But I've got my own ideas on that.'

'What?' Rich whispered.

Agnes stopped swaying. She stared down at him. 'You don't want to know.'

'You're just making this up, anyway,' he muttered.

She smiled. 'The Madman Stan will settle for men and women. And he likes little girls very much. But more than anything else in the whole wide world, he likes little boys. They're his favorite.'

'Sure,' Rich said.

Billy nudged him with an elbow. Rich elbowed him back, harder.

'Like I told you, I don't know what the madman does with them. But they're never seen again. Ever. Folks who live over by the graveyard say they hear screams, sometimes. Horrible screams. And sometimes, they hear digging sounds out there.'

'Like fun,' Rich muttered.

'Not much fun for those he snatches,' Agnes said. 'Not much fun at all, I should think. That's why we all lock our doors up tight, here in Oakwood. Like I told you, I've never seen Madman Stan over by the graveyard. But I've seen him other places. Plenty of times. Always late at night. I'll be looking out a window at the street, or I'll be walking home after a sitting job, and I'll see him. I've even seen him right here on Fifth Street. Do you know what he's doing?'

Rich didn't make any crack. Billy felt a little breathless and Sick.

'The madman is walking from block to block, from house to house, going up to each and every door and trying the knob. He's looking for a door that isn't locked. And when he finds one, in he goes. And that's the last of someone.' Agnes nodded and grinned. 'Off to bed, children.'

'That's all?' Rich asked. 'That's no story.'

'That's my story. Now, to bed with you. I want you to go

straight to sleep, children.' Her grin suddenly grew so large that her cheeks pushed against the bottom of her glasses and the round lenses drifted upward. 'If I hear so much as a peep out of either one of you . . .' Unfolding her arms, she pointed past the end of the couch toward the front door of the house. 'I'll unlock it.'

'Rich?'

'Shut up,' Rich whispered.

Billy braced himself up on his elbows and squinted through the darkness. His brother's bed, just on the other side of the night table, was a dim blur. He thought maybe the small pale area near the headboard might be Rich's face. 'It wasn't true, was it?' he asked.

Low on the pale area, a dark spot moved when Rich said, 'Don't be a dork.'

Billy was seeing Rich's face, all right. That was a relief. He said, 'It kind of sounded like it might be, you know?'

'She was just trying to scare us.'

'Are you sure?'

'There's no madman going around trying doorknobs. Are you kidding? The cops'd be all over a guy like that.'

'Yeah, I guess.'

'So forget about it and . . .'

The bedroom door flew open, slamming the wall. Billy flinched. He jerked his head toward the light.

Agnes filled the doorway, fists on her hips. 'What did I tell you children about talking?'

'We weren't,' Rich argued.

'I'm not deaf, sweetie-pie. I told you what I'd do, didn't I? You bet I did! And that's just what I aim to do.'

She jerked the door shut, cutting out the light.

Billy clutched his pillow to his face. He clamped his lower lip between his teeth. He tried not to cry.

He listened.

Listened for the quiet clack of Agnes unlocking the front door.

He didn't hear it. That was awfully far away.

But soon he heard quiet sniffing, gasping sounds. They came from the other bed.

'Rich?' he whispered.

'Shut up.'

'Are you crying?'

'None of your business. It's all your fault, you little crud.' He made a wet, slurpy sniffle. 'Why'd you have to go and open your big mouth?'

'I'm sorry.'

'Now she's gone and unlocked the door.'

'You said you didn't believe in Madman Stan.'

'I don't.'

'Then what are you crying about?'

'I'm not. It's just she's such a bitch.' Another loud sniff. 'How could Mom and Dad leave us with a bitch like that?'

Billy shrugged, even though he knew Rich couldn't see it. 'Linda had that date.'

'Hope she had a rotten time.'

'Don't say that, Rich.'

'She should've been with us.'

'You're telling me.'

'Shut up before *she* comes back.'

'Okay.' Billy rested his head against the pillow and shut his eyes.

He heard soft, muffled sobbing.

Jeez, he thought. Rich is even more scared than me, and he doesn't even believe it about the madman.

430

Bet he *does* believe it.

'Mom and Dad'll be home pretty soon,' he whispered.

'Oh, sure. Pretty soon. Like two or three hours.'

'I bet she didn't unlock the door, anyway.'

'Like fun she didn't. Shut up, huh?'

'Okay.'

Billy rolled onto his back. He stared at the ceiling. He listened to his brother cry.

After a while, the crying stopped.

'Rich?' he whispered.

No answer.

'You asleep?'

It seemed impossible. How could *anyone* fall asleep with the front door unlocked and everything?

Soon, Rich started to snore.

Billy felt deserted. It wasn't fair. Rich shouldn't leave him alone like this.

He wished *he* could fall asleep. But his eyes felt locked open.

My bed's closest to the door, he thought. When Madman Stan comes, he'll get me first.

He had an urge to watch the door. But fear stopped him. What if he turned his head to look and just then the madman smashed the door open?

So he kept on staring at the ceiling.

He wished Rich would wake up.

I could wake him up, he thought. We could sneak out the window and get out of here.

If we do that, we'll be outside where *he* is.

Billy considered hiding under his bed.

That's probably the first place a madman would look.

Besides, what if I hide and he gets Rich instead of me?

For a while, he wondered how things would be without his

431

brother around. Rich teased him a lot and started fights. But sometimes he was okay. Billy sure didn't want the madman to get him and take him to the graveyard and do things to him that even a rotten bag like Agnes wouldn't talk about.

Rich called her a bitch.

He'd get in trouble if Mom or Dad found out.

Well, she *is* a bitch.

Billy suddenly had a thought that made him smile.

If Madman Stan comes to the house and the door is unlocked and he comes in . . . won't he get Agnes first?

Doesn't she know that?

Is she a stupe, or what?

Billy had another nice thought.

The bitch didn't unlock the door, at all.

He knew positively that Agnes had lied about unlocking the door.

He just wished he could be sure.

Heart slamming, Billy eased open the bedroom door until a strip of light came in. He peered through the crack. The coast was clear.

He slipped into the hallway. Getting down on his hands and knees, he made his way to the dining room. He crawled between a chair and a table leg.

What'll I do if she sees me? he wondered.

Sometimes, Mom and Dad caught him under the table. But plenty of times they hadn't. He and Rich had both gotten away with watching late TV shows from under here while their parents watched from the couch, just out of sight because the edge of the doorway blocked them out.

Billy halted when he could see the television. It wasn't on.

What's she doing anyhow? he wondered.

Maybe reading a magazine, or something.

If she was reading, he might be able to sneak by and get to the front door.

He crawled slowly toward the far end of the table, turning his head and gazing out through the bars of the chair and table legs. Finally, the bottom of the couch came into view. He inched upward, leaned forward, and peered around a chair back that was in the way.

Agnes was lying down on the couch.

A big mound of pink, hands folded on the hill of her stomach.

Her eyes were shut. She didn't have her glasses on.

Billy spotted her glasses on the lamp table between the end of the couch and the front door.

Okay, he thought.

He didn't *feel* okay. He could hardly catch his breath and his heart was thundering and he felt like he needed to use the bathroom bad.

But this was his chance.

He crept out from under the table. Staying on his hands and knees, keeping his eyes fixed on Agnes, he crawled into the living room.

*Wait'll I tell Rich*, he thought.

'You what?' Rich would say.

'Yeah, I just crawled over to the door and made sure it was locked.'

'And Agnes was there?'

'Yeah, right on the couch.'

'Wow, Billy. I didn't know you had that kind of guts.'

'Wasn't any big deal.'

'How did you sneak by without her seeing you?'

'Indian style.'

'Was she asleep or something?'

'I don't know. She could've been playing possum.'

Billy's fantasy fell apart. *What if she is playing possum?*

He halted and stared at Agnes.

Her eyes were still shut. Her mouth hung open. Her chin looked like a golf ball someone had shoved into a pile of raw dough that was heaped up where her neck was supposed to be. The front of her sweatshirt slowly rose and fell.

She *is* asleep, Billy told himself.

But he wasn't sure of that, any more than he was sure she had lied about unlocking the door.

If only she would snore.

Billy forced himself to start crawling again. He was halfway to the door when a floorboard creaked under his knee. He cringed. A hand slid down the slope of Agnes's stomach. It fell off the edge of the couch, taking her arm with it. Billy scurried forward, knowing she would wake up, praying he could get past the head of the couch before she opened her eyes.

His spine froze as she mumbled something.

Her eyes stayed shut.

At last, the stuffed arm of the couch blocked Billy's view of her head. He slowed down, and crept past the lamp table. When he was even with the front door, he turned to the right and crawled toward it.

Staring at the lock.

It had an oblong brass gizmo that you turned between your thumb and forefinger. It was straight up and down. But it always was. By looking, you couldn't tell whether or not the door was locked.

Billy would have to try the knob.

Bracing himself up with his left arm, he raised his right hand toward the knob.

*What if Madman Stan's right outside?* he thought.

*What if he's reaching for the knob right now?*

Billy's fingers fluttered as if he were having a spaz attack. He closed them around the doorknob. The knob rattled. He heard a soft whimper slip out of his throat.

Holding his breath, he turned the knob.

He pulled.

The door wouldn't budge.

The dirty pig hadn't unlocked it, after all.

Behind the dining-room table again, Billy got to his feet. He pressed a hand against his chest. His heart was kicking like a wildman.

I did it, he told himself.

*I did it and she didn't catch me.*

He stared at Agnes, still sleeping on the couch.

He felt a smile stretch his mouth.

Then he tiptoed toward the bedroom, hoping Rich might be awake so he could tell him about it.

Billy woke up in the dark, terrified, hot urine shooting down his leg as something bashed the bedroom door again and again and Rich shrieked, '*Yaaaaaaaah!*'

More bashing. The door opened wider with each bash as the straight-backed chair under its knob scooted a bit more on the carpet.

'Boys!' Dad shouted.

Billy had never heard him sound so scared.

'Boys! What's going on!'

Billy hurled himself out of bed. He rushed toward the door, wet pajama pants sticking to his groin and left leg. He pulled the chair out from under the knob and backed away.

Dad came in. He hit the light switch. He was out of breath, eyes bulging as he looked quickly from Billy to Rich. 'They're okay!' he called over his shoulder.

'Oh, thank God.' Mom lurched through the doorway, weeping.

'What's been going on around here?' Dad asked. 'Jesus! Where's the babysitter? Why was the door blocked? What's going on?'

Rich had stopped screaming a few seconds ago. Now, he was sitting up in bed, crying and shaking his head.

'Agnes was *horrible*,' Billy blurted.

'Well where is she? How could she go off and leave you guys? What the hell . . .?'

Mom, Billy noticed, was holding Agnes's glasses down by her side.

'We come home,' Dad went on, 'and the Goddamn baby-sitter's gone and the front door's standing wide open! What the hell happened?'

'Madman Stan got her,' Rich whimpered through his sobs. 'Oh geez! She unlocked the door so he'd get *us*, but . . .' Then, he was crying too hard to say more.

Billy looked up at his parents and shook his head. He decided not to tell who had really unlocked the door.

# Bad News

The morning was sunny and quiet. Leaving the door ajar, Paul crossed the flagstones to his driveway. He sidestepped alongside his Granada, being careful neither to tread on the dewy grass nor to let his robe rub against the grimy side of the car.

As he cleared the rear bumper, he spotted the *Messenger*.

Good. Nobody had beaten him to it.

Every so often, especially on weekends, somebody swiped the thing. Not this morning, though. Getting up early had paid off. The newspaper, rolled into a thick bundle and bound by a rubber band, lay on the grass just beyond the edge of Paul's driveway.

On Joe Applegate's lawn.

Crouching to pick it up, Paul glanced at his neighbor's driveway and yard and front stoop.

There was no sign of Applegate's paper.

Probably already took it inside, Paul thought. Unless somebody snatched it.

Hope the damn redneck doesn't think *this* is his.

Paul straightened up, tucked the paper under one arm, and made his way up the narrow strip of pavement between his car and the grass.

Inside the house, he locked the front door. He tossed the newspaper onto the coffee table, started away, and thought he saw the paper wobble.

He looked down at it.

The *Messenger* lay motionless on the glass top of the coffee table.

437

It was rolled into the shape of a rather thick, lopsided tube. The wobble he'd noticed out of the corner of his eye must've been the paper setting from the toss he'd given it.

It shimmied.

Paul flinched.

A rat-like, snouted face poked out of the middle of the folds. Furless, with white skin that looked oily. It gazed up at him with pink eyes. It bared its teeth.

'Jesus!' Paul gasped as the thing scurried out, rocking the paper, and rushed straight toward him, claws clicking on the table top, teeth snapping at the air.

Paul staggered backward.

*What the fuck is it?*

The creature left a slime trail on the glass. It didn't stop at the edge of the table. It tumbled off, hit the carpeted floor with a soft thump, and sped toward Paul's feet.

He leaped out of its path. The thing abruptly changed course and kept coming.

Paul hurled himself sideways, lurched a few steps to his easy chair and jumped up onto the seat. His feet sank into the springy cushion. He teetered up there, prancing for balance as he turned around, then dropped a knee onto the chair's padded arm.

He watched the thing rush toward him.

Not a rat, at all. It had a rodent-like head, all right, but beyond its thin neck was a body shaped like a bullet: a fleshy, glistening white cylinder about five inches long, rounded at the shoulders, ending just beyond its hind legs without tapering at all as if its rear was a flat disk. It had no tail.

At the foot of the chair, it dug its claws into the fabric and started to climb.

Paul tore a moccasin off his foot. A flimsy weapon, but better than nothing. He swept it down at the beast. The limp leather sole slapped against the thing's flank, but didn't dislodge it. It kept coming up the front of the chair, eyes on Paul, its small teeth clicking.

He stuffed his hand into the moccasin and shoved at the thing. Its snout burst through the bottom, a patch of leather gripped in its teeth. He jerked his hand free, losing the moccasin, and sprang from the chair. Glancing back as he rushed away, he saw the creature and moccasin drop to the floor.

At the fireplace, he grabbed a pointed, wrought-iron poker. He whirled to face the beast. It worked the rest of its body through the hole in the slipper and charged him. He raised the poker.

Something brushed against Paul's ankle. A furry blur shot by. Jack the cat.

Jack slept in Timmy's room, curled on its special rug beside the boy's bed. The commotion out here must've caught its attention.

'Don't!' Paul blurted.

The tabby leaped like a miniature lion and pounced on the creature.

*Stupid cat! It's not a mouse!*

Paul's view was blocked by Jack. He bent sideways, trying for a better angle, and saw the blunt rear and tiny legs of the thing hanging out the side of Jack's mouth.

'Nail the bastard!' he gasped.

Jack worked his jaw, biting down. His tail switched.

'Paul? What's going on out there?' Joan's groggy, distant voice.

Before he could answer, the cat squawled and leaped straight up, back hunching.

'PAUL!' Now alarmed.

Jack went silent. All four paws hit the floor at once. The cat stood motionless for a moment, then keeled over onto its side. Its anus bulged. The bloody head of the beast squeezed out.

Paul stared, numb with shock, as the thing slid free of Jack's body. It came at him, a tube of red-brown mush flowing out of its stubby rear.

'Christ!' he gasped, stumbling backward. 'Joan! Don't come in here! Get Timmy! Get the hell out of the house!'

'What's going . . .?' The next word died in Joan's throat as she stepped past the dining room table. She saw Paul in his robe dropping to a crouch and whacking the floor with the fireplace poker. The hooked end of the rod nearly hit a yucky thing that she thought for a moment was a rat. It scooted out of the way.

It wasn't like any rat that Joan had ever seen.

She saw the cat, the carpet dark with gore near its rump.

'Oh dear God,' she murmured.

Paul gasped and leaped aside as the creature darted toward his foot. It chased him across the carpet.

Joan took a step forward, wanting to rush in and help him. But she stopped abruptly. She had no weapon. She was barefoot, wearing only her nightgown.

'Shit!' Paul jumped onto the sofa, twisted around and back-stepped, the poker raised overhead. The thing scurried up the upholstery. 'Do like I said! Get Timmy out of here. Get help, for Godsake! Call the cops!'

The little beast suddenly halted.

It looked back at Joan.

Ice flowed up her back.

She whirled around and ran. Straight to Timmy's room. The boy woke up as she scooped him out of bed. 'Mommy?' He sounded frightened.

'It's okay,' she said, rushing out of the room with Timmy

clutched to her chest. Hanging onto him with one arm, she snatched her purse off the dining room table. She raced into the kitchen, putting him down while she opened the back door, then hoisted him again and ran outside.

'What's wrong, Mommy?' he asked. 'Where's Daddy?'

'Everything's fine,' she said, easing him down beside the Granada. 'A little problem in the house. Daddy's taking care of it.' She fumbled inside her purse, found the car keys, unlocked the driver's door and opened it. 'You just wait here,' she said, lifting Timmy onto the seat. 'Don't come out. I'll be back pretty soon.' She slammed the door.

And stood there at the edge of the driveway.

*What'll I do?*

Go back inside and help him?

He's got the poker. What'm I gonna do, go after the thing with a carving knife?

*She cut off its tail with a carving knife.*

That was no damn mouse.

He said to call the cops. Oh, right. Tell them a *thing* is chasing my husband around the house. And then when they get here in ten or fifteen minutes . . .

Joan snapped her head toward Applegate's house.

Applegate, the red-neck gun nut.

She crouched and looked through the car window at Timmy. The boy wasn't stupid. He knew that, somewhere in the house, shit was hitting the fan in a big way. His eyes looked huge and scared and lonely. Joan felt her throat go tight.

At least you're safe, honey, she thought.

She managed a smile for him, then whirled around and rammed herself into the thick hedge beside the driveway. Applegate's bushes raked her skin, snagged her nightgown. But she plunged straight through and dashed across his yard.

She leaped onto his front stoop.

The plastic sign on Applegate's door read: THIS HOUSE INSURED BY SMITH & WESSON.

What an asshole, she thought.

Hoping he was home, she thumbed the doorbell button.

From inside came the faint sound of ringing chimes.

Joan looked down at herself and shook her head. The nightie had been a Valentine's Day present from Paul. There wasn't much of it, and you could see through what there was.

Applegate's gonna love this, she thought. Shit!

Where *is* he?

'Come on, come on,' she muttered. She jabbed the doorbell a few more times, then pounded the door with her fist. 'Joe!' she yelled.

No answer came. She heard no footsteps from inside the house.

'Damn it all,' she muttered. Being careful not to slip again, she hurried to the edge of the concrete slab. She stepped down, took a few strides across the dewy grass, then made her way into the flower bed at the front of Applegate's house. He must be home and up, she thought; his curtains are open. He always kept them shut at night and whenever he was away.

Joan pushed between a couple of camelias, leaned close to his picture window and cupped her hands around her eyes.

She peered into the sunlit living room.

Applegate was home, all right. But not up. He lay sprawled on the floor in his robe and a swamp of blood.


Paul leaped off the end of the couch. He landed beside the front door.

*Get the hell out!* he thought.

Sure, and leave the thing in here? You come back and can't even find it.

I've gotta kill the bastard.

He lurched sideways as the creature sprang off the arm of the couch. He was almost fast enough. But he felt a sudden small tug on his robe, and yelped. The thing was hanging by its claws near the bottom of the robe, starting to climb. Paul threw open his cloth belt. He twirled to swing the beast away from his body, and jerked the robe off his shoulders. It dropped down his arms.

He let go of the poker so his sleeve wouldn't hang up on it. The poker thumped against the carpet. With one hand, he gave the robe a small fling. It fell to a heap, covering the beast.

He snatched up the poker. For just an instant, he considered beating the robe with the iron bar. But the rod was so thin, he'd be lucky to hit the beast.

Squealing 'SHIT!' he sprang onto the cloth bundle with both feet. He jumped up and down on it. Shivers scurried up his legs. He felt as if cold fingers were tickling his scrotum. The skin on his back prickled. He thought he could feel the hair rising on the nape of his neck. But he stayed on the robe, dancing on it, driving his heels at the floor.

Until his right heel struck a bulge.

He screeched, 'Yaaaah!' and leaped off.

He whirled around, poker high, and bent down ready to strike.

The robe was too thick, too rumpled, for Paul to locate the lump he'd just stomped.

*Gotta be dead*, he thought. *I smashed it. Smashed it good.*

Then realized he hadn't actually felt it squish.

He whacked the robe with his poker. Stared at it. The rod had left a long, straight dent across the heap. Nothing moved. He struck again. The second blow puffed up the old dent and pounded a new one close to where it'd been. He struck a few more times, but never felt the rod hit anything except the robe and the floor.

Paul stepped a little farther away, then leaned forward and stretched out his arm. He slipped the tip of the poker under a lapel, jostled it until a heavy flap of the robe was hooked, then slowly lifted.

The blanketed area of carpet shrank as he raised the robe higher. No creature.

Then the end of the robe was swaying above the carpet, covering nothing at all.

Still no creature.

It came scurrying down the slim rod of the poker toward his hand.

Paul screamed.

He hurled the weapon and ran.

Racing up Applegate's driveway toward the rear of his house, Joan wondered if she should try next door. An older couple lived there. She didn't actually know them. Besides, they might be dead, same as Applegate.

And what if they didn't have a gun?

Applegate had plenty. That, she knew. She and Paul had been in his house just once – enough to find out that he was not their kind of person. A Republican, for Godsake! A beer-swilling reactionary with the mean, narrow mind of his ilk. Anti-abortion, anti-women's rights, big on capital punishment and the nuclear deterrent. Everything that she and Paul despised.

But he did have guns. His home was an arsenal.

Dashing around the corner of his house, Joan spotted a rake on the back lawn. It had been left carelessly on the grass, tines upward. She ran into the yard and grabbed it up, then swung around and rushed across the concrete patio.

She skidded to a halt at the sliding glass door. With the handle of the rake, she punched through the glass. Shards burst inward, fell and clinked to the floor, leaving a sharp-edged hole the size of a fist. Reaching through the hole, she unlatched the door. When she pulled her hand out, a fang of glass ripped the back of it.

She muttered, 'Fuck.'

Not much more than a scratch, really. But blood started welling out.

I'm ruining myself, she thought. But then she remembered how Applegate had looked, remembered Paul scampering over the couch with that little monster on his heels.

He could end up like Joe if I don't hurry, she told herself.

Why doesn't *he* get the fuck out of the house?

Deciding to ignore her bleeding hand, Joan wrenched open the door. It rumbled on its runners. She swept it wide, and entered Applegate's den to the left of the broken glass.

There was the gun rack on the other side of the room. She hurried toward it, holding the rake ready and watching the floor.

What if Applegate hadn't been killed by one of those horrible *things*? Just because we've got one . . . Maybe he was murdered and the killer's still . . .

One of those horrible *things* Scurried out from under a chair and darted straight for Joan's feet.

She whipped the rake down.

Got it!

The tines didn't pierce its slimy flesh, but the monster seemed to be trapped between two of the iron teeth.

Joan dropped the rake.

She rushed to the gun rack. A ghastly thing with the weapons resting on what appeared to be the hooves of deer or stags.

Wrinkling her nose, she grabbed the bottom weapon. A double-barreled shotgun?

She whirled around with it just as the monster slithered free of the rake tines.

Clamping the stock against her side, she swung the muzzle toward the thing, thumbed back one of the hammers, and pulled the front trigger.

The blast crashed in her ears.

The shotgun lurched as if it wanted to rip her hands off.

The middle of the rake handle exploded.

So did the monster. It blew apart in a gust of red and splashed across the hardwood floor.

'Jesus H. Christ,' Joan muttered.

Then, she smiled.

Paul slammed the bathroom door. He thumbed in the lock button.

An instant later, he flinched as the thing struck the other side of the door.

Just let it try and get me now, he thought.

Then came quiet, crunching sounds. Splintering sounds.

'Bastard!' he yelled, and kicked the bottom of the door.

He pictured the beast on the other side, its tiny teeth ripping out slivers of wood.

If only he hadn't lost the poker, he could crush its head when it came through.

Rushing to the cabinet, he searched for a weapon. His Schick took injector blades. They'd be no use at all. He grabbed a pair of toenail scissors. Better than nothing. But he knew he couldn't bring himself to kneel down and ambush the thing. Not with scissors four inches long.

If only he had a gun.

If only the cops would show up.

He wondered whether Joan had managed to call them yet. She'd had plenty of time to reach a neighbor's phone. Applegate himself might come charging over with one of his guns, if she went to his place.

The door rattled quietly in its frame as the creature continued to burrow through.

There must be something useful in here!

The waste basket! Trap the thing under it!

Paul crouched for waste basket. Wicker. Shit! They'd had a heavy plastic one until a couple of weeks ago when Joan saw this at Pier One. The bastard would chomp its way out in about a second.

He looked at the bottom of the door, and two tiny splits appeared. A bit of wood the width of a Popsicle stick bulged, cracked at the top, and started to rise.

He heard a faint boom like a car backfiring in the distance.

The flap of wood broke and fell off. The snout of the beast poked out.

Paul whirled. He rushed to the bathtub and climbed over the ledge. The bathmat draped the side of the tub. He flipped it to the floor.

The shower curtain was bunched at the far end, hanging inside.

With no rug or shower curtain to climb, the thing couldn't get at him.

He hoped.

I don't care how good it is, he thought, it can't climb the outside of the tub.

'Just try.' he muttered as the thing scurried across the tile floor. It stopped on the bathmat and looked up at him. It seemed to grin. It sprang and Paul yelped. But the leap was short. The beast thumped against the side inches from the top. Its forelegs raced, claws clittering against the enamel for a moment. Then it dropped. Its rump thumped the mat. As it keeled backward, it flipped over and landed on its feet.

Paul bit down on the scissors. He crouched. With both hands, he twisted the faucets. Water gushed from the spout. As it splashed around his feet, he stoppered the drain. He took the scissors from his mouth, stood up straight and looked at the floor beside the tub.

The beast was gone.

*Where . . .?*

The waste basket tipped over, spilling out wads of pink tissue. It began roiling toward the tub.

'Think you're smart, huh?' Paul said. He let out a laugh. He pumped his legs, splashing water up around his shins and calves. 'BUT CAN YOU SWIM? HUH? HOW'S YOUR BACK-STROKE, YOU LITTLE SHIT?'

The waste basket was a foot from the tub when the beast darted up from the far side. It landed atop the rolling wicker. Paul threw the scissors at it. They missed. The creature leaped.

He staggered backward as it flew at the tub. It landed on the ledge, slid across on its belly, and flopped into the water. It splashed. Then it sank.

'GOTCHA!' Paul yelled.

He jumped out of the tub. Bending over, he gazed at the beast. It was still on the bottom, walking along slowly under a few inches of water.

He jerked the shower curtain over the ledge so it hung outside.

The beast came to the surface, glanced this way and that, then spotted Paul and started swimming toward him.

'Come on and drown,' he muttered.

It reached the wall of the tub. Its forepaws scampered against the enamel. Though it couldn't climb the smooth wall, it didn't seem ready to drown, either.

Paul backed away from the tub.

On the counter beside the sink was Timmy's smurf toothbrush standing upright in its plastic holder. He rushed over to it and snatched it from the Smurf's hand.

He knelt beside the tub.

The beast was still trying to climb up.

Paul poked at it. The end of the toothbrush jabbed the top of its head and submerged it. But the thing squirmed free. It started to come up. Before its snout could break the surface, Paul prodded it down again.

'How long can you hold your breath, asshole?'

It started to rise. He poked it down again and laughed.

'Gotcha now.'

Again, the beast escaped from under the toothbrush and headed for the surface.

Paul jabbed down at it. His fist struck the water, throwing a splash into his face. As he blinked his eyes clear, something stung his knuckles.

He jerked his hand up.

He brought the creature with it.

Screaming, he lurched away from the tub and shook his arm as the thing scampered over his wrist. It held fast, claws digging in.

He swiped at it with his other hand. It came loose, ripping flesh from his forearm, and raced up *that* hand.

Raced up his left arm, leaving a trail of pinpoint tracks.

Swinging around, he bashed his arm against a wall. But the beast merely scampered to its underside. Upside-down, it scooted toward his armpit.

\* \* \*

'PAUL!'

Joan twisted the knob. The bathroom door was locked. From beyond it came a horrible scream.

She aimed at the knob and pulled the trigger.

As the explosion roared in her ears and the shotgun jumped, a hole the size of a fist appeared beside the knob. The door flew uopen.

Paul, in his underpants, stood beside the bathtub shrieking. His left arm was sheathed with blood. In what remained of his right hand, he held the monster.

He saw her. A wild look came to his eyes.

'Shoot it!' he yelled, and thrust his fist toward the ceiling. Blood streamed down his arm.

'Your hand!'

'I don't care!'

She thumbed back one of the twin hammers, took a bead on her husband's upraised bleeding hand, and pulled a trigger. The hammer clanked.

'My God! Shoot it!'

She cocked the other hammer, aimed, jerked the other trigger. The hammer snapped down. The shotgun didn't fire.

'RELOAD. FOR GODSAKE RELOAD!'

'With *what*?' she shrieked back at him.

'IDIOT!' He jammed the monster into his mouth, chomped down on it, yanked, then threw the decapitated body at her. It left a streamer of blood in the air. It slapped against Joan's shoulder and bounced off, leaving a red smear on her skin.

Paul spat out the thing's head. Then he dropped to his knees and buried it in vomit.

In the living room, he put on his robe. They hurried outside together.

450

Timmy was still in the car, his face pressed to the passenger window, staring at the woman in curlers and a pink nightgown who was sprawled on the sidewalk, writhing and screaming.

From all around the neighborhood came the muffled sounds of shouts, shrieks and gunshots. Paul heard sirens. A great many sirens. They all seemed far away.

'My God,' he muttered.

He scanned the ground while Joan opened the car door and lifted Timmy out. She kneed the door shut. She carried the boy around the rear of the car.

'Where're you going?' Paul asked.

'Applegate's. Come on. We'll be safer there.'

'Yeah,' he said. 'Maybe.' And he followed her toward the home of their neighbor.


# The Tub


'Hello?'

'Guess who, Kenny.' She spoke into the phone using her very most sultry voice and that, she knew, was exceedingly sultry.

'All *right*!'

'Whacha doin?'

'Nothing much. Hanging around. How about you?'

'I'm languishing in bed.'

'Yeah?' Joyce heard his husky laugh. 'You sick?'

'I'm sure running a fever,' she said. 'I'm hot. I'm just so hot,

I had to strip myself stark naked. I don't know *what* could be the matter with me.'

'Have you got a temperature?'

'I just don't know, Kenny. I don't have the strength to get up and fetch the thermometer. Why don't you come over and bring yours? That big one you've got between your legs.'

Silence for a moment. Then Ken asked, 'What about Harold?'

'Oh, don't you worry about him.'

'That's what you said the last time, and he almost caught us at it.'

'Well, it's absolutely safe tonight. I can guarantee it. He went off to New York, New York and he won't be back till Sunday evening.'

'When did he leave?'

'You *are* a nervous nelly.'

'I just don't want any trouble.'

'Well, he left this morning. And you needn't worry that he missed his flight. He phoned me just a few minutes ago from his room at the Marriott. He's three thousand miles away, so I'm sure there's no danger whatsoever of him popping in on us.'

'How do you know he didn't call from a pay phone a mile away and *say* he's at the New York Marriott? Maybe he's at the Brentwood Chevron.'

'My, aren't we paranoid?'

'Why don't you phone the hotel? Just make sure he actually did check in, then call me back. If he's there like he says, 'I'll come right over.'

Joyce sighed. 'Well, if I must, I must.'

'I'll wait right here.'

She rolled sideways, cradled the telephone, swung her legs off the bed and sat up.

What a nuisance.

Harold was in New York, just as he'd said. He had been nominated for a Bram Stoker award for that disgusting novel of his, and he certainly wouldn't miss his chance to bask in the glory. Tonight, he would be sopping up liquor in the hospitality suite with Joe and Gary and Chet and Rick and the others, yucking it up and having a ball. Joyce would be the farthest thing from his mind.

Even if he did have his suspicions about her – even if he didn't care a whit about chumming around with those other writers – even if he weren't nominated – he *still* wouldn't have the balls to pretend he'd gone to New York so that he could sneak back to the house and catch her with Ken.

Such a gutless wonder.

Such a wimp that even if he walked in on her by accident and caught her in full rut with Ken, he would probably do no more than blush, say nothing, and walk away.

Silly of Ken to worry about him at all.

What did he think, Harold might shoot him? Harold was terrified of guns. He probably wouldn't use one to save his own life, much less to blow away his wife's lover. And without a gun, Harold wouldn't stand a chance against Ken.

Ken, a 290-pound giant, all hard bulging muscles, could take care of little Harold without breaking a sweat.

She waited a while longer, then picked up the telephone and tapped Ken's number. He answered after the first ring.

'Hello?'

'Hello yourself, big man.'

'Is he there?'

'According to the front desk, he checked in at six o'clock this evening.'

'All *right*. I'm on my way.'

'I'll leave the front door unlocked. Just come right in and see if you can find me.'

'*Ciao*,' he said.

'Yuck. Don't say that. That's what Harold always says. It's sooo pretentious.'

'See you in ten minutes.'

'Much better. See you then.'

She hung up, stepped to the closet and reached for her satin robe. Then she decided not to bother with it. She *was* feeling hot. Though she would have to walk past windows to reach the front door, it was unlikely that anyone would see her. There were no other houses within viewing range, and hedges made it impossible to see her house from the road.

She left the bedroom, walking swiftly, enjoying the soft feel of the air stirring against her skin and the way her breasts jiggled just a little when she trotted down the stairs.

At the bottom, she saw her dark reflection in the window beside the front door.

She imagined a peeping Tom gazing in at her, and felt a small tremor. Not a tremor of fear, she realized. For the benefit of the imaginary voyeur, she brushed her thumbs across the jutting tips of her nipples. The touch made her breath tremble.

She unlocked the door.

Her heart thumped and she trembled even more as she considered opening the door and stepping out onto the stoop. Waiting there for Ken. In the moonlight, in the open, the warm night breezes licking at her.

Some other time. Maybe later tonight, they could go outside together. But not now. She had already decided on her method of greeting Ken and she didn't have much time.

She hurried about, turning off all the downstairs lights before rushing upstairs. At the top, she shut off the hallway lights.

Now, the entire house was dark except for the master bedroom.

She entered, flicked a switch to kill the bedside lamps, then made her way carefully over the carpet to the bathroom. She put the light on, but only for the moment she needed to find the matchbook and strike a match.

She shut the door and fingered the switch down. Then she touched the flame to the wick of the first candle. That was enough for now. She shook out the match. The single remaining flame was caught by mirrors that covered every wall and the ceiling. The bathroom shimmered with fluttering, soft light.

Joyce smiled.

Harold has his damned tub, I have my lovely mirrors.

When they'd remodeled the bathroom, she had wanted a spacious sunken tub. Harold had insisted on his white elephant. It was a hideous ancient thing that stood on tiger feet in the middle of the floor. Like a showpiece. And he did enjoy showing it. He would bring his friends upstairs to the master bathroom so they could admire the monstrosity while he told them the whole long boring story of how he'd gotten it at an estate sale in Hollywood. Some bimbo actress from the silent screen days had supposedly slit her wrists while she was in the thing. *Cashed in her chips*, Harold liked to say. *In this very tub*.

What a schmuck, Joyce thought as she bent over the tub and turned on its faucets. Water gushed from its spout. When it felt good and hot, she plugged its drain with the rubber stopper. She straightened up and wiped her wet hand on her thigh.

At least I got my mirrors out of the deal, she thought.

She had let him have the stupid haunted tub, and he'd let her have the mirrors.

She admired herself in them as she made her way around the bathroom, lighting more candles.

The wavering mellow glow made her eyes shine, her russet

hair sparkle and gleam. Her skin looked dusky and golden. When the last candle was burning, she set down the matches and stretched, turning slowly, arms high.

She was surrounded by Joyces, all of them shimmering and mysterious. She gazed at their sleek, arched backs curving down to the perfect mounds of their buttocks. She gazed at the velvety backs of their thighs, legs tapering down to soft calves, delicate ankles. Still turning slowly, she lowered her arms and interlaced her fingers behind her head. All the Joyces did the same. They had such long, elegant necks. Shadows were pooled in the hollows of their throats and above the bows of their collar bones. Their breasts were high, the color of honey, tipped a deeper hue of gold. Below them, the rib cages were maybe a little too prominent. Harold certainly thought so. *Why don't you eat!*

The bastard.

I'm perfect the way I am.

She brought her hands down, savoring their touch and excited by the view of all the Joyces caressing their breasts, gently squeezing their nipples, sliding their hands down their ribs (which are just fine, thank you), down the slim smoothness of their bellies, lower until their thumbs pushed into soft, gleaming coils of hair.

If Ken walks in and sees me like this, she thought, he'll never let me make it to the tub.

She hurried over to it. The water was high. She shut off the faucets and listened, wondering if he might already be in the house. She heard only her own quick heartbeat, her own ragged breathing, and quiet plops of water dripping from the spout.

But Ken could be just outside the bathroom door.

Gripping the high rim of the tub, she swung a leg over. Hot water wrapped her foot. Almost too hot. In the mirrors, she watched other Joyces climb into the tub, hold onto both sides, and slowly lower themselves. Then only their heads and the tops of their shoulders still showed.

Joyce slid herself forward. Her rump squeaked once against the porcelain. When she was submerged to the chin, she stopped her slide by raising her knees and pressing her feet flat against the bottom of the tub.

The damn thing was too long. She could never just stretch out in it, feet against the far end to keep her head out of the water. Which meant she could never truly relax. She had to keep her feet planted. Either that, or brace herself up by spreading her legs wide enough to brace her against the sides of the tub.

A royal pain.

But this is one damn cloud with a silver lining, she told herself. The fucking tub's just the right size for fucking. Big Ken would be able to fit right in.

'Gonna do it right in your precious tub,' she muttered. 'How do you like *them* apples, Harold?'

She waited, savoring the water's heat, caressing herself. The ceiling mirrors reflected candlelight down into the tub. She watched her hands move, her body writhe as she squirmed with pleasure.

She flinched at the sound of a floorboard creaking.

He's here!

In the bedroom?

She scooted backward, sliding herself up the rear of the tub until she was sitting. She rested her arms on the edges. She wanted to look just right when he entered, and the mirrors showed that she did. The water covered her like a sheer blanket from the belly down. Her arms, shoulders and chest were wet and shiny.

She turned her eyes to the bathroom door.

What's taking him so long? she wondered . . . and heard a faint, muffled footstep.

Definitely a footstep.

*What if it isn't Ken?*

A shiver crawled up Joyce's body. She felt her skin tighten and tingle with goosebumps.

*Anybody might've walked into the house.*

It had seemed like such a grand plan – leaving the front door unlocked, making the house dark, secluding herself in the bathroom so he would find her in candlelight, naked and gleaming in the tub.

Stupid!

But it has to be Ken.

It doesn't *have* to be.

Christ!

But if it's a stranger out there, maybe he thinks the house is deserted. Maybe he won't find me. Maybe . . .

The door flew open.

Joyce gasped and flinched.

Ken strode into the bathroom as if parading onto the stage at a body-building contest.

He had removed his clothes. He had oiled his skin.

'It's you,' she whispered.

He began to pose. He turned this way and that, moving and pausing and flexing with slow, graceful elegance. His muscles bulged and rippled and bounced. Joyce watched, breathless. She had seen him do all this before, but never in the fluttering gold of candlelight.

He looked magnificent and strange. A gorgeous, hairless monster of dancing mounds and slabs.

When he strutted to the rear of the tub, Joyce didn't have to turn her head. She watched him in a mirror, watched him bend and reach down and slip his hands down her breasts. They touched her only for a moment. Then he pranced backward, curling his arms and twisting his torso.

He twirled around. With coy glances over his shoulder, he came to the side of the tub. He raised his arms and flexed, displaying the bands of muscle criss-crossing his back, the hard mounds of his rump. Joyce smiled when he made the buttocks bounce. One side at a time. She reached up and stroked one slick cheek.

He gently swatted the hand away as if offened, strutted away from the tub, then whirled around and sashayed back to her. Hands on hips, he bent his knees. His rigid penis, inches from her face, jerked up and down. He hopped closer. Joyce twisted toward him, rolling onto one hip, clutching the rim of the tub with both hands. Her breasts pushed against the cool porcelain wall. She opened her mouth. He brushed against her lips, teasing her, not entering. Then he pranced backward.

'Quit it,' she gasped. 'Get in here. I want you *in* me.'

He returned to the tub. Peering down at her, he whispered, 'You look delicious.'

'You look pretty good yourself.'

'You seriously want me in the tub?'

'There's plenty of room.'

'The bed would be more comfortable.'

'But not as exciting.'

He shrugged his massive shoulders. Bending over, he clutched the side of the tub and climbed in. He stood at her feet, glanced down at her, then turned his head slowly, surveying his images in the mirrors.

'Quit admiring yourself and fuck me.'

He sank slowly to his knees, flinching a bit when the hot water met his scrotum. Joyce slipped down into the warmth. As it wrapped her to the neck, her feet met the slippery skin of Ken's thighs.

'You don't want me on top, do you?'

'Of course I do.'

'You want to drown?'

'I want to be crushed.' She lifted a foot out of the water and stroked him. 'I want to feel you on me, that whole gorgeous body pounding me senseless.'

He moaned. He nodded. He muttered, 'Let's lose the water.'

'Hurry. Just hurry.'

He reached down behind his rump. Joyce heard a quick sucking gurgle, then the soft rush of water flowing down the drainpipe.

She spread her legs. Ken crawled forward slowly. His hands glided up her thighs, caressed her hips and belly, moved up the slope to her ribcage. They cupped her breasts. As they squeezed, she lifted a hand out of the water and curled her fingers round his penis.

'In,' she whispered.

His hands slid away and down her sides. Bracing himself above her, he lowered his face into the water. His tongue flicked her right nipple, swirled and pressed. His mouth opened, and she felt his lips around her breast. He sucked. He sucked it deep into his mouth.

'God!' she cried out. She let go of his penis and clutched his back.

He let go. He came up, gasping. His dripping face smiled at her, then plunged down again. She felt lips on her other breast. They were like a soft, plaint ring encircling her nipple, making a tight seal. This time, they didn't suck. They blew. Blew like a kid making fart sounds on his arm. Lips and air and water vibrated against her nipple. Bubbles erupted on the surface.

Gasping, she pushed his head away.

'Did it hurt?' he asked.

'No. Just . . . quit it and fuck me . . . *now!*'

He struggled, trying to reposition himself. Joyce realized that their differences in size were causing him problems. That, and the water. He was still worried about drowning her.

Suddenly, he reared back onto his haunches, dragging her up out of the water by the armpits, lifting her, planting her down on him, impaling her.

A club shoving high up into her.

She cried out and shuddered and clamped herself tight to his chest as spasms quaked through her body.

Spasms also quaked Ken.

He dropped forward, driving her down. Her back splashed, then slammed the bottom of the tub. Her head snapped down and thunked. Lights exploded in her vision as water rained down on her face.

When the exploding lights went away, she realized she was sprawled beneath Ken, her chin resting against the top of his shoulder.

'Christ,' she gasped. 'You hurt me.'

He didn't apologize.

He didn't say a thing.

She realized that he couldn't. His head, next to her own, was face-down in the water. The level was lowering, but slowly. The heat enclosed Joyce's head like a warm hood, only the front of her face in the air.

So Ken's face had to be submerged.

*He's going to drown!*

'Ken!'

He didn't stir.

He wasn't making bubbles. He wasn't breathing.

461

His chest was mashed tight against Joyce's chest. She felt a raging heartbeat. Whether *his* was beating, she couldn't tell.

Though she was pinned down by his weight, her arms were free. They'd been around him at the moment of the fall. So she made fists and pounded on his back.

'Ken! Ken, wake up!'

*He's not sleeping, you idiot!*

'Ken! Get your head up! Ken!'

She kept hammering her fists down against his back. They made meaty thuds. She had no idea whether pounding on him would do any good, but she'd seen it done on doctor shows. Also, in a way, it felt good. Each blow sent quick little tremors through his body. Like rapping a water melon at the grocery store. The tremors made him vibrate on top of her. They gave Joyce a tingle.

The blows even jostled his penis a little.

It was still buried in her. Still erect.

'I *know* you're faking,' she said. 'Now, come on. Dead guys don't have boners.'

He didn't move.

'Come on, Ken. This isn't funny. I bumped my damn head. Besides, you scared me. I thought you were dead or something.'

He still didn't move.

'All right. You're asking for it.' She jabbed the long nail of her forefinger into his back. She felt it pop into his skin. He didn't flinch.

A sick, icy chill snaked through her bowels.

'Oh, my God,' she muttered.

She nudged his head with the side of her face. It moved easily. She bumped her cheekbone against his ear. His head swung away, then flopped back and hit her as if trading blows.

'Shit!'

He's dead! The bastard's *dead*!

Joyce squirmed under his terrible weight.

This won't be easy, she thought.

She took a deep breath, then attacked. She bucked, she twisted, she shoved and tugged at Ken, she kicked and thrust at the bottom of the tub with her feet, she clawed at the sides with her hands. But she couldn't roll him off. She couldn't lift him. She couldn't writhe her way out from under him.

All her efforts hardly moved him at all.

Finally, she was too exhausted to continue the struggle. She lay beneath him, limp and sweaty, arms at her sides, fighting to breathe.

Calm down, she told herself.

Right. Calm down. I've got a fucking *stiff* on top of me. Not to mention . . .

Don't even think about that.

There has got to be a way out of this.

A way out of it *fast*!

Use your head, use your head.

The problem – the *major* problem, is the damn tub. The way it's holding us in. Of course.

If only we'd done it on the bed! I could've just rolled him off me . . .

If only. A lot of good that'll do you.

If only he hadn't *fallen* on me, that's what.

What happened to him? A heart attack? An aneurism? Who knows? Who cares? The jerk was pumped up with steroids, probably fucked up his system.

And now *I'm* the one who's fucked.

For the first time since she'd landed on her back under Ken, Joyce noticed the overhead mirror. She stared up at it.

No wonder she was trapped. She could hardly see herself.

Only her face and legs were visible. The rest of her was hidden beneath Ken's massive body. She raised her arms. They came up into view below Ken's armpits. They looked so small.

Her legs looked useless. Beautiful, useless legs, with their knees in the air – legs spread wide and painfully apart and jammed against the walls of the tub by Ken's thick thighs.

She tested them. She was able to unbend her knees. She could straighten her legs, lower them, and raise them high.

When she moved her legs at all, Ken seemed to shift position deep inside her, probing and exploring.

She didn't let that stop her. She watched her legs in the mirror and kept on testing their maneuverability. She found that she could kick around pretty well, but mostly just from the knees down. What she couldn't do was bring her legs together. Though she tried, they remained tight against the walls of the tub.

Maybe . . .

She lifted her right leg high, hooked its calf over the edge of the tub, shoved her right elbow against the bottom, and struggled to raise and turn herself, hoping to roll Ken off. She couldn't budge him.

Okay. This doesn't work. *Something* has to work.

She lowered her leg. She tried to relax.

I can't actually be *stuck* here.

But I'm certainly *being* stuck.

At least I should be able to do something about that, she thought.

She slid her open right hand into the tight crevice between her belly and Ken's. His skin was slippery against the back of her hand. She shoved downward. Their pelvises, locked together, stopped her fingertips. She tried getting to him from the side of her groin. No way.

'Great,' she muttered.

Then she screamed and kicked and pushed and twisted and squirmed, determined to get him off her, out of her, knowing she could do it – she had to do it and she could – mothers picked up cars, didn't they, when they had a kid trapped under a wheel? – and she could lift Ken. She would. She would hurl him aside and scamper out of the tub.

When she found that she couldn't, she wept.

Sometime later, the candles began to die. One by one, they fluttered, flared brightly and went out. She was left in darkness.

Just as well, she thought at first. Nothing to look at, anyway, but a dead guy pinning me down.

She didn't feel that way for long.

Terror began creeping through her.

A dead guy. A *corpse*. I'm trapped by a corpse.

What if it starts to move?

It's only Ken, she told herself. It's not any fucking ghoul or zombie or spook, it's just Ken. And he's dead, kaput. He isn't about to start *moving*.

But suppose he does? Suppose he wants revenge? I'm the one who killed him.

He threw a heart attack or something. Wasn't my fault.

Maybe he doesn't see it that way.

Shit! He doesn't see anything. He's dead! Besides, he died happy. What a way to go, right? He came and went.

She heard a laugh. It sounded a trifle mad.

He didn't come, she reminded herself.

*Coitus interruptus croakus.*

She laughed again.

It went silent, frozen in her throat as she imagined Ken lifting his head, kissing her mouth with his dead lips, whispering 'I've got some unfinished business,' and starting to thrust.

It took the light of morning to ease her terror. She slept.

She woke up aching and sweaty, her rump numb, her legs lifeless. She flexed her muscles, kicked and squirmed as much as she could. Soon, circulation came back. Her buttocks and legs burned. They felt as if they were being pricked by thousands of needles.

When she felt better, she noticed the odor.

The overhead mirror revealed its cause. Down between Ken's feet, a turd was hanging over the edge of the drain.

'Shit,' she muttered.

She closed her eyes.

Don't sweat the small stuff, she told herself.

Think, *think*.

Okay, it's Saturday. If he doesn't miss his flight or something, Harold will be getting back tomorrow evening. Around seven. That gives me better than a full day to get out of here. Or hubby'll get the surprise of his life.

How's *this* for a horror story, Harold? Write this one up, why don't you? Maybe you'll win a fucking award!

Won't happen. I'll be out of this mess long before he gets home.

Right. How?

*I can float Ken off me!*

She thought about that for a while. If she filled the tub, wouldn't the rising water lift him? Sure it would.

I might drown in the process.

But if I can hold my breath long enough . . .

She raised her legs, stretched them out, tried to squeeze them closer together. And came nowhere near the bathtub's faucets.

So much for great ideas.

There has to be a way. There . . .

'Get off me!' she shrieked, and fought the body. It was rigid with rigor mortis. It felt even heavier than before. Finally, exhaustion made her quit.

There *is* no way, she realized.

I'm gonna be trapped under this Goddamn stiff until Harold gets home.

After that, she spent a long time crying. Later, she dozed. When she woke up, her butt and legs were numb again, but she no longer felt the horrible desperation. She felt resigned.

'When rape is inevitable,' she muttered, 'relax and enjoy it.' What asshole thought up that one? she wondered.

This isn't the end of the world, she told herself. It may be the end of my marriage, but that's no great loss. Harold will come home tomorrow and get me out of this.

It's awful and disgusting, but I'm not going to die from it.

Later in the day, the stench got worse as her own excretions joined Ken's.

When darkness returned, so did her terror.

She lay motionless, hardly daring to breathe, waiting for Ken to stir. Or to speak.

*Joyce.*

*What?*

*I'm hunnnngry.*

She imagined his head turning, nuzzling down against the side of her neck, biting.

When she finally did feel him move, she shrieked. She screamed until her throat felt raw and burning.

Later, she convinced herself that Ken hadn't come back to life. The motion had probably been caused by something natural. Like decomposition. Shifting gasses. Tendons or muscles turning soft. Gross. Disgusting. But he wasn't coming back to life. He wasn't going to start talking to her. He wasn't going to bite her. He wasn't going to start humping her.

Just make it through the night.

Later, as she was starting to drift off, Ken moaned.

Joyce gasped. She went rigid, goosebumps squirming over her skin.

It's just escaping gasses, she told herself.

He did it again, and she whimpered.

'Stop it,' she whined. 'Stop it. Get off me. Pleeease.'

She exploded into another frenzy of struggles, then lay sobbing under his bulk and prayed for daylight.

When the first gray light of dawn came into the bathroom, Joyce's panic subsided and she closed her eyes.

It's Sunday.

Harold will come. He'll be here around seven. Before dark.

There won't be another night under Ken.

Exhausted, she drifted into sleep.

The jangle of the telephone startled her awake.

Who is it? Maybe someone had heard her screams in the night and was calling to check on her. When I don't answer . . .

Fat chance.

Nobody had heard the screams. Probably just a friend calling to chat. Or a salesman.

Or Harold. Harold calling to say he'd missed his flight, or he'd been bumped, or he'd decided to stay on another day or two in New York to meet with his agent, his editor.

'No,' she murmured. 'No, pleeease. Harold, get back here. You've got to.'

*I can't go through another night!*

It's all right, she told herself. He'll come. He'll come.

A few more hours, and he'll be here.

She wondered if Harold would be able to get her out from under Ken. Probably not. Such a weakling. He might have to call the fire department. *I hate to bother you folks, but I'm afraid my wife is stuck in the bathtub. It seems she was screwing this muscle-man and the fellow pitched a coronary or something.*

The idea of it made her laugh. The laughing made her chest hurt. Worse, it jostled her insides and jiggled Ken's penis.

She groaned.

There's nothing funny about this, she thought.

But if Harold can't get me out, the fire department will. It'll be a little embarrassing, but so what? I'll be free.

She imagined herself running down the corridor, butt naked, the firemen gaping in shock and maybe just a bit turned on. Running to the other bathroom, the big one, the one with a shower.

First, she would drink cold water. Fill her parched mouth with it. Drink till her belly bloated. Then she would take the longest shower in history. Sudsing and scrubbing until there was not a trace left of Ken's foul dead touch. Douching, too. Getting rid of his death.

Afterwards, cocktails. Vodka and tonic. Ice clinking in her glass. A twist of lemon. Drinking until her head was full of soft, cozy cotton.

Then, a steak dinner. A thick slab of rare filet mignon, charcoal broiled.

I'll have to broil it myself, she thought. Harold isn't likely to be in any mood to cook for me. If he sticks around at all.

Thinking about the steak, her mouth watered. Her stomach growled.

I'll be eating soon, she told herself. In just a few more hours

. . . if that wasn't Harold on the phone, calling to say he wouldn't be home.

It wasn't.

Please, it wasn't.

He'll be here. He'll come.

He came.

Joyce, lost in daydreams about his arrival, heard nothing until the bathroom door swung open.

'Harold!'

'Joyce?'

She heard his quick footsteps. Then he was gazing down at her, at Ken. His face turned a shade of gray almost the same color as Ken's back. His mouth drooped open.

'Get me out of here!'

He frowned.

'My God, quick! I've been pinned under him since Friday night!'

'You can't get up?'

'Would I be here if I could?'

'Jeez, Joyce.'

'Get your thumb out of your ass and get me out of here!'

He kept staring down into the tub, shaking his head slowly from side to side.

'Harold! Get me out of here!'

'Uh-huh. Right.'

He turned and walked away.

'*Ciao*,' he said. The bathroom door bumped shut.

Harold flew to Maui and spent a week relaxing on the beach, reading horror novels written by his friends, dining at fine restaurants. He ogled some beautiful women, but he stayed away from them. He didn't need any more traitorous bitches in his life.

Upon his return, he stepped into the house and called out, 'Joyce, I'm home.'

She didn't answer.

Grinning, Harold trotted upstairs.

The smell was not good. It made him gag. It made his eyes water. With a handkerchief over his nose and mouth, he hurried across the bedroom and entered the bathroom.

He went numb.

He dropped the handkerchief.

He stared.

The tile floor near the bathtub was strewn with body parts.

A bloody orb that he recognized as a head. Part of a head, anyway. It was missing its jaw. The ragged stump of its neck looked *chewed*.

He saw an arm. Another arm. Big, muscular things. So much missing from around their tops. The knobby ends of the humerus bones looked as if they'd been licked clean.

The floor was littered with other pieces. Curving slats of rib bones. Chunks of flesh. Slabs of stringy muscle. Slimy gobs that might have been interior organs – parts of lungs, maybe, or kidneys – who knows?

Harold *did* recognize a heart among the assortment of litter.

Over the rim of the tub hung coils of intestines.

Harold threw up.

When he was done, he approached the tub, careful not to step on any mess.

Joyce wasn't in it.

Her boyfriend was. Some of him. From the ass down, he appeared to be in fine shape. Excellent shape.

Most of his torso, however, had been hollowed out. He was

an armless, headless husk sprawled in a swamp of blood and puke and floating bits of God-knows-what.

'Welcome home. honey.'

Harold whirled around.

Standing in the bathroom doorway was Joyce. Clean and fresh and smiling. Wearing her red satin robe.

'My God,' was all he could say.

She grinned and clacked her teeth together. Then she brought her right hand around from behind her back. It was holding a jawbone. 'Ken has good, sharp teeth. He was of enormous benefit.'

'My God.' Harold muttered.

She tossed the jawbone, caught it with her forefinger behind the front teeth, and twirled it. 'Let's talk settlement,' she said. 'I get the house. The tub is yours.'

# No Sanctuary

## Richard Laymon

Rick would do anything for his girlfriend, Bert. He'd even spend his vacation in the wilderness, walking the trails around Fern Lake – though after what happened last time, it's the one place in the world he'd prefer not to go. But Bert is a woman with a passion for the outdoors – and a passion for other things too. Rick would follow her to hell and back – which is what he's about to do . . .

Gillian is off on vacation too, only her idea of a holiday is a little weird. She likes breaking into people's homes while they are away and living there. Pity that this time she chances on the home of a serial killer. The kind of guy who likes to take his female victims out into the wilderness for his fun.

Rick and Bert are not the only ones heading to Fern Lake . . .

'If you've missed Laymon you've missed a treat' Stephen King

'A brilliant writer' *Sunday Express*

'No one writes like Laymon and you're going to have a good time with anything he writes' Dean Koontz

0 7472 6730 8

**headline**

Coming soon in the **Richard Laymon**
Collection and available from your bookshop
or *direct from his publisher*.

FREE P&P AND UK DELIVERY
(Overseas and Ireland £3.50 per book)

Volume 1:                                           £7.99
The Beast House Trilogy

Volume 3:                                           £7.99
Night Show & Allhallow's Eve

Volume 4:
Beware! & Dark Mountain                             £7.99

TO ORDER SIMPLY CALL THIS NUMBER

**01235 400 414**

or visit our website: www.madaboutbooks.com

Prices and availability subject to change without notice.

ENDEAVOUR BOOKS